RULED BY SILENCE

Bree Rathbone

The characters and events portrayed in this book are fictitious and are for entertainment purposes only. Any similarity to real persons, living or dead, is coincidental and not intended by the author.

This novel features a deaf FMC. I tried my best to accurately portray this charachter and her struggles as a person with a cochlear implant. This is a work of fiction and shouldn't be taken as fact in regards to the deaf/hard-of-hearing community.

ISBN-13: 9798994252000
Cover Design: Disturbed Valkyrie Designs

For all of my readers who want to be thrown over a desk and thoroughly fucked.

CLASS IS IN SESSION.

XOXO

CONTENTS

TRIGGER WARNING

This novel contains mature themes/content that is intended for audiences over 18 years old and may be distressing to some readers. The provided list below contains some key triggers that may also be considered spoilers. The list will likely not cover all triggers.

PLEASE READ AT YOUR OWN DISCRETION.
Your mental health matters.
When in doubt, don't read.

Triggers:
Death
Grieving
Violence
Mentions Domestic Violence
Addiction
Alcohol Use/Abuse
Drug Use/Abuse
Mental Health Struggles
Mass Shooting
Murder
Depression
Bullying
Suicide

HOTLINES

If you or a loved one are experiencing emotional distress or a suicidal crisis of any kind, there is help.

988lifeline.org

Text: 988
Call: 988
TTY: 711

If you or a loved one are experiencing struggles with *substance use and/or abuse,* there is help.

findtreatment.gov

Call: 1-800-662-HELP (4357)

PLAYLIST

Love Me Leave Me by Lovechild
Perpetual by Yannick Lowack
Fire Up The Night by New Medicine
Killing Me Slowly by Bad Wolves
Zombie by YUNGBLUD
You Don't Own Me by SAYGRACE ft G-Easy
Pompeii by Bastille
Riot by Hollywood Undead
Tension by Conley
Don't Go by Letterday
I Found by Amber Run

PROLOGUE

-SAWYER-

Three Months Ago

My mind felt like absolute sludge. Kids these days had no drive. Especially the students of Oak Valley High School. The need to burn the essay dangling from my hand just so I didn't accidentally catch the stupidity like herpes was overwhelming. I didn't know how the fuck I was supposed to grade assignments for AP English when they weren't speaking any kind of english that I recognized.

I glanced back at the paper in my hand to read the first few sentences again, hoping for a different outcome.

What Elijah did was brave and innovative. Fax, no printer. When he sacrificed himself for the sake of society, I was absolutely shook. To come to that kind of decision was so selfless and inspirational. He absolutely ate and left no crumbs.

Fuck, it was worse reading it the second time around. Teachers don't get paid enough to educate these little assholes but we definitely deserved a stipend for the regression of our own knowledge that we paid thousands for in private colleges.

I placed the paper down and tried to rub away the dark circles that I was sure were visible under my eyes. I had stayed up late watching bullshit movies while Victoria had taken her sweet time getting home from happy hour with her girlfriends. She told me she would bring me home dinner from the restaurant, but I would have declined had I known I would be waiting up until 11 PM when I had to be up at 5 AM the next morning.

The framed sketch of her that I had drawn sat displayed

on my desk. Who wouldn't want to display her beauty and poise? I straightened it and just looked mindlessly over the marks on the page and the shading of her face. There were a few strokes that weren't perfect though, and I couldn't help getting agitated every time I looked at it.

The bell shook me out of my daze and I glanced at the clock unsure of how much time had passed. Victoria's class had just ended so I knew it was time for our regular lunch meet-up in the faculty lounge. Dragging myself out of the chair, I left my ungraded papers, dying for something more stimulating than that bullshit.

My eyes tracked through the lounge and I eventually found her sitting at the table alone, already digging into her salad. I grabbed my BLT from the fridge and gave her a kiss on the cheek before taking the seat across from her.

"Only 2 more weeks until summer break. I can practically smell the beach already," I said around a bite. She smiled and continued to nibble at the crisp romaine leaves with raspberry vinaigrette. The smell was pungent, almost making my eyes water, but I continued. "How were your classes this morning?"

She lifted one shoulder in a shrug. "The usual. I have some grading I have to finish before my last classes begin so I will be cutting our lunch a tad short. As long as I don't have to take assignments home to grade, I will be happy."

I nodded as I savored the bacon swirling around in my mouth. "That's fine. I would rather have you all to myself after work anyway. My stack of papers isn't exactly light either."

She beamed and threw me a wink. "You know I wouldn't trade a free moment with you for the world. Maybe we can snuggle up on the couch and watch a movie. My choice?"

I shook my head with a smile. That meant I was going to be stuck watching some sappy romance about a girl dying of cancer or something. But for her, I'd do it.

"Your choice, baby."

At that moment, Benjamin Tenford, came strolling in to grab a mid-day cup of coffee.

"Hey Vicky, Sawyer." He nodded to both of us in greeting. "Did you see the mandatory faculty meeting update? I heard it's about potential budget cuts. Just what we need, less teachers and more workload."

Victoria and I nodded in agreement and continued to make small talk with him before he went on his way. Victoria wiped away the crouton crumbs from in front of her and fixed her makeup with her compact mirror before gathering up her belongings to head back to the classroom.

"Meet you in the parking lot after the last bell?" She asked, looking over at me..

"Works for me. Now go get those papers graded, Ms.Trexler." She smiled, giving me a soft peck on the lips, then walked away. I watched the sway of her hips in her pencil skirt, appreciating the way that it hugged her body perfectly.

After a few minutes of finishing my meal in silence, I began cleaning up my trash. The contrast of baby blue against white had my eyes flicking to the floor. I crouched down to grab the piece of plastic that must have fallen off of Victoria's shirt during lunch.

I took a second to admire her beautiful smile on the front of the ID badge. She looked every bit like the school teacher she is.

Soft and inviting.

I walked a few halls over to drop her badge off to her since her classroom wasn't far from mine at all. I knew she would be ransacking her bag trying to find it eventually. Gripping the handle and pulling her door open, I walked straight in. I was expecting her to be busy so I was planning to make it quick and get back to my own work.

What I wasn't expecting was to see her pressed against the chalkboard with her skirt hiked up around her waist while the man in front of her ate her pussy like it was his last goddamn meal.

When he heard the door slam shut behind me, his head reared back and focused his wide surprised eyes on me. Benjamin fucking Tenford.

I didn't say a word. I just moved my steel gaze to Victoria where I could already see tears threatening to spill from her eyes. "Sawyer, please lis–"

I held up my hand and let my gaze trail to the wall to my left to avoid seeing the visual reminder of what I had just witnessed. My stomach was beginning to churn as bile crept up my throat. But I pushed every sensation down and asked the only question that I wanted to know.

"How long?"

"Not long," she said.

"Four months," Benjamin stated at the same time.

My head snapped back in Victoria's direction and I finally let her see the fury rolling off of my body. Four months. Four fucking months.

This fucking bitch.

It's ironic, because if she had waited another four months before spreading her legs for Benjamin dweebus Tenford, she would have watched me get down on one knee to propose. Maybe she would have realized what she was doing was a mistake. But she didn't. Now I had a ring in my glove box that was going to be either swiftly returned or smashed with a hammer. I hadn't decided which yet.

"I'll head home early to grab my stuff from the apartment. I'll stay with my brother until I find a more permanent place," I said sharply, allowing no room for argument.

With that I turned my back to them and walked out with my head held high and hands clenched into fists, ready to start swinging. I could hear her sobs follow me until the end of the hallway.

Fuck her.

I dug my phone out of my pocket and called the one person that always had my back.

"This better be good, big bro."

I sighed. "Good? No. An absolute trainwreck? Yes. Long story short, can I stay at your condo in Elmwood until I secure a new place?"

The silence stretched and I could tell he wanted to ask. I sighed again in agitation, not wanting to further piss myself off with the recurring image of his head between her thighs.

"She cheated. I refuse to stay there while I figure things out. I don't want to hear a damn word out of her mouth again. It would be better if I could stay somewhere far away from her and this fucking town. So, can I stay at your place?"

"Man, that blows. I'm sorry. On the bright side, I'm out of town on business so I likely won't even be at that condo for another few months anyway."

I relaxed my shoulders, thankful that he took a huge weight off of my chest. I really didn't want to stay in a motel that was likely infested with bedbugs until I figured my shit out.

"Thanks, Connor. I'll owe you one."

He snorted. "Yeah, and you bet your ass that I will collect." I could hear the sound of crunching metal in the background and had to pull the phone slightly away from my ear at the screeching sound. "Hey, I gotta go, things are getting dicey at the moment."

"Alright, be safe. Later."

He hung up and I checked that one task off of my mental checklist. One problem down, a million to go.

Awesome.

CHAPTER 1

-HALEN-

The spray of water pounded on my sore skin as the sweat was swept away with it. The flow of water grazing over my toe made me wince. I was hard on my feet and they were definitely overdue for an ice bath session.

I missed a cue on the stage during rehearsal and punished myself as a result. As a dancer, you are already trying to prove your worth, but to be a deaf dancer requires you working even harder to meet the minimum expectations.

I shut the water off and dried my body with the fluffy white towel hanging on the hook. The other girls were all in different states of recovering as well. Some were already putting a fresh coat of makeup on and others taking their sweet ass time in the shower.

I threw on my classic daily outfit of a pair of torn up black jeans and a band tee. After pulling my hair out of the tight bun, I felt almost instant relief from my screaming scalp. I was already beginning to feel like myself again. I was barely hanging on to my spot here in the company as it was. Every single day, like today, I was so fucking ready to quit. It wasn't *me*. It never was me.

My cochlear implants sat on the vanity in front of me just waiting to be put back in. The lack of chatter was welcome more times than not. With that thought, I threw them in my duffle bag and dragged my beaten up body to my Lexus RX in the parking lot.

This car was not at all what I would have chosen for myself, but I didn't pay for it. My parents did, as they did everything else concerning me. It's not ever a choice for me. They chose and we had a reputation to maintain, after all.

I agreed to this particular car with the exception that it was blacked out everywhere. The matte black wrap was badass and the tinted windows made it even better. The tint was technically against the law, but it was worth the tickets.

Love Me Leave Me by Lovechild blared through the speakers as I ripped through the parking lot. Not that I could hear it, but I knew. The vibrations were very distinct. I couldn't wait to finally get to Nicky's house. Nicky and Evan had blown up my phone all day asking when I was finally going to get there.

Needy bastards.

I spotted his house off in the distance and decided to park in the driveway. His dad, Rick, was rarely home. Which was a blessing. He spent about 90% of his time either at the bar or barely making it through work shifts. The other 10% was reserved for taking his rage out on Nicky.

His mom left years ago and fucked off to God only knew where. Rumor was that she was slutting it up with a business owner somewhere in Cleveland but I didn't know if it's true or not. Deep down I couldn't blame her for leaving the toxicity of Rick's behavior, but to turn her back on her own son, I could absolutely blame her for.

Without knocking, I plowed through his house and finally spotted them laying on the bed in the room at the end of the hallway.

"Hey, butt plugs! I'm here. Now what is so important that it warranted thirty text messages? One of you better have been on the ground bleeding out."

I threw my bag onto the chair and pulled out my implants. Once I heard the signature hum and background noise trickle in, I turned to give the boys my full attention again.

Evan had his hands up in mock surrender. "Sorry babe. It was urgent. Still is. Guess what we got today?" His smile lit up his face.

He glanced at Nicky who pulled something out from his bedside table. I waited patiently as he held up the signature green Xbox disc case. My heart sped up when I saw the label on the front.

"No. Fucking. Way. How?! Combat Strike: Defcon One won't be released until tomorrow!" I said with my mouth hanging open.

Nicky huffed a laugh. "Casanova over here flirted with the cashier at the game store. She was a beached whale and ate that attention right up. She was so worked up by his charm that she let him snag one early."

I looked over to Evan who was smiling impossibly bigger. "Evan... you didn't."

"What?" He asked with a laugh. "I don't mind when they are a little more on the squishy side. I love a good cake eater."

"I am not even going to dignify that with a response. But just tell me you didn't trade sex for a video game or break that girl's heart. Did you?"

"Nah," Nicky cut in. "He just did some light flirting and she utilized every second of it. I'm sure she walked out of that interaction feeling twenty times better about herself. Consider it an ego boost."

"Yeah, what he said. I mean, look at me," Evan said, gesturing to his model worthy face. "I'm hot as hell. I'm sure I boosted her self worth at least a little. But seriously, like I said, I actually don't mind a woman like little miss thickums."

I rolled my eyes and groaned, but I still looked back to Nicky's sparkling dark brown orbs. He knew I would break in a matter of seconds.

"Come on, Halen. Play with us. Don't make me go all *Daddy Nicky* on you and put you in time out until you finally give in."

My cheeks heated at the double meaning but I just gave him a wink and jumped on the bed in between them, not letting either of them think they won. "Fine. Fire it up, Daddy

Nicky."

With a chuckle, he got the game up and running and placed controllers in our hands. We began shooting enemy players which were clearly bots since the servers weren't going to be actually available until midnight for the official release.

"Are you both ready for tomorrow?" I asked while throwing a grenade into the enemy base.

Nicky groaned. "No. I've quite enjoyed not being around all of our dumbass classmates for the summer." He sighed a long breath before murmuring, "bunch of fucking assholes."

"Agreed, but it's our senior year, so I am actually trying to make the most of it. You know? I want to go out with a bang," Evan said before cursing at being killed in the game.

I nodded. "Yeah, I get it. I plan to keep my head down and spend more time in the library. I am definitely not looking forward to Katherine and her group of skanks talking about me as if I can't hear them."

Their hands both halted their clicking on the controllers as they leveled me with a look. I smiled. "You know what I mean you sass-holes."

They both chuckled and resumed wrecking shit on the screen. We played for hours until we heard the door slam and a slew of grunting and cursing. Once we heard the unmistakable sound of a bottle cap hitting the kitchen counter, Evan and I got up and grabbed our things. Nicky didn't like us seeing his father when possible. Things often got heated and he didn't want our judgement or pity.

I gave him a hug and Evan squeezed his shoulder before we snuck out the front door and into the night. Evan lived next door to Nicky so it was just a few steps to his place.

However, tonight he walked with me to my car and got up on the hood where he let his back rest on the windshield. I climbed up beside him and snuggled into his side with my head resting on his arm while he held me close.

We watched the clear starry sky and embraced the silence. I loved nights like these. I loved the quiet. Had it been my choice, I don't know that I would have actually gotten the implants. I am proud of who I am and most definitely don't see my lack of hearing as a disability. I prefer the lack of noise most times.

"Tomorrow's gonna be great, babe. I can feel you stressing. We have our entire lives ahead of us. Let's just go wild this year. Fuck the haters." He flicked his eyes over to me. "Okay?"

I nodded and huffed a laugh. "Fuck the haters."

I took my time driving home, enjoying the warm breeze that caressed my skin. I wasn't ready for the winter months. Snow plows, salted roads, shoveling your car out of a snow mound, and my personal favorite, the seasonal depression from the lack of sunlight.

Ugh, At least I got to go through the autumn months before then.

Apple cider, pumpkins, apple cider donuts, sweaters, pumpkin spice lattes, all of it. My lips quirked at the thought of snuggling up next to the fireplace with a good book and a mug of hot chocolate.

As I walked through the front door, I let it shut behind me with a slam, harder than I meant to. I winced a little and kept walking towards my room. My mother slid up next to me like the quiet serpent she was.

"Halen, good you're home. I know tomorrow is your first day of school." I was surprised she even noticed. "Don't forget to behave yourself. I have a friend with a son that I'd like you to meet and it's best to make a spectacular first impression. Dinner is at 6."

Ah, there it is.

"*Mom, do I have to?*" I asked while signing the words.

"Please don't do that tomorrow." She gestured towards my hands in a waving motion. "It's distracting. Use your implants and try not to draw negative attention. This boy might end up being the one that your father and I recommend for arrangement."

I clenched my jaw tight. "Okay."

"Wonderful. Now run along to bed, you don't want to have dark circles on your first day," she said as she turned away to head back in the direction of her room.

After crawling into bed, I set my implants on the nightstand and grabbed my book. At least my schedule had an hour that I am free to be in the library helping out. Nothing quite felt better than being in a place that is *supposed* to have a lack of noise. I'm not different there. Everyone is quiet, therefore I am not the weird quiet one the people immediately want to pick on.

Whatever, I didn't give a shit. I'd just throat punch them. I deserved a peaceful senior year.

Sure, Halen. Sure.

CHAPTER 2

-SAWYER-

My classroom here was way nicer than those at Oak Valley. I was surprised to walk in and see how clean everything was and how unmarred the desks were. Since Black Grove Academy was downtown, in the middle of some rough spots, I just assumed it would be more torn up.

I was pleasantly surprised.

After I got settled into the area behind my desk, I waited for the first bell to ring. A large crowd of students came barreling into the classroom and claimed seats right as the tardy bell rang out over the speakers.

Half of the students were groaning, with eyes drooped, showing they were still half asleep. While the other half were chipper and excited to be amongst friends again after a long summer break. It was to be expected from a senior class.

I got up and moved around to the front of the desk to lean my butt against the edge of it, with my legs kicked out and crossed at the ankles. I crossed my arms over my chest as I studied the faces before me.

I was sure I could have nailed down every clique. The populars, jocks, theater geeks, mathletes, goths, burnouts, and so forth. They were all here in one room, separated by their own hierarchy. I knew they were assessing me just as much as I was assessing them.

"Get up," I said calmly.

They all glanced around at each other waiting for someone to grow a brain cell and stand first. I cocked my head to the side as one of the goths, surprisingly, was the first to get up.

The rest followed.

"My name is Mr.Bennet, and I will be your English teacher for the year. This period is not going to be your *blow off class* for you to just mingle with your besties for the resties," I said mockingly. "I'm here to prepare you for next year. It's a big step and I need to give you all of the tools to not only be ready but to succeed."

"Dang, this sucks. Mr. Bend-me-over is kind of strict," I heard a girl whisper to her friend.

I let it slide because I didn't want to deal with the awkward sexual nature of her comment only 30 fucking seconds into my first class. Giving her attention would have only encouraged her to make more unnecessary bold comments.

I rolled my eyes and said, "Everyone come up and grab a popsicle stick from this cup, and find the desk with the number that matches the popsicle stick that you drew."

They wandered up and each drew a stick. Some were happy with their assigned seat in the classroom. Most were definitely annoyed that they were now mixed up to interact with those they normally wouldn't.

Once everyone was seated I clapped my hands together once. "Great. Now let's get started."

The hours ticked by faster than I expected as I breezed through my class periods. I had a lot of students this year but still a smaller student to teacher ratio than previous schools I had taught at. It made it much easier to actually get to know the students individually and help them with their individualized learning.

One thing that bothered me over the years was how easy it was for students who actually wanted to learn to slip through the cracks and eventually fail. Sometimes they just needed extra guidance, but were never given any.

"Knock, knock," a feminine voice filled the small classroom.

I peaked up from my laptop and saw a blonde bombshell just inside of the doorway holding a basket of candied apples.

Stretching out my hand, I offered her a shake. "Hey, I'm Sawyer, I don't believe we have had the pleasure of meeting yet."

She giggled. "Hay is for horses."

Oh, god.

"I'm Ellen Ferrier, and my room is just right across the hall. Sophomore English. I'm passing out candied apples to help the faculty start their day off right."

I gave her a smile and took the apple that she offered out to me. "Thanks, Ellen. This will definitely brighten my day."

"You should know that we do happy hours on Fridays at Canal Brewery. Sometimes it can get a little crazy but it's the perfect place to blow off steam after a long week," she said as her eyes made a pass over my body.

"Ah, yeah, I'll be sure to try to catch the next one. It definitely wouldn't hurt making friends in the area."

She beamed and began hopping in place with excitement. Her dress definitely did nothing to hide her very large and very plastic tits. Even I can admit I was having a hard time concentrating when I was worried she was going to accidentally knock herself out with one. Not surprisingly though, they stayed nearly frozen in place with no bounce. Definitely fake.

She suddenly stopped and her brows shot up. "Oh you're new to the area too? Where did you relocate from?"

I swallowed, hoping she wouldn't ask anything beyond that. "Chicago."

"I've never been, but If I plan to go, I guess I'll have the perfect person to ask for travel tips."

I nodded and told her of a few nice places to go if she were to visit. I glanced at my watch and noticed I had been standing here chatting for twenty minutes already. I quickly thought of a way out so I could get back to the pile of lesson plans that I needed to sort through.

Looking down at my watch again, I made a big show of being shocked at the time. Not a complete lie. "Oh wow, I better get back to work. I don't want to be working too late on the first day."

She nodded and rubbed the side of my bicep in a friendly gesture. *Very* friendly. "Sure thing, Sawyer. Thanks for your time!" As she began to walk out, she stopped right at the door and turned around. "Oh! And don't forget, you're *apple-so-lutely* going to crush it this year!"

Jesus. Kill me now.

I hammered out plans for the next week and felt good about where I was at enough to stop and take a break.

My lunch hour began a few minutes prior and I had a wave of anger and nausea roll through me. It had been months, yet here I was, still letting Victoria's actions dictate my emotions. I wouldn't let her take the credit for damaging me. I'd already been damaged long ago.

After slamming my laptop shut, I got up and made my way to the teacher's lounge. It felt good to roam around the school and get my bearings on the campus grounds. The layout was unique and clearly built with funding limitations not being an issue.

The atrium was beautiful. The glass roof let all of the natural light shine through, to illuminate the area. There were indoor benches and assorted potted trees. If I was in high school, I would have happily parked my ass right in the corner, away from walking traffic but still around the ambiance.

My hand twitched with the eagerness to sketch the area. I didn't get the urge to do so often. Only with things that I knew would take up my headspace for longer than it should. I begged for mental clarity and peace daily. Maybe I should have begged my doctor for Lexapro instead.

I passed by the cafeteria as I continued walking and saw the mass of students shoveling food into their mouths and surely talking about who broke up with who. All of the cliques were at their designated tables.

A group of girls were hanging on the jocks. Typical. At another table, a few guys and girls were just staring wordlessly at each other.

What the hell?

One of them turned to scan the cafeteria and I immediately recognized the glassiness and red rimmed edges of his eyes.

Ah, burnouts. Got it.

I continued watching the groups and was able to identify the theater kids, scholarship kids, and geeks. At the table closest to the exit, I saw two students smiling and eating. I couldn't quite place them.

They were both dressed like average seniors. One looked almost like he could easily fit in with the popular kids. His hair was a blonde medium length that definitely screamed *pretty boy*. He smiled, showing off his blindingly white teeth, and I was positive he would eventually end up as a frat boy in college, that's elbow deep in pussy.

The boy across from him had a more intense edge to him. His hair was dark brown and short at the sides but tousled on the top in a messy way that exhibited how little he probably given a fuck. His lips were tugged down in a frown. Everything about him said *fuck right off*. His right fist was clenched while the other dipped a fry into a mayonnaise and ketchup mixture.

Gross.

I wasn't sure where they fit into the whole clique system, but I started walking away trying to push the curiosity out of my head. Kids had a tendency to piss me off. I only showed interest in those that actually cared to learn and grow as a person. I wasn't going to let stupid curiosities sit in my head for no reason.

I turned a corner and ended back at the atrium. Shit. Did I walk in a circle? A few doors down I noticed the double doors that had the words *LIBRARY* stamped above them.

Instead of wasting more time trying to find my way, I walked inside in search of a librarian or stray teacher that could point me to the teacher's lounge.

The only person in sight was a young woman with

auburn hair. She was dressed in black skinny jeans and dark green fitted tee. Her Vans looked a tad scuffed up but overall looked taken care of unlike some of the other ratty shoes gracing these halls.

She continued shelving books and hadn't turned to face me upon my entrance.

"Excuse me, can you help point me in the right direction?" I asked quietly even though there wasn't another soul in sight. We were in a library after all.

Silence.

I spoke a little louder, assuming she didn't hear me the first time. "Excuse me, do you know where the teacher's lounge is?"

Silence.

She continued shelving books like she didn't give a shit who I was or what I wanted. No care in the world but the books in front of her.

Getting agitated, I spoke firmer and louder. "Young lady, I'm speaking to you."

Silence.

Now crossing over into pissed off territory, I stomped over to her, ready to get in her face and assign her detention.

She looked down at her feet and then turned to face me right as I got into her personal space so she was forced to look at me. My face was surely red with irritation and I know for certain I was sporting my best asshole look.

She was slightly startled but she stayed silent and waited for me to speak. "Young lady, I don't know how you were raised, but when someone speaks to you, you acknowledge and listen. I need help finding the teacher's lounge or a faculty member that can help me. Where is the librarian?"

Her eyes darted to my lips as I spoke and I immediately stepped out of her space. I didn't want to give this little brat the wrong idea. I already had to deal with a handful of flirting attempts by students today. I was not interested in that kind of attention from them.

From a skanky divorcee at the bar? Absolutely. From a student? Hell no.

She continued to stay silent but her eyes narrowed to slits. She inhaled a deep breath through her nose and I could hear her hands grip tighter on the dust jacket of the book in her hands.

She gently placed the book back onto the cart.

Her hands came up and for a moment I thought she was going to try and smack me. But in a way worse turn of events, she began angrily gesturing with her hands that I quickly realized was signing. I couldn't be sure what she was signing, but I caught the last two signs that I would try to look up on google later.

Then her soft voice hit me. "Maps are above all of the fire extinguishers." She pointed to the one closest to us, and sure enough, a map was mounted to the wall above it.

Once I turned back to face her, I saw she had already grabbed her stuff off of the nearby table and made it to the exit. I continued watching, stunned, with only the sound of the door closing behind her echoing throughout.

Fuck.

CHAPTER 3

-HALEN-

My body was practically vibrating with rage as I exited the library without another word. I put my cochlear back on with a huff of annoyance. What an absolute asshole. It was even more annoying that he was beautiful as sin. The pretty people always had absolute trash can personalities.

Who did he think he was? That entitled prick. Through all of my anger, my lips tugged up slightly, remembering the shock on his face when I started signing. If I had a polaroid camera, I would have absolutely captured that for my *mic drop scrapbook.* If such a magnificent thing existed.

It would have been placed in the perfect spot, right next to Raya's horrified face when I told her she was trashy for making out with Chad at the local cafe last spring. It was only scrapbook worthy because I had said it right in front of Astrid, who happened to be her BFF who was also dating Chad at the time.

In a disgusting show of dominance, Raya took me blasting her secret as her sign that the air was cleared and she could begin dating Chad publicly. Katherine, Raya and Astrid remained the *twat trio* as if no betrayal had even taken place.

I walked up to the cafeteria doors and looked through the window to scan the crowd. After spotting my guys, I whipped out my phone and shot off a text to Nicky.

Me: I'm outside of the cafeteria. Finished early in the library.

I watched Nicky glance at his phone and then speak to Evan. They both looked over at me and I jutted out my bottom lip. Evan smiled and shook his head at the same time that Nicky gave me a smirk.

I watched them both get up and discard their trays before walking out to meet me. The moment that they made it through the doors, I brought them in for a group hug. Sometimes a hug was all I needed. Just something to show that people cared.

"Thanks guys. I'm sorry for making you end your lunch early. I just needed someone to keep me from getting suspended or even arrested," I huffed a humorless laugh.

Evan's smile dropped. "What happened, babe?"

Nicky just stared at me, waiting for a response. I could tell he was getting angry. He knew it was going to be something about me being deaf. It was the one thing that could really trigger my fight or flight.

Biting my lip, I told them what had happened in the library. They were both quiet for a moment.

"Oof, a teacher?" Evan asked. I nodded.

"Teacher or not, if I was in there and heard him talking to you that way, I would have beat his ass," Nicky said with his eyebrows scrunched together, creating hard lines between them.

I pressed my finger to the space between his brows to get him to relax. He immediately released some of the tension that had him coiled up.

We walked to the atrium and took a seat while we waited for the lunch period to end. Right as we sat, Evan spoke up. "You know you could just unplug and join us in the cafeteria when you want to, right?"

I shook my head and let my gaze drift to the floor. "You know I can't do that, Evan."

His lips pinched into a tight line. "Why? If you unplugged, you could just–"

"No," I snapped. "They will gawk at me like the assholes that they are. Then on top of it, I will drag you both down with me. No."

Nicky snapped his fingers in front of my face. My downcast eyes flicked back up to his.

"Do you think we give a shit about what people think," he signed. My eyes held his black ones in a sad stare off for another beat. "*We learned for* you."

I looked over to Evan with watery eyes.

"He's right, you know," he signed.

I exhaled a shaky breath and pulled myself together again. This wasn't me. I was proud of who I was. I had no issues with signing and being the way that I was. I did have a problem with dragging my friends down for my sake though.

People in everyday society were usually fairly accommodating to the deaf community. They were usually curious, but not unkind. Teenagers in high school? Unkind as hell.

The bell rang out and we all stood to head to our next class. Nicky and I had English together, thankfully. Evan gave us fist bumps before walking in the opposite direction to his art class. Nicky tugged me into his side and kissed my temple as we walked.

Right when I looked up at the classroom door we were approaching, my throat began to tighten.

Fuck me, and my fucking luck.

The entitled prick.

He stood just outside of it with his hands over his chest and watched us approach with an uncomfortable expression. If I had to guess, it was a mixture of embarrassment and authority. A deadly combo in a man.

"Welcome to English. Find your assigned seat, and get your syllabus out," he said in a curt snap.

Nicky nodded and began to pull me inside of the classroom without a response. But I didn't break my glare from the asshole as I walked past him, tucked under Nicky's arm.

After finding our assigned seat with a horribly old-school approach involving popsicle sticks, I pulled out my syllabus and a pencil, ready to be done with this stupid class.

I got stuck at the front while Nicky was on the other

side of the classroom and more towards the back. I didn't mind being closer to the front so I could hear better. But the thought of being next to him more than I needed to made me want to punch someone.

The teacher, or prick, closed the classroom door behind him as he entered. The door's quiet click sounded off like a shotgun blast. I had a feeling that this was going to be an hour long disaster.

"My name is Mr. Bennett and you will have the honor of residing in your current seat for the rest of the year while attending my class." Some groans sounded throughout the room. "With that being said, I'd like everyone to take a turn introducing themselves. I would also like you to share something that you are good at. Starting with you." He pointed to a nerdy kid at the front.

Students began chiming off their names and skills. When Nicky's turn came, a smile stretched my face.

"My name is Dominic and I am good at creating chaos."

I shook my head in silent laughter when his eyes flicked over to mine and he gave me a wink. That little brat thought he was *all that.* He kind of was in a way. People either feared him or wanted to be him.

"Right... next." Mr. Bennet said, unimpressed.

More kids shared with the class. My heart began to beat faster as my turn approached. What would I have even said? Ballet? I was skilled at it, but I didn't enjoy it by any means. It was just something that my mother pushed me into as a way to keep me classy.

The person behind me finished their turn and I could feel the sweat beading my brow. Why was I so nervous? I never got this way. I chalked it up to anxiety around the first day of school.

Who *wouldn't* be nervous?

I cleared my throat and lifted my gaze to focus on Mr. Bennett. He was leaning against his desk with his feet crossed at the ankles. His hands gripped the edge of the desk as he waited for me to speak.

Ocean blue eyes stared down hard at me, waiting patiently for me to open my mouth to speak. The light stubble around his jawline moved slightly and I caught the ever so slight tic in it as he clenched.

Gathering every ounce of courage, I straightened my spine in my seat. "My name is Halen and I'm a skilled dancer."

"Yeah she is," the dumb jock a few rows over shouted out in a slimy provocative tone and winked.

Mr. Bennett's head snapped in his direction. The tic in his jaw now looked to be a full on grind. If he wasn't careful, he would have cracked teeth in no time and dentures to show for it.

Old fart.

"Mr. Jones, if you can't be respectful to others, then I will make sure to turn the other way when you find yourself in a situation where someone is being disrespectful to you. Understood?"

Jackson Jones slumped down into his seat, losing all bravado. I could feel my cheeks redden at him coming to my defense. There were very few people that did. One was also in this classroom.

I glanced over to Nicky who was glaring daggers at Mr. Bennet. I crinkled my brows together trying to figure out why he would be upset at him for punishing someone who was being rude to me.

I looked back over to Mr. Bennett who had his eyes focused right on me. They didn't budge as he projected his voice to the class. "The same rules apply to *all* of you. Golden rule and all that. Got it?"

The class mumbled varying agreements, but his gaze never wavered away from me. Once it became almost unbearable and incredibly awkward, he snapped.

"Next!"

CHAPTER 4

-SAWYER-

I began teaching the class and the time was moving fairly quickly. Students in their final year usually felt the urge to slack since they were already getting their college acceptances in the mail. So I wasn't sure what kind of students I would have in my class until I really saw them working in action.

I watched as the class independently read Cormac McCarthy's *No Country For Old Men* at their desks. I wanted them to read a few chapters so they could have a structured Socratic discussion.

It was a rough read but for a senior class I liked being able to grab their interest in reading right out of the gate. This tended to be the book to grab the attention of both the boys and girls.

I saw a few people slacking off here and there, but for the most part, everyone was buried in the book. Each class period I tried making a mental note of each student's general interest in the class.

Directing my attention to the right, I noticed a boy staring into space. His eyes were tinged red like he had an untreated case of pink eye. He also had a half eaten tub of orange marmalade. Clearly a burnout, and just trying to stay awake by this point.

I wondered how much he had to smoke to become that numb. I hadn't touched the stuff since college but with how my life had been going down the shitter, it was almost worth a try. Maybe I would finally let go of some of my resentment and hurt toward Victoria.

Unlikely.

After giving everyone a chance to finish the assigned chapters, I split the classroom in half and let them go at it with free discussion over what they had read. I sat down and answered some emails while listening to key points made.

Knowing I could hear everything and re-direct if needed, I sat and began working on assigning future chapters and discussions for the students to do next time. I never believed in assigning homework, so I tried to allow for more allotted time during class for them to complete everything needed.

Assigning kids homework to read a book outside of class, that I chose, wasn't going to help a kid fall in love with reading. It was going to piss them off and they would either resent it due to time wasted or they would blow it off and fail. Neither have sat well with me. Regardless of what school rules state.

A nerdy kid, Trey, was spouting off his opinion of the writer's odd writing style.

Out of the corner of my eye, I watched as a pair of legs as they dangled, swinging from front to back in a carefree way. She was sitting on the desk portion so her feet didn't come close to meeting the ground.

The urge to draw them and put them on paper was strong. I remembered when I was that carefree and young. The act was so innocent and showcased how she had the whole world and the rest of your life at her fingertips. It was easy to be pulled into those nostalgic thoughts as you got older. My eyes focused on her swinging legs again.

Back and forth. Back and forth. Back and forth.

"I've really enjoyed the tones and language used so far. You can easily identify whose point of view it is even if it wasn't clearly outlined in the chapter," a familiar female voice said.

My eyes snapped up from the pair of legs to the face of

the owner of said legs. I realized what she had said and continued to study her for a minute. She sounded genuinely interested in the topic. I had found her in the library earlier so it should have been obvious that she likely loved to read.

After I realized I was spending way too much time focusing on her, I went back to my emails and continued to listen. I didn't want to show any students special attention. Specifically female students.

The bell rang loudly throughout the room and students rushed to gather their things to leave. "Miss Knox," I called out. "Please stay behind for a moment, I'd like a word."

So much for avoiding special attention.

She pursed her lips and finished gathering together her binder and notes. The boy at her side was wearing a pissed off scowl but finally turned her way before signing something. She smiled and shook her head gently. He nodded and gave her arm a squeeze before leaving without a backwards glance.

She had an annoyed look pasted on her face as she stared at me silently, waiting for me to say something. I was going to have to just swallow my pride and get it out there, or else I was no better than the little punks in this place who pretend they did no wrong.

I was meant to lead those who wanted guidance, and show them the difference between right and wrong. Or show them what to do when you were wrong and you needed to kiss the feet of a little seventeen year old pistol with a mean mug like she could rip your face off with her teeth.

I could tell she was angry. What I couldn't figure out was if she always had an undertone of anger, or if she was just particularly angry with *me*.

I cleared my throat. "Right, well... Please accept my apologies for my outburst earlier. I admit that I handled that part rather poorly."

"That part?" She crossed her arms over her chest, and my eyes dropped to the motion. "What part, specifically, do you think you did handle correctly?"

I walked around to the front of my desk and leaned against it before mimicking her arms crossed at the chest. Another silent moment passed as we held each other's gaze in a stand off.

Silence except for the occasional laughter or slamming of a locker in the hall.

"Why weren't you wearing your things," I asked as I gestured my finger to the side of her head.

I saw her stand straighter with a fierce as hell look on her face. I lifted my hands in a placating motion and tried to clarify before she stabbed me with one of my grading pens.

"I just mean, why did you take them out, and block out the world," I asked, genuinely curious.

Her anger slowly faded from her face and she looked to the side to cover the small smirk gracing her lips. I wasn't sure what was so funny about my question when she was ready to rip my head off over it five seconds ago.

Her eyes drifted back over to mine but the small hint of her smirk remained.

"Well, Mr. Bennett, it seems you answered your own question." She cocked her head to the side and watched me. After realization dawned on me, she must have seen it in my face because she couldn't hide the smile now.

"You *want* to block out the world," I stated, not questioning it.

She nodded.

"Sometimes."

"Why, though?"

"Life is loud. Messy. Chaotic. Sometimes, it's just too much." She looked down to the floor. "Everything has sound. The scrape of your pencil as you drag it across a piece of paper. The hum of the 20 year old mini fridge that Mrs. Lowell has tucked behind her desk in the library. The freshman kid blowing his nose into his tissue as he passes me in the hallway. The squeak of my Vans on the heavily polished school floors. Your breathing." She gestured to my chest.

Right at that moment, I realized that my breathing had indeed picked up in pace while she was speaking. Her words hit me like a train at full speed. I didn't realize how zoned in she was to everything around her. Hearing all those things you weren't used to must be exhausting.

I willed my breathing to calm as I continued to watch her. Though, I couldn't help but secretly listen to the sounds around me that I so easily blocked out every single day. The things that I could easily disregard… haunted her.

"So it's your way to take a break? To shut it off?"

She nodded slowly. "I may be ruled by silence. But I thrive in it."

I nodded thoughtfully. "I think I understand. I'm sorry, Halen. You're the first person I've met with this disa– I mean, that is deaf. I didn't really understand, but I want to. So if I am missing something from here on out, please tell me. Help me understand. I will try my best not to make any assumptions."

She smiled then and nodded her head before moving to the door.

"Halen?" I couldn't help it. It was eating away at me.

"Yes?" She asked as she stopped and slightly turned her body to face me.

"What did Mr. Ressner sign to you as he was leaving?"

She let out a chuckle before smirking at me. "Wouldn't you like to know. Maybe learn some signs and next time you can properly eavesdrop."

With those words hanging in the air, she left the classroom, presumably to her next class. I stayed fixed in my place as I let them fully sink in. Truth be told, I did. I really wanted to know.

CHAPTER 5

-HALEN-

"What did Mr. Bennett want?" Nicky asked as I laid on his bed reading my book.

I shrugged even though he couldn't see it, his head buried in his computer. "He just wanted to apologize for being a dickhead in the library earlier today."

He scoffed and swiveled in his computer chair to face me. I paused my reading and placed a finger on my stopping place because this story was really starting to get good and I didn't want to lose my spot. Lifting my eyes to meet his, I saw the disdain clear as day.

"He was the teacher that made you feel like shit? Our English teacher? Fucking great. I already didn't like him, but now I have a genuine reason to want to bury him."

I sighed and gave him a soft smile. "It's okay. I'm okay. He was actually very kind and interested in learning about my implants once we began to speak openly to one another."

"He was interested in you?" His hands went into light fists on the arm rests of the chair and the seriousness was heavily taking over his face. Nicky cared about me more than anyone I knew. Sometimes it could come off as over the top, but I always knew it was from a place of love.

I was only worried about what would happen when I finally started dating. Or worse, when I finally lost my virginity. I would probably need Evan's help as a buffer on that one. He would absolutely flip.

As much of a wild card I could be, Nicky had always made it a point to keep me innocent. He never wanted to see an asshole hurt my heart, or take my time away from him or Evan. For the first year of our friendship as our unbreakable trio, I actually thought that both Evan and Nicky would be my boyfriends.

I was naive, but it was understandable, given that I was 12 years old. But nothing ever came from our friendship. We had always been more than friends, but less than romantic. Just a mini family, I suppose. Evan and Nicky were beautiful, don't get me wrong, but none of us ever made that push. I always kind of figured that they didn't want a deaf girlfriend, but deep down I think they might have just wanted to preserve our tight bonds.

Grabbing one of his pillows from behind me, I chucked it at him with a laugh. "Not like that, you idiot. About being deaf and having the cochlear. Now, where is Evan? I thought he would be here by now."

I pulled out my phone, ready to text him when Nicky spoke up. "He was flirting with some girl in our statistics class. They made plans to get coffee after school."

My brows shot up to my hairline at hearing that. Not like Evan wasn't a total golden boy with an angel face. His face was beautiful in all society deemed ways. But it was only the first day! One day in and he already had a date and potential future girlfriend.

Prick.

"That boy wasn't kidding about going all out this year," I said as I settled back into a laying position. "I can't wait to find someone. Maybe it will be easier next year at Gallaudet."

He let out a sigh and scooted his rolling chair over towards the bed. Reaching for my hand, he kept his eyes on mine. "Don't worry about dating right now. All guys our age are after one thing only. Just wait. Use your time at Gallaudet to find yourself, and to see me on the weekends, of course." He winked.

I squeezed his hand and brought it to my mouth to kiss the knuckles. "I know, but you *do* know I will start dating eventually? I can't find Mr. Right if I'm always pushing boys away," I whisper.

His smile was tight but he slowly nodded his head. "Of course. Just remember that I hold my ground, and I personally don't think anyone is good enough for you. I don't like the idea of your innocence tainted."

He rolled back over to his desk and I huffed a laugh as I went back to my book. In all the years he had known me, it still baffled me that he considered me innocent. Sure, I followed the rules growing up and usually didn't give too much lip. But I also pushed boundaries with my clothes, my friends, and hopefully soon by quitting dance.

Dance is a beautiful form of art. Truly. It's just not me. I always wanted to be plain and simple Halen. My parents had more interest in shoving me in socially appropriate hobbies than listening to what I wanted for myself.

Granted, I didn't know that I would have picked anything if they had given me the choice. I would have rather soaked in the tub or lay under a weeping willow with a good book. But at least I would be happy. Didn't that count for something?

My phone buzzed with text notification and I paused my reading to glance at it. Maybe Evan needed help getting out of his date.

Mom: Get home, NOW. You have to freshen up before dinner this evening. I know you likely look like a wreck.

"Ah, shit! I gotta go."

Nicky turned and looked at me with furrowed eyebrows. "What's wrong?"

"Um. Nothing. Just a dinner with family friends. Nothing important, but as a Knox, I am obligated to be there and look like the perfect cookie cutter daughter that has a five foot rod shoved up her ass."

Nicky gave a low whistle at my outburst, and turned back around to his computer. "Right, well, give them hell. Call me later and give me all of the gossip."

"Of course, and give Evan a kiss on the cheek for me. Tell him I will catch him later," I yelled out as I started running out of his bedroom door.

"I'm not kissing Evan for you, little twerp!" I heard him shout as I barreled out of the front door and to my car.

After racing home, I managed to throw on my designated dress and run a razor over my legs in record time. I touched up my makeup and spritzed myself with my favorite Burberry perfume.

Walking down the stairs to the main dining room, I could hear music playing alongside the mindless chatter. As I got closer, the sounds of Perpetual by Yannick Lowack filtered through the air. While I could hear the beauty in some parts, the ringing tones in my ear could only be described as painful to listen to.

My cochlear struggled to pick up certain sounds and pitches. I typically enjoyed music more without it. Just feeling the vibrations around me in that special rhythm was more than enough for me.

I elegantly joined my parents who were speaking to a couple of people. My mother turned her head to look at me. I watched her eyes track down my body as she surely ticked off everything possible wrong with my outfit in her head.

"Halen, dear. I was wondering when you would finally make it. Let me introduce you to the Jaffly family. This is Mr. Edward Jaffly, and his wife, Eleanor." She gestured to the immaculately dressed couple. Edward was on the much older side. If I had to guess, I would probably place him in his late 60s.

I wasn't able to place Elenor's age if I tried. She clearly had enough botox and facial fuckery to try to fool everyone. When did it become such a crime to age gracefully?

I reached my hand out to Mr. and Mrs. Jaffly in a friendly shake, and I heard my mothers sharp intake of breath. While I was positive I was the only one who heard it, I was still surprised as to why. The handshake was spot on in terms of etiquette. Not too firm and masculine, not too flimsy like a dead fish.

I looked up towards her discreetly and saw her lips pinched tight.

Oh yeah, she was annoyed for sure. Why? No fucking clue. Pushing her dramatics aside, I listened as Edward went on and on, asking me about what I had planned for my future and about my interests.

For a moment, though fleeting, I forgot the reason that these people were here. My arrangement. It seems that their son was on the list of candidates to tie me down with a Harry Winston rock.

"Ah, darling, there you are," Eleanor said sweetly. Though strangely, her mouth barely moved. "Please come meet Mr. and Mrs. Knox, and their delightful daughter, Halen. Halen, this is my son, Gregory."

I turned around to look at who she was speaking to and saw a young man walk up with Enzo, our butler. I had to admit, the man was beautiful in an uptight, stick up his ass kind of way. If he could carry a conversation, I figured it wouldn't be a total disaster of a dinner.

I continued studying him. His brown tousled curls that were pulled back by entirely too much hair gel, his face that was fully bare of facial hair, and his honey brown eyes that danced with amusement. He smirked as he caught me assessing him.

My cheeks flushed but I stood my ground. He thought he had the upper hand by making me uncomfortable. I didn't like feeling like the fish in a tank with a shark. I grew up feeling that way everyday with my parents, so any chance I had to remedy it, I took.

He finally approached with his hand outstretched to mine and a dazzling white smile. "Miss Halen, a pleasure."

I gently placed my hand in his which he promptly brought to his mouth to place a kiss on top. Here was my chance. It was go time, baby.

I pulled my hand back gently and brought both of my hands in front of me.

"The pleasure is all mine," I signed.

His smile fell instantly and he shifted uncomfortably on his feet looking at both my parents and his for direction. His cheeks flushed crimson and he cleared his throat, clearly trying to stall for a moment.

Checkmate, bitch!

"Halen!" My mother snapped. "We have guests. Don't speak other languages that they don't know, it's rude." She looked at Edward and Eleanor apologetically.

A look of relief passed over Gregory's face and he exhaled a quiet chuckle. "Ah, you're bi-lingual? That's very impressive. I'm multi-lingual in German, Spanish, and Japanese."

I gave him a warm smile. "Yes, I am, because I'm deaf."

His face fell again. "I'm, um, sorry to hear th–" I held up my hand to stop him mid-sentence.

"No need to be sorry. I'm not. It's who I am, and I am proud of who I am."

He smiled uncomfortably. "Yes, well, it's lovely to meet you, Halen." He looked at my mother and father. "It is also a pleasure to meet both of you Mr. and Mrs. Knox. You have a stunning home. Thank you for inviting me."

"Of course, Gregory. We are honored. Shall we take a seat for the first course to be brought out?" My mother asked the Jafflys.

Everyone nodded in agreement and we took our seats. Time slowly passed as I listened to the practically snooze worthy discussions of politics and gossip. I occasionally caught Gregory watching me with a mixture of interest and uncertainty. I had definitely caught him off guard and thrown him off his game earlier.

I couldn't tell if he was still interested in me, or grossed out. His expression was hard to decipher. It didn't really matter though. I wanted to marry for love. As much of a show as my parents liked to put on regarding my marriage, if the time ever arose for my arrangement to be sealed, they would have to drag me down the aisle by my hair.

Until then, I was going to try to find a way out.

CHAPTER 6

-SAWYER-

Classes were beginning to find a steady rhythm as the weeks went on. I was beginning to truly feel settled in at the school. I did have to deal with the occasional run in with Ellen, but I could tell she meant well.

I finished my cup of coffee while I prepped for the first period class. Fire Up The Night by New Medicine filtered through my classroom. Having some upbeat music was always a nice way to start my mornings. Caffeine also helped. A fuck ton of caffeine.

I always felt like Wednesdays were worse than Mondays. You're far enough into the week that you can feel the weekend, but still too far from that blissful break to get excited. It's like seeing land on either side of you but not having a life raft to get to either one quick enough.

A throat clearing had me whipping my head from my computer to meet the vibrant green eyes of one of my best students recently. Upon meeting her, I was sure she was going to be a pain in my ass or simply one of the students that simply blew everything off.

I was rarely wrong in my assumptions, but every assumption I had made of her to date, was wrong. Even the kids that were still saveable in the eyes of education, I was able to point out. She went against the rules I had built in my head.

I knew she hung out with a few questionable kids, including one of my other students, Dominic Ressner. She also dressed like she would either light up a joint or hop on the back of a crotch rocket with her college aged tatted up boyfriend.

I didn't actually know if she had a boyfriend, but she looked like that would be the scenario if she did. My eye twitched at the thought of her getting on the back of a Ducati with a reckless frat boy. I pushed the unwanted thought away. I was only feeling that way because seeing a high school kid on a motorcycle would make anyone nervous. Especially a teacher. Yeah. That must have been it.

"Halen," I said with raised eyebrows. Checking my watch I noticed it was still an hour before the first period. The halls were still mostly quiet with only a few teachers roaming passed here and there. "You're at school really early. What can I help you with?"

She smiled and it was at that moment I realized just how beautiful she truly was.

Seventeen, you fucking perv.

"Good morning, Teach. I actually wanted to chat with you about our reading assignments going forward, if you don't mind."

My eyes practically shot up to my hairline. She wanted to discuss her assignments going forward? Why did I feel like I was the one about to get schooled. My eyes narrowed as I recalled her nickname for me. Teach. I'm not sure I liked it, or I liked it a lot. I couldn't tell.

I gestured to the seat next to mine behind my desk that I kept there for one on one mentoring during class while other students read. She rounded the desk and dropped her back pack to the floor before taking a seat.

"Okay I'm just going to come right out with it. I'm not satisfied with your performance," she said with no humor in her voice.

I choked on my coffee and spluttered my caramel macchiato everywhere while trying to regain my senses. Not satisfied with my performance? What the hell? I eyed her as we stayed staring in silence for a moment. Something I was quickly realizing we did often.

Her words from a few weeks ago filtered back into my

mind.

"I may be ruled by silence. But I thrive in it."

I also found a strange comfort in the quiet moments my entire life. My brother and I were always alike in that regard. While he has always had a rough edge to him, I liked to think I was a bit softer. I had to be, given my profession.

I couldn't imagine a world where Connor actually taught high schoolers. He would absolutely kill one by accident. I've never had the outright knowledge of what he did for a living, but I knew it suited him. And to not ask questions.

But this girl in front of me, she was soft. Everything about her style screamed edgy, but I could tell that her mind and soul was lighter and fluffy. Bright. It was just trapped underneath a sharp attitude and bitterness. From being deaf? Neglect? Trauma? I didn't know which.

"I have never had complaints about my performance before, Miss Knox. Please, enlighten me."

Wow, way to sound like a fucking predator.

A smirk graced her face like she knew exactly what I was thinking. As quick as it appeared though, a serious expression took over.

"Well, consider me your first, sir," she said in a more hushed tone. Before I could even let the sentence take my mind places that it really fucking shouldn't go, she continued. "I need more. I have finished all of the books on the syllabus and need some more recommendations to keep me occupied. I like the variety of genres that you have picked so far. I want to branch out even more and find some authors and sub-genres that will really pull me in."

I let her words sink in for a moment, nodding in understanding. She shifted in her seat as she crossed her left leg over her right. My eyes tracked the movement as she placed her hands back on her black pleated skirt, in her lap.

Snapping out of it, I met her eyes.

"Right, well, I can make an exploratory list for you of books that you might enjoy from different genres. What have you found to be the most enjoyable so far?" I asked as she cocked her head in thought.

"Probably romance. Cliche, I know. But I think I want to look into the kind that is dark or less conventional. I loved Wuthering Heights and Jane Eyre that you gave us. But I would like to try darker, maybe. Or even some fantasy."

"Fantasy? Like, what? The Lord of the Rings?"

She nodded. Okay then. She really did blow through my syllabus. I was kind of surprised that she actually managed to plow through that many books so quickly. Did she even have a personal life?

"Alright, I will see what I can put together by the end of the week. Come see me after school on Friday and we can go over it. How does that sound?"

"Perfect! Thank you."

I couldn't resist asking. "How did you get through the list so quickly? Or more importantly, I should ask, why?"

She shrugged. "Escapism probably. Some people snort coke, I read shameless fu-" she stopped abruptly, suddenly clearing her throat. "Romance."

I lifted a brow but I couldn't stop the smile from stretching across my face. I didn't know if I was supposed to scold her for talking about snorting coke in front of a teacher, or that she was clearly readying filthy bodice rippers during free periods.

Her smile matched mine and we both chuckled before none other than Ellen came waltzing in. I saw her boobs enter the room approximately fifteen seconds before the rest of her body appeared.

"Sawyer, good morning! Happy hump day!"

This woman's goddamn timing couldn't have been any fucking worse. I shouldn't have been thinking about humping just moments after speaking with Halen about fucking books... And books about fucking.

Halen's eyes met mine in a brief glance, both of us trying to hold in our smirks at the innuendo that only we were privy to. I saw Halen stare at her lap for a moment before rolling her lips inward.

Don't you dare laugh, little girl. I won't be able to stop mine.

I looked back to Ellen, plastering on a fake smile. "Miss Ferrier, it's good to see you. I was just speaking with Halen about reading materials. What can I help you with?"

Her eyes flicked over to Halen momentarily before drifting back to me. "Well, I thought I would remind you that we have a happy hour this Friday. I wanted to give you a few weeks to settle in before mentioning it again. But we can carpool from here if you are interested in going."

My thoughts were scrambled as I tried to think of a quick and believable excuse. I didn't exactly want to come right out and say I would rather jump off of the school roof.

The truth was that I didn't know whether I was ready to move on or not. Victoria and I were together for so long that it felt improper to not give myself time to grieve time wasted and memories I will never make again. I was livid at what she had done, for weeks. My heart felt content moving on and letting go afterwards, except for the bitterness of her making a fool out of me.

I guess I was just confused on what it was that I really was feeling. Ellen's eyes held mine as I watched her shuffle from foot to foot with nerves. I couldn't come up with anything quick enough.

"Sure, um, I think I can spare a Friday evening amongst co-workers." God, I sounded like a douche. "Why don't we meet here at 4PM?"

She beamed at me and clapped her hands together excitedly. "Wonderful! I'll see you then." She glanced at Halen and her smile faltered for a split second before reappearing, firmly back in place. The door of the classroom clicked shut with her departure.

I turned back to Halen and saw she was twisting her fingers in her lap, chewing on her lip. "I'm not big on school functions, so next time I'd appreciate it if you bailed me out.

You kind of left me hanging there. So thanks a lot."

She snapped her head up with her mouth hanging open and a slight annoyance firing in her eyes. When she registered the smirk firmly in place, she barked a laugh and shook her head. "Not a social butterfly, Teach?"

I shrugged. "Not typically. Especially not with people that I hardly know." Silence stretched in the air. "As I was saying earlier, drop by on Friday before 4 PM and I will have that list ready for you."

She smiled and grabbed her backpack before standing up. I watched her tuck an auburn strand behind her ear, revealing her implant. I'd completely forgotten that she had them for a bit. Her speech was perfectly smooth and free of wavering.

"Thank you. See you then."

With that, she sashayed around the student desks and out the door. My mind was stuck on her for an extra moment. She was not at all what I had expected. But it felt nice to have such an easygoing conversation with her.

I didn't want it to end. It had been so long since I had genuine sparks of organic conversation with someone. Thinking back it was probably a year or two before I ended things with Victoria. Even while we were still together, we lost interest in talking with one another. But with Halen, it was easy, natural, and just *right*.

And *that* was dangerous.

CHAPTER 7

-HALEN-

"Halen, Halen, Halen..." Katherine snorted. "Did you hear about the halloween party coming up in three weeks?"

I began to speak but was rudely interrupted.

"Of course you didn't. You should probably adjust the antennas on those things or something. Doesn't matter anyway. It's not like you fit in with the crowd anyway. You also wouldn't even be able to enjoy the music. Maybe it's a blessing, honey."

My blood boiled with anger but I tried to keep my face from flushing with fury. What a thunder cunt. I inhaled slowly trying to slow my heart rate. I couldn't start throwing punches in school.

My mother would keep me from seeing the boys. She had always seen them as a bad influence. I believe her exact words were *barbarians without class*. I refused to give her a reason, even though I was going to be eighteen soon.

"As if I would be interested in attending a party where body odor wafts in the air and innocent girls are roofied. While you're dry heaving in a toilet with half of your fake lashes hanging off your eyes, I will be cozied up with my guys, enjoying a peaceful night. But by all means, have fun girlie." I winked as I stepped around her.

Nicky watched as I approached him and Evan with a dramatic eyeroll. When I got within whispering distance, I heard Evan speak in a hushed voice. "Wait, does this mean we aren't going? Babe, come on. It's our senior year. Pretty please? I'll do your laundry."

"My mother hired people to do our laundry a long time ago."

"I'll do your homework," he said quickly.

"I actually want to pass."

"I'll… I'll tell everyone that you sucked me off better than anyone ever has. Including Katherine."

"Ew, don't remind me that you let that happen." My nose scrunched up at the reminder of his drunk encounter with her during a game of truth or dare our freshman year.

I thought about what he said for a moment longer. Not the drunk mistake, but him doing it in a subtle way to make Katherine look bad. She had made it her mission to torment me since I moved here. She was pissy that I was the shiny new toy with something unique about me, when she was as plain as they come. All the attention I got, specifically Evan's, set her on a warpath to make me a social pariah.

God, she really was a twat. Maybe this was my chance for a little harmless payback.

"Fine," I said as I smiled at him. "But not only do you need to talk me up, but you also need to drag her down a little."

"Hell yeah. Deal."

"I don't like this," Nicky mumbled. "If you are sucking any dick, it should be Daddy Dom's, remember?"

I leaned into him as we continued walking. "How could I forget? Love you Nicky."

I felt his arm band around my shoulder as he placed a kiss into my hair. My smile grew as I finished walking the boys to the cafeteria. This was where I usually split off to head to the library.

A sense of peace washed over me when I walked into the quiet room filled with rows and rows of books. I traced my finger along the spines of a few hardcovers that had caught my eye. Pulling them from the shelf, I walked to the checkout station and scanned my library card.

Tugging the cochlear from my ear, I stuffed it into my backpack and continued to fully immerse myself in the silence.

With a deep breath I sat down at one of the floor to ceiling windows and grabbed one of my selections from my bag at random.

Shatter Me by Tahereh Mafi.

I couldn't hear the spine cracking as I opened my book, but I could feel the stuttering vibrations on my fingers as I stretched the book apart to get a full view of the pages.

Looking at my smart watch, I saw that I had about twenty minutes remaining until lunch period ended. I didn't waste another second before diving into the first page.

With a start, I felt my watch buzz and I realized how quickly the time had passed. I was already so invested in the story unfolding before me. I knew I was going to have a hard time putting this one down.

I pulled a pin from my hair and slipped it onto the page to mark my spot before closing the book and stuffing back into my backpack. With a stretch of my arms and legs, I took the moment to take in the surroundings of the library.

That's when I noticed the back of a tall man exiting through the double doors. Studying his muscular arms and firm ass filling the khaki pants, I had a feeling I knew exactly who it was.

Firm ass? Really? No. Bad Halen. Bad.

Shaking my head I rushed to gather my things and head towards the cafeteria. It was already shaping into a long day.

"Excuse you, young lady. Watch your mouth! Richard, are you hearing this," my mother asked in a sharp tone.

My father sighed and pressed the bridge of his nose between his thumb and index finger. I could feel his high blood pressure expanding his arteries from here. One day I figured his heart would go, pop! Bursting like a fake tit in a de-pressurized cabin.

"Jennifer, she knows her obligations. She is just acting

like a teenager. We were all one once, even you.. When the time comes, she will follow through."

"What part of, 'I am done being a pawn in your gold digger matchmaking games', did you both not understand? Here, hold on, I understand the problem better than anyone."

My hands raised in front of me, and I cracked my knuckles for added dramatics. My mother had a way with theatrics so I was definitely speaking her language now. Loud and clear.

"Tell Gregory, the trust fund baby, that I would rather jump in front of a taxi than endure a date night out with him." My hands finished signing as I swear steam began to rise from my mother's ears and nostrils. Holding in my smile at her fury was harder than I thought it would be.

"Halen. Stop it right now. I won't force you to bond with Gregory on the date your mother arranged, but you *will* be marrying him. The contract is supposed to hit my desk by Sunday. So, consider it in your best interest that you start finding common ground with that young man. Otherwise, only you will be suffering the consequences of losing time becoming friends first."

My dads words felt like a judge's gavel being struck against polished wood. What if I failed to find a way out? I really would be fucking myself in the long run. Maybe I should've been playing the long game a little smarter. Having to deal with this shit would definitely be an ugly reminder of my future. But maybe it would continually fuel my fire.

Maybe… it could be used as a bargaining chip for something I want to rid myself of right now. "Fine, I will go on the required outings with him, without fuss, on one condition."

"Of course," my mother huffed in annoyance.

Her icy glare settled back on me where I smiled with my full mocking innocent grin and looked between her and my father. "I want to withdraw from dance."

"What? Absolutely not!" My mother fumed. She opened her mouth, fully ready to run through her whole list of reasons why hell would freeze over before she allowed me to drop it. We were both stunned as my father's intense stare on me continued, and he sliced a hand up in the air towards my mother, silencing her.

We all stood there with the quiet surrounding us for a moment. Nothing but the sounds of the neighbor's landscaping crew running the lawnmower next door and the ticking of the grandfather clock in the living room.

With his hand still raised in her face, he exhaled a long and deep breath. "I think that is... reasonable. Dumb, but reasonable."

I waited for the outburst of my mothers tantrum to take over, but thankfully it didn't come. At least someone had the ability to get her to shut the fuck up when needed.

She didn't have another choice really. She signed an iron clad prenuptial agreement when she married my father. She would never risk him leaving her. I also happened to know that she turned a blind eye when he came home with lipstick on his collar, or wearing a different outfit than what he left the house in.

She never said a word. She would go out and plow through 100k on his credit card in a single afternoon, but she never had anything to actually say on the matter. Was she playing her own long game? Nah. She definitely wasn't smart enough for that kind of long term planning. Nor was she patient.

I knew she genuinely loved my father. But I think her love for greed, power and status outweighed any kind of love or affection a human being could give her. That was the real difference between me and her. I would beg someone on my knees to take away the unnecessary wealth, status, and obligations that comes with being the daughter of a well known wealthy family if it meant finding my true love.

This wasn't me winning the war, by any means, but it was a small victory, and for that I would be thankful .

I smirked and made eye contact with my very red faced

mother. “Tell him to pick me up tomorrow after school, and to dress in jeans and a tee.”

My father finally relaxed and nodded before walking away to his office, leaving me and the she-devil in the same breathing space.

I watched her tense muscles restrict even further as if she was posing to strike. I didn’t cower, because she didn't scare me. Piss me off? Yes, always. Scare me? Never. She wouldn’t do anything to me out of risk of damaging a perfectly manicured nail.

Materialistic bitch.

“You better not ruin this, Halen. You act on your best behavior and treat that boy like the gentleman that he is. If I find out that your little felon friends are hanging around him, or that you are giving him a hard time, there will be hell to pay. I could always match you with Eric Eisner. Recognize that me pairing you with Gregory was a courtesy that you clearly don’t deserve.”

CHAPTER 8

-SAWYER-

Friday rolled around and I spent it exactly how I always did, jamming out in my classroom in the early morning before all of the grumbling teenagers flooded the halls. Killing Me Slowly by Bad Wolves surrounded me as I tapped my foot to the beat.

Reading through essays, I made a hefty dent in my grading pile. This set of essays weren't nearly as bad as some in the past, but if I had to read the word 'dude' or 'slay' one more time, I was going to jam this #2 pencil straight into my eye socket in the hopes of a botched lobotomy.

The students were instructed to argue their opinions on the ending that takes place in the classic *Of Mice and Men*. I was convinced that half of them only watched the movie instead of read the book, but points for trying, I guess

Little did they know, I planned to show them the movie at the end of our essay deadline anyway. Looks like they would be watching it twice. My leg continued to bounce and I grabbed my coffee to calm myself down a tad.

You would think it would do the opposite, since caffeine is supposed to give you a boost, but the warm cozy liquid always had a way of unwinding me. Especially when I felt myself beginning to rush with tasks. It was just a simple comforting reminder to take a second, enjoy your drink, and get back to work with a clearer focus.

I graded more essays and checked the clock on the computer to see how I was doing on time. One hour until the herd would arrive. Plenty of time to knock out the rest of these.

"Teach?" The whisper in my ear from behind, tickled the hairs on my neck and sent me shooting up out of my seat with a startle. As I began to turn around the pen slipped from my shocked fingers and clattered to the ground.

Kneeling down to the ground, I grabbed the pen on instinct before actually looking to see who it was that caught me by surprise in the first place. Deep down, I knew. But I didn't really process it until I made the crucial mistake of kneeling down right in front of her. Only one person called me Teach.

Halen.

She was rattling my mind a little bit lately. It made me uneasy. There was no reason to see her any differently than every other high school girl that walked these halls. But she had a maturity about her. Mature with a rebellious bite. It kept things interesting. Her essays always had a tone to them that kept me on my toes. That was rare for students these days.

With one knee on the ground in a kneeling position, and the other bracing my arm clutching the dropped pen, I chanced a look at the thick black loafers standing directly in my line of sight. They were spotless and shiny. Possibly designer. I wouldn't know though considering teachers had pennies for a salary.

My eyes began to lift from the shoes, up the toned legs. I traced the smooth edges of creamy white calves that looked soft as silk. Followed the glide of her bare and exposed thighs right up to the edge of... oh, hell... a pleated tartan skirt.

I felt a pang of disgust at my instant attraction to the beautiful woman's body before me. She was seventeen. I needed a slap in the fucking face. Regardless of the fact that she was older than the age of consent, she was also my student. Double no.

Snapping my gaze away from her pressed thighs, I rose to my full height and finally met the jade eyes that could bring me right back to my fucking knees.

Nope. Jailbait, kinda. Your student. No.

"Halen," I said with a raspy edge to my voice. Clearing

it, I continued. "Are you going to make a habit of these early morning visits?"

She shrugged and smiled. "Maybe. I wouldn't mind having a place to work on my assignments where I'm not alone but I'm with someone who understands I want to unplug." She mimed the action of pulling her hearing aids off.

Without thought, I touched her chin and slightly turned her head to the side. Her eyes remained fully focused on mine the entire time, wide and unblinking. Her lips parted, on the quietest gasp that I wasn't even sure if she realized it. I then slowly shifted her head to the other side, getting a good view of both implants.

Realizing I was holding her chin in a rather tender grasp, I yanked my hand back like it had been burned. Man, I was really fucking up this morning.

Way to go, Merv the perv.

"Go ahead and sit wherever you like. Will it bother you that I have music playing?" I pointed to the overhead speaker.

Her lips thinned as a stony expression took place.

Panic rushed through my system as I realized what I had just asked. Of course it wouldn't bother her, she was here to unplug. She wouldn't hear a thing. Silence.

She must have recognized the second I put the pieces together because she barked a laugh so abruptly, it caught me off guard. It was a genuine laugh full of understanding and humor that I couldn't help my own chuckle from slipping through my lips, my shoulders relaxing a bit. Her laugh was infectious, in the best possible way. Like sunshine while you can still smell the rain permeating the air.

"Yeah, I guess I didn't really think that one through first," I said, rubbing the nape of my neck.

Her laugh died down but her smile remained fixed in place. "It's fine. We all have those moments. I don't want you to treat it like it's something you need to walk on eggshells around. I don't see it as a hindrance, so neither should you. I won't be able to feel the vibrations of the music either since the speaker is so high up, so I highly doubt it will be an issue in being a distraction."

She walked towards her usual desk in the front row and took a seat. I watched her pull her textbook and assignment out before pulling her cochlears off and setting them at the top of the desk.

I sat back down and pulled another sip from my mug before focusing back on my work. She was quiet and her assignment had her full attention, however I struggled to maintain my progress.

Every few minutes I would be reminded of her presence with the shift of her legs, crossing from one side to the other. Disturbingly, it took restraint not to watch the action. Every heavy sigh would pull me from my grading with the urge to ask her if she needed any help with her work. I refrained. She said she wanted quiet, so I tried to give her that.

We continued to work that way until the early bell rang to signal the arrival of students. I waved my hand over at her, catching her attention before pointing to the door. She saw the students walking by, realizing her time was up. She quickly packed her things, plugged back in and strutted towards the door, while I kept my eyes on the papers in front of me.

"Hey, Teach?"

My eyes snapped up to meet hers, and I waited for what she had to say.

"Thank you, for letting me chill in here." She gestured to her seat. "Did you have that list of book recommendations for me?"

I did have them. In the bottom drawer of my desk. "Not yet, I just have a few more to add to it that completely slipped my mind. But if you come back after the last bell, I can have it by then. Promise."

She grinned. "Alright. See you then, Mr. Bennett." She turned around and sauntered out of the door and into the hall that was quickly filling with hormonal teens.

What the fuck was I doing?

◆ ◆ ◆

Towards the end of the day, I decided to make a trip through the halls to stretch my legs. Sitting at a desk all day made me feel weak and pained. I could literally feel my muscles atrophying by the hour. God, I was getting old.

The thought of being in my forties in only a few months made me nervous. I wasn't ready to feel the time ticking by so quickly. I felt like I had hardly even lived, but life after forty seemed to be a minefield. Prostate checks. Colonoscopies. Saggy skin. Muscle breakdown. Osteoporosis. Damn, the thought alone made me shiver.

As I passed through the atrium, I saw a fellow teacher watering the plants that gave the area the perfect burst of life. I hadn't seen him before, but he looked to be around my age, maybe a tad bit younger.

"Were all of these plants your idea?" I asked softly to avoid the open space catching my echoing voice.

He looked my way and gave a smiling nod. "Indeed they were. I figured they would really give a natural pop of color. Nature intrigues me. Calms me. I figured this would be a great place for the kids to have something beautiful during the doom and gloom of the winter months here."

I looked around at all of his potted greenery. "It was smart. It definitely caught my eye when I first saw it. I've sat in here a good few times myself to grade papers."

"Oh, that's right! Where are my manners? My name is Brent Putnam, I am the choir director. I heard you started this year after moving from Chicago, is that right?" He reached out a hand for me to shake after setting the watering can down.

I clasped his hand and shook it. "Nice to meet you. Yeah, I needed a fresh start."

"Ah. Your wife left you too, huh?"

I reared back in shock, wondering how the hell he knew of my relationship complications. Was the gossip really that bad here? I hadn't gotten to know anyone really besides Ellen, but even that was conversational only. Interested in what he knew, I answered with caution.

"Um no. Not exactly. Not my wife and I was the one that did the leaving." I'm not sure why I was being so honest. Maybe I was so sick and tired of dishonesty that I didn't want to put in the effort for fake stories.

"Oh, wow. That blows. I'm sorry to hear that. For what it's worth, mine left me just before the school year started, so I am in a similar boat as you. Though, to be fair, mine left for reasons unknown, so occasionally I do struggle with the lack of closure." He shrugged.

Cocking an eyebrow, I asked the question that would be bothering me all day. "She just ghosted you?"

His laugh echoed through the atrium, bouncing off of the windows making it so much louder than normal. "Yes, actually."

I waited, seeing that he was going to speak more on the topic but didn't want to interrupt him.

"She's dead."

My breath caught in my chest and I could feel my face instantly fall. That was not at all what I was expecting. Usually people say those kinds of things with more finesse. He said it so matter of factly. Almost with no emotion behind it.

Letting the pieces click together, I finally realized what he was telling me. He had just openly told me that his wife committed suicide without even knowing me for more than five minutes. People in this city were weird.

I suppose I shouldn't have been surprised. It was literally known for being the *city of good neighbors*. For east coasters having the dickhead reputation that they had, most people here seemed to be kind and inviting. Unless you were driving during rush hour. But that came with the territory anywhere.

"Oh. I'm sorry for your loss." I said, feeling uncomfortable with the change of conversation direction.

He looked around at his thriving plants. "Thank you.

While it's been hard, I am healing. People in those situations don't understand the wreckage that they are leaving behind. I forgive her for it though. On a lighter note, are you going to the happy hour after work? I haven't seen you atend one yet."

Oh, shit. I had forgotten.

"Yeah, actually. Ellen invited me to carpool over. I would have completely forgotten if you hadn't reminded me. So, thanks."

He gave me a nod. My phone buzzed in my hand interrupting my conversation.

"Well I will let you get back to your day, but I'll see you this evening," I said as I scanned the name on the screen.

He gave a wave and walked off with his watering can. What a strange guy. Kind, but strange. It was still better to know someone with an odd personality than a manipulative one.

Opening the lock screen on my phone, I clicked on my texts.

Connor: Hey bro, I'm gonna be back in town in a couple of weeks. Not sure when I will be back on assignment again.

Quickly responding, I let him know that I would be sure to have all my hookers out of the condo for his return then continued my walk through the school and back to my barren classroom.

Before I knew it the dismissal bell rang and I gathered the jar I made for Halen. I added a few additional book recommendations during my lunch period. It was crossing a line to add them. I couldn't help it. She wouldn't connect any dots. She would just assume that they are coincidental among the other ones I had in there.

Pacing my classroom, I wanted for her to arrive soon, hoping that she would beat Ellen, since it would be quite awkward giving this to her in front of another teacher.

I felt her presence before I looked towards the doorway. Her auburn hair was strewn in a somewhat messy way like she had run a marathon to get here.

"Did you... run here?" I asked.

Her eyes sparkled with amusement. "I didn't want to miss you before you left. I've been eager for that list. I want to shop for some of them over the weekend.

Smirking, I nodded towards my desk and she followed behind me obediently. Obedient student. Obedient girl. Woman. I mean, an obedient woman.

I reached into my bottom drawer while maintaining eye contact with her. She swiveled her body from side to side anxiously while fidgeting with her fingers in front of her like she was about to open a christmas present.

"There are rules with this." I said, giving her a stern look. "First rule, you can only pick three out at a time to shop for. It will ruin the experience if you pick too many at once. Second, you have to unplug while you are reading. Don't let the outside world creep into your personal experience with these characters and their stories. Third, you have to message me your thoughts as you read through these. You have a unique mind, and I would love to hear your opinions on them."

She released a nervous breath and nodded eagerly. "Okay, okay. Deal. Just give it up, Teach!"

Chuckling, I pulled the jar out and held it in front of her. The jar was matte black with white roses scattered throughout. You couldn't see inside the glass, I made sure of it.

She looked like she was holding her breath but gently took the jar from my grasp. Her gaze never left the jar. She smiled widely and opened the lid.

"Remember the rules." I reminded her.

She gave me a sarcastic look followed by an eyeroll. "I know the rules." Pulling three popsicle sticks out she looked at each one to read what they said.

Each popsicle stick contained a book for her to read. There should have been enough to hold her over until the end of her senior year. I made sure of it. Though, seeing how fast she plowed through books, I was wondering if I should have added more just in case.

Her smile grew even more. I couldn't help the smile that was plastered on my face either.

"I made sure to add a few different genres and subgenres so see what interests you the most. I wanted to give you variety but still stay within your preferences."

She looked at me with such eagerness that I had a hard time gauging what she was thinking. I could tell she was happy, which I was thankful for. I was just surprised that something so simple made her so... giddy.

She clearly had money, so I guess I thought that when she wanted something she just bought it. But seeing her reaction to something like this made my mind trail off, creating theories. Maybe she didn't receive gifts for religious reasons. Maybe she loved the effort people put into more sentimental things. Maybe people didn't give her many gifts because she was neglected emotionally.

That last thought made my anger spike. Surely she was loved. She was a brilliant woman and so full of life. At the very least she had Ressner who stuck to her side like glue.

"Thank you," she whispered and locked eyes with me.

"Sawyer darling, are you ready to hit the road? Those drinks are calling our names."

Our moment was broken by Ellen's untimely arrival. Though she was actually on time, it was untimely for *me*. I strangely wanted more time with Halen. More time to look into her mind. Know her history. Make her... smile.

I met Ellen's eyes across the room and smiled gently. "Yes, of course. I was just wrapping up." Turning to Halen, I gave her an apologetic smile. "Remember the rules. I'll see you Monday, Squid."

Her brows furrowed, but she quickly masked her expression and gave Ellen and I a polite wave before exiting.

I looked at the overly eager Ellen. "Ready when you are."

CHAPTER 9

-HALEN-

Walking out of the school's main entrance, I saw the person I was secretly hoping wouldn't show. I almost did a double take when I realized it was him standing at the curb, because he wasn't sporting a douchey car with a custom paint job.

No. He was standing next to a beautifully loved motorcycle. My interest was now slightly piqued. Cocking my head to the side, I studied him. Maybe I judged him too quickly? He seemed to be interested in the more fun things in life. I walked his way and stopped right in front of him.

He dressed how I asked him to. Sporting a casual pair of jeans and a crisp fitted tee, I had to admit that he did look like quite the eye candy.

Gregory smirked and straddled his bike before handing a helmet over to me. I pulled my cochlear off and stuck it in my bag for safe keeping. I made sure my backpack was tightly fastened to my back before hiking a leg over the seat of the bike and grabbing ahold of his waist.

I had never backpacked someone before, so I was definitely eager for this adventure. I felt the bike rumble to life. After a few moments, I felt him rev the engine a couple of times, sending vibrations skittering throughout my body. I clutched on tighter and he gave my hands a courtesy squeeze before knocking the kickstand up.

With a deep breath, I looked around my surroundings, waiting for the moment that the buildings would speed by in a blur. Instead I saw the hard fixed glare of Mr. Bennett. He was standing at the front entrance with Ms. Ferrier, fists clenched at his sides. Was he upset with me? Maybe Ms. Ferrier had said something that pissed him off.

Gregory revved once more and the motorcycle lurched forward before he righted us and began to speed off. I was quickly reminded I was wearing completely inappropriate attire for this ride when I felt the wind caress my ass as we began to move. I reached back and tucked the hem of my skirt under my butt to keep it from flying up again.

With one final look behind me at the 2 teachers, I saw a disapproving expression on Ms. Ferrier's face and Mr. Bennett looked downright murderous. Damn. Clearly they weren't motorcycle lovers. Oh well.

I focused on my journey ahead as Gregory weaved in and out of traffic. He was lane splitting like a mad man and most definitely speeding. I was having a blast either way.

After about 15 minutes, he pulled in front of a dive bar called, Raw Dawgs. Charming. I was so shocked by the turn of events, that I had to admit, I was quite excited to see where tonight would go. Who would have thought that Gregory had a wild side like me.

As we entered the bar, the smell of boiled meat and beer wafted across my nose. It was disgusting. I loved it. I smiled at Gregory as he pointed to a high-top table, returning my smile. After sitting, I unzipped my backpack and retrieved my cochlears.

I saw his smile drop slightly before he fixed it firmly back in place. The sounds of the bar hit me all at once.

Clattering glasses.

Masculine laughter.

Chairs scraping against the floor.

"You look like you have questions. Or that my deafness makes you uncomfortable. I would prefer honesty to fake pleasantries, so please, ask away."

He winced. "It doesn't make me uncomfortable, that much. I'm just not used to it. I haven't met someone that is deaf before. Are you fully deaf?"

"Yes. Without the implants, I hear nothing. With it, I hear almost everything you would. Though some things are hard to hear correctly, like music."

He nodded slowly, clearly trying to wrap his head around it all. An awkward beat of silence passed before he finally spoke. "Okay, well, I only have one testicle if it makes you feel better. We are both kind of broken, huh?"

Anger surged through me. "I'm not broken. Maybe you ar–" I halted my sentence abruptly. "Wait. You have one testicle?"

His mouth twisted before nodding curtly.

A laugh bubbled out of me before I could stop it. Oh. This poor guy. He seemed to actually be trying to connect. I felt bad for assuming he was being malicious, but he was just misunderstood and also misunderstood me and my view on being deaf. Easily corrected. I realized I was being bitchy with the thought he was judging me without even knowing me. But in reality, that's exactly what I was doing to him.

Wiping a tear from my eye and taming my laughter, I met his eyes. He had a stern look, but I could tell he was going to crack a smile any second.

"We aren't broken, we are just different." I said with a lingering chuckle.

"I suppose you're right. Let's start this night off right, without the expectations of our future engagement lingering over our heads. What do you say?"

I nodded and looked over the menu. The waitress came by and grabbed our drink orders before leaving us in peace to chat some more.

Time flew by. We had stuffed our faces with a variety of hot dogs. I felt like my stomach was going to burst. I was more and more shocked each second I got to know him. He clearly wore a mask around his parents and family friends. But the Gregory in front of me was kind and quite funny. In another life, we could have been good friends that raised hell together.

We played a few rounds of darts and had very few awkward gaps in conversation. For the most part everything flowed naturally. Before we left for the night, I made sure to snag a selfie with him at our table so my mother would see I was making a genuine effort and get off my back about it.

After a thrilling ride to my house, he walked me to my door. I wanted to ask him the question that was burning a hole in my brain. If things ended up not going my way, I would be walking down the aisle with him at the receiving end, and I needed to know.

"Do you plan to take over your father's empire? I imagine you will be running everything at Jaffly Corp," I asked quietly. I didn't want to risk my mother's eavesdropping.

He stood silently in thought for a moment. "Yes."

I nodded. "You know he is kind of beginning to be seen as a villain around here right? He has manipulated people into selling their homes, land, and businesses. He is basically monopolizing the area."

"How is that any different from your father with The Knox Group," he asked.

Good question. "It isn't. But that's the problem. Since their only competition is each other, our union will control everything. Everyone. Are you a person who will use that power wisely, or will you fall to the temptation of greed like our fathers and grandfathers?"

"I don't know yet, if I am being honest."

I gave him a nod. At least he wasn't trying to hide behind the mask he used with others when talking to me. Just because I didn't like the answer, didn't mean I couldn't trust him.

"Thank you for being truthful. I admire that above everything else. And thank you for a fun evening. I was shockingly surprised. You rock the casual look way better, even though I am still thinking you starched your shirt."

He laughed. "My maid definitely did. Your welcome, Halen. I'll text you. Okay?"

I gave him a hug and walked upstairs to my bedroom,

trying to avoid any unwanted interactions with my mother. The last thing I wanted was her pressing me for details tonight. I was doing what she wanted, but that didn't mean she got a front row seat into our private conversations.

I took off my clothes and jumped into the steaming shower to rinse off the long day. I felt slightly sticky from the bar and sweaty from holding onto Gregory's body so tightly on the way home.

After cleaning myself from head to toe, I wrapped a towel in my hair and threw on my robe, then jumped onto my bed to scroll through social media for a few.

Before I could even open any of my apps, I saw I had a few missed text messages. One from Nicky asking if we could meet up tomorrow. I sent him a quick reply letting him know I was free after 1 PM. I had to give myself proper time to sleep in. It was going to be Saturday morning, after all.

The next text was from my dance studio, confirming my request to drop my spot. They also included that an exit interview would be necessary before processing withdrawal. Great. I knew I was in for a guilt trip.

The last text made my eyebrows scrunch together in confusion.

Unknown Number: That better have been apple juice in your cup.

My cup? I racked my brain for a moment trying to figure out if this was a person with the wrong number or if I had a conversation with someone that I somehow forgot about.

Me: I think you have the wrong number. I don't drink apple juice.

I began scrolling through social media and within a minute, my phone buzzed with a notification.

Unknown Number: Don't mess with me, Squid. I saw your Instagram. You're underage, so why were you at Raw Dawgs of all places, drinking with that punk?

My heart rate picked up. *Squid.* I remembered the nickname that Mr. Bennett called me earlier in the day. Why did he call me that? I thought I had misheard, which wasn't uncommon given the situation, but now I knew I heard correctly. I texted back, trying to be vague just in case.

Me: Teach?

Unknown Number: Some have been known to call me that.

My irritation rose for some reason. Some? I figured he was too grumpy to really have any students give him nicknames. But to also be so unoriginal that someone else called him that made me slightly annoyed.

Me: Some?

Unknown Number: One.

With that admission, I quickly changed his contact info in my phone and clicked back into the conversation. My heart was pounding with anxiety. Why was he texting me? How did he even get my number? These were all questions I fully intended on him answering.

Me: Good to know. For your information, it wasn't apple juice. But it wasn't beer either. I sipped on sweet tea the whole time.

His response was immediate.

Teach: Better have been. I have another question, a statement really, but it's delicate and I need you to understand it's coming from a place of concern.

Me: Hit me with it, old man.

A minute passed with no response and I wondered if he had fallen asleep or maybe chickened out of asking. It wasn't unusual for teachers to occasionally reach out to students, but this wasn't school related. So, maybe we were walking a line here.

Teach: Watch it. I'm not old. I'm in my 30s, you know. But... I do turn 40 in February. Back to the important stuff; Be careful riding on the back of that death bike, especially when you are wearing outfits that might cause a ruffle.

I snorthed. A ruffle.

Me: I wasn't expecting him to pick me up on a bike, or

else I wouldn't have. But if it bothered you so much to see my undies, you should have looked away. It was just a simple error.

I rolled my eyes with irritation. He better not have been one of those guys to think that wearing certain outfits meant that we were asking for certain attention. Some of us just liked the freedom of expression in what we wore. Mine was a statement of rebelling against my parents usually. Didn't mean I wanted guys giving me 'fuck me eyes' all the time.

His texts came in one after the other with barely a second of time in between.

Teach: I couldn't.

Teach: Look away, that is.

Teach: Because you were in my line of sight.

Teach: Not because I was staring at your black laced underwear.

Teach: I'm just saying to be careful.

Holy fucking shit. Ignoring everything else that was clearly needing analysis in this conversation, I focused on one thing. He knew the type and color of my panties. He saw and he remembered enough to specify. He thought about it.

I might have been grasping for something that wasn't there. But the pieces of this puzzle were starting to click more into place. I kept my reply nonchalant.

Me: I will. Thank you for looking out for me. I'll keep you updated on my findings, per your rules. Goodnight, Teach.

I attached a photo of the jar sitting on my nightstand next to a stack of books that I had already burned through earlier in the week but hadn't had a chance to move to my bookshelf.

Teach: Goodnight, Squid.

I plopped back on my bed and got cozy under the covers. As I drifted off into my relaxed sleep, I thought of the one thing I shouldn't have. Forbidden thoughts of a certain teacher.

An older teacher.

A sexy as hell teacher.
My teacher.

CHAPTER 10

-SAWYER-

What the fuck was I thinking? I could feel myself balancing the tightrope that was my professionalism. Why did Halen seem to interest me so much all of a sudden? Well, I guess it wasn't sudden. She interested me the moment she put me in my place in the library. But the need to get to know her better was manageable then. It felt overwhelming now more than ever.

The knot that formed in my stomach when I saw her straddle that bike and hang on to that little punk ass bitch like her life depended on it, had me fuming. Granted, her life did kind of depend on it since she was backpacking on a crotch rocket.

To clearly punish myself some more, I checked her social media frequently throughout the night, hoping to catch a glimpse of where she was and what she was doing. I told myself it was because I was worried about her safety. But even I knew that deep down it was so much more than that.

My skin crawled when I finally refreshed her feed while I was nursing a glass of whiskey, watching the traffic below from Connor's high rise.

She was sitting next to that fuck face, with a glass of what I assumed was beer, but thankfully was only sweet tea. Thank fuck I had already had some alcohol coursing through my system from happy hour with Ellen, Brent and a handful of other overworked educators.

I lost my cool and pulled her phone number from the school database that us teachers have access to in case we need to contact our students or a parent in an emergency. It was an emergency in my book. If she was drinking, she sure as fuck wasnt going to go riding on a bike on my watch.

Realizing how brutally clouded my thoughts were, I walked into the bathroom and stripped down out of my clothes and walked under the scalding spray of my shower.

Cracking my neck, I tried to loosen my muscles and let myself fully relax. As the water glided down my body, I felt the tingle of arousal prickle my spine. It wasn't because of my borderline flirty conversation with Halen. Not at all. I was just a little tipsy.

Needing to relieve myself of the shame and sexual frustration, I gripped my cock firmly in my hand. I slid it up and down, from base to tip, making myself rock hard. My brain was running a marathon while the strokes continued in a pleasant rhythm.

Halen's pleated skirt popped into my mind's eye and I began to tug harder, and faster. Shit. Realizing my error, I pushed the thought aside and tried to think about something I was supposed to like more.

Ellen. Her tits were basically hanging out of her top the entire evening. Fantasizing about grabbing one in my hand, I winced at the thought of it being fake and with little bounce. I could feel myself softening.

Fuck. That wasn't working. I drifted to Victoria. God she pissed me off, but she was beautiful and the only work she had done was regular botox injections which looked more on the natural side.

I worked myself faster as I pictured her on her knees, in her pencil skirt, taking me into her hot mouth. I could feel her bobbing up and down on my length.

As I drew closer to my climax, her hair started to transform from a rich brown to the auburn that I knew all too well. I didn't stop my frenzied stroking. If anything, it had become more hurried.

Focusing on her face in my mind's eye, I realized the

vibrant orbs staring back at me weren't dark brown, but green. My breaths were coming in breathy pants as I pulled at my cock and leaned a hand against the shower wall.

Picking up Halen, I threw her over the edge of my desk on her stomach and hiked up her skirt. No panties. *Fuck.*

Lining myself up to her entrance, I teased her by rubbing my head against her slit. She let a breathy whimper fall from her lips. I couldn't hold back any more.

With my hips stuttering, I fucked my fist a few more times before ropes of cum hit my shower wall while I moaned her name aloud. While the sins of what I had just done washed down the drain, I began to feel something similar to guilt rising inside of me.

She was turning eighteen. She was above the age of consent in New York. Technically I hadn't done anything illegal, but there had to be a line, and I felt way too close to it for comfort.

I wasn't going to touch her. She was still my student, even if she was approaching her birthday. It would risk my job, her education, our reputations, and any respect.

Cracking my neck and letting my shoulders sag with exhaustion, I walked into my closet and threw on a comfy pair of boxer briefs before sliding under the covers. I pulled up a few of my 'continuing education' videos from a class I had recently enrolled in for online study. Before I knew it, my eyes were slipping closed and I drifted to sleep with defeat.

Rubbing my eyes, I tried to push the fatigue from my sockets. News flash, it didn't work. Sometimes it felt like I was aging like a fine glass of curdled milk. I stretched my calves for a moment, easing the ache deep in them.

Other joggers passed me by as I began running again at a steady pace while sweat started to trail down my cheeks and back. I managed to get in a couple of miles before calling it and washing up for the day.

Feeling more energized after the run and a hefty triple espresso, I grabbed my sketchbook and headed out for some fresh air. A Parisian inspired coffee shop I wanted to try was just a few blocks away, so I headed straight there and found a seat next to the window. After ordering a delicious almond croissant and a hot chocolate, I sat back and opened my sketchbook.

The first few pages were filled with nature inspired scenery that I had come across on my runs or when I was trying to soak in the warmer weather outdoors before the cold snap hit. It was October, so it was a matter of days. I could already feel the slightest nip in the air.

Flipping through the pages, I stopped when I came across one that I had sketched of Halen recently. She was ethereal. Her body was tucked into a ball on the floor with her side braced against the floor to ceiling window of the library. Light made her already vibrant red hair and skin glow, like an angel. The auburn locks cascaded down her back in soft bouncy curls, as the front stayed put, tucked behind her ears.

I could tell she wasn't wearing her cochlear when I sketched it. The thought made me happy. It's what made me add that rule to the jar I had given her.

When I saw her reading without them, lost in her story, I also knew that I didn't want her to experience her reading any other way. I also knew I had to capture it, so I sketched her from the corner of the library as she flipped from page to page.

I needed to clear my mind of her. She was already invading every free moment of it. I knew it wasn't healthy with a regular woman, let alone one of my students.

Trying to distract myself, I sketched for about an hour. An elderly couple sitting on a bench across the street caught my eye, and I fell into my peaceful rhythm. They seemed so content just sitting there, not talking, remaining quiet as they waited for their bus to come to the stop.

Once it did, they stood and smiled at one another before

the older man gave her a gentle peck. He then helped her up the steps of the bus to find a seat together. It was beautiful.

My phone buzzed right as I saw the bus pull away. I saw the sender and my heart began to race.

Squid: Starting my first book from your list. Be ready for updates.

I smiled to myself and my breath hitched as a photo came through. It was a selfie of Halen with her book cracked open and her hair in a messy bun. I looked at the cover of the book and knew immediately what it was. It was a good pick for her first selection.

This one was a romantic fantasy with some dark elements to it, but still not too dark. I shot out a quick reply giving her a thumbs up emoji and closed my sketchbook before heading back to my place. I really needed to get a fucking life. I was starting to become a little too interested.

CHAPTER 11

-HALEN-

Soaking in the words on my page, I became quickly engrossed in the fictional world. A girl my age had the capability to wield below freezing shadows while the male love interest was able to blast scalding light. They were supposed to be enemies, but were coming to realize that they actually cared for each other.

My body jostled from being nudged accidentally. After a glance, I refocused on the page in front of me, finding where I left off. Once I got a few sentences in, I felt another body rocking nudge.

I slammed my book shut and sat upright.

"*Evan!*" I aggressively whipped his name sign in front of his face. "*Sit fucking still! Every single time you move, I lose my spot, and my focus.*"

He poked his bottom lip out like the big baby that he was and faked a quiver. "*It's not my fault, I swear, these dweebs wont fucking revive me in Combat Strike. They are either stupid or I'm playing with a bunch of eight year olds,*" he signed quickly.

I had been following the rules that Mr. Bennett gave me, and remembered to unplug when I had opened the book. He was right about it giving me the opportunity to create a peaceful environment to really take in the world unfolding in the pages.

I huffed. "*Evan,* you *are an eight year old.*"

His mouth fell open in a mocking gasp as he placed his hand on his chest. So dramatic.

"*I'll let that go since it's your birthday, but only for today, babe."*

At that moment, Nicky walked in with three cans of soda and a bowl of popcorn. The buttery delicious scent hit me and I salivated. He set down the cans and bowl before looking between Evan and I with a brow raised. He landed his irritated stare on Evan.

"What did you do? I could hear Halen's aggressive hands slapping from across the house." Nicky always made sure to sign when I was unplugged. If we were around others that didn't know the language, he would sign and talk at the same time. I truly didn't give him and Evan enough credit for including me in every way since becoming friends.

Evan shrugged. *"She wanted to cuddle and was rubbing her body all up on me but got mad when I told her we couldn't fuck in your bed."*

I took a calculated step forward and while I couldn't hear it, I saw the panicked scream leave Evan's mouth as he jumped off the bed and darted behind Nicky. He knew when my wrath was something to fear.

"Pussy," I signed as Evan's head peeked around Nicky's body.

My eyes met Nicky's and his danced with amusement. If there was one thing that he loved, it was when I put other men in their place. As long as it wasn't him. Me picking fights with other people, specifically men didn't happen often, but when it did, he would always be there watching with a smirk.

His head jerked towards the bed.

"I'll lay between you and Evan so he doesn't bother you. You can snuggle me instead while I watch him play and listen to music," he signed with a soft smile.

We did just that. It was a simple birthday, but those were the ones that I loved the most. No extravagance. I was born into extravagance and those memories weren't always fond.

I rested my head in the crook of his arm while I read chapter after chapter. I knew I needed to check in with Mr. Bennett on my thoughts so far, but it felt risky doing that around the boys. Especially Nicky. If he even got a whiff of the tension, he would blow a fuse.

"Happy birthday, Halen," hands signed in front of my face.

I looked away from my book to glance at Nicky. He held a cupcake out to me with a single candle lit in the middle. Evan was smiling, watching and waiting for me to make my wish.

I smiled and shut my eyes tightly as I thought about what I wanted to spend my wish on. Was I supposed to wish for happiness? For a chance to marry someone I love? For my teacher?

I could feel the heat from the candle near my face, taunting me to hurry up. After a few more seconds, the wish formed in my head, and I lightly blew the candle out. Smoke tendrils lifted from the lifeless stick of wax.

Wasting no time, I took a big bite, passed it to Nicky who copied me, and then passed it to Evan. Evan's blonde strands fell over his eyes as he shoved the remainder of the massive cupcake in his mouth.

We resumed our snuggling and fell into our comfortable silence.

At some point I must have fallen asleep because the room was fully dark. I shifted around and saw Nicky still cuddling me. Evan's body was draped across both of our legs like a damn dog. My book was closed on the nightstand with a bookmark settled inside. One of them must have taken it from me when I drifted.

With exhaustion still tugging on my eyelids, I decided to get snug again and allow my body to drift once again into a silent slumber.

Monday morning came so much quicker than I thought it would. I was annoyed because I wouldn't have as much free time to finish my book, but at the same time, I was eager to see Mr. Bennett again and fill him in.

I texted him a few times throughout the weekend referencing page numbers and my thoughts on the incredibly action packed plot. He kept the responses brief and a tad cold. He was so warm and inviting on Friday but as the weekend flew by, he would only react to my messages with a single emoji of a thumbs up signal, or a three word response with no emotion. He also didn't mention my birthday, but I figured he just didn't realize it had passed.

Stop making this into more than it is.

The hallways were empty and there didn't even seem to be one teacher in sight. I arrived two hours early instead of one. I figured if he wasn't here yet, I would just read in the atrium.

As I got closer to his classroom in the dimmed hallway, musical notes pierced the dead silence of the echoing hallway.

Recognition hit when the chorus to Zombie by YUNGBLUD got louder. I ducked into the classroom quietly, not wanting to disturb him. He was in his classic white button down shirt and perfectly ironed pants. His focus was unwavering as he stood behind his desk and looked through a stack of papers.

When my backpack dropped to the floor, he finally looked up and gave me the most panty dropping smile. I could feel my cheeks heating. I was already feeling better about the simple responses he was sending me. Maybe he was just a shitty texter sometimes.

"Squid."

I narrowed my eyes but they held no heat. "You haven't told me why you call me that." I hopped up and sat my ass right on my desk and crossed my legs, waiting for a response.

I saw his gaze drop down over my body. I wasn't wearing anything revealing. I was actually quite dressed down today. The pair of jeans I was sporting had holes at the knees and I paired them with a black cold shoulder sweater and sneakers.

He walked around his desk, right towards my seat. I watched him carefully as he pulled a student desk next to mine, so that they were only 6 inches apart, and dropped into the seat.

"Did you know that squid can't hear?"

My eyebrows flew up. "Really?"

"Well, that's what scientists used to think at least. Now they believe that they can hear but only at certain frequencies. But some scientists still have their doubts on that. Either way, they are hearing impaired at a minimum."

I sat completely still. I wasn't sure what I was supposed to be thinking. He broke my thoughtful silence.

"It's not meant to be disrespectful, but endearing. I learned about that little squid fact when I was doing some continuing education. It made me think of you."

I knew I should have probably been offended that he compared me to a slimy oceanic creature, but in a weird way, it was sweet. I stared at him expressionless, and knew he was waiting to see my complete reaction.

After a moment, I couldn't hold my smile any longer. I saw his shoulders finally relax in relief and his lips kick up at the sides.

"Well," I said playfully, "I like that you have a pet name for me."

I watched him go completely still as his smile dropped a tad, but his eyes were still laser focused on mine. Neither of us said a word. The tension was thick and the space between us was quickly filling with the things left unsaid. But they didn't need to be. We were definitely both feeling this... sensation.

"Are you trying to stay hip with the music choices, old man?" I pointed to the overhead speaker.

He scoffed. "I'm not an old man. And if you are so all knowing, what would you have recommended to bridge the gap?"

I didn't waste a beat. Hopping down from the desk, I walked behind his teaching desk and pulled up a song that I thought he would recognize but is still relevant.

Walking back in front of the desk he was sitting in, the music started playing while he remained seated. He watched me like a hawk. Or a predator.

The beat of You Don't Own Me by SAYGRACE ft G-Easy picked up and I took that as an opportunity to begin doing what I did best. Dance. Even though I gave up on the hobby, it didn't mean I didn't enjoy it on my own terms or wasn't good at it.

I began working through moves more aligned with contemporary ballet. But as the song became more intense and the heat of Mr. Bennett's stare nearly burned my skin, I adjusted into something more loose and easygoing.

I started rocking my hips and dancing slowly with myself. Gathering my tousled curls, I lifted my mane from my shoulders and let myself become fully focused on the beat with my eyes closed.

After a minute, I opened my eyes, and found him breathless, utterly still. I was so shocked by the sight that I nearly faltered in my now sultry dancing.

He didn't move a muscle as I continued to dance, and leisurely made my way in his direction. It wasn't until I was standing right in front of him that I noticed his hands in tight fists resting on the desk and the muscles along his clenched jaw.

Was he mad?

The song came to an end and I slipped into my desk next to him. It was at *that* moment that I was given the direct vantage point to view the hard bulge tenting his pants while he remained sitting for a moment longer.

I wanted to gasp for a few different reasons. The size being one of them, but also the fact that he had such a forbidden reaction to me dancing in front of him. The same reaction I felt when in his vicinity. The dance wasn't meant to be sexual, but even I could admit I was feeling myself by the end of the song. Words of caution rang in my ear while we continued in silence.

Forbidden.

Forbidden.

Forbidden.

I'm not sure how much time had passed, but if I had to guess, maybe a couple of minutes. It wasn't until my cochlears picked up on his sudden intake of breath that my eyes drifted up to his which were boring into me.

I had been staring at his...

Oh my god.

I had been staring at his fucking dick this whole time. And he fucking caught me doing it!

His lips were slightly parted, but he still remained silent. The heat rose in my cheeks and I am sure they were vibrantly displaying how this whole thing was affecting me. I shifted in my seat and pressed my legs together tighter.

The action most certainly didn't skate by his attention on me. He was observant. Always so observant.

"Mr. Bennett, I'm so–" I whispered but was quickly cut off.

"Sawyer," he whispered, his blue eyes still holding mine in suspense. "When we are alone, call me Sawyer. Or Teach."

"Sawyer." The name rolling off my tongue felt *right*. "I'm sorry if I overstepped. I didn't mean to make you uncomfortable or look at me differently. Negatively."

He huffed a laugh. "Halen, I do see you differently. But it's because I see you the exact opposite of negatively that I am holding on by a thread here. As you could clearly see."

I let out a small whimper but quickly reigned it in by biting down on my bottom lip. His gaze darted down to watch as I pulled it in between my teeth. Agonizingly slow, he reached up and pulled it free with his thumb.

Without having as good of a hold on my own emotions as him at the moment, I instinctively dipped my head and brought his thumb between my teeth and nipped it. His hiss rolled into a growl from his chest. I could almost feel the vibrations from where I was sitting.

He brought his barely injured thumb to his mouth and sucked it into his mouth as if he was trying to stop a bleeding wound. I definitely didn't bite him hard enough to bleed.

His eyes closed for a brief moment before making a low guttural sound. "Fuck."

As if the heavens hated me and wanted to see me unhappy and miserable, Katherine walked in looking like a chipper skanky housewife. She was sporting a mini skirt and a blouse that showed off her cleavage.

"Hi Mr. Bennett, I was hoping I could steal some tutoring time this morning over the essay that I am writing. I am struggling with it."

"Sure, Katherine. Take a seat wherever you would like and I'll sit next to you while we review what you have so far," Sawyer said professionally.

Sawyer.

I glanced down at his lap and noticed the bulge wasn't visible any longer. With a sigh of relief I pulled out my book and took off my cochlears to begin reading while he made his way over to Katherine.

Thankfully I couldn't hear her pathetic flirting so I wasn't constantly distracted while reading, but I knew it was happening.

I deep dived into the story until I felt a masculine hand slide over my shoulder. Looking up, I saw Sawyer standing above me and Katherine nowhere in sight. Glancing at the door, I could see students passing by the classroom in the hallway.

"The arrival bell rang."

I nodded and then snapped my attention back to him.

What the fuck?

He smirked at me, but didn't make any moves to further explain.

"Did you just sign to me?"

He winced and nodded. *"Go slow, Squid. I'm still learning."*

My smile stretched so far across my face I felt like my cheeks were going to crack. He gave me a megawatt smile in return that was enough to make my heart skip a beat.

"Get to class before I give you detention."

I laughed and grabbed my stuff before heading to my first period class. If I wasn't careful, I was going to cross some lines with him. I was secretly hoping I would.

CHAPTER 12

-SAWYER-

After an excruciatingly long week, I had finally received some feedback from the school board, which was typical for first year teachers at Black Grove Academy. Even though I had been teaching for years now, they had a different set of expectations as most schools. Thankfully there weren't many negative critiques.

Halen had come to visit me every single morning since our overly intimate moment last Monday. We managed to stay purely friendly since then. She respected my wishes in calling me Sawyer in private. Hearing my name from her made me feel something similar to butterflies flapping their wings in my stomach. But not butterflies, because that's girly as shit.

Moths.

She made me feel moths.

"Yeah bro, she swallowed my dick so well that I came the longest I ever had. She's got the face of an angel and a mouth like a Hoover, unlike Katherine who was all teeth."

I kept walking past the group of boys and a few girls. They were spreading stupid gossip that was definitely not anyone's business, but that was just how high school was.

A girl I didn't recognize chimed in. "Halen sucked you off better than Katherine? Oh, I can't wait to spread that shit like wildfire. Katherine got Raya to spread a rumor that I have crabs. Vengeance is mine." Her giggle was one of malice.

I stopped dead in my tracks so abruptly that the squeak of my shoes against the atrium tile made the group look over in confusion. Once they realized I had turned to glare at them, they scattered like mice.

Red covered my vision as irritation surged through me. I felt an odd sense of possession over her. I had no claim to her, but I couldn't push away the feelings. They were burning through me.

My phone buzzed and I pulled it out to see an unknown number calling me. Getting a number in a new area code always meant that I was getting telemarketer and robotic calls.

Normally I would have ignored the obnoxious intrusion on my personal cell, but I really wanted to rip someone's head off and this seemed like a good way to burn off some frustration.

"What," I snapped.

A soft female voice gasped and there was a brief pause. I would normally feel bad. Especially doing that to a female, but right now I was too fucking pissed to give a shit.

"Sawyer?"

I recognized the voice. It was one that I had become familiar with for years. One that I remember crying tears of sadness and joy.

Moaning my name.

Cursing at my male stupidity.

Cherishing me as the love of her life.

Or so I thought.

"Victoria. What do you want?"

I heard her loud exhale then her soft voice spoke once again. "I've been trying to reach you, but you blocked me and cut me out of every way to contact you. I want to talk. I took some time off to visit Buffalo. Maybe we can have a civil dinner?"

I could hear the pleading in her voice, clear as day.

"Victoria, I don't th–"

"It would be much easier for us to just meet at a mutual place rather than me visiting Black Grove. Don't you agree?"

It didn't sound threatening, but having her show up here was a disaster waiting to happen. I needed to keep her separate from the new life I was building.

"Fine. When and where?"

"Yay! Okay, how about Great Lakes Grill on Sunday at 7 PM?"

"Okay." I went to hang up but held off for a moment. "Victoria, you do know that this will be a strictly friendly dinner, right? And even that is exaggerating."

"I respect your boundaries, Sawyer. I'll see you then. Have a good evening." The call disconnected without allowing another word.

She had fucking terrible timing, that's for damn certain. I was already fuming and ready to break shit. Her calling just felt like adding gasoline to an already out of control fire.

I made my way home after a few goodbyes to co-workers, including Brent who chatted my ear off about the benefits of taking chlorophyll supplements. Walking into Connor's condo, I stripped down to my boxers and immediately poured a deep glass of whiskey. Once the hum of the buzz hit my system, I pulled my phone out, not being able to resist anymore.

Me: I heard a rumor about you today.

Squid: Is that so? Was it about how Samuel Yates kept playing different frequency sounds during class so that I had to keep yanking off my implants? Which then pissed Nicky off so bad that he punched Samuel in the face? Yeah, not his finest moment. But the asshole deserved it.

My brows rose at the amount of information I wasn't expecting to dissect.

Squid: Am I allowed to say the word asshole to you?

Squid: Eh, I'm gonna do it anyway.

I chuckled at her comfortability with me. She was being herself, without the barriers. Remembering why I had reached out to her in the first place, my smile dropped and I typed out a response.

Me: I'm sure he did, Squid. Had he not been a student, I would have done the same thing. I heard a student talking after school today, and he said that he had some experi-

ence with you. Experience where you... pleasured him. Just thought you should know.

This most definitely wasn't about just letting her know. I was selfishly trying to get answers from her on the issue. I was also now completely crossing a line.

Cross it. Cross it.

I drained my whiskey glass and filled it again before getting comfortable on the couch. Minutes flew by with no response and I was suddenly worried that she was going to ignore me or confront the other guy about the rumor and forget to respond to me.

Right as my body was going from buzzed to tipsy, my phone rang with a video call request.

Fuck, this wasn't good.

Abort. Fucking abort!

Maybe it was just a butt dial. I could have just rejected the call so it went to voicemail. She probably would have thought I fell asleep.

Being the fucking idiot I was, I answered.

Her beautiful smile lit up my screen. I could see her hair was twisted into a messy bun and she was free of all makeup, which really highlighted her natural beauty.

"Who was spreading the rumor?" She asked, as her smile became slightly more hesitant.

"I have no idea what his name is. But he had blonde hair that was a little longer on the top."

Her chuckling caught me off guard."Alright, what did he say, word for word?"

I repeated what I had heard and tried my best to hold a straight face. This was already feeling like a severely inappropriate conversation, but I didn't want her to hear what people were saying behind her back while least expecting it.

She gave a belly laugh. "Oh wow, that's great," she wiped under her eyes. "I didn't think he would actually do it. Best news ever. Thanks for telling me."

I watched her in stunned silence, trying to fit the very

confusing pieces together. I must have been silent for far longer than typical because she chimed in again.

"It's not true, Sawyer. Evan made it up, with my permission of course. There is a party on Friday and it was a payment so I would go with him and Nicky. Katherine has been giving me a hard time for years, so I took the bait on him humiliating her. I know it's childish, but I couldn't resist. She's a cunt."

I choked on a laugh and her smile returned with a wicked edge to it. I tucked his name away in the pits of my mind for future digging.

"Just to be abundantly clear. I'm a virgin. I've also never given a blowjob before. As embarrassing as it is to admit that to someone, especially you, I just want you to know that I'm not some tramp blowing guys under the bleachers."

I remained quiet for a moment letting her words soak in. I didn't know how to respond but it didn't take long for my boxers to become tented. Thank fuck she couldn't see it over the video call.

Images flashed through my mind, of her licking the head of my cock and sucking me as far as she could. The mouth that hadn't touched another man's cock. So fucking hot.

She was so... comfortable in her own skin. Comfortable with not giving into the temptations of the horny little jock bros around her.

The whiskey was well running through my bloodstream now. This was dangerous. Hanging up would have been the smart thing.

"Have you ever touched one before?" I asked quietly.

She still heard me.

She leaned back in her bed and got comfortable as her chest started rising and falling quickly.

"Sort of. By accident. Nicky and I often nap and have sleepovers together. Occasionally his morning wood is rammed into my backside."

A rumble worked its way up my chest but I tried to squash it. She had sleepovers with Ressner? What the hell?

"You let Dominic Ressner grind his dick into your ass while you both cuddle in bed?" My words were firm but they weren't harsh. It was written all over her face that she knew what I was asking, and why.

She bit her lip. My eyes darted to it and the action transported me back to when she nipped my thumb in my classroom.

"Like I said, accidentally. But I've never seen one in real life. Not hard at least. I've occasionally caught Evan and Nicky's when they changed, but they were always unaroused. I've only seen a hard dick in porn."

I almost moaned as I squeezed my hard cock through my boxers at her confession. The idea of her watching porn sent blood rushing to it, ready for my hand.

But I couldn't do that. Not while she could see. Although it would have made me her first hard cock. We weren't technically even around each other so there was no risk of touching.

"You watch porn, Squid?"

She nodded, her eyes half lidded with lust. I knew that look, very well.

"Have you ever watched one where the guy jerks off?"

She shook her head.

"Want a recommendation?"

Another nod.

Swallowing hard, knowing that I was probably going to regret this for the rest of my life, I let the alcohol push me to continue. I could tell she was interested. She was saying as much, too. I guess I was just giving a middle finger to all of the other rules we were breaking.

I leaned over and rested my phone against the whiskey glass on the coffee table so that it was propped up and facing me at a lower angle.

She was now able to see that I was naked except for my boxer briefs. They did nothing to hide the steel pipe of an erection.

I leaned back and made eye contact with her on the

camera, and waited for her signal. I wouldn't cross this line until she gave me her full consent.

With her breathy voice sounding like music to my ears, she broke the silence with her whisper. "Touch yourself, Sawyer." A pause. "Please."

I smirked at her and slowly lifted my hands to my waistband and slid them down until they hit my ankles. My erection sprung free and slapped my abdomen, begging me to relieve the pressure

I leaned back against the couch cushions to get comfortable but still within clear view of the camera. Her eyes widened into saucers while he studied my cock as my hand started to slowly stroke.

"It's like, really big," she said.

I breathed a laugh. "Big enough to make you hear colors, Squid."

I stroked up and down from base to tip while occasionally paying attention to my slit as I rubbed the precum around my shaft.

Her breathing was the only thing I could hear and it was like throwing gasoline on a fire for the lust that was pulsing through me. I picked up my pace, all while maintaining eye contact.

I saw her move around slightly before leaning back against her headboard. She had her camera fully focused on her face so I couldn't see what she was wearing or what her comforter even looked like.

I stilled my movements on my cock as I narrowed my eyes at her. "Are you touching yourself, too?"

Her eyes got even wider as she realized she had been caught. I started moving again and stroked harder and faster while my jaw clenched tight.

"Show me. Now."

She hesitated for a minute but ultimately pulled her black and grey comforter off of her naked bottom half and angled the phone downward to expose her spread thighs and glistening pussy.

I moaned as my strokes started to become frantic. "Keep touching yourself. Don't stop on my account. Just let me see. I want to see the way your pussy weeps for me like my cock does for you."

Her whimper went straight to my balls as they began to tighten. I rocked my hips up to meet my frantic hand movements. I was so close.

Her hand traveled to her pussy as she started rubbing fast tight circles around her nub while watching me. The sight alone was a masterpiece. I couldn't imagine how it would feel to touch her. Lick her. Taste every inch of her.

Another moan slipped through my lips as she began panting and making small mewling sounds. I began to see the trickle of wetness drip down onto her sheets and I lost all self control.

"Come right fucking now. Damn, you're so wet baby. Come, now!"

Her back arched and she threw her had back as liquid gushed from between her legs. The sounds of her moaning filled my living room through the phone's speaker.

Cum shot out of me as I followed immediately after her. "Halen... Oh, fuck." My cum had coated my abdomen as I finally began to come down from that extreme fucking orgasm.

I picked up my phone from the coffee table and focused it on my face again as she did the same. Her smile was breathtaking.

"Holy shit," she said between breaths. "That was amazing."

I winked at her and let out a loud sigh. I was absolutely beat. I had never felt such an erotic moment in my life, and she wasn't even within touching distance.

She shook her head with a small laugh. "Get some sleep. You look like you're barely hanging on."

I nodded. "You're right. You need to rest too. I'll see you tomorrow in class. Goodnight."

"Goodnight, Teach." She lifted the two fingers she used to rub herself to her mouth and sucked on them right as she ended the call.

Holy fucking hell.

CHAPTER 13

-HALEN-

"Halen, your father and I would like to discuss something with you."

I pushed the overcooked chicken around my plate and glanced over at my mother who was watching me with an irritated expression, like she was waiting for a response. She didn't ask a question, so I wasn't sure it warranted one, but whatever.

"Okay."

My mother straightened in her seat and smiled brightly at me like she often did when we had guests over. I had to survey the room just to make sure I didn't miss someone. Finding the room empty except for my parents and myself, my eyebrows pinched together.

"Richard, would you like to share the wonderful news?"

My father cleared his throat and looked at me. "It took longer than we were expecting to find the perfect agreement, but we finalized the contract as of yesterday. The only signatures that are needed now are yours and Gregory's after you wed."

"Did you hear that dear?" My mother asked with excitement in her tone. "Now we can move on to wedding planning!" She clapped her hands together excitedly.

My pulse roared in my ears. I knew this was coming. It's always been expected and he had even told me that contracts were already at play. I was just surprised that they were actually going to make me go through with this. That they wanted to rob me of a chance of marrying for love.

All for greed.

I bit my tongue. Arguing with them over it would only cause problems. It was the same argument we always had, and I was almost old enough to free myself and leave it all behind.

My father took a long sip of his scotch and began digging into his food again. His words kept coming even though he was no longer looking at anything but the food in front of him.

"I had my assistant reserve a table on Sunday to celebrate the upcoming union.

I watched my mom wiggling in her seat with happiness. It was almost hard to watch. She genuinely thought that this was normal. My father's phone rang as I took a small bite of the jerky textured chicken.

"I have to take this. You ladies have fun talking about girly wedding stuff." He briskly walked off, barking commands into his phone.

After another agonizing hour of listening to my mother, I finally had made it upstairs. I needed to get the fuck out of here. I felt like my world was imploding around me. I had a plan, but deep down I wondered if I was going to actually be able to pull it off.

Pulling my phone out, I dialed the one person I was nervous to tell all of this to. I wasn't sure how he was going to react.

"Hey, Twerp."

I smiled sadly even though he couldn't see it. "Hey. Do you and Evan want to go somewhere? Some things have happened, and I think it's time that I filled you both in on it."

There was a beat of silence, but then he spoke, relieving me of my immediate stress.

"Sure thing. Meet us at Wingin' It in 20 minutes. Evan smoked too much. He has the munchies and said he is craving something meaty."

"Bro, don't make it sound so fucking gay." His voice sounded a little far away but a rustling of the phone assaulted my ears before Evan's voice came through clearly. "Hey babe, I didn't say I wanted meat. I said I wanted something mouth-wateringly salty."

I chuckled. "Yeah, Evan, I hate to break it to you, but that isn't much better. Don't worry, we all know you love pussy too much to swallow any salty dicks."

"So true. We leave the dick loving to you."

"Alright, that's enough," I heard Nicky say before speaking into the phone again. "We will see you in a few."

After a fairly quick drive, we all sat in the booth at the restaurants and I could feel Nicky's hard stare and Evan's questioning gaze, trying to understand what was going on while his brain was currently fried.

"I just wanted you both to know that even though I am actively working to get out of this, my parents informed me that I am officially arranged."

"Arranged?" Nicky asked.

"To be married."

Evan's wandering gaze snapped back to me, as if the words suddenly sobered him completely. His eyes were wide and unblinking.

"You're getting married?" He asked quietly.

I nodded.

Nicky's knuckles were drained of blood flow as they gripped his cup without mercy. His face was nothing short of furious. I reached across to place my hand on his but he pulled it away and glared harder at me.

"How long have you known, Halen?" Nicky asked in a deadly calm.

"I just learned that the contract is ready tonight at dinner."

He shook his head. "No. Not happening. Not fucking happening."

Evan started to look a little uneasy as he watched the slow spiral begin to happen with Nicky. They didn't happen often but when they did, it was hard to talk him down. Once his mind was in *struggle mode*, it was nearly impossible for him to truly hear us.

I grabbed his hand and squeezed. “It’s okay. Like I said, I kind of have a plan in place. My father should be releasing my inheritance now that I am eighteen and my acceptance to Gallaudet should be any minute hopefully. After that, they can't make me do shit.”

Evan placed his hand over mine that was clutching Nicky's. With a few minutes passing in silence, Nicky’s breathing returned to normal and he finally met my eyes again.

“Okay. Don’t worry, Twerp. We won’t let this happen. Hell, *I’ll* marry you.”

I sat back, shocked. “What?”

He shrugged a shoulder feigning casual indifference, but growing up deaf, I had learned facial expressions at an expert level. He was serious. There was *feeling* there.

The thought was too much for me to dwell on at the moment, but his offer was kind and amazing either way. These boys always protected me. They were always my beacon to something brighter.

I gave Nicky a smile as I tried to fight off tears forming in my eyes. He kissed the knuckles on my left hand and just like that, the worry started to disappear.

We spent the evening trying to clear our minds of the chaos that was taking over my life. I nearly barfed a couple of times watching a very high Evan clear the bones of our wings. You would have thought he hadn't eaten in a week with how he managed to put them in his mouth, twist it a few times and pull it out completely bare of meat. Gag.

The next morning I threw on a cute black skater dress to pair with some chunky combat boots. The weather was quickly getting cold, but sometimes you had to suffer goosebumps for the sake of looking nice. I would have been lying if I said that I wasn’t dressing for the male gaze. A specific male’s gaze.

We hadn’t done or said anything sexual since that night

over video call. My muscles tensed up and my thighs pressed together at the reminder. We had crossed a line. And I was hell-bent on crossing it again.

Opening the door to the school, I was hit with the smell of cinnamon and maple. The cafeteria workers must have been already working hard getting breakfast ready for the masses.

I quickly made it to Sawyer's classroom and found him at the window, staring out at the passing cars and slowly rising sun. The gloomy season was among us, but there was a small break in the clouds that let the beautiful orange and pink tones paint the sky.

I quietly set my stuff down and walked over to him. I heard his pencil stop scraping against the paper as he felt my presence. I was deaf, but I knew how to be quiet on my feet. No way he heard me.

As if he could read my thoughts he glanced over his shoulder down at me and gave me a wicked smirk. "Your perfume gave you away."

My brows crinkled together and I cocked my head at him in confusion. "I'm not wearing perfume."

His eyes slipped shut and his groan filled the space between us. I moved closer and peeked at his book. There was a half-finished sketch of moving cars and rays of light bursting through the clouds. It was gorgeous.

"You're so talented," I whispered. "May I?"

I reached my hand out in question, to which he placed the sketchbook on my palm. I saw the uncomfortability take over his face.

I flipped through a few pages slowly. A couple sitting at a bus stop. A worn down boat traveling across the water of Lake Erie. A window overlooking the city with raindrops sprinkled on the glass. So many different beautiful scenes of life.

I saw the clenching of his fists across his chest and looked back at him, wondering what had triggered him. His face became flushed. My question was answered when I flipped to the next page.

A girl with bouncy curls, sitting next to a window that had sunshine streaming around her. A book was on her lap as she leaned into the window and read quietly. Bookshelves surrounded her with different stories to be told occupying them.

It was *me*.

I looked up at him in shock and awe. Flipping to the next page, I found another one of me. I was sitting at my desk with my pencil in hand, clearly working on an assignment while students surrounded me. The other students' faces were void of expressions or depth, but mine was full of detail.

He stepped closer to me and I lifted my eyes to meet his intense blues.

"I sketch things that I find beautiful beyond reason." Another step. "Things that aren't supposed to catch my attention, but do." One final step and we were nearly touching, with only a few inches separating our bodies.

He lifted his hand and caressed my cheek. I felt a shiver rush across my body and my hairs raise. He saw the goosebumps littering my skin and his lips parted with a deep exhale.

I kept my eyes trained on him and saw the moment his went from admiration to something else. I hadn't seen anything close to it before except for maybe in Nicky every so often. But this was more intense. More raw.

Hunger. Pure desire.

This was my moment, and I told myself I was going to take it when I had the opportunity. After feeling the connection with him over a phone screen, I was dying to know what the real thing felt like.

I took the final step so that our bodies were flushed against each other. His head whipped to the side and he quickly started marching off. *Away* from me. I was left confused and a bit hurt.

The sting of rejection hit me like a shitty Buffalo city bus. It was a fatal crash, no survivors. Just my sad heart left as carnage.

I heard his classroom door shut and my gaze finally dropped to the floor in disappointment. I misread the situation, or pushed him too far.

Hurried footsteps met my ears and I looked over at the door in confusion to see him walking rapidly towards me with no intention of stopping. I continued to hold his sketchbook as I looked at him with curiosity and a tad bit of fear. Exciting fear.

His strides didn't falter. He finally made it to me and pushed me back against the window before crashing his lips to mine in an earth shattering kiss.

The sketchbook dropped from my hands to the floor and I threw my arms around his neck. The cold glass pressed into my back through my dress yet all I could feel was a burning heat.

His arms dropped from my hips and reached behind my thighs as he lifted my legs from the floor. I instinctively wrapped my legs around his hips as he pressed harder into my body.

His lips were soft but consuming. He was ravenous with the need to touch and feel me. My heart was pounding against my ribs.

The very solid length of him rocked against me and I couldn't hold back my gasp. He took that opportunity to plunge his tongue into my mouth with fervor. I moaned as his silken tongue battled mine for dominance.

Holy hell. This fucking man.

CHAPTER 14

-SAWYER-

Her moan made my already rock hard dick begin to throb. I was desperate to taste every inch of her. She was perfect in every possible way.

Her hips began to meet mine with hunger and we grinned back and forth trying to find pleasure in each other. I must have rubbed the perfect spot because her mouth pulled away from mine and her head tipped back against the window.

"Sawyer," she moaned.

A rumble was pulled from my chest as I tried to hold myself together. With her neck exposed as her head was tilted towards the ceiling, I sealed my lips to the skin above her collarbone.

Her hips continued their relentless rocking with mine. I laved my tongue up her neck and to her ear before nipping at the lobe. I felt her legs begin to shake. She was close.

Fisting a handful of hair, I moved her mouth to mine again and swallowed the sounds that were starting to pour from her. With each moan, my cock leaked more.

I wanted every single bit of her. Every smile. Every moan. Every thought. Everything. With an intense jerk, her legs began to convulse as her release gushed from her underwear clad pussy all over the front of my slacks.

The warmth quickly penetrated the fabric and had me panting in her mouth as I followed quickly behind her. White flashed in my vision and the breath was stolen from my lungs. I shuddered and gritted my teeth to keep from calling out her name. My hips finally fell still against hers as we just stayed there in an embrace with her head resting against my shoulder.

I held onto her as I peeled her away from the window and sat her on top of my desk. Pulling back, I could see the absolute mess we had made of ourselves. Reality hit, real fast.

I had just blown my load in my pants like a fucking teenager and I had class in about 30 minutes. What the fuck was I going to do?

Remembering I kept a spare change of clothes for myself in the event of a coffee spill, I pulled out the bottom drawer to my desk and retrieved the folded pair of boxer briefs and black slacks. I was already wearing a black button down, but black on black could be edgy. Especially with the right belt.

Pulling my soaked underwear and pants off of my body, I slipped into the fresh ones. She remained sitting where I left her, watching me with a curious expression.

I walked back over to her and stepped between her legs. Brushing a stray hair from her face, I looked directly into those blindingly beautiful green eyes.

"Do you have spare clothes in your locker? You've made a mess, Squid." I couldn't help the smirk that pulled at my lips.

Her face took on a mischievous expression. She pushed me back gently as she hopped down from the desk. Keeping her eyes planted on mine, she bent down and pulled her black lace panties down her legs. I couldn't tear my eyes away.

After stepping out of them completely, she balled them into her fist and moved her hands towards me. Our eyes were still locked. I felt the movement of her fingers as she shoved the balled up fabric into my pants pocket.

"Souvenir."

My sharp exhale was audible, even to her. "Fuck, baby, you're trying to kill me."

Her smile fully took over her face. She loved me calling her that. Noted.

Pompeii by Bastille broke the moment we were stuck in. She walked over to her backpack and pulled out her phone.

After looking at the name on the screen, she looked towards me and gave me an apologetic smile.

"Go ahead," I gestured to the phone, "I'll just busy myself with something."

She swiped to answer the call as I went to the window to grab my sketchbook. My cheeks felt flushed at the memory of her flipping through the sketches I had of her. Little did she know, I didn't intend on them being the last.

"Hey! You're calling early. Is everything okay?" She spoke gently into the phone.

I got comfortable at my desk and kicked my feet up leaning back. I watched as she walked the perimeter of the room aimlessly. She bit at her nail, listening to the person on the other end of the line.

"Yeah, that works for me. I'm not happy about it, but a deal is a deal. Tell Nicky I'll drive myself there and catch an uber home."

If the floors were made of carpet, she would have burned a trail into them by now with the pace she was keeping. Why was she so nervous?

Maybe because you just dry humped her against the window of the classroom, you fucking pervert.

"Okay, I will. Love you too. Bye."

My stomach immediately dropped. Love? Who the fuck does she love? I don't know who was on the other end of that phone call, but it sure as fuck was a male voice. Her dad, maybe?

"Sorry about that," she said, this time directed at me.

I gave her my most reassuring smile even though deep down I could feel rage pulsing through me. But I had to play it cool.

"No worries, Squid. Your dad?"

She shook her head. "Evan."

Her words from earlier in the week flashed in my mind, making my anger surface even more, though I tried my best to keep it contained.

I've occasionally caught Evan and Nicky's when they changed, but they were always unaroused.

"You love him?" I had to know. I couldn't play this shit cool. The last thing I needed was another woman fucking with my head when her heart was somewhere else.

"Yes."

Ouch.

She bit her lip then continued talking to clear the silence. "But only like a brother. Evan and Nicky are family. The family I chose, not the family I was born to tolerate. We've never crossed any lines... if you're wondering."

Ease washed over me. She must have seen the tension I released from my shoulders because she giggled and I swear my heart palpitated briefly.

"Good." I said sternly. "I don't share. Understand, Miss Knox?"

"Understood, sir."

Fuck. *Sir*. Here I was, getting fucking hard again.

"Right, well, the bell is about to ring Miss Knox. Better be on your way."

She tucked a stray strand of hair behind her ear and grabbed her backpack. Quietly, she walked to the closed door and opened it, letting the scent of food from the cafeteria fill the area.

"I'll see you in class," a pause, then she whispered, "Sawyer."

The day moved at a painfully slow pace but as Halen's classmates filtered into the classroom, I tried to remain unaffected as I scouted for her. She finally made it inside with Dominic Ressner's arm draped across her shoulders.

Evan and Nicky are family.

I pushed down my jealousy that was already overtaking my thoughts. She wasn't like Victoria at all. She was a good girl. Soon to be *my girl* if I had anything to say about it. When the time was right.

Everyone took a seat and I called out the next book

assignment for the class to read. Some groans could be heard from the jocks, but for the most part, everyone seemed okay with the book selection. You would have thought that they were being asked to read a novel over economics with how some of them reacted.

The classroom quieted as I put on a classical playlist over the speakers to have as white noise as they read their chapters.

I was writing a letter to a parent regarding their son failing the class, when I glanced up to make sure everyone was focused. My eyes met Halen's as she sat in her front row assigned seat.

Her smirk was not sweet. It was something else. I couldn't pinpoint what made it so different. She looked like she was a mixture of nerves and sneakiness.

I kept my eyes trained on her discreetly. She stood from her desk, catching me off guard. Walking to me, she put on a full innocent act as she asked her question in a whisper.

"May I borrow a pen please? I forgot to bring mine to annotate."

Hmm. I looked at the pen I was using for the parent notification and immediately passed it to her. She beamed at me and said her thanks before returning to her seat.

What are you up to, Squid?

I kept my head down as if I was proofreading the paper on the desk, but my eyes were fixed on her. Always her.

She scribbled a few things on a sticky note that was marking a spot in her book. I noticed over the past few weeks that she used literally anything as a bookmark. Receipts, gum wrappers, and pens. Literally anything she could get her hands on.

Then she slowly pulled the pen away and let it drift down the front of her body. The clicking side of it scraped down the valley of her breasts. Most of her cleavage was covered but the anticipation alone was enough to keep me watching, mesmerized.

Her hand eventually hovered underneath her desk but above her lap, waiting. My eyes remained fixed on her hand until the rapid clicks of the pen had me locking my eyes with hers.

Her smirk was seductive and wicked. This was a new side of her. She mouthed the words *I've been bad* as her hands started shifting again. I had a full view of her crossed legs from where I was sitting.

My cock jumped in my pants as she parted her silky smooth legs and gave me a view of her glistening pink pussy. No underwear. The lacey material was burning a hole in my pocket. She went the whole day without any panties on? I figured she had an extra pair in her locker. Definitely bad girl actions.

I watched the pen with rapt attention as she slid it lower and lower until the end of it slid through her slick center. She teased the area for a minute, rubbing it slightly in and around her core.

Eventually she moved the pen slowly up to the bundle of nerves and began making circles. I had to remind myself to close my mouth multiple times due to the spell I was currently under.

Occasional coughs and sneezes echoed through the room alongside the classical music as the students quietly continued reading. No one was likely paying attention to her movements thankfully. But I couldn't find it in me to look away to be sure. I didn't want to miss a single second.

I noticed a small shake of her left leg. So faint, but noticeable to me. I looked to her face to find her half lidded eyes locked on me. My cock twitched at the intimacy that we had so quickly fallen into. It was as if we had one dose of whatever this was between us and threw our middle fingers up to the rules.

I alternated glances between the pen playing with her dripping pussy and the expression she wore on her face that made her look like even more of a goddess.

The shaking got more intense but she quickly locked it down as she began to ride the wave of ecstasy she found herself in.

My dick strained so hard against my pants that I pressed down on my crotch just to give into the sensation for a moment. To pretend it was her hand there instead of mine.

Her eyes shuttered closed and she moved the pen to her center again and lightly pushed it in and out. I could see the moisture reflecting off of the blue plastic from the classroom's fluorescent lighting.

Jesus Christ.

After a moment, she opened her eyes again and lifted the pen back above the desk. With a quick glance around the room, she noticed that nobody was looking, until her eyes connected with Ressner's dark ones.

His brows were pinched in confusion as he cocked his head to the side, watching her. He saw her. I could tell that he didn't quite understand what had just happened, but he was trying to click the pieces into place.

"Ressner, focus on your own work," I barked.

With a grumble, he finally looked back down to the book in front of him. Halen easily got up and placed the pen down on the desk before giving me a wink.

"Thanks. All done now," she whispered as she quietly held the blue pen out to me. I wasted no time grabbing it from her like it was something naughty that the students would see.

Her lips tipped up at the edges and she sat back down. Clearing my throat, she glanced up. Her mouth gaped as she watched me pretend to study the paper in front of me and bring the pen to rest on my lips.

I darted my tongue out to lightly connect with the plastic and her breathing hitched. My eyes nearly rolled into the back of my head at the ever so faint lingering essence of her. It wasn't enough. But it was just enough to crave more.

"Back to work, Squid."

Her eyes widened in shock then morphed into confusion. I didn't get a chance to sign more to her because Ellen walked in to ask if I could cover her hallway duty after school for her, and the bell rang before our conversation ended.

Time. I would get her, in time.

CHAPTER 15

-HALEN-

Friday had finally arrived and school was the average boring redundant teaching, except for *his* class. He kept his eyes and thoughts to himself for the most part. I knew he didn't want to risk something happening on school property again. We had already been careless with the rules. But we did text back and forth about the book I was currently devouring.

I hadn't texted him in a couple of hours though. I had obligations that needed my attention and focus. These kinds of events always gave me anxiety. You never knew what you were going to stumble into. Especially when it came to the *twat trio.*

Looking at my outfit in the mirror, I smiled, feeling content in my decision. I knew that Nicky wasn't going to dare show up dressed in something other than his usual jeans, tee and leather jacket. Evan was a wild card. Not even I knew what he had planned.

My black sequin dress barely covered my ass. I paired it with a pair of sneakers and a full beat of makeup. Any excuse for a dark smokey eye was good enough for me. I rarely got the chance for edgy makeup around my mother.

I was eager to get the party over with, but at the same time, I really needed to let go. I was beginning to find understanding in what Evan said about finishing this year with a bang. So much was hanging in the air. My future marriage. Graduating. And *him*.

With one final look at my reflection, I grabbed my phone and keys. I didn't want to worry about dragging a purse around with me so I tucked enough cash for an emergency in my shoe. I usually just used my phone to pay for everything anyway.

Jumping into the front seat, I rolled the windows down, and push-started the car. The engine purred to life. The vibrations gave me the boost I needed. Traffic was thankfully minimal as it was now approaching 9 PM. The streets were nearly clear as I started to leave downtown Buffalo and make my way into Orchard Park.

The party was at Katherine's which I knew was going to be a risk. She didn't leave any opportunity to taunt me open. A true fucking bitch. Mean for sport. It wasn't going to be any easier trying to fight off her bitchiness when Evan was likely going to be dancing with Nicky and I. Half of me always wanted to poke the bear and make her more jealous, while the other half feared the confrontation deep down. As much as I pretended to be unbothered by people's opinions of me, it still hurt.

The god awful mansion came into view. Lights throughout the lawn illuminated the rows of maple trees colored in vibrant yellows, reds, and oranges. This time of the year was unmatched. It was half of the reason why I even agreed to go to this. I could smell the apple cider donuts wafting into my car from the gate.

I parked the car among the massive herd of heavily abused Toyota Corollas. As I walked to the front door, I saw Evan's car parked and empty. I could tell it was his based on the sticker on his bumper.

Wanna take a look under my hood? I'll show you mine if you show me yours.

I huffed a laugh and rolled my eyes as I kept walking. Music was booming and the chatter of people began to get louder as I drew closer. As I stepped into the house, my mouth wanted to drop open from jealous amazement. I would never admit it, but she knew how to throw a party. The home was filled with all different kinds of stations. Axe throwing. Face painting. A witch brewery. Even a kissing booth, featuring a very drunk looking Chad. My nose screwed up.

That surprised me. Wasn't he with Raya? Well considering how he actually began his relationship with Raya, maybe it wasn't that surprising. I loathed the girl, but sheesh, that guy was a prick.

I continued surveying the crowd for a sign of my boys, but didn't see anyone so far. I did catch sight of Astrid. She was standing in a corner listening to a boy ramble on and on about something. Her head was nodding as she listened, but just one look told me everything I needed to know. She wasn't listening.

Her eyes kept darting over to Chad as he collected ticket after ticket. Kiss after kiss. The pain on her face was evident if you were really paying attention. Though it seemed that everyone in this home was so self absorbed that they didn't seem to notice.

As her eyes tracked back to the guy she was speaking to, she halted her movements when she caught me observing. I was expecting her to raise her chin and curl her lip, but I was shocked when she gave me a doleful look instead.

I pinched my lips together for a moment trying to figure out which direction my moral compass was going to point. Deciding to go with my gut, I tapped the back of my hand underneath my chin twice, and inclined my head.

Chin up.

She cocked her head at me before giving a brief nod. Her face changed from one of sadness to confidence and power. Then inclined her head.

Smiling to myself, I walked out onto the grounds at the back of the mansion. I didn't think it was possible for the music to be louder than it was inside, but I was wrong. There was a raging bonfire blazing in the distance. People were either standing around talking or grinding their hips into one another.

I spotted Evan nearly immediately. My hand instinctively shot up to my mouth as I watched the disaster taking place in front of me.

"Yeah. We definitely need to start approving these

things before we let him out into society." The words shocked me but I quickly relaxed as I registered the dark and deep voice.

"Why... did he pick *that*? Sure it's crazy, but it's so random," I said, shaking my head. He was sporting a full ass chicken costume. It was way over the top and clearly not a sudden last minute pick. That boy put thought into it.

He chuckled and pulled me in for a hug. I could smell the whiskey pouring off of him. His face fell into the crook of my neck for a moment. Then he mumbled, "he keeps asking women if they like his cock."

My laughter echoed out into the chilly night air before I could stop it. His breathy laugh tickled my neck and made goosebumps pop up along my skin. It was like a 50-50 mix between the colder temperature and the sensation.

He pulled away but just enough to look into my eyes at a very close proximity. I was stunned by the sudden seriousness in his face. My brows drew together, trying to read his mind.

"What's wrong?"

"You're just looking really fucking edible tonight, Halen. Part of me wants to throw you over my shoulder and march you back home for wearing something so revealing, while the other half wants to throw you against that wall over there and taste you."

My eyes widened at his admission. He was always protective but we had never done anything like this. Ever. We would joke about sexual intimacy, but it never held any truth. At least I didn't think it did.

"You... you... want to taste me?"

He let out a groan and pressed his body close to mine. His answer was crystal clear. The hardness between his legs pressed against my thigh.

"I saw you the other day, you know. I didn't fully comprehend it because I was so distracted by the expressions on your face. But after a few hours of replaying it in my head, I knew what it was."

I looked at him as I tried to understand what he was

talking about. Realizing what he was referencing had blood rushing to my cheeks. I was sure they were bright red.

"Um, uh, well–"

"It's okay, Twerp. Really. You know I don't think anything is wrong with it. In fact, I have been thinking about that moment quite a bit. You're beautiful. You deserve the world and you know I would give it to you in a heartbeat. I even offered to marry you. It wasn't just out of obligation. You know I love you, right? You and Evan are my entire reason for existing."

Swallowing back the lump in my throat, I nodded at his vulnerability. I knew he loved us. We were family, and we always would be. I loved him too. But this seemed more like an admission of *true* love.

I was so stunned that I didn't even know what to say. My fingers twined in front of me as my brain tried to reset. Before I could form a coherent thought, I said the first thing that came to mind.

"Do you want a drink? I really need a drink."

He chuckled at my nervous gesture. "Yeah. Let's go get Evan and get fucked up."

I nodded eagerly, trying to get away from the situation so I could think it through later. Feeling uneasy about it all, I unlocked my phone and sent off a message that would hopefully keep me from looking like someone who was playing the field.

Me: Hey, I know it's late, I'm sorry. I just wanted to let you know that Nicky is very drunk. He shared some things with me that caught me off guard. He's been more touchy feely than usual too. Just wanted to be transparent so there isn't any mis-communication if word was to get around.

Hitting send, I darkened my screen and followed Nicky to the bar. I was gonna need a strong one.

Music blared around me, making me wince at the pain it was causing me. I tugged my implants off and set them on one of the outdoor couches before heading back into the horde of writhing bodies. The vibrations on the soil beneath my feet from the car sized speakers were more than enough for me to enjoy the music around me.

At some point I had lost my sneakers. The cold grass and dirt tickled my toes but the alcohol flooding my veins made it almost feel therapeutic. Some people called it grounding. Maybe they were on to something.

I was also pretty shit faced, so I could have been dancing to Beethoven over a pile of horse manure for all I cared. I could feel myself sandwiched between Evan and Nicky as we pressed our swaying hips to the music. The crowd began to jump around like it was a Jersey Shore nightclub, so I peeled out from between the boys and began fist pumping, likely incorrectly.

Evan was howling with laughter as Nicky's smile was wide, eyes filled with amusement. I felt the vibrations taper down to transition into the next song.

"Holy shit! Look at that McLaren dude! Come on, let's see if they will take us for a spin," Evan signed to Nicky.

Nicky's eyes jumped to mine with raised eyebrows. *"You coming?"*

Shaking my head, I started leaning into the rhythm of the music. *"I'm fine, go ahead. I'll be here connecting with the earth!"*

Nicky nodded. *"We won't be too long."* Then I watched as Nicky and a very oversized chicken walked into the night towards the group of cars. If I hadn't known about Evan's costume before arriving, the image would have made me wonder if I was having hallucinations from the alcohol.

Shaking my head, I went back to dancing among the rubbing bodies as Riot by Hollywood Undead boomed around us. I only knew that was the song because the song title and artist was displayed on one of the speaker screens.

A body pressed against my back as we all swayed with

no room in between. The scent of sandalwood and leather filled my nose just as firm hands grasped my waist. I knew that smell. Though I could have been trying to manifest something that was highly unlikely to be true.

With the fantasy of it being him flowing through my mind, I swayed my hips against his, as I felt his erection dig into my ass. The vibrations in this chest felt a thousand times stronger than the bass on the speakers shaking the ground.

I felt his nose run along my collarbone and up the side of my neck before stopping at my ear. I couldn't hear anything, but I didn't need to. His breaths wafted across my lobe and made me shiver. Then, without warning, he nipped it.

Turning my head I saw a man in a black jacket with the hood drawn over his head. The fire light danced along his skin and briefly illuminated his face. Or rather, his mask. A mask from Phantom of the Opera to be specific.

Even with him concealed, it was everything I needed to know. I knew the smell. I knew the lips. I knew the sharp jawline with the small prickling stubble running across.

He was staring into my eyes as we held still in the moment. Lifting his hand, he pushed the hair away from my ear. Observing. Then he tucked the hair behind my ear to keep it out of my face.

"Teach," I whispered. I knew he couldn't hear me over the thundering music, but he recognized that name on my lips. His smirk told me that much.

"Hey, Squid," he signed.

CHAPTER 16

-SAWYER-

She looked absolutely fuckable, and it was nearly snapping any grip I had on myself. Though I knew she was a virgin and she deserved her first time to be special, definitely not while she was intoxicated. And likely not with me.

Wait, it was absolutely going to be with me. She was mine.

Pushing away my aching thoughts, she nudged her ass right into my crotch. I knew she could feel every inch of my restraint. My desire. My proof of how badly I wanted to take her into the thick trees and slam her back against the rough bark.

"Where is the boyfriend?"

Her eyes narrowed. *"He's not my boyfriend. He's just drunk I think. The three of us have always been touchy but never in a sexual way that didn't have humor behind it. I'm not really sure where his head is at."*

My brows crinkled. I was picking up the language really well but I was nowhere near an expert at understanding what she was communicating at such a fast speed.

"Do you want to come back to my place where we can talk openly? I'll make you a late night grilled cheese. How about that? Mine are the best."

Waiting for her answer, my heart was pounding against my chest. I wanted her to say no. To say yes. I don't know what the hell I wanted.

She was everything I couldn't have, but was going to take anyway.

She bit her lip in thought for a moment before glancing

at an area of cars in the distance.

"I'll drive," I interrupted her potential thoughts of driving in this condition. *"I'll bring you back tomorrow to pick up your car."*

Shaking paused for a moment, then nodded and slipped her arm into mine. I instinctively clutched it closer.

Mine.

"Aren't you worried someone will see us together," she asked with a panicked glance around.

I gestured to my mask. *"Good thing it's Halloween and my identity is safe for the night."*

She grabbed her cochlear and then my arm once again before I ushered her to my Ford Raptor. Even in the cold, warmth radiated from her body. I wanted to drug her under my bed sheets to keep me cozy and do things that I would absolutely be fired for.

She hopped into the passenger seat and got comfy as we left that madness behind us. Now it was time to show her my temporary home. I was hoping to have already moved out of Connor's but it was convenient and free.

I didn't realize how much of my paycheck went to Victoria's bullshit facials, clothes, shopping and makeup hauls until I actually stopped paying for them. Now I was renting from Connor temporarily while saving back up the damage that was done on my credit card.

It wasn't mine, but it was home for now.

Maybe I could buy a home with Halen after she graduates.

The thought hit me like a strike of lightning. Live with her? I barely knew her. She was my student. What the fuck was I thinking? Though I didn't know every little detail about her, I had learned the important things. Maybe this weekend would be a good time to ask her to open up. But I would also have to be someone willing to open up. That would be tricky.

Her eyes widened in shock when I pulled into the parking garage of the high rise condominium building. I knew she came from money. Maybe she was doing the math and wondering how I could afford this on the salary of a teacher.

"You are full of surprises, Sawyer."

My name on her lips made me want to do unspeakable things. Like have her screaming it as I lick–

She spoke again. "I expected something more like a small suburban home. Nothing quite this opulent." A pause. "Can I ask you a personal question?"

"I plan on us speaking about all kinds of personal things while you stay with me, so please, by all means," I said as I pulled into my designated spot.

"Do you come from money?"

I quirked a brow at her. Usually that statement coming from someone meant that they had a specific interest in it. Or more like a special interest in obtaining it. I knew that wasn't the case since she probably had more money than I could make throughout my entire career.

"I'm comfortable, but not wealthy. This condo belongs to my brother, Connor. He works… as a private contractor. I'm just staying here to save some money while my brother doesn't use this place often anyway. He has multiple landing spots across the world."

She nodded her head. Clearly the thought of owning homes in different countries wasn't foreign to her. But my curiosity *did* poke at me.

"Are you wealthy, Squid?"

She rocked her head back and forth in thought, trying to find the right words. "Yes, and no. My parents are wealthy. And while I do have a trust fund coming my way any moment, I don't have access to it at this moment. So, I'm not wealthy at the moment. Just my parents."

I hummed my acknowledgement and led her to the elevator. The ascent to the top felt like the longest of my life. These elevators really moved at a fucking snail's pace.

The ding echoed throughout the claustrophobic box and slid open. She walked in slowly, waiting for me to take the lead. Curious about her opinions, I gestured for her to look around at her own leisure. I wanted to know her likes, dislikes, everything. Her steps were a little wobbly, likely from the massive amounts of alcohol filtering through her system.

"This is a beautiful view. I bet it will be even more stunning when the snow starts falling. It will be any day now."

She continued walking through the kitchen, running her fingertips along the marble island countertops. Everything was 'white glove clean'. It was only me here, so there wasn't much for me to clean after.

"Cute aesthetic. I like it," she said as she walked towards the hallway. She found the master bedroom in a matter of seconds then she pushed the door open.

From the side profile of her face, I saw the moment her nose scrunched up and lips pursed. Glancing at the bedroom, I scanned over everything from the bed to the leg on the dresser trying to figure out what it was that would cause such a reaction.

"Halen?"

"You have brothel sheets."

Looking back to the bed my brows knitted, trying to piece together what she wasn't saying.

"Brothel sheets?"

She pointed to the king sized bed. "Brothel sheets. Blood red. You only see red sheets in brothels, Teach."

Shaking my head in shock, mouth agape. I looked back at her, staring at me with a raised eyebrow. "Where do you even come up with this stuff?"

"Look it up! Find any brothel scene in any movie or show. Red sheets. Guaranteed. The only exception is for people that have BDSM rooms or something like that. Otherwise, it's not normal for people like us. This is definitely giving a prostitute vibe."

I couldn't help the laugh that escaped me, and her smirk let me know she liked the sound of it. I knew I didn't nearly laugh enough, but it seemed to come easier around her.

"Okay, buy new sheets, noted. Are you hungry for that

grilled cheese?"

The sound of her stomach rumbling stopped her in her tracks. She bit her lip, assuming in embarrassment.

"Let's go, Squid," I chuckled.

After some time cooking up my infamous dish, I placed the grilled cheese sandwiches down in front of us. She examined it for only a second before diving in. Her moan as she chewed instantly hardened my dick.

"Oh my god! This is so fucking good. What did you put on here that makes it so sweet? What's the red stuff?"

I swallowed my bite with a smirk before answering. "Jellied cranberry sauce."

Her eyes rolled back into her head as she moaned again through another bite. "You probably think I'm reacting this way because I'm coming down from being drunk, but I swear I'm not. This is the best thing I've eaten in my life."

"I'm glad you like it. It's definitely a comfort meal of mine. I probably make it once or twice a week. It was my mother's specialty. I guess that's why I enjoy eating it so much. It reminds me of her, and her love for me everytime she made it when I was sick, hurt, or just needing a little extra attention."

I watched her features soften as my vulnerability. "That's really sweet, Sawyer. What was her name?"

Swallowing the lump in my throat, pushing past the urge to throw up, I took it as an opportunity for her to see me. The real me. The damaged parts and all.

"Alva." I kept drawing every bit of strength I could from within. "She was one of the most wonderful people I have ever known."

"Will you tell me about her?" She asked hesitantly.

"Let's finish eating, and get you tucked in, and then we can talk, okay?"

She nodded. "So, I finished another book from your jar. I plan to pick a new one tomorrow. Be ready for incoming thoughts. That last one you picked just pissed me off. I didn't want to text you too much about it because sending you texts cussing you out would have looked bad. I planned to do it in person."

I snorted at her odd way of thinking, thankful for the change of topic until we could properly chat. "Never be afraid to text me, Halen. Ever. I want to know what's going on with you, what you're reading, what you're doing, who is touching you and professing their love." The last statement was pointed, and we both knew it.

As if the universe was trying to send me warning signals left and right, her phone chimed on the countertop. With a glance, she shot out a quick reply and placed it back down.

"Parents?"

"Nicky."

My fists clenched. He wanted her. He had known her for years longer than me, obviously putting me at a disadvantage. He was her age. So many things were trying to pull us apart.

Not if I stop every single one of them.

"He's just a fr—"

"Friend. I get it," I interrupted.

Her eyes narrowed. "Yes. My best friend. My family. But there won't ever be a time when he is more than that. I have taken a special interest in someone else."

My eyes couldn't help bouncing to hers. Waiting.

"Someone else?"

"Someone older." She whispered. "Someone forbidden. Someone who I fantasize about constantly."

I swallowed down the animalistic hunger coursing through me at her words, desire dripping from them. She wasn't making it easy to keep my hands to myself.

Even through the thickness that was permeating the air, she took another huge bite of her sandwich. Pulling the bread away from her lips, a thick and melty string of cheese stretched out between her mouth and the grilled cheese.

"That was probably the longest and sexiest cheese-pull I have ever seen." I chuckled.

Her cheeks blushed from the praise or the embarrassment, I'm not sure. The red hues against her alabaster skin fought for dominance. The flush could have also been exacerbated by the copious amounts of alcohol.

After we finished our food, stealing glances in between bites, I led her to the guest bedroom and watched her climb in. These sheets bathed her skin in a dark forest green that made her eyes even more pronounced. I'm sure my arousal was evident in my pants.

Refusing to strip down my clothes at the risk of what would happen, I excused myself to change into a pair of sweats and a tee. Upon returning, I found her snuggled up, with the covers pulled up to her chin, staring at me like she was counting the seconds for me to return.

Crawling into the bed next to her, I let her drape her head on my shoulder as I inhaled a sharp breath. Coconuts and waterlilies. It was all her.

"She died when I was one month into being eighteen years old." I said to the dark room. I could tell she was awake based on the tickle of her blinks against my fabric clad chest, but she remained quiet.

"I had just taken my brother out to his first party. He was sixteen at the time. I was only a few months away from graduation, so he wanted me to bring him into the popular crowd to make introductions before I left."

I licked my dry lips, and continued. "By the time we got back home that night, the cops were already there, rolling out a gurney with a big blue bag on top."

Her sharp intake of breath let me know that she was putting it together. "A body bag."

"Yes. After going through some identification verification with the police officers, they allowed me to identify the body. I felt instant relief when I saw it was our step-father."

She lifted her head to try to make out my expressions in the darkness. Only the moon assisted in illuminating our faces. "Not... not your mother?"

I swallowed down the rising bile. Brushing my fingers

against the silky skin of her cheeks, a wave of calmness rushed over me.

"It wasn't until I was done identifying Ken's body that I saw them wheel out the second blue bag. It took three police officers to hold Connor back as he screamed. That moment broke him. It broke us both, but as I went to therapy to heal, he channeled his anger in other ways. He never went back to that boy who just wanted to be accepted by the popular crowd. He became the guy that the popular crowd feared."

Playing with the strands of her hair as she continued to study my face, she finally asked the question. "How did they pass away? Was it a break in?"

My little detective.

Bopping her little button nose, I smiled sadly. "Those books are turning you into a little Nancy Drew, huh? Maybe I should add more murder mysteries to the jar." A moment of silence.

"It was a murder suicide. He shot her for threatening to leave, then turned the gun on himself when he realized he had just killed her. He was on heavy drugs, so that likely had a play in his erratic decisions, but either way, we had nobody. I became a parent at the age of eighteen. For two years at least."

She rested her head back on my chest and released a long sigh. "I'm so sorry Sawyer. Nobody deserves to lose their life or someone they love that way."

After a few minutes of holding her to me, her even breaths filled the silence, indicating she was asleep. I pulled off her cochlear implants, and rested them on the nightstand before laying her head greatly on the pillow.

With one more glance full of longing, pain, joy, and everything in between, I cracked the door and walked to my own room. Where I belonged.

CHAPTER 17

-HALEN-

A sudden jolt to my senses woke me from a dead sleep. The dryness of my mouth had me licking my lips for relief. The sensation felt like sandpaper rubbing across my skin. Cracking an eye open, I saw that it was still dark outside but the pink and golden hues were just starting to glow in the distance.

With a small groan at my body's uncomfortability, I sat up and threw my legs over the side of the mattress. If I didn't get some water down, I was surely going to feel like dog shit. I saw my cochlear placed nicely on the nightstand. Sawyer must have taken it out for me after I had fallen asleep.

The cold tile floor of the bathroom made me shiver. I rubbed my arms to give myself some warmth, but it was minimal. I took my time breaking the seal on a gallon's worth of pee from all of the alcohol, and took hydrating gulps from the tap. After quenching the deadly thirst residing in my mouth, I walked back across the hall to the guest bedroom with squinted eyes. I was so tired.

Sawyer had crawled into the bed while I was in the bathroom. His back was facing me as his large body rose and fell with each breath. My mother would often tell me how loud I could be when getting up in the middle of the night due to not hearing the slam of a cabinet door or the lid of a toilet seat.

I must have woken him enough with the noises I created to check on me. The warmth stretched across my belly at the realization that he came back into my room. I knew he was a rigid rule follower, but seeing him break them for me, did things to me. Bad things. Wonderful things.

Lifting the covers, quiet not to disturb him, I crawled in behind him and continued to listen to the deep inhales and exhales. With some courage, I scooted closer to him, almost making him an oversized little spoon to my big one.

He smelled like male musk and spice, making me scrunch my nose. It wasn't his usual scent, but I always saw him in a professional school setting, likely wearing cologne.

Pushing my thoughts away, I reached my hand over and pressed our bodies close together. Within a flash, he had me flipped to my back with his front pressed to mine, and a knife to my throat.

My eyes widened with fear and confusion as I took in the features hovering so close, his minty breath skating over my face. The snarl was evident even in the extremely dimmed lighting. Similar features but nothing compared to the sexy as hell teacher that I had become obsessed with.

It wasn't Sawyer.

I barely swallowed my sob. His lips moved, but in the cover of darkness, it was hard to make out exactly what he was saying. My bones were rattling beneath my skin in fear. I could feel the nerves rushing through my body, almost making me want to chatter my teeth. If I hadn't already peed, I definitely would have at this moment.

Finally, after another shake of my body from his rough handling, I screamed.

"SAWYER!"

I didn't hear him. I couldn't. I didn't hear the thunderous steps pounding down the hallway. I didn't hear the bedroom door slamming open and crashing into the wall. No. I didn't hear a sound. But I felt it. Every vibration of his panic and anger as he barreled his way through the condo to get to me.

Within under ten seconds of calling his name, the man on top of me was being pulled off and thrown to the floor. Sawyer straddled him and landed a hard looking punch to his face. I couldn't hear what they were shouting to each other in the darkened room, but my body stiffened the moment they both went deadly still. Realization dawned between both of them.

What realization though? I had no fucking clue, but I was still too shaken to move my hand over you the nightstand to grab my implants. Feeling the whimper leave my lips, I watched cautiously as their heads both snapped towards me.

I scooted back towards the headboard. I wasn't afraid of Sawyer by any means, but him giving benefit of the doubt to this fucking psychopath had me nervous about his capability to keep me safe.

I saw Psycho jab a finger towards me, shouting something again, and Sawyer's head slowly turned toward me. His hands moved but I couldn't see what he was trying to say, so I communicated out loud.

"I don't know what you're saying dammit. I can't see!"

Jumping to his feet, Sawyer hit the overhead light and faced me again with a face made of fury. Fury at *me*. My attention was pulled back to the stranger when he threw his hands up in a *what the fuck is happening* gesture.

"That doesn't make sense. Oh... is she... special?" I saw Psycho ask.

"Yes, she's special." Sawyer snapped. I could tell it was said with a bark to it because his chin jerked forward as his lips moved and then we quickly clenched his jaw. Tight.

"Ah, shit. This is so fucked up," Psycho said staring into space. He glanced at me again. "I'm sorry, Red. I didn't know Sawyer had someone staying here with a disability."

"I'm happy the way I am! I don't have a disability!" I exploded at the stranger. I didn't bother signing because he wouldn't have understood me anyway.

"Right. Well, it's okay either way. Autism is nothing to be ashamed of." His lips mouthed.

Sawyer slapped a hand over his mouth to stifle a laugh and my head slowly turned fully in his direction. He immediately threw his hands up as if he was trying to calm a lion about to pounce on a little dickhead who was going to have his head torn off.

"*Squid,*" he said out loud as he signed so that everyone understood. With a laugh he continued to sign. "*This is my brother, Connor. Remember how I told you about him? This is his condo.*"

My mouth gaped as I looked between the two brothers in front of me. The similarities were there for sure, but where Sawyer was tall and fit, Connor was shorter, bulky and all muscle. I jumped to my knees and crawled over to the nightstand to grab my implants and put them in.

"You're Connor?" I asked him.

He nodded, looking equally confused and tired as hell. The bags under his eyes and split lip from Sawyers punch had him looking pretty fucked up. I almost smiled at the damage done to him from Mr. Protective.

Looking back to Sawyer, I pointed at Psycho. "Your fucking brother tried to slit my throat! Then, he had the audacity to call me autistic! What the hell, Sawyer?"

His annoyingly radiant smile made me want to punch him, but it quickly turned serious as he looked at his brother then back to me.

"He said you tried to make a move on him in his sleep."

With my nose scrunched hard, I looked at Psycho. " I thought you were Sawyer. Don't flatter yourself."

Sawyer's shoulders sagged with relief. I hadn't even realized how hunched they were around his shoulders. He was nervous and angry at the thought of me touching Connor. Why? I wasn't trying to seduce him. He must have known it was accidental and I would never do that, right?

You are about to be engaged to another man.

With that awful thought in mind, I had to reassure him. I was going to need to tell him about Gregory soon enough. He was going to find out eventually. But he needed to know it wasn't going to actually happen, and that I just needed time.

"Sawyer," I said lightly to him. "I thought you decided to crawl back into bed with me. That's all."

With a nod, he glanced between us then said, “Let’s get some rest. We can talk over breakfast.”

I nodded. “Okay, I’ll just grab a blanket and sleep on the cou-“

“No.” Sawyer said. “You’ll sleep next to me. My system is all fried after hearing you scream. I need you to sleep close to me. Next to me. I promise I won’t touch you.”

My hope fell a twenty story plummet to its death. He wasn’t going to touch me.

Super.

Sawyer led me to his room where he watched me crawl into bed and snuggle under his duck feather comforter. The mattress was still cozy warm from him sleeping in it.

Turning my head into the pillow, I managed a sniff of his scent. The correct scent. Not the one Connor was sporting earlier. I inhaled deeply, soaking it in.

Sawyer turned off the lamp and crawled underneath the covers beside me. His body heat was radiating off of him. With the colder weather rolling in, it made me want to burrow into him and snuggle against his body like a cat.

I refrained.

The moonlight illuminating the guest room was a stark difference to the pitch black darkness of the main bedroom. I saw the large blackout curtains when I had walked in so I knew it was going to be dark, but this was pure lack of light aside from the digital clock on the nightstand. The only thing that told me that Sawyer was here with me was his body heat and the light breathing.

I decided to take my cochlear off and place it on his nightstand, removing yet another connection from me to him in this room. Now, I was only left with the warmth that threatened to pull me in. I knew I would be powerless to stop it.

After an hour, based on the illuminated clock next to me, I still laid motionless, laying on my side. The heat I was feeling slowly became something completely different as I watched the sixty minutes tick by on the clock. It went from the pure science of wanting the warmth against my skin, to my own skin becoming flushed with desire and eagerness.

Desire for *him*. The man sleeping next to me. He said he wouldn't touch me. He promised. But did that mean that I couldn't touch him? I could tell he was facing me because I could feel his measured breaths as they hit between my shoulder blades. He was close. But not touching.

I slightly scooted back, one small movement at a time. After about five moves, my ass finally nudged perfectly into his crotch as my back pressed against his chest.

I made no movement, feeling content with him already so close to me. Touching me, without actually *touching* me. It wasn't until I felt a small jolt against my ass cheek that I realized I would feel his very hard length pulsing.

As if caught in a trance, I rocked my hips once against his crotch. The rolling vibration of his chest and jump in his boxers were the only thing that told me he felt what I had just done. With another roll against him, I felt him stop my hips in place, then bring his mouth to my ear.

I wasn't sure if he was going to try to speak to me, or not, but I learned the answer to that question quickly as he ran his fingers through my hair and over my ear to feel around for my implant.

Once realizing it was out, he edged his mouth closer to my ear and nipped the earlobe. I let out a shuttering breath and resumed rocking against him. I felt his mouth move against my ear with the vibration in his chest, so I knew he said something, but I was too caught up in lust to care what he said.

Feeling brave, I reached behind me and grabbed his hard erection through his boxers. His panting danced across my earlobe making me shiver in excitement. He was all hard muscle, manly scents, and pure lust.

The spell was broken when he jolted against me and pulled back as if he had been burned. In the dark, I couldn't make out anything or hear anything, obviously. Looking around for an answer, I saw the blinking light on his clock that illuminated the early hour. 6 AM flat.

He reached over to smack at it then jumped out of bed to draw the curtains back. The sunrise was much higher in the sky now. It was daylight savings this weekend, so it was going to be much darker for a while. I knew I needed to soak up the light while I had it.

Amongst other things.

CHAPTER 18

-SAWYER-

"Sawyer, can you tell your brother to stop staring? It's making me feel violent," Halen said sharply.

Connor scoffed. "You don't even know the meaning of violence, Red." He bit into his croissant while he continued to eye her.

I smacked him on the back of the head. "Quit it."

"Ow. It's almost as if you forget who I am, *brother*. Don't forget to remind Miss Special Ed here," he gestured to Halen, "that I once fucked a man up with this one single finger." He held up his left index finger to show us the offending digit.

"Oh, you fucked a man with your finger?" She asked Connor then clicked her tongue. "You should have told me you swung that way! Of course it was scary having a woman in your bed last night! Silly me."

I rubbed the space between my brows, trying to ease the sudden headache. These two bickered back and forth more like siblings than me and Connor did. Then it hit me. Halen didn't have siblings, just her guy friends. This was all new for her.

The reminder of Ressner's love confession from last night sent a whole throbbing wave to my temples. Frustration bubbled inside me at the unknown future that awaited Halen and I.

Connor and Halen continued to shoot eye daggers at one another for the rest of breakfast but remained verbally civil.

"I didn't know you were coming home, Con. I would have slept in the guest bed. How long are you staying?" I asked while I picked up the empty plates in front of him and Halen.

"Not sure. Could be just today or could be a few days. I'll chat with Blake and see today to see when our next contract is expected."

Halen's phone started buzzing with an incoming call. Her smile was full of genuine love as she looked at the incoming caller's name and photo.

Not being able to refrain from looking, I glanced at the screen. A photo of the blonde little shit from school was plastered on the screen. The one who was bragging about her cock sucking skills.

Evan Saunders.

I tensed at both the caller and the images running through my head of me shoving my cock deep down Halen's throat. My cock began to press against my jeans with excitement.

For fuck's sake. You're acting like a damn teenager.

"Excuse me for a moment," she said as she walked towards the master bedroom.

My phone chimed with an alert as Connor made himself comfy on the couch.

Victoria: Can't wait to see you this weekend!

Oh. Right. I had forgotten about that. I wasn't necessarily looking forward to going but it seemed like the right thing to do for closure. For her. For me.

I typed out a vague response confirming I would be there and set my phone down to join my brother. I hadn't seen him in a while. He was always busy running jobs across the globe. I worried about him constantly, but was proud of how independent he was. He did bad things, but for the right reasons. That was something I was positive of.

Halen returned with a sheepish look. "Sorry, I've got to jet. I forgot I have plans with Evan and Nicky today. Talk later?"

I nodded and got up to walk her out. She turned to Connor as if remembering to say something. "I would say it was a pleasure to meet you, Psycho, but I don't like to lie." Her smile could eat any boy alive. Thankfully Connor was forged from malice.

He scowled at her before returning his gaze to the tv. "Whatever, Short Bus. Try not to hump any strangers on your way home."

She huffed and turned to continue walking to the elevator. It was clear that they were similar in attitude but different in their views of others.

"I told you I would take you to get your car. If you give me a minute, I can grab my keys." I said as I stopped.

"No worries, the Uber is already waiting."

"Oh. Okay. Well, send me an update if you make any dents in your reading jar."

"Got it, Teach." She said with a two finger salute. I watched her thoughtfully as she pressed the lobby button. The doors began to slide closed. I couldn't help it. She was captivating my entire headspace.

"Well finish what we started next time, Squid."

Her sharp intake of breath was the only indication that she had heard me. The metal doors sealed shut tightly as the elevator descended. I watched the numbers above as they ticked all the way down.

With a sigh, I returned to the couch.

"I like her."

"Hands off, Con." I warned.

His smile was acidic. I could've sworn he could read every thought. He wasn't going to touch her, but he sure did love poking people where it hurt. I wasn't an exception.

I received a few texts throughout the day from Halen. She filled me in on her thoughts about the book she was reading. She had started one that highlighted a professor's relationship with his student.

Perfect timing.

She was quickly becoming someone I didn't want to let go of. Someone that saw the parts of me that nobody else could. I eventually fell asleep that evening with her on my mind and the eagerness to hear her voice again.

The next evening I threw on a pair of dark jeans and a button down shirt for a casual yet classic look. I wasn't dressing to impress Victoria but I also didn't want to look out of place at such a nice restaurant. The navy fabric stretched against my chest, emphasizing my toned muscles.

A ding at the elevator informed me of someone's arrival. Assuming it was Connor, I walked out to let him know I was leaving but wouldn't be out late. I had no intention of dragging this out.

Walking into the main area, I didn't see Con anywhere. What I did see, however, was a very nosy Victoria poking around the place, dressed in a jewel tone purple dress that molded to her body like a second skin. As mad as I was at her for the betrayal of her actions, she had a knockout body. It was a shame that it did nothing for me anymore.

"Victoria." I said plainly. "I thought we were meeting at the restaurant."

"Yes, well, I didn't want you to come up with an excuse to back out. I figured we could carpool." Her grin was full of lust and longing.

"Alright. Might as well since you're already here. Let's get this done."

My short response was clearly not what she was looking for if her wince was anything to go by. I didn't care all that much. Though the wounds were healing, more rapidly with Halen around, I still harbored a loathing for what she had done.

Who would cheat on someone in the same workplace as their spouse? It's asking for trouble but also leaves the victim to deal with the rumors and humiliation. No, I didn't want to get back together. But I knew that it's where this conversation was headed.

Walking into the dimly lit restaurant, we approached the hostess who was waiting with a beaming smile.

"Reservation?"

I nodded.

"Name?"

Victoria chimed in with the reservation details. The hostess grabbed our menus and led us to our table. As we walked between the tables, she slipped her arm through mine and held on tight while I led us to follow the hostess.

Candles flickered against the white linen tablecloths throughout the large area, with low chatter from different patrons. A harp was being played gently in the corner so that it could be heard throughout, yet subtle enough to not overpower the talking volume.

Looking from table to table, my gaze tugged back on a party of six I was passing by. They were indulging in glasses of red wine while they looked over their menus. I knew that burning red hair. I knew those fuckable lips. I knew her. *Halen.*

I also knew the boy she was sitting next to. The little cocksucker with the motorcycle. My steps faltered as my mind caught up with what I was seeing.

"You alright, darling?" Victoria asked with worry lacing her words.

Halen glanced up at the voice. For someone who struggled hearing things, it seemed she caught more than most. She had mentioned she heard every small click and tick and it sometimes drove her crazy. I shouldn't have been surprised she was as observant as she was.

Her eyes widened in surprise then flicked between Victoria and I. Her brows pulled together in confusion but shifted to uncomfortability just as quickly. Adjusting in her seat, she looked around the table to make sure no eyes were on her before focusing her attention on her menu.

I clenched my jaw tight and tugged Victoria along again to the table the hostess had for us. As luck would have it, it was in clear view of Halen's table. I was still far enough away to only hear light laughter but close enough to see everything.

"I think I would like a Cosmopolitan, please," Victoria said as she took the menu from the waitress who filled our water carafe.

The waitress, Gemma, based on her name tag, looked at me in question.

"Oh, right. I'll have a Manhattan. Thanks."

She nodded and left quietly.

"Thank you for meeting me. I've been wanting to reach out these last few months, but I had some things I was trying to work out first before making contact."

I grunted a response and took a sip of water. Halen never left my field of vision. She was sitting close to dickhead. I could only see the top of her dress, but it looked to be a one shoulder black satin slip. She was fucking stunning.

Victoria cleared her throat. "So, what do you say?"

I hadn't realized she was talking the whole time. The waitress dropped off the cocktails and left again while we continued to look through our menu.

"Sorry, what?"

"I was saying that I accepted a contract with Black Grove Academy," I paused with the rim of the glass pressed to my mouth. "I wanted to be sure I was offered the contract before reaching out. To show you how much effort I'm putting in. I made a mistake with Ben and I've regretted it every day since."

I blanched at his name. Benjamin Tenford. Fucking prick. Reality slapped me in the face and I suddenly felt physically ill.

"You accepted a job at *my* academy?"

She huffed a laugh. "Well it's not yours, but I understand your meaning. Yes. I spoke with the principal a few weeks ago and just wrapped up my contract back in Chicago."

The urge to stand up and leave was suffocating. Was she serious? She just decided to move her life to follow me? After no contact for months? After her affair with fucking Ben

Tenford?

My mind was glitching and my attention drifted back over to Halen as the motorcycle punk stood from the table and walked around to her other side. I jerked up, ramrod straight in my chair, as I saw the scene unfolding before me.

No. Fucking. Way.

I already knew that this night was about to get a fuck ton worse before he did it. But when he finally knelt down on one knee and grabbed her left hand, I felt the ten ton boulder crushing my chest as I struggled to inhale a steady breath.

Whispers and coos from around the restaurant filled the silence. I couldn't hear what the boy was saying, but I saw every nervous twitch in her eyes as she flicked them to me. Victoria finally understood what I was looking at and turned with a hand to her chest.

"Oh, how precious! She is absolutely stunning," she whispered. "She is going to make a beautiful bride. Aw, young love."

The salad fork in my hand began to bend at an unnatural angle as my grip tried to press every ounce of anger into it. I was fucking livid. My eyes stayed fully trained on my Squid. She looked panicked. Likely from everyone watching.

Her eyes darted quickly between the four other adults at the table, to the douche, and then *me*. I saw her long defeated exhale as her shoulders slumped slightly. Then she did the unthinkable.

She nodded.

Fucking nodded.

Wine glasses clinked around us as the onlookers tapped their silverware against their glasses. I looked around at all the busy-bodies I wanted to strangle at this moment.

The douche placed a ring that had a striking sparkle, even visible from here, on her left finger. Then he pushed up from his knee, grabbed her face with both hands, and kissed her. My eyes were hot and burning with fury I had never felt before. Not even after walking in on Victoria and Benjamin.

"Do you agree?"

Thinking back to her statement about Halen being a beautiful bride, I muttered my agreement in a hoarse voice. Before I knew it, Victoria grabbed my hands in hers and leaned over the table to place her lips on mine. I was caught off guard so I jerked back after the initial shock wore off.

"I'm so glad you agree. I was worried you wouldn't want to try again, even after me giving it my all by leaving Chicago."

I must have missed something in between her talking about Halen and that kiss, because I was starting to realize that I think I had just agreed to a fresh start.

Looking at Halen, I quickly realized she saw everything. Her face was flushed and jade eyes were more vibrant than ever. I could tell that she was holding in tears. Regret maybe. Regret at me finding out or even starting something with me to begin with, I was unsure.

I pinched my lips together and sent her a glare that definitely communicated the malice I was feeling. She deserved to see me kiss Victoria after her little show. I didn't have a right to claim her as we weren't exclusive. But to have someone propose meant you were obviously involved with them beforehand.

"*Can we talk,*" she signed subtly from across the dining room as her eyes flicked between me and Victoria.

My skin was beginning to sweat through the emotions. Pain, jealousy, hatred, and so much more rose to the surface. Victoria kept rambling in about our future but I wasn't able to retain a single damn word.

I just shook my head at Halen slightly.

To keep Victoria from realizing I was signing with the newly engaged woman across the room, I only risked responding one word.

"*No.*"

CHAPTER 19

-HALEN-

Fuck. Fuck. Motherfucking fuck.

My blood was boiling, but it didn't ease the amount of guilt I felt inside for my part in tonight. What was I thinking? I knew I should have told him sooner.

Nausea punched through my stomach as I replayed the kiss. His kiss. My kiss. Our unspoken battle from two sides of the expensive, yet gaudy, dining area. The sconces on the walls flickered as if the suffocating shadows I was feeling around me were physically draining life from the air.

I sat silently throughout most of the dinner. The weight of the diamond pressed down on more than just my finger. I refused to look back up after his denial to speak with me. I wouldn't show him how hurt I was. How sorry. How fearful I was to lose what didn't even have a chance to start.

The bisque was tasteless. Who was she? All I could see was the pin straight haired brunette whose body was wrapped in a purple dress that made my jealousy grow to dangerous levels. I couldn't see her face, but the rest of her was stunning. I was sure her face was no less beautiful.

Trying to gasp for air, I realized I wasn't being exactly inconspicuous when a masculine hand slid under the table to squeeze mine that was resting in my lap. Looking up, I met eyes full of curiosity and nosiness, but also sympathy.

Gregory leaned in, pressing his lips to my ear. "Excuse yourself to the ladies room and freshen up. I'll keep the conversation going." I squeezed his hand back and excused myself quietly.

With a well mannered departure, I nearly sprinted the last twenty feet into the ladies room where I stood in front of the mirror and gave myself the pep talk of the decade. While fixing some running mascara, a woman stood next to me at the neighboring sink and began to wash her hands. Her face was perfectly pampered, lips stained a vibrant red. I hadn't realized someone else was in here. I smiled at her through the mirror as I fixed my face.

"Congratulations. You look lovely. The running mascara from the tears of joy only makes your eyes pop more." She smiled.

I gave her a small sad smile in return that I tried to pass off as shy. "Thank you."

"Your proposal actually gave me the courage to rekindle my relationship with my fiancé. Life is short, so I took charge of the moment."

She smiled triumphantly at herself. Proud of her second chance with her love. I was jealous of her ability to love who she wanted. And she took it with no hesitation. I should have done that with Sawyer. I was eighteen, and there was nothing *really* stopping me except for my greed for attending Gallaudet and getting my inheritance.

"Well, I better get back out there so we can get the bill early, if you know what I mean." She winked and grabbed her clutch as she walked away and out the door.

It wasn't until she was already gone that my brain caught up with me and nearly seized.

Her dress was purple.

I walked back to the table with my head held high and my fury flowing so strong, I could have sworn that steam was billowing from my ears. Not giving a flying fuck anymore, my eyes drifted to Sawyer's table as I watched him sign the check and place it back on the table and smile at the woman before his eyes flicked to mine.

His smile immediately faltered as worry creased his brows. I'm sure he had read every emotion written on my face like the little book snob he was.

Read this.

I turned my head to look at the table where my family and future family sat, as I lifted my middle finger to Sawyer as I passed by. He didn't need to be an expert in ASL to understand that. I didn't look to him to see his reaction. I did, however, hear a table clunk and the faint sounds of Miss Purple's voice.

"Everything okay, darling?"

I rolled my eyes. Though the nausea was back in full force. He might have been alright, but I sure as fuck wasn't. I sat back down next to Gregory and gave him a thankful smile. With my chin lifted a little higher with confidence, I finished my dinner.

The next two weeks were brutal. I didn't seek him out before school, nor did I text him updates on my reading thoughts. Instead, I pulled out a blank journal and wrote down all of my feelings about the characters and their story as if I were still talking to him.

I purposely avoided looking at him in class, but the few times I did, I occasionally caught him glancing at my oversized Harry Winston sparkling on my finger.

The bell for the end of school rang and I ran out of class to meet up with the boys. Nicky had been acting weird since I told him I was officially engaged. We knew it was coming, but it was still hard to process. He was irritable and antsy. I knew it hurt him to see me being taken away by someone else, especially after our drunk conversation at Katherine's Halloween party. But he hadn't brought it up again.

"Hey, Twerp," Nicky draped an arm over my shoulder as we walked.

"Hey, let's get the hell out of this place. Have you seen Evan?" I looked around to see him speaking with a few guys at their locker then quickly shove his hand in his pocket. My eyes narrowed as he walked towards us with a little too much pep in his step.

"Hey guys," he said as he reached us.

"What was that about?" I asked, gesturing to the group of guys.

"Just scored some party favors for tonight." He wiggled his eyebrows at me, and I pinched my lips into a tight line.

"Just weed, right?"

"Right." His face had the dopiest grin. I cocked an eyebrow.

"Hell yeah, man. Let's go," Nicky said as he led us out.

The drive out to the overlook took about thirty minutes, but we arrived two hours later than normal because they decided we needed to eat our weight in food first. Our bellies were busting the buttons on our pants after munching down on not one, but three pizzas.

The sun had already set due to the winter being so fucking dark all of the time. The sun set at like 5:30 PM and rose around 8 AM. But tonight, there were surprisingly no clouds in sight, and the stars were sparkling something beautiful. That was rare for Western New York this time of year.

I inhaled the woodsy scent of the trees around me, embracing the burn of the chill inside my nostrils. We laid on the hood of the car, bundled together in a blanket with me sandwiched between them. Like always.

We were talking about how to get me out of my engagement, college, and how often we wanted to meet up. We were family. Just because we were going to be living in different areas for a few years, didn't mean we would be any less connected.

My phone buzzed with a notification.

Teach: Are you awake?

My pulse quickened but I was still so full of hatred, that I sent back something that I was hoping would hurt.

Me: Yes, but I'm out. Can't talk.

His response came immediately.

Teach: Where are you?

Me: The Overlook with Nicky and Evan.

After five minutes of no response, I figured I wasn't

going to get one. I wanted to beg him to keep talking but was relieved that he was probably understanding that losing him wasn't bothering me.

Liar, liar.

"Guys, I'm gonna catch an Uber home. I'm not feeling so well," I said as I pulled up the app.

"Are you sure? It's only midnight." Nicky said with a small pout to his voice.

"Yeah, I'm just gonna curl up in bed with my book."

"Okay. Well, how about Evan and I pick you up for breakfast tomorrow? The diner?"

I smiled and leaned in for a long hug. His hugs were the most comforting. Familiar.

Evan stole me away for a hug of his own before topping it with a sloppy kiss on the cheek. I made a show of wiping all of his slobber away.

"You know, you're gonna miss my smooches when you're off at your fancy college, babe." He said with a playful nudge.

"Yeah yeah." I rolled my eyes at him but smiled at his usual playfulness. We took a few selfies together that we posted to Isnta before the Uber pulled up and I got up to leave.

"Behave, boys. Love you."

"Yes, mommy." They both grumbled in unison.

With a chuckle I walked away but heard them as I made my way to the beat up Honda Civic with an older gentleman in the driver's seat.. "Time to break out the good stuff."

Ugh, boys and their bongs.

The Uber got me home in record time with nobody else on the road. I didn't even take off my makeup before falling face first into my pillows and letting sleep claim my mind.

When the light woke me through my eyelids, I stretched like a cat. Glancing at the clock, I was shocked to see how late I had slept. 10 AM. I slept better than I thought I would. It likely had to do with spending some time with the boys to ease my nervous system.

With a shiver, my feet padded against the cold wood floor as I walked to my window. A light blanket of white stretched across the streets. The first snow of the year. The first time was always magical. Everything after was just annoying.

With a yawn, I grabbed my cochlear and got it placed correctly. My messy bun had me looking like I stumbled out of a meth lab, but it was the weekend so I had no plans aside from reading and watching trash tv. I grabbed my remote and flipped through the channels. Nothing was on besides info-mercials trying to sell egg cracking tools and cellphones for old people. Leaving it on the news, I wandered off to take a shower and get dressed.

While putting my favorite pair of black skinnies on, I heard the news anchor asking the public for help in finding a girl who had run away. Glancing at the screen, I saw a photo of her with a banner of her name illuminated underneath.

Evelyn Steele.

She was gorgeous. Scoffing, I pulled an edgy black top over my head. I was jealous of a random runaway girl. She had the right idea. Maybe I should have taken notes on what she did, so I could copy them if this marriage seemed impossible to escape.

I grabbed my phone that was still in my bag from last night and my eyes widened at the notifications.

34 Missed Calls

16 Text Messages

13 Voicemails

What the fuck? Starting from the most recent voice-mail, I held the phone to my ear and listened with confusion setting more every second.

"He is out of surgery, sweetie," she sniffled. "They have him in the ICU until the fluid is cleared from his lungs. He will be on ECMO until he heals a little more."

My body flushed with panic immediately. Ringing in my ears had me pulling my cochlear off to shake it and place it back on. Reading the caller ID of the voicemail, I whimpered. Helen.

Evan's mother.

With shaking fingers, I thumbed through the text messages to start from the beginning.

Nicky: Did you make it home?

Evan: You should have stayed, babe. We just saw a shooting star!

Nicky: Save me. Evan is dancing in the falling snow. Naked.

Nicky: Crisis averted. He put his clothes back on.

Evan: Have I ever told you that your skin is like heavy cream? Super silky and soft.

What the hell?

Evan: Are you awake? Nicky is wondering if you made it home or not. He said psychopaths hide in plain sight, usually as Uber drivers.

Nicky: We are going to head home. Please text me in the morning that you are safe.

That message was at 2:30 AM. A little over two hours after I had left them at the overlook. Worry had me pausing my scrolling to take a shaky breath.

In.

Out.

Teach: I don't want to argue with you. Please talk to me.

Teach: I want an explanation. How could you do the things that we have done, and be on the road to engagement simultaneously?

Teach: Was I just some adrenaline rush for you?

Teach: Where are you?

Teach: I just got a call from Principal Howard that some of our students were in a critical car accident at the overlook.

Teach: Halen, I am not fucking around. Answer your goddamn phone!

Teach: HALEN!

Teach: Fuck. Please.

Teach: I will search every fucking hospital if you don't answer me.

The last message had come through thirty minutes ago. Understanding of what happened had taken every ounce of my attention. An accident took place at the overlook.

Nicky and Evan.

I threw on my shoes and a jacket before rushing over to Mercy Hospital. Helen had mentioned the ICU so at least I had an idea of where I was going. Hope fueled me as I briskly walked through the halls, until I saw something that would be forever burned into my mind.

A woman on the floor, her face buried in her hands, begging for the doctor in front of her to check again.

"Please! He's just weak. The pulse is there. Check again!"

Danny, Evan's father, squatted down next to Helen and placed his face in the crook of her neck. I could tell by the shake of his shoulders that he was also crying.

No.

CHAPTER 20

-SAWYER-

The rain fell from the sky at the same pace that salt-water fell from the eyes of the mourners around me. Whimpers and wails filled the cemetery as they lowered the casket into the quickly dampening soil.

The crowd consisted of a large volume of teachers, students, and family of the deceased. He wasn't one of my students directly, but I felt an obligation to attend. Not just to the family, but to *her*..

She stood across the six foot hole in the ground. Rainwater cascaded over her hair and face, making it hard to tell whether or not she was crying or just soaked from the unrelenting skies. When she tipped her head to the onslaught of water, I saw her ears free of any tech. She was unplugged. She didn't hear a single word said during the eulogy.

Wanting to get her attention was going to be harder than simply calling out her name as people began to leave. Ressner stood by her side with his arm in a sling. His face revealed no sadness. Not an ounce. Just pure anger.

I watched as he laced his fingers through hers and clasped them tight. I felt like a piece of shit for the jealousy that made my stomach roll. I was at a fucking funeral.

Halen had a moment of shock play over her face as she turned to study Ressner. Her free hand went to his face as she stepped right into his line of sight. People were beginning to leave, but I stayed cemented to my spot, watching the scene in front of me. She released his cheek and signed in front of his face. I couldn't tell what she was signing with her back to me, but I could tell it was repetitive.

This continued for a good three minutes before he finally snapped his attention to her and his mouth pulled even more downward. Without a word, he released her hand and pulled her into a bear hug, placing his face into the crook of her neck.

A growl rumbled from my throat but I faked a coughing episode as an older woman next to me was basically clutching her pearls. Halen was too focused on comforting her friend that she didn't meet my eyes once. Not while they cried, not while they walked to the line of black sedans, not when she gazed back to the now filled hole and closed the car door.

She was gone. And I wanted nothing more than to comfort her. I had spent the morning of the accident blowing up her phone and calling hospitals. It wasn't until I started seeing the social media posts with Evan's image photoshopped with angel wings floating around on Facebook that I was able to get some answers.

I sifted through endless comments and conversations from students asking what happened and who was involved. A few had mentioned that Halen and Ressner were with him in the car, and were also pronounced dead. I dry heaved over the toilet when I read it. After another hour of cold sweats and heartache, fellow students started pouring in with more reliable information. Halen had gone home early that night. Ressner was with him but sustained only minor to moderate injuries.

Looking once more at the plot, I said a mental prayer, that he was no longer in pain. The car had wrapped around a tree on one of the curves at the overlook. The speed they were traveling was a huge factor in the severity of the wreck. There was a small layer over ice on the road that also had a play in the spin out.

I swallowed my sadness for the boy that would never have a future. The anger at Halen for being there that night followed by relief that she wasn't involved in the tragedy when it happened. I was still confused and livid at her lack of communication regarding her fiancé. But I couldn't say that it wasn't slightly lessened at the worry I had felt when I thought I had lost her.

After arriving home, I saw grocery bags littering the counter and a beautiful woman cooking dinner in my kitchen. She was wearing a pair of khaki pants and a fitted pink blouse. It was all wrong. No edgy black tones. No vibrant red hair. No emerald eyes.

"I figured I would make something nice for us to eat together after the hard day you've had."

I nodded, ignoring the urge to ask how she got in without a key, and did the one thing I could think of to ease the bitter disappointment of Victoria's presence in my personal space. I poured a heavy glass of bourbon.

My phone chimed from my pocket and I swiftly pulled it out, hoping it was Halen. Maybe she needed me. Wanted me.

Connor: Had to leave on an assignment. Not sure when I'll be back, but I'll keep you updated. Also just a heads up that Icky Vicky was arriving at the same time I was leaving. She said she was dropping off groceries for you.

I sighed, typing a quick response.

Me: A little late, Con. I've got it handled. Be careful.

A week passed and it was hard to focus when I was painfully aware of Halen's absence. I wasn't surprised. Both she and Ressner had lost their best friend, their family member based on what she said regarding their relationship. My mind struggled to stay focused. Thankfully the week off for Thanksgiving followed and gave me some time outside of the classroom.

More time passed and my worry hadn't reduced any. If anything, I was feeling a severe itch to reach out to her.

Engaged. She's *engaged*.

"I have to go get sweet potatoes from the grocery store for the casserole. Did you want to come with me?" Victoria looked at me expectantly while she straightened the pillows on my couch. She had been hovering recently, clearly trying to show her usefulness in my life. I wasn't completely mad at her presence, as it did get occasionally lonely. But she left no room for me to be with my own thoughts.

"Actually, I told Brent I would meet up with him for drinks. I'm about to head there now."

She jutted her bottom lip out. "Should I tag along? I will be his coworker starting next week, after all."

"Next time. This is an outing for the guys only. But I'll try to ask him for some time for all of us to go out. They do happy hour every Friday. Maybe we can catch the next one."

Her smile stretched wide as she clapped her hands together. "Yay! Okay, well don't stay out too late. I could use some help stuffing the turkey for tomorrow." She pecked me on the lips with hers, something she had become more brazen about it in the past few days. I wanted to let her in again, mostly out of pain and the urge to hurt Halen like she hurt me.

I basically darted out of the condo and met up with Brent at a local burger joint. We were three beers deep already and laughing over horror stories from our teaching years so far. He had told me all the different cat fights he had to break up over girls fighting for lead vocals in certain shows.

My mind was itching to ask him something useful to me. "I'm buzzing hard, so I am just going to come right out with it. How did you handle the grief of the loss of your wife? Did the constant missing her ever lessen?" I wanted to know how to cope with the empty feeling I was fighting everyday without *her*.

He rocked his head from side to side in thought. "Grief is like a new houseplant." I held my eyeroll at his plant reference. He really loved his fucking plants. "It's something that's new to your life but eventually it settles into your everyday surroundings. You know it's there, and sometimes you can't help but to pay it attention, pruning the dying parts, but it usually just sits on the sidelines and becomes something you don't quite forget but isn't a main focal point of your routine."

"What was she like?"

His smile was pure but sad. "She was everything a wife should have been. Made meals. Cleaned the house. She went and hung out with her girlfriends at the nail salon."

"But?" I asked, sensing more.

"But she was always pre-occupied. She did everything ideally a wife would do, but we rarely spoke. We didn't date. We didn't exchange stories of our day. We only managed the basic pleasantries before going to our own area of the house." His eyes darkened. "I didn't find out she had an affair until a couple of weeks after her death. Never learned who it was with, just that she had emotionally checked out of our relationship."

Stunned by the change of direction this was taking, I comforted him the best I could. I knew what it was like to be cheated on, but to not even be able to hate her because she was dead was a type of non-closure I wouldn't wish on anyone.

"I'm sorry. I can't imagine. How did you find out?"

He inhaled sharply and snagged the waitress over to order a few rounds of shots. Clearly he needed some liquid courage to take this up a notch.

He explained how he went through her phone and found messages between her and a man. She had referenced days that they had spent together, and intimate moments, in detail.

He threw back one of the shots immediately after the waitress brought them over. Shrugging a shoulder, he quirked a smile. But I saw the sadness in it.

"We didn't have a big spark in our marriage, but we did our best. I wish she didn't betray my trust, but I am just learning to focus on myself for now. I'll always love Geneva for the happy moments that she *did* give me."

I clapped a hand on his shoulder and threw a shot back alongside him."Well, we don't have to teach tomorrow. What do you say about getting fucked up?"

His chuckle lightened the mood immediately. "Cheers to that."

◆ ◆ ◆

The room spun around me as I tried to get my feet to steady themselves. We had stayed out until the bar's last call. I was surprised how easy friendship with Brent was. He was nothing like me, yet we had so much to talk about. I was shocked at how genuine of a person he was. I needed more people like that in my life. People like him. Like... Halen.

After knocking a vase off of the entry table, I figured I was a lost cause. I groaned as the glass shattered to the floor. The glass could wait until tomorrow to clean up, right? The lights were out in the condo, so surely that had something to do with my equilibrium.

After finally making it to my bedroom, I stripped down to my boxers, and threw myself onto my bed. Red Sheets. There was *nothing* wrong with red sheets, I thought. Screw her. What did she know about brothel sheets anyway? She was a virgin.

With Halen's virginity on my mind, I slipped into a better place. A place full of dreams that had her vibrant hair and green eyes. At some point in the night, my dreams gave me exactly what my subconscious was looking for.

The warm and wet glide of Halen's tongue ran up and down my cock as I moaned. She made sure to pay special attention to the head, flicking her tongue against the slit.

My fingers slid through her silky strands and tightened them into my fist as I began to buck my hips upward. The room was void of sound except for my heavy breathing and the sloppy wet sounds of her mouth sucking hard.

Why did this have to be the only place that I could have her? Why was life so cruel that it would dangle a carrot of potential happiness in front of my face, just to tell me it was forbidden and I would never be able to take a nibble. Suddenly I had a perfect understanding of Eve's temptation with the apple.

I wondered if it would have been easier to be together if I left the academy. There still would have been the stigma to fight, but the potential legal aspects of being her teacher would no longer pose an issue. Remembering her as she kissed her fiance *at the restaurant, my stomach turned, so I tried to grasp back onto the fantasy that my mind allowed me to partake in.*

I dug my head back into the pillow as she continued to assault my dick with her hot fucking mouth. I dreamed of her beautiful eyes locking on mine. I could feel the rock of her hips as she straddled my shin while blowing me. She was trying to get herself off, while getting me off

Dirty girl.

"Fuck. Good fucking girl, Squid. Just like that, baby." I continued to thrust my hips, basically fucking her face now in full force. My body had begun to tingle as I could feel my orgasm approaching.

"God, fuckkkkkk. Halen! Yes, baby!" My orgasm pulsed out in what I imagined were hot thick ropes as they poured down her throat. She was becoming everything to me, yet she was currently nothing to me.

Sleep must have really pulled me under because after releasing all of that tension, I didn't remember a single thing until the sounds of clanking dishes in the kitchen woke me.

The headache radiating from my skull told me everything I needed to know about the night before. I had way too fucking much to drink, and I was likely severyly dehydrated. Licking my lips, I confirmed the latter instantly. With a few moans and groans, I threw my legs over the bed and made my way into the bathroom. Letting the hot water flow over my skin in a cocoon of warmth took away the headache for a whole five minutes before it came back in full force as I threw on my outfit for the day and brushed my teeth.

When I entered the kitchen, I was greeted with Victoria running around like a crazy person, trying to juggle cooking seven different things at once. Uncooked pies, casseroles, a stuffed turkey, and bread rolls littered the kitchen counter, waiting for their turn to bake. Admittedly, the smell made me want to vomit. Though, that was likely due to the hangover instead of her cooking capabilities. She was a good enough cook, but I can say with confidence that I was better. But her effort was clear.

"Good morning," she chirped as I sat at the island bar stool. Her face was full of excitement as happiness. Definitely too much for this early in the morning, but I wasn't going to say anything.

"I was wondering when you were going to stumble out here," she continued, "I know you had your fair share of drinks last night. No worries though, I managed to get the turkey stuffed alone."

My eyes crinkled as she placed a mug of coffee in front of me. Oh, sweet delicious, overly sweetened coffee. "How did you know I was shit faced last night? I didn't realize you stayed over. I tried to be quiet as I passed the guest bedroom, but I guess I wasn't quiet enough. Sorry."

I took a sip of the warm liquid which caused my eyes to filter closed. It was the only thing fueling my existence for the moment. Whoever invented coffee needed a statue in their honor. The vanilla flavors swirled around my taste buds and my eyes nearly rolled into the back of my head.

"No, silly. I slept next to you, remember?" My coffee mug hung in the air as my brain started rapidly shuffling through scattered memories. "Don't you remember me taking care of your little friend?" She pointed down towards my crotch and I placed my mug down quickly before straightening my spine. Shock and unease rolled through me.

"What do you mean?"

She giggled. "You were definitely plastered, honey. You were saying things about squids and Van Halen. I don't know. But don't worry, you definitely enjoyed yourself."

With a salacious wink, she went back to handling the different sides for Thanksgiving lunch. I was hit with another wave of nausea that made my stomach churn, but I knew it had nothing to do with the hangover.

CHAPTER 21

-HALEN-

The pillow cradling my head was practically stained with varying layers of dried tears. Evan was gone. Sawyer was gone. Nicky was spiraling. I was lost.

Evan was gone.

Gone.

I would never watch the stars with him again. Never feel his kiss against my temple as we walked in between classes. Never hear him calling me babe after his outlandish words of wisdom. He was a whisper of something that no longer existed and never would again.

My eyes were crusty from the nonstop saltiness falling from them. I got a whiff of something unpleasant, and hesitantly sniffed my underarm. I crinkled my nose in disgust and debated if I had the energy to do something about it. With an annoying huff, I finally showered and immediately crawled back under my covers.

There.

I had showered.

Progress.

My phone blinked from the nightstand, indicating a call. I didn't answer. It rang again. This time I peered over my massive pillows at the name illuminating the screen to make sure it wasn't Nicky. He had been quiet, but I was giving him space to cope. After the funeral, we had video calls with each other but we let the silence fill between us.

We didn't need words to express how we were feeling. We were in the same boat with grief. We lost a part of us. I knew he also felt guilty for not seeing the accident coming, and mad for allowing Evan to drive when he was in that state. He hadn't said it, but I knew it.

I didn't place any blame on him, and neither did Helen or Danny. I planned to tell him as much, but my own mourning ended up taking all of my free mental space. I really needed to tell him soon, though.

Gregory's name flashed on the screen. Based on the notifications counter at the top, it looked like he had called a few times. Pressing my face into my pillow, I let a scream rip from my throat. I think the pillow, surrounded by egyptian cotton, muffled the sounds enough to keep anyone from hearing.

Only dad had checked on me, and it was sporadic as he was away from home every couple of days. Mom didn't even bother. Thanksgiving had come and gone without notice as there was no one here to make anything. I thanked the Lord for the empty home.

I realized I had fallen asleep with my face buried, when a hand caressed the hair from my face and crawled into the bed next to me. When his hand reached around to spoon me, I glanced at the knuckles grasping my abdomen.

Those were most definitely not Nicky's hands.

I also knew based on the smell that they weren't Sawyer's either, but I mentally reprimanded myself for even considering that he would be here to comfort me. We hadn't spoken.

Fuck, not this *again*.

I jolted upright and turned my head to look at the culprit. My eyebrows shot to my hairline as I took in the sad smile of my fiance.

"Gregory." I said in a hoarse voice. I couldn't hear it but I could sure as fuck feel it. I hadn't really spoken in a while, so it was clearly raspy from no use. Remembering I didn't have my implants in, I grabbed it from the nightstand and placed it on.

"What are you doing here," I asked hesitantly.

"I tried calling you, but you weren't answering."

"For a reason," I snapped.

A flash of hurt crossed his face, which had me groaning and dragging my hands down my face.

"I'm sorry," I said. "Its been hard."

"I know, Halen. I heard, and I'm so sorry about your friend. I wanted to come sooner but I figured you needed time alone. Sadly though, we are out of time."

My brows pulled together as my head whipped to face his. "What do you mean?"

"My parents have been talking with your mom. My dad wants to get a date down for the wedding. Preferably in the next 6 months."

"What?" I screeched. "I won't even be a high school graduate yet!"

He patted my hand then grabbed it to hold. "I know, I know. I asked my dad to at least allow you to graduate first in the interest of our image. It wouldn't look right if I was marrying a high school senior. It would do more damage than good."

My shoulders relaxed and I gave him a grateful nod. "Thank you. I need time to get this all figured out."

"Just so that we are on the same page, you're not interested in marrying me, right? You're looking for a way out?"

I squeezed his hand that was still holding mine. "Yes. We both deserve marriages much greater than the ones decided for us by the omnipotent Knox and Jaffly parents."

He smiled then. "Yeah, okay. But I do enjoy spending time with you. I wouldn't mind if we continued. In fact, I would prefer it. Maybe it would also keep them off our backs if we stayed in touch more." He jabbed my ribs with a finger and I giggled.

It was the first time I had laughed in far too long. I was thankful for his distraction. Truth be told, his presence was calming. I wasn't sure about him at first, but I was starting to learn how easy he was to be around and open up to.

"Want to go get some lunch?" I asked with a raised brow.

He pulled his lips between his teeth to stifle a laugh. "It's

8 PM."

Well, I guess I had smothered myself in my pillow for a few hours longer than I had originally thought.

"Dinner?" I asked with a wince.

"Abso-fucking-lutely." He laughed and dragged me out of bed.

I was surprised at how much better I felt after going out to dinner with Gregory. He asked me about Nicky and Evan, even though it was a hard topic to get through. He also asked about school and how I was doing. He couldn't help but ask if I had my eyes on anyone. I wasn't interested in anyone anymore. I lied through my teeth, even to myself.

We stopped at a cute bookstore bar just outside of the city. It was the perfect hidden gem with soothing ambiance and the light scent of draft beers. I thought heaven might look and smell like that. Maybe I'd eventually get to see it with Evan.

After he dropped me off, I pulled an outfit aside for the morning, knowing that I was going to have to face school again. Completing my outfit choice, I pulled out a short black pencil skirt, a cropped Van Halen tee and a pair of vans, then plopped on my bed and texted Nicky.

Me: Check in.

No response came for a couple of minutes.

Nicky: I'm good. Are you going tomorrow?

Me: No choice. Besides, he would be mad if we gave up and were destined to flip burgers forever.

Nicky: True. I'll meet you in Mr. Bennet's class. I'll be arriving a little later than normal, but I promise I'll be there.

Me: K. Goodnight.

Nicky: Night.

Darkening my phone and placing it on the charger, I contemplated my next move in the quiet space. Shutting my eyes tightly, and opening them again with determination, I pulled out my journal and drew a popsicle stick from my special jar. With a heavy sigh, I found the right title on Kindle and finally curled up into the covers and began reading.

◆ ◆ ◆

The stack of books in front of me was nearing my max allowable limit for the library, so I checked out and placed them in my backpack. The first bell hadn't chimed yet, so I knew I had some time to sneak in a chapter or two.

Snow danced beyond the floor to ceiling windows, but the chill of the glass didn't deter me from taking my usual reading spot next to the window. I felt a shiver run down my body and pulled a cardigan over my cropped tee. Before I knew it, I was captivated by a world where love conquered all, even when it was forbidden. A tale as old as time, I guess?

Whispers flew through the halls, ricocheting off of the metal lockers as I passed by students mingling and pouring into classrooms.

"She's back. I wonder if that Dominic guy is too."

"I heard it was Dominic who pressured him to take the drugs."

"His body was so fucked up, his mom could only identify him at the hospital by the birthmark on his shoulder blade."

"Has anyone talked to Katherine? She must be heartbroken, since they were in love."

The last two had my anger simmering just below the surface, ready to pluck the eyeballs from anyone that looked at me wrong or for too long. At the same time, I wanted to duck my head and rush out of the school to head home and cry.

"I'm really sorry for your loss," a feminine voice whispered from behind me.

I turned, expecting to see a teacher who had seen us walking the halls together often. I wasn't even close to guessing that it would be one of my enemies.

Astrid.

My lips pinched into a tight line as I studied her face, looking for signs of insincerity. I found none. Only traces of sympathy and even pity. I thought of Evan. Everyone loved him and he never held a grudge. I felt him around me, imploring me to take a chance.

"Thank you, Astrid."

She looked uncomfortable as she shifted from one food to the other. "He was a good guy. Everyone knows that Katherine wasn't involved with him. Not really, at least. They know you and Dominic were family to him. Ignore the chatter."

She tapped the underside of her chin twice with the back of her hand, and gave me a small smile before stepping around me and walking to her next class.

Chin up.

I was still angry and filled with sorrow that felt like acid burning through my chest. Clearly my painful emotions didn't extend to all, because my eyes met beautiful blue ones and I felt my gaze beginning to drop in avoidance.

Sawyer didn't say anything when I walked into his classroom. I could see Nicky already sitting in his seat with a murderous look plastered all over his face. When his eyes met mine, the features instantly softened.

He must have registered my worry for him because he quickly signed, "I love you. I'm okay."

I nodded and gave him a soft smile before sinking into my seat. My phone vibrated in my pocket and I glanced at it before putting it back in my bag.

Nicky: Come over after school. I miss you. You've been MIA.

I turned to look at him and saw pure vulnerability on full display. I didn't bother texting him back, but instead signed to him from across the classroom with eyes clearly trying to read into it.

Fuck them. I wasn't ashamed of who I was and they could fuck right off with the judgement they projected. The last of my concern for what shitty people thought died the moment my best friend took his last breath.

"I know, I'm sorry. I've missed you so much. You're all mine

this afternoon."

He didn't sign back, which I was anticipating due to his healing arm in a sling. But he smirked and winked. It was the closest to the old Nicky that I had seen in a while. Maybe this was the step in the right direction to feeling myself again too.

Turning my head to the front of the classroom, I saw Sawyer glaring daggers right at me. His eyes flicked over to Nicky who was oblivious, and then back to me. The sudden reminder knocked the air from me as I realized what just happened.

Sawyer had been learning to sign. He wasn't quite fluent but he was damn good with his signing so far. If he didn't catch it all, he surely caught the gist of it.

Well, shit.

CHAPTER 22

-SAWYER-

I wanted to wrap my hands around her delicate little throat and squeeze until she turned blotchy. Then when she knew she was under my full control, and accepted it, I would release. The thickening in my pants had me pushing away the thoughts that were equal parts rage and lust.

I missed being around her. Touching her. Listening to her. Signing to her. Watching her eyes drift from line to line as she read. Why did she have to put us in this situation? Why did *I* have to? Remembering where I was, I blinked out of my rapidly wavering thoughts and glanced around the class.

Thankfully only a few students were trying to figure out what was happening. Playing it off, I snapped out a demand in the hopes of keeping attention off of the inappropriate tension between Halen and I.

"Miss Knox, please see me after school for detention. Alright class," I said, addressing everyone. "Let's get started, shall we?"

Her eyes nearly bugged out of her head and then immediately turned to slits. Goosebumps trailed along my skin as I felt her attention so fiercely on me. I felt so conflicted with our situation, but I decided right then and there that we would have it out in the open. Finally.

After a long day of instruction, the final bell finally rang out and students poured from classrooms into the hallway in an escape to leave. I spent a few free minutes sketching, waiting for Halen to arrive. I didn't normally sketch things based on fantasy, but I had already sketched not one, but three different scenes in my book. They weren't real scenarios, but still purely *her*.

The first was of her sitting on my desk as her legs are crisscrossed, a book resting in her lap as she devours the pages before her. The second was filled with wispy hair filling the page as her face peeks through the tendrils, a small smile on her face. I even added the cochlear poking through a few strands of hair. The last one was my favorite, and also something that would have me fired in an instant.

My cock began to harden as I studied the nearly done image of Halen leaning over my desk, glancing back at me waiting for her spanking. The skirt didn't reveal any nudity, but it was suggestive enough to imply that only a few more centimeters, and her glistening pussy would be on display for me to see. She was biting down on her lip, trying to contain an anxious smile.

The scrapes of my pencil came to a halt when Victoria came prancing in like a giddy school girl as the last students trickled throughout the hallway. Halen was going to be here any minute.

Clenching my teeth, I tried my best to appear unbothered by her presence. "What are you doing here?"

Her smile slipped a little but she quickly recovered. "Oh. I thought we could grab some takeout or something and grade papers together at home. What do you think?"

"Um. I'm actually holding detention for a student and then I am meeting up with Brent for a few. He just lost his wife recently, and is lonely."

Using the dead to cover your tracks? Ugh, you suck.

I popped my knuckles to try to alleviate some tension from my body.

"Oh no, how terrible!" She lifted her hand to her mouth to cover her shock and then nodded. "Okay, take your time, I suppose. We can always catch up tomorrow over breakfast or something."

I gave her a tight smile and nodded. She blew me a

kiss and left the room without another word. My shoulders instantly relaxed and I blew out a breath. I didn't realize just being around her put my body in a state of physical stress.

Why was I even humoring her idea of being together? It started out of anger at Halen, but why continue? It obviously wasn't helping anything.

Cause you're a fucking idiot.

I cleaned up the student desks and removed everything from my own desk to clean off. After the last streak of Lysol was cleaned away, I heard the unmistakable huffing of a stubborn eighteen year old girl. My gaze slowly lifted to hers with a raised brow.

What I saw wasn't what I was expecting. She was standing there by the door, looking like sex on a stick. A skirt tightly fitted to her body, and a band crop top that had me screaming internally, *delicious sin.*

"Sit." I said, pointing at her desk, masking my thoughts.

She obeyed but not without an eye roll and slamming the door shut, a little too hard to be civil.

"Implants out."

Her eyes jumped to mine and held them with confusion written on her face. I wasn't the best at communicating her way, but I wanted to be. I was decent enough now with the hours upon hours of studying, but I needed immersion. I wanted to be able to speak her language with ease. I didn't stop learning during my free time just because I was mad. I think I secretly knew this moment was coming.

She listened and removed her implants, setting them on the desk. I smiled.

"Good girl."

Her scowl almost made me burst out laughing. I continued with my objective before I chickened out. Looking right at her, I sat down in my own seat behind my desk and asked the question I had been dying to know.

"How long have you been with your fiance? What's his name?"

"Gregory." Hmm, chatty.

"What a nice name. Gregory." I signed, admittedly the spelling of his name took longer than I would have liked.

Her scoff was very audible, though I wasn't sure she realized.

"You can use his name sign," she harshly signed, then showed me slowly the motion for his name. I sent up a prayer to God because it was so much easier than spelling out. *"And I'm not with him. I'm arranged to be married to him, for now, but he is nothing more than a friend."*

I felt the crease between my brows wrinkle. *"I don't understand."*

She started signing slower like I was a toddler who was learning the signs for 'poop' and 'eat'. I cut her off.

"No. I understand what you said. I don't understand why you are being arranged to marry. That practice is archaic."

She shrugged her shoulders. *"It's most definitely not archaic to wealthy families. Greedy families. Our families."*

"You said that you are engaged for now. Does that mean you won't be engaged for long? As in, getting married soon, or are you going to call off the engagement?"

That stretch of conversation was harder for me to get through. The emotions mixed with not knowing the correct sign for certain words. I spelled what I couldn't remember. Thankfully Halen seemed to understand everything.

The silence continued between us as she bit down on her lower lip in thought. I could see her trying to arrange whatever was running through her head. I'm sure after Evan, it was likely a mess. Her face hardened as she worked through the varying emotions rushing her.

"Why do you think you have the right to ask me about my engagement up on your high horse, when you haven't shed any light on your own, S—?" She sent me a withering glare. I couldn't make out the last word that she signed. Pushing my pride down, I just came right out and asked.

"What was that last word? I don't think I know it." It al-

most looked like the sign for '*stupid*' but the letter s was pointing outward in an awkward way. I had a feeling it was similar to stupid, but I wasn't sure. I'm sure it wasn't good, either way.

Her smile gleamed with pure anger. *"It's* your *name sign."*

I pursed my lips and scrunched my nose. *"No, I don't like it. I want it to be something like this."* I signed the letter s while circling my face like you would with the word '*handsome*'.

It was her turn to scrunch her nose in distaste. This time she both spoke, quite loudly I might add, and signed at the same time.

"That is not how this works, Sawyer!" She definitely put emphasis on my name sign now. Even if she wasn't verbally spitting the words, I would have known she was pissed. "Only a deaf person can give you a name sign. I'm deaf. I think you're stupid. So I think it fits beautifully!"

She plopped back down in her seat, realizing she had stood while she was angrily signing and yelling at me. Thank fuck the school was empty. The last thing I wanted was someone overhearing our argument.

I waited for her eyes to meet mine. She was currently shutting me out from communicating with her by staring at the ceiling with her head tipped back. Taking heaving breaths and long moments between blinks.

Her head finally drifted back to eye level and she stared straight at me, waiting. I didn't waste another moment. I was tired of the things that went unsaid. The silence within the silence.

"I don't know what you're talking about, but I'm not engaged to anyone."

Her eyes flashed. *"Really? Then who was the woman who you kissed at the restaurant?"*

I shifted in my seat but held her gaze, remaining firm as I responded. *"She is my ex-girlfriend. It was a dinner for closure. We split quite some time ago and she wanted to speak with me over dinner. Turns out, she was looking to reconcile, but I wasn't inter-*

ested. I'm still not interested."

With the cock of her head she studied my face, clearly looking for telling signs that I was lying.

"Not according to her."

My eyes narrowed on her and my lips parted. Had she overheard about Victoria's recent sexual interaction with me? How would she have even heard about it? Did she know she was basically living with me?

Fuck, I really needed to get that bitch out of the condo. Out of my life, actually. Halen read the confusion on my face like a book and took pity on me, thank fuck.

"When I saw you kiss her, each time was like a blow to my chest. More painful, I would guess. I was put in an uncomfortable situation. You chose to be a prick in return." She swallowed, and though she was signing with a cold fluidity that showed confidence in her words, I knew she was hurting. *"With the small dignity I felt I had left, I excused myself to the ladies room to freshen up. That's when your fiance cornered me at the sink and told me she is also engaged."* Her eyes were hard and unforgiving. *"Imagine my surprise."*

"I don't have to imagine your surprise. I experienced the same shock, Squid." I pleaded with my eyes, begging her to see reason. Thankfully after a moment, she managed a small nod.

"So, is that why you gave me detention? For a truce? Weird way to start a ceasefire."

Fair enough.

"I'm getting Victoria out. She just kind of barged back into my life. Believe me when I say I am going to make this right, by the end of the week. To make sure there are no misunderstandings, we have never been and never will be engaged. I'm not sure what psychosis she was in during that conversation with you."

Halen's eyes softened as she watched my hands move. "Did–" A pause. "Did you sleep with her?"

I winced. Trying to think of the best way to answer her, I didn't even get a chance, because she threw on her cochlear and was out of her seat in an instant. She clearly read my hesitation wrong. Her face resembled granite, unmoving and stoic. She wasted no time grabbing her stuff and rushing towards the door to leave.

Without a second thought, I jumped out of my seat. She wasn't going to leave. Not after we had truly started to straighten things out. I couldn't continue on the track of us hating each other anymore. It was going to kill me.

Reaching her right before she made it to the door, I grabbed her arm and spun her around. Her gasp only encouraged me more and pushed me further than I had originally planned in the fifteen seconds that I thought it all through.

She dropped her bag as I pinned her body against the wall. Leaning down so she could clearly see that I was not fucking around. I made myself as clear as I could.

"I thought she was *you*."

Halen's eyes widened in shock, clearly not expecting that response. I continued to clarify.

"I was basically blacking out from being so fucking drunk. I was desperate to dull the pain of my mind constantly thinking of you. I stumbled into my bed, expecting to sleep it off and start again the following day." I clenched my teeth, remembering Victoria's part in that night.

"I thought I was dreaming. Of you. I didn't even know until the next morning that–"

"That you fucked her?" Halen's chin wobbled.

I shook my head. "No. I didn't fuck her. But she did... suck me off." I swallowed hard. "I was sleeping, Halen. Or I think I was? I don't even fucking know."

I pinched the bridge of my nose but made no move to release her from between me and the wall keeping her here. I didn't plan to either.

Her eyes looked over my face, looking for signs of deceit. She wasn't going to find any. Her green eyes were intoxicating, like a siren's would be when calling sailors to tip over the edge of their ships into the abyss of no return.

And I was about to tip.

Her eyes were brimming with tears but I could tell she wouldn't dare let me see one fall. She was strong and stubborn. Fierce. But the moment her eyes flicked to my lips, I fucking broke.

Into the abyss I went.

CHAPTER 23

-HALEN-

His lips crashed down on mine with the delivery of a starved man. My surprised gasp only made him groan as he plunged his tongue into my mouth. As much as I thought I was a baddie with a backbone, I didn't stand a chance against Sawyer. I folded so fucking quick.

I was still angry at him for his part in our pain, but I was equally mad at myself for the same reasons. The circumstances were not ideal for either of us. My hands trailed up his chest and snaked around his neck. With that gesture, he knew I had just given him permission to continue. His growl into my mouth said as much.

His arms skated down my sides and slipped behind my thighs as he hiked me up and wrapped my legs around his waist. After a moment, I felt us moving as he expertly navigated through the desks in the classroom.

My ass thudded against the stained wood of Sawyer's desk. Though I was wearing a skirt in the middle of the fucking cold season, I felt like my skin was physically burning with his touch. Not a painful fire, but a heat that I wanted to push myself into. Like the prickles of a barely too hot shower as the water pelts your skin. Intoxicatingly comforting.

His lips began a trail down my throat, as one hand rested in the mess of my hair and the other pressing firmly into my hip. My head tipped back as he continued to make his way lower, over my collarbone. At his annoyed huff, I glanced down to see he couldn't kiss any lower without my shirt obstructing his path.

He didn't even appear to think twice about it as he pulled the hem up and guided the shirt over my head. Tossing it aside, his eyes were a swirling mixture of anger and unguarded temptation.

"No bra? Your shirt was cropped," he snipped.

I sat there, bared completely from the waist up, nipples stiffening under his assessing gaze and the cold temperature. I leaned back on my forearms, feeling stacks of papers underneath me. Lifting my legs from their dangling position I set the pads of my feet on the desk and spread them wide.

His sharp inhalation of breath was all I needed to hear for my arousal to begin pulsing from me. No underwear either. His eyes flicked to mine as he stood leaning over the desk, waiting for me to back out. Begging me to.

Not a goddamn chance.

I gave him a smirk and the last thread of patience he held onto was severed with the slash of his lips on mine. His hands roughly began pushing my skirt up around my waist as his tongue slid against mine in heated kisses. After a few minutes of claiming my mouth, he pulled my ass as far to the edge of the desk as possible and pushed my bent knees apart as far as they would go. It was similar to the position I had been in once before at my first pelvic exam.

My anticipation had my body vibrating with need and excitement. His blue eyes were bouncing between my pussy, my eyes and my breasts, trying to decide how to mentally catalog them all, I'm sure. He slid to his knees, now at eye level with my surely glistening core.

"Fuck, you're dripping on my desk," he whispered. "This is so much fucking better than my imagination."

My back arched off the desk as his tongue made the first swipe through my slit. His hum of approval made me moan due to the vibrations it caused there. I raked my fingers through his perfectly styled hair and began to chase that tingling feeling that was creeping up on me.

"I knew you would taste like this. Heaven. Sin. All in

one. You shouldn't have tempted me, Squid."

He slapped my pussy and my yelp of pleasure had my eyes rolling back for a moment. Holy shit.

"Sawyer, please."

I didn't know what I was begging for or why, but was pleased when he flicked the bundle of nerves, sending a jolt through me. I fixed my hips against his face as he laved my clit that was throbbing for attention. His tongue was relentless in its mission to draw my desire from me.

I couldn't contain the sounds that were leaving my mouth. Nobody should have been here anyway. So without holding back, my moans echoed off of the classroom walls as my toes curled and my hand tightened in Sawyers thoroughly messed up hair.

A gust of liquid pulsed from me as I rode the euphoric wave that threatened to carry me away. I barely had a second to come down before a feral sound ripped from Sawyer's throat and he stood over me.

I could distantly hear the metal clinking of his belt as he yanked it off. His lips claimed mine as he multitasked with freeing himself from his pants. My body was shaking with nerves and the trembles of post orgasmic bliss.

I could taste the essence of myself on his lips, causing another moan to pull from me, right into his eager mouth. He pulled away, and with his eyes locked on mine, he slid the head of his cock from my clit to my slit. Back and forth.

With oceanic blue eyes still fiercely focused on my green ones, he pinched his lips together tightly and then spoke with a scary calm. "Last chance, baby. There is no coming back from this. You'll be mine. And that fiancé of yours can fuck right off."

I nodded wordlessly, bobbing my head rapidly like an idiot. "Please, Mr. Bennett."

His eyes dilated as he began pushing in immediately and my gasp was loud in the quiet empty classroom. He stopped for a moment to let me adjust to his size as he peppered my face with kisses.

Another inch.

Kisses.

Another inch.

"Halen, fuck," he sighed in pleasure. I felt the physical resistance at the same time he did and he stopped before lifting his head from the crook of my neck.

"It's going to hurt. But I promise it will feel better once your body adjusts. Do you trust me?"

"*Always,*" I signed, looking right at the eyes that held me in a trance.

He slammed his hips forward, burying his cock so deep that my back bowed off of the desk and my howl of pain echoed in the small space. He didn't stop though. He kept thrusting at the same speed, as his mouth whispered reassurances in my ear.

"You're so beautiful." *Thrust.* "Do you like having your teacher's cock buried in you?" *Thrust.* "God you're so fucking tight, baby." *Thrust.* "You're gonna milk me dry. Damn."

The pain began to shift into pleasure as that familiar tingle started to return. Sweat beaded at his brow as he pumped in and out, holding my legs tight like I would disappear at any moment.

I watched his gaze trace every angle of my body. The softening of his face as he continued to map every inch of me made my stomach flutter with butterflies. Once his gaze reached the apex of my thighs, his lips parted on a silent gasp followed by a feral groan. He watched with each push and pull of his hips and promptly picked up in delicious speed.

When I looked down at the sight, I realized why he was so mesmerized moments ago. My thighs were coated in blood. It was everywhere. As he drew his cock back out again, I saw that it also covered the entirety of his length, further lubricating the area.

Writhing my hips up to meet his thrusts, I threw my head back with a moan as heat and prickles raced along my skin. I'm sure I was panting at this point. The sensations were everything I hoped that they would be, better even. The fact that the man pumping into me was my teacher made it even sweeter.

"Please, Sawyer. God. I can't take it. I'm so close," I whimpered through a mixture of pleasure and need.

He smiled a wolfish grin and pounded harder as he trailed one of his hands in between my thighs, and brushed his thumb across my clit. I shuddered with the contact, letting my loud cries and begging fill the space around us.

"Fuck, baby. Just like that. Your pussy is sucking me in with how hard you're gripping it. Keep going. Fuck, keep going."

His words sent light flashing before my eyes and the tingle turned into a full spark of electricity, lighting up my system. Sawer's mouth slammed down on mine, absorbing the sounds of my ecstasy rushing through me. Every slide of his tongue against mine had me pushing through the orgasmic wave, fighting for the next one.

Sawyer read my body's signals and pinched my clit as he sat up and watched me come undone for a second time. This one had liquid squirting from where we connected, coating my thighs.

"Holy shit. Flood my cock, Squid. God fucking dammit!"

Nothing could have prepared me for the absolutely stunning face of Sawyer coming undone. His sharp jawline made him look scary and full of authority, while his *just fucked* black hair gave him a softness that seemed to contrast his edges.

His cock pulsed hard inside me as he panted out the remainder of his release, painting my insides white. I was short of breath and absolutely wrecked, but I felt the most alive that I had felt in… ever.

I just had sex. With my teacher. I gave him my virginity. What did this mean? Did he just want the sex? Was he interested in more with me? What about his girlfriend that he still needed to break up with? There was so much up in the air that my stomach began to twist at the uneasy thoughts of where this was going.

"Stop thinking so loud."

I looked up as his voice cut through my mental spiral and found him watching me with adoration and a touch of concern.

"Did I hurt you? What are you thinking?" He pulled his softening cock from my center and tucked it away beneath his perfectly pressed slacks. I couldn't hold the slight wince from the release of pressure. It was tender, but that experience was everything I had hoped it would be. *More* than I had hoped it would be.

I shook my head. "No, not at all."

His smile was so gentle that it nearly took my breath away. "And your thoughts?"

I bit my lip and looked towards the empty desks facing our direction. Just sitting there waiting for the next herd of students to plop into them.

"I– I don't know what to feel. I feel everything right now. And that scares me. I feel on display, but I don't want to just be on display. I need substance. Something to hold onto, so that I can look back on this fondly instead of with sadness and yearning."

His brows pulled together as I looked back at him, waiting for the uncomfortability to show on his face at the awkward post-sex topic.

Smooth, Halen. Real smooth.

It didn't come. He was lost in thought for a moment but quickly recovered. "I guess I didn't make myself clear, Halen. So let me be crystal, now. Things with Victoria are going to be cleared up this week. I want you. Exclusively. Yes it's risky, but we only have a handful of months before you graduate. If it really comes down to it, I'll quit. You won't yearn for anything, because I'm not letting you go."

I looked at him with wide eyes, confused as to why he would throw away his career for me. He was wearing a determined seriousness across his face, so ready for a battle. I couldn't even determine if it would be *with* me or *for* me. Either way I was stunned into silence once again while I centered the thoughts flying through my mind, a vortex of *what ifs* and *what abouts*. I shut the door to the mess in my mind and took what I wanted.

"Okay. Yes." The smile that stretched across his face had me wanting to jump on him for round two. "But, I do plan on leaving here after graduation. I have had a dream since I was little, and it was always Gallaudet. I need to see it through."

"Who the fuck is Gallaudet?"

It was my turn to smile. Jealousy was leaking from him but I didn't want to prolong the suffering for too long. "You mean *what* is Gallaudet?" I chuckle. "It's a university that specifically caters to deaf and hard of hearing students. Hearing students can attend too, but the college is a safe haven for people like me to learn, meet others, and live without barriers in communication."

His lips pinched. "Where is it located?"

"Washington, D.C."

"Okay."

"Okay?"

"Okay." A pause. "I'll start looking for teacher postings in the spring when they release them for the following school year."

I cocked my head at him, watching sincerity flood his features. "Have you thought about not teaching? Or teaching something else? You look miserable grading essays sometimes. Are you happy?"

"What would I even do? Flip burgers? I don't know."

I thought for a moment. "What about art? Have you thought of going back to school to be an artist?"

He shook his head. "Shitty pay. We would live on scraps while I tried to sell shit. I'm not interested in that rough version of life."

I let his worldbuilding of us living together slide, because the truth was, I wanted him to continue piecing his future together. Specifically with me in it.

"Alright, what about teaching art?"

He thought about it for a good minute. Getting lost in the possibilities rolling through his mind. Then he looked at me and raised his hands in front of him.

"Teaching still doesn't pay great, but I suppose I really would enjoy teaching students something I secretly love. I love teaching English too, but students are here because they have to be, not because they want to be, like they would with art. I like it."

I beamed and jumped into his arms, stretching my arms around him. Pressing a kiss to the tender part where his vein pumped beneath the skin of his prickly neck, I felt him shudder. I smiled again and pulled back to sign.

"Want me to catch you up on the books I've read in your absence?"

His chuckle was a breath of fresh air. He pulled me tight against him for a hug and signed in front of my face that was tilted to the side, without letting me budge.

"Yes. Always."

So we did. Everything else was forgotten.

It wasn't until I got home and saw the texts ranging from kind, to worried, to pissed, that I realized I had stood up Nicky. His last few texts seemed frantic but in an incoherent way that I could almost not understand.

I called him, but it went straight to voicemail.

With a sigh I let it go, and told myself I would reach out to him the following day. For now, I was going to fall asleep, willing dreams to feature a certain teacher who made my heart skip a beat.

CHAPTER 24

-SAWYER-

"Sawyer, darling, I was wondering what you thought about me moving my stuff into the main room with you. It's time, don't you think?"

Victoria's hopeful voice cut across the dining table as we ate breakfast together. I was wanting to break things off the previous night during dinner but she had already been asleep due to a migraine.

Biting into my poached eggs a little more aggressively than I had anticipated, I let all the previous hurt she caused me, rush to the surface. It felt like armor I was plating over me as a way to feel less guilty for letting her back in, than being no better than her by fucking around behind her back. All of that just to finally close a door I was ready to be fully shut months ago.

Truth is, I wouldn't have given her a moment to believe it was possible if it wasn't for seeing Halen that night at dinner. Her fiance, presenting an huge as fuck diamond. That anger and fire for wanting someone I shouldn't want sent a sense of calm over me. I wanted Halen more than I wanted to breathe. She was becoming everything.

The only thing.

The memories of making her truly mine had my cock slightly stirring in my pants, but that couldn't happen right now. If Victoria even thought for a moment that I wanted something sexual from her, she would never unleash her claws from me. While she had no problem letting me go months ago, to fuck around with another man, she was never good at taking 'no' for an answer. I knew with no doubt that she would put up a fight.

"We need to talk."

She straightened in her seat and paused with the fork halfway to her mouth. Runny eggs dripped off the prongs as she sat motionless. "Those words mean something, Sawyer. Tell me you aren't doing this again. Tell me you aren't pushing me away for no reason."

I glared her way. "You know damn well that I had every reason the first time—"

"First time?" She shrieked. "So there is a second time? You're really doing this? Why? I haven't done anything besides show you love and affection. What else could you possibly want?"

My lips thinned into a tight line as I looked away. I felt a surge of emotion for doing the same thing to her that she had done to me. Cheat. Fuck someone in the classroom. Find happiness elsewhere. But if I was being honest with myself, I didn't feel bad that it was to her, but that I stooped to her level.

Karma. That's all it is for her. Sweet, justified karma.

I was choosing Halen. I wasn't waiting for Victoria to find us fucking in a classroom. I was breaking things off before she found out. It wasn't like we were together that long for this second stretch, anyway.

It was like she saw every detail written across my forehead because her next words were biting and full of venom. In true Victoria fashion.

"Who?"

I blinked, feigned ignorance. "What do you mean?"

Her scoff told me she didn't buy an ounce of my bullshit. "Who is she?"

I kept my face neutral. "Not someone that you need to concern yourself with."

Truth.

She tightened her hands into fists. I could see the cherry red acrylic nails making indents into her palms as she held them firm and got up. She slowly began walking over to my side of the table. I stood up to face her head on. I wasn't going to let her tower over me like she had any power in this situation.

"Sawyer, I'll ask one more time. Who?"

"You don't know what you're talking about. I'm not sure why I agreed to restart things with you, but it was never really something that interested me. I apologize for giving you the wrong impression, but I feel that it's best if we just have a clean break. It worked well last time."

She gasped. "So that's it? You have no interest in even trying? I started a new contract at Black Grove for you! I moved my whole life just to show how serious I am! For what? A petty little affair that meant nothing? I even gave you some time away to regain some clarity."

I snorted. "Yeah, I definitely regained some clarity."

Her eyes narrowed to slits. "What the hell is that supposed to mean?"

"It means that my life actually didn't change that much when we split. You were rarely home to begin with, likely too busy fucking up against a printer in the teacher's lounge, or spending money that we really didnt have to spend. Leaving you meant that my bank account was more full, my time was better spent only cleaning up after myself, and I had the opportunity to meet people that actually bring happiness to my life. You contributed very little, and it sucks that it took me walking in on you acting like a slut to realize it, or else I could have had years of my life back."

The sound of the slap registered before the actual pain spread across my cheek. I must have had adrenaline surging through my body from my hateful declaration because I could even taste blood across my tongue. The light metallic taste had me looking at her in shock. It wasn't a real shock that she hit me, but damn, she had a fucking swing on her.

"How dare you? I made one mistake–" *A four month mistake.* "– and it's not right that you judge me for one wrongdoing. We all make mistakes, Sawyer. You included. I can tell you are hiding something from me, and I will figure it out. But just know that I'm not asking out of my contract at the academy. You'll just have to accept that I will be in your life whether you like it or not."

Little did she know I was willing to back out of my own contract at the drop of a hat. If people found out about Halen and I, or the moment she drove off to college, I would be putting in my resignation.

"Fine. Doesn't matter to me."

She inhaled long and deep, and released her fists, revealing the half moon shapes lingering on her skin. "I'll just pack up my stuff."

"I have to get to work early anyway. Just leave any keys on the entry table." I didn't spare her a glance or bother listening to her mumbling as I walked away.

Thank fuck that was over with.

Later that day I felt like a whole new man. The boulder that was lifted from my chest had me feeling lighter and more free. I think I was unknowingly harboring hostility at the situation with Victoria because I never really put it out there how her bad side outshined her good side. I couldn't deny that I was hopeful for a future with her, but that was only because I didn't know what it felt like.

Talking to Halen, and learning everything about her had changed everything I knew about what it meant to be happy. I felt more at home in my life with Halen snuggled in my arms, simply existing, than I ever felt with Victoria.

Walking through the halls, I heard a feminine voice call my name with the rasp of vocal fry that singed my eardrums. I guess it was a good thing that I was kicking ass at learning sign language. I had been practicing every single day for my classes, and tried to immerse myself whenever possible. I always did exceedingly well in school, and I think it had to do with my photographic memory. I was going to soon be able to hold full conversations with her with no issues.

I turned to face the voice calling out to me. I was greeted with the overwhelming sight of cleavage nearly popping the top button of the yellow blouse. "Good morning! I haven't really seen you around much lately. I guess I was just wondering if you wanted to go out this weekend. Maybe a movie?"

I had to admire her confidence, because it took guts to put yourself out there like that. She seemed very sweet. She was full of an ungodly amount of the same plastic that they probably put in storage containers, but she was kind and still pretty. She just wasn't the kind of woman that I wanted. Especially considering I only wanted one.

My attention was solely on an eighteen year old deaf girl with parent issues, a fiance, a dead friend, and a best friend who loved her.

Shit. I definitely had a fast pass to hell. Skip the line, zero wait time.

"Right, um, I'm actually involved with someone at the moment, so it wouldn't be right for me to lead you on in any way."

A frown tugged at Ellen's lips. "Oh. I see."

As if the heavens had opened up and offered me the best idea I had conjured in a long time, I saw movement across the atrium. Brent was finishing up his plant watering and about to leave, presumably back to class.

"Brent!" I called out before I could even think it through. His head snapped towards me and started sauntering my way with a wave.

I glanced at Ellen's face and saw confusion written all over it. Praying that I could pull this off, I did something that I wouldn't normally do. I meddled.

"Brent, have you met Ellen?" I looked between them as they shared a look with each other, but Ellen's face softened as she saw Brent's hand stretched out to her for a shake.

"Hi Ellen, I've seen you around but I don't think I have

had the pleasure of actually meeting you."

She placed her hand in his, and like the goddamn stallion that he was, he brought her hand to his lips and kissed the top. A blush immediately flushed her cheeks.

Damn Brent, I didn't know you had game.

"It's nice to meet you, Brent. I didn't realize you and Sawyer were friends. You teach choir right?"

"I do, yes." His eyes sparkled with interest in a way that they always did when he was speaking to another friendly person. But I could tell there was a tad deeper of a twinkle there.

"He is also the one who set up this atrium to look as beautiful as it does," I chimed in.

She bit her lip, either not realizing her hand was still clasped in Brent's, or she just didn't care. Either way, this was working out exactly like I had hoped.

"What did the geeky plant lover say to the beautiful woman in front of him," he asked Ellen.

She remained quiet in thought, trying to puzzle out the punchline. After the shake of her head, she finally gave up.

"What?"

"You're beautiful. Apologies if I'm *roughage* around the edges."

Jesus Christ.

Ellen's laugh echoed due to the nearby atrium and I took that as my sign that I had not only dodged a bullet but also potentially introduced Brent to the female version of himself. She was eating right out of his hand, but he was equally as interested. He deserved happiness after the shit hand life had dealt him.

"Right, well, I'll give you two some time to better get acquainted as I have some things to attend to," I said as I walked away to make my escape.

Damn, I was killing it today.

I could feel Victoria's absence the moment I walked into the condo that evening. It was like going from breathing stale suffocating air to smelling fresh new oxygen. I'm sure Halen's presence would make it feel like I was pulling in air from a rainforest after a storm. Crisp and divine.

I could basically picture her sprawled out on the couch reading one of the books I assigned to her jar. I would likely need to nudge her because I made it a rule to take out the implants when reading.

With the image playing over in my mind, I went to find my sketch book to forever keep it in there as something I could reflect on, and manifest. After twenty minutes of searching, and coming up empty, my phone rang from the kitchen counter.

I rushed into the kitchen, secretly hoping Halen was calling. Instead my brows furrowed as I saw Connor's name on the screen.

"What's up, Con?"

"Hey, man. Something has come up. I am going to be out of state for a while."

He never reached out to me like this unless he was somewhat worried about not returning. We had plans in place if or when that was to happen. I could count on one hand how many times I had received this phone call, and it never felt easier. He was my little brother, and it was my job to take care of him.

Yeah, okay, he could lay you on your ass.

"Can you tell me where?"

"Maine. That's all I can give you, Sawyer. Just remember the folder in my safe. The code is mom's birthday."

I inhaled a deep breath and nodded even though I knew he couldn't see it. "Yeah, man, I know. When will I hear from you next? Are you with others?"

"I'm going to be with my team, so no solo runs. I'll try to check in once a week but I can't promise anything. Just know that what I'm doing may seem bad on paper, but it's for the greater good. I promise."

"Con, I have never doubted that. I know you do shit you probably shouldn't but I also know that you do way more good than bad. I love you, man. Try to keep in touch. Stay safe."

"I have Blake on the phone with some info," I heard male a voice in the background say.

"Yeah. Got it," he responded to the man before addressing me. "Listen, I've gotta go. I love you too. I'll try to reach out. Talk later."

I hung up feeling a tightness in my chest that had everything to do with worrying for his safety. There were two people in my life that were quickly becoming everything I couldn't afford to lose.

Connor had been that way since his birth. I could say that Halen started to become that when I kissed her for the first time, but realistically it was the moment she snapped at me in the library. I was hooked immediately.

I knew I was falling hard.

And fast.

CHAPTER 25

-HALEN-

I felt my watch vibrating with a phone call as I tried to bury my face deeper into the pillow. I was dreaming of Sawyer, damn it! Groaning, I flipped my body over to my back and brought the watch within an inch of my eyes. The light illuminating had me squinting my eyes shut again momentarily.

Ow, my retinas!

Cracking one eye open, I looked at the screen again right as the buzzing stopped. Nicky's name was highlighted in red three times indicating this wasn't the first call I had missed. Dimming my watch, I leaned over and grabbed my phone, realization dawning that it was 4:30 in the morning.

He answered the video call immediately and I flicked on my disgustingly bright lamp so that he could see me. There was darkness surrounding him, but headlights were illuminated over his body up enough to see clearly.

He set his phone down on an elevated surface behind him, if I had to guess, a small boulder. Snow dusted the ground around him as I saw his whole body sitting in view with his knees pulled to his chest. A small red glow orbed throughout the screen as he brought it to his face and back down out of view behind his knees.

"Nicky? What's wrong?"

"Nothing. Everything. I'm flying high, baby."

"Are you sitting on the snow? You're going to freeze to death. Go sit in your car and talk to me," I snapped.

His hand movements were sloppy. A giveaway that he was either drunk out of his mind, high beyond comprehension, or both. Why was he outside this early?

"If only," He muttered before looking away. He didn't sign it, but I saw his lip movements well enough to make out the two words. My brows pulled together as I watched him stare off into the distance in thought.

I snapped my fingers at the screen to get his attention back on me. I couldn't communicate with him constantly looking away without plugging in. I think he had forgotten I was sitting on the call with him for a moment.

"Hang on, let me get my implants." I said quickly.

"No. No. I'm sorry. I'm paying attention."

Ignoring his plea, I grabbed the cochlear and them put in place. The moment the sounds came rushing in, I was greeted with something that tore my heart in half.

Whimpering.

His whimpering sobs.

He was looking away from the camera every time one broke free. The barrier protecting my heart and mind began to chip away with every sound that came from the phone.

"Nicky," I whispered. "What's going on? Where are you? I'll come to you. Wait, are you at The Overlook?" My heart thudded in my chest with a mixture of panic and sadness.

"Twerp, I'm about to leave, so don't worry. I just– I just needed you. To ground me." I didn't believe him entirely. His surroundings were dark, but my instincts were screaming that he was at our spot. The spot we all last hung out. "You keep me level. Especially now that Ev– it's just the two of us."

Now that Evan is gone. That's what he was going to say. Now that the third to our trio was ripped from us, and we were both just hanging on to the scraps of this world that made us happy.

If the timing of Sawyer pulling me back into his orbit didn't happen, I can't say that I wouldn't be right there next to him, looking for ways to drown myself in grief. But, I did have Sawyer now. He brought a happiness to my life that made me forget about the pain, even if it was only for a minute.

"Nicky, I'm sorry I didn't go over to your place earlier. I got caught up with detention and school stuff. Forgive me?"

He nodded his response, but remained quiet. I could always read him like a book. His gaze was caught on something in the distance out of view, deep in thought.

"Want to come over before I have to head in for school? You can rest in my bed. My parents are out of town, vacationing in Florida with Gregory's parents."

I could see his smile as he looked at me through the screen. It was subtle but the hook of his lips had me feeling confident that I had him.

"I'll even order us some croissants and coffee from the cafe before we head into school. Though you might need to sit out today if you haven't had any sleep."

"You're probably right," he slurred a little.

"I'm sending a ride-share to you. You aren't driving like this. We can pick up your car after I get out of school tomorrow."

His annoyed huff was something that would piss off any other person, but to me was music to my ears. This was the Nicky that I knew and loved. Sassy and intolerant of anything that wasn't his way.

"Fine. Hurry up, it's fucking cold out here."

Half an hour later, he walked into my room smelling like a mixture of stale beer and something else I couldn't quite place. As he sluggishly padded towards me, I noticed how gaunt his face truly was.

Where his skin used to be full and glowing with mischief, was now hollowed and shadowed by dark pigments. His undereyes had the worst of it. Bags and greys made his dark eyes look even more clouded.

Pressing my palm to the side of this jaw, I gave him my best and most convincing smile. The stubble on his jawline poked at my palm, tickling the skin.

"Come on. Let's get you to bed. We will worry about getting you showered in the morning. Sleep first."

I led him to my bed and cautiously watched as he plopped himself onto it, not even bothering to crawl under the covers. Grabbing a nearby throw blanket, I placed it over his lower half to shield him from the bitter cold that was making this house feel arctic.

His snores almost immediately filled the room, finally allowing me to release a breath that I hadn't realized I was holding. Crawling under my comforter, I snuggled next to him and watched his chest rise and fall. I closed my eyes as a tear tracked down my face and dripped onto the pillow. They fell until I drifted into a deep sleep.

Upon waking, I saw Nicky still passed out beside me. I quickly ordered some breakfast as I went to get cleaned up for the day. My phone chimed with the delivery of the food on my porch. I ran down the stairs and opened the door to retrieve the items before quickly returning to the room. Nicky hadn't budged.

Rubbing his back and calling his name, his eyes fluttered open. A small smile broke out on his face. I returned the smile but worry still settled like a concrete block in my stomach.

"Are those the croissants you promised?"

"Yep. They even had some of your favorites."

He quirked a brow at me and reached into the bag I was holding, pulling out both double chocolate and tomato basil croissants.

"Sweet and savory. Just like you." I bopped his nose with my index finger and grabbed two cups from the nightstand that I had set down.

"Also," I said, drawing out the word, "I didn't forget the most important part."

He was beaming now. Without a word, he quickly snatched the cups from my hands and opened the lids. After inspecting each liquid, he took multiple big gulps from each one, then dumped the smaller cup into the bigger cup, combining the liquid into a new concoction.

"That's foul." I scrunched my nose. "I'll never get used to seeing you do that."

"Oh don't be a diva, Twerp. It's just like a mocha."

He stuck his finger inside the cup and twirled together the coffee and Parisian hot chocolate. It did in fact make the coffee super creamy. But I would never admit that to him.

"I have to go to school before I'm late. Do you feel rested enough, or do you think you need to take a day?"

His eyes narrowed, glancing at the clock. "Late? It's an hour and a half before the first bell. And no, I'm staying back today."

Looking away to keep him from seeing the blush on my face, remembering Sawyer taking me on his desk, I gave him as much truth as I could.

"Yeah I'm supposed to see Sawy– Mr. Bennett, this morning about an assignment."

As I turned to glance at Nicky, I saw him watching me with a frown. He could always tell when I was lying. I told him a majority of the truth, but even with that, he seemed to be able to see right through me. Or was suspicious at a minimum.

"You've been spending a lot of time in his classroom."

Crap.

"Just the usual. He has a few students who he mentors. I happen to be one of them. That's all." I shrugged my shoulders, trying to show him it wasn't a big deal.

Yes it is, liar.

"Any update with Gregory?" I welcomed the change in subject until I realized there wasn't really any good news on that topic either. I hadn't officially told my parents to fuck off yet, hoping I could bide my time until necessary. Until I found a way out of it, I'd be Gregory's fiancé. Even though we now had an understanding.

"Um no. Not really, considering everything… It's been hard trying to find a loophole or a way to get my parents to see reason. I might be graduating as a homeless person."

His shoulders hunched up around his ears as his eyes

looked at me dead on. They had darkened and even the air around us felt more intense.

"Have you kissed him?" I pinched my lips tightly together.

"Nicky–" I started but was quickly interrupted.

"Don't let him kiss you, Halen. Just say you're saving all of yourself for marriage."

I flinched at his demanding tone. I knew he wasn't trying to be threatening or anything. But his voice offered no room for argument. He was always protective of me, but even I had to admit that this was the first time that he had a certain frightening edge to him. Even to me.

"Trust me. Please. Trust that I am trying to get out of it with the least amount of fall out. I really don't care if I don't manage to salvage the relationship with my mom, but I would like to at least try to keep a relationship with my dad. He tries, in his own way."

Nicky's shadows receded a little. "Yeah."

I glanced at the clock again, which did not go unnoticed by him. I stuffed down my eagerness to race to the school. The sooner that I got there, the sooner I could see Sawyer. But my friend needed me, and that needed to be put first.

"Go. I don't want you failing because of me. You're not getting into Gallaudet with shitty grades," he smirked as he bit into the savory croissant.

Releasing a relieved breath, I huffed a laugh and gave him a kiss on the cheek. "You're right. But text me if you need me, and I'll ditch. Understand?"

I leveled him with my harshest glare as I waited for his nod of understanding. After receiving it, I quickly walked out of the door, giving him one last glance before darting down the stairs.

He would be okay. He was mourning. We all were. Even the people that barely knew Evan were suffering from his loss. He was loved by everyone, from rejects like Nicky and I, to popular thunder cunts like Katherine. I was still plagued with nightmares occasionally, though I was learning to cope with the hole that was left in my heart from where his love had been.

I knew Sawyer had something to do with that. He was placed in my life at the right time. Otherwise, I had a feeling that I would have been worse off than Nicky. While Nicky always dabbled in questionable drugs and spiraling. I had very few people in this world, and to have one taken away was like chipping a piece of my heart from my chest. I was no longer complete.

Sharing my love for Nicky and Evan with Sawyer, made Evan's missing chip just a little less unlivable.

CHAPTER 26

-SAWYER-

Snow fell from the sky in a lullaby that couldn't be heard by anyone. This is what it must have felt like to be Halen for everything. Seeing and observing the beauty in everything, even with the silence surrounding you.

My pencil sketched the beauty that the sky was presenting me with on the new sketchpad I had bought. A cold quiet that was unbothered and undisturbed due to me being probably the only person at the school this early. Thankfully I was able to observe such tranquility from the comfort of my own classroom.

The headlights of a Lexus swerved into the parking lot at an alarming rate. The snow had just started to come down but the ground was coated in decent slabs of ice patches. They really needed to slow the fuck down.

As they pulled into the student lot, and slid into a parking spot, my brows furrowed. Of course it was a student. Always so reckless. Black Grove had quite a large student body for a private academy, but if I could pinpoint exactly who was driving like a bat out of hell, I could lay into them, or demand a visit with the principal, but then remembered he took Christmas break a few days early. My heart slammed to a stop while my anger surged to the front.

That. Little. Brat.

My eyes caught the tight black leggings, tucked into a pair of combat style snow boots before they raised to the slightly oversized black alt sweater with purposeful rips and tears. She was a sight I wanted to commit to my memories forever. She was always sporting such an immature grungy style, and yet, on her it was like anything else would look foolish. Her style was unapologetically perfect.

I was going to spank her little ass so hard that welts marred her skin. Maybe with a paddle. No, scratch that, I wanted to feel every shudder and twitch from the pain and pleasure beneath my palms as they connected with the bare milky skin.

I watched as she slung her bag over her shoulder and started darting across the lot, not looking might I add, and headed straight for the entrance. That was going to be another five slaps for not watching her surroundings. She knew she had to be more observant using her sight than most. So fucking reckless this morning.

God, if I had believed in him, had unleashed a punishment on her before I could even attempt to. Before she could even make it to the sidewalk, her legs flew up in front of her as her ass smacked the asphalt.

Holding up my sketch pad, I began to trace the outline of her silhouette as she remained seated on the lightly snow and ice covered parking lot, cursing at the sky.

I couldn't hear her, but the middle fingers she was holding up to her surroundings as she spouted off words I couldn't hear from here told me everything I needed to know. I was able to get the basic outline drawn before she finally huffed and stood up.

I continued to fill in the blanks based on memory as she walked out of view and into the building. I likely had about five minutes before she made it to my classroom. She usually stopped at the library to drop off her books every other day. Based on the bulging from her bag, I imagined it was stuffed with ones that she had read.

Sure enough, at about the four minute mark, she came blasting into the classroom like a fucking hurricaine, and slumped into her seat at her desk.

"Something wrong?" I asked in a slightly mocking tone.

She caught the smirk I was sporting, and as her eyes took in my position in front of the window and the area that it looked out to, realization smacked her right in the face… or ass.

She huffed, ignoring my question, before standing up again to pull the jar I had made her form her bag. There was only about a quarter of the popsicle sticks left. She really *did* blow through books.

As I watched her bent over, closing the zipper shut on her backpack, I caught the slightly darker rounded spot on her leggings. Her whole ass was wet from her slip. I barked a laugh but quickly smothered it.

She shot up straight and looked right at me. My hand was covering my mouth, but I knew she was reading the humorous scrunch of my eyes. Hers narrowed.

"Your pants are wet from your acci–" Her hand shot up as if to silence me.

"Don't even finish that sentence, Sawyer. It makes me sound like I pissed myself. You're already on borrowed time."

My hand dropped to my side and my eyebrows shot up as I took in her grumpy threats. She was most definitely not a morning person. But today, she was even more on edge than usual. I felt my length thickening in my trousers as I couldn't tell if she wanted to fuck me or yell at me.

The tight material somehow clung even tighter to her skin. A rumble began to travel up through my chest but I tampered it down, thankful that she didn't hear it. I didn't want her thinking I only wanted sex from her. That was so far from the truth. Honestly, I thought about her far too much for my own good.

"What's wrong, Squid?" I walked over and squatted next to her desk that she had sat back into. "Do you want to talk about it?"

To my surprise and displeasure, a single tear slipped from her eye as she avoided my questioning gaze. I opted to sign to her since I knew she wouldn't be able to resist looking over to see what I was saying.

"I am going to get you some tissues from the supply closet. One second, baby." Walking over to the stocked closet, I quickly located them and grabbed a box to set out as well as a small pack for her to keep in her bag if she needed them today.

The door clicked shut behind me. Gentle, but deafening in this small room. The darkness fell around me, aside from the dim emergency light. A soft feminine hand traveled up the ridges of my abdomen from behind until she made it to my pecks.

My cock was fully pulsing with desire, and every thread of patience was quickly snipped. When one of her hands quickly traveled south and squeezed the bulge in my pants, I tossed the tissues aside and whirled around before slamming my mouth down on hers. She was like coming home from a trip after being homesick. She was *home.*

Groaning in her mouth, I pushed her against the shelf, savoring every inch of her mouth. Our tongues slid against each other's as my hand wound into her hair and gripped tightly. Her whimper was a melody to my ears. One I wasn't planning on forgetting anytime soon. Secretly I wanted to hear it everyday going forward.

"Want me to make you forget whatever is haunting you, baby?" I kissed her again, not allowing her enough time to respond. But she didn't need to. Her nod and moan was answer enough..

I flipped her body around so her chest was pressed against the shelf as my chest was heaving at her back. I trailed my hand up her front and firmly, but not painfully, gripped her throat and turned her head to the side for another searing kiss.

I couldn't get enough of her. Not her taste. Not her scent. Not her sounds. It was all a puzzle piece clicking into place, showing me all that I had been missing with other women. I may have gotten off with others in the past, but it sure as fuck wasn't filled with this kind of hunger and adoration.

Tugging down her leggings to her knees, her needy

panting filled the silence surrounding us. "Sawyer, please, hurry, I want it."

I smirked at her begging. She was a firecracker one minute and my delicious little begging girl the next. I dropped to my knees behind her and ducked my head as I ran my tongue from her clit to her ass.

She yelped but it quickly turned into pornographic whine as she leaned as far forward as she could and pressed her dripping pussy right back into my face. I fucking devoured her, licking and groaning while I used a hand to press down on my own cock. It was leaking from my tip at an alarming rate.

Twirling my tongue around her clit, I felt every shudder as she gently rocked into my face, begging for a release that I could give her. No one else. *Me.*

Her sobbing release gushed from her as I lapped and lapped at her. Once I was sure she was thoroughly cleaned, I stood and ripped my belt off, shoving my pants down just enough to yank out my throbbing cock.

"Are you sure about this, Squid?" I gave my cock a few good punishing strokes.

"Yes. Hurry the fuck up, Sawyer. Do it. NOW."

I didn't need to be told twice. I slammed my length inside of her and my head fell forward to rest between her shoulder blades as I tried to calm my breath.

"You're so fucking tight. I'm going to make myself look like a foolish old man if I don't give myself a second."

Her chuckle was a balm for my jaded and miserable soul. "You could never look foolish to me."

I melted at her words, and began pumping in and out of her slowly, lovingly. We had rushed into this with so much need for each other that it was hard to pace correctly. But now, it just felt *right.*

She moaned as she met my thrusts. I kissed the spot between her shoulder blades, up her neck, along her earlobe. Her skin was vibrating, teetering on a knife's edge. As much as I wanted to crawl into a bed with her and rotate between slamming my cock into her pussy and soaking in as much of her gentle touch as possible, I knew that the bell was going to ring soon.

Students would be shuffling and groaning in protest through the halls, as they made it to their homerooms. I almost didn't give a shit if I got caught at this point, but I cared about what trouble that would bring Halen.

Any scholarships she applied for, her admission to Gallaudet, her family, friends, her smile. She played a good game when it came to hiding her pain, but I saw it. I could read her like the books that she drowned herself in.

The shelf we were pounding against kept banging the wall in a constant and steady rhythm.

Thud. Thud. Thud. Thud.

She masked the pain that the kids around her caused. She hid when she could, always implying that she preferred it that way, when in reality, she just didn't want the ones she loved to feel uncomfortable with the stares that always followed her.

Some of these kids had gone to school with her for years. They still stared. They still teased. I heard the occasional whisper, especially after Evan died. Black Grove wasn't short on gossip. But when he passed away, it seemed that Ressner and Halen were the hot topic of conversation.

"Will she date Dominic now?"

"I wonder if it was Dominic's drugs that killed Evan."

"I heard Evan was forced to be her friend by the school at the request of her parents."

"She barely even knew him, so why did she sit front and center at his funeral?"

"I heard she pretended to be deaf to gain his attention. He was such a giver."

So much misinformation. So many bratty little shits that ran their mouths without realizing the consequences it could have on someone's self esteem, mental health, reputation, and so much more.

Her cry of ecstasy pulled me from the depths of my thoughts as her pussy began to flutter around me, tightening around my girth.

"Fuckkkk," I groaned and let my head tip back.

"Im so close. I'm almost – Shit, I'm coming. Holy–" She cried out as I pounded into her from behind, her body thudding against the shelf.

The tingle at the base of my spine zapped up through my body, covering my skin in goosebumps as bliss poured from me.

I exploded inside of her, as her pussy clamped down hard on me, milking every single drop. I gently pulled out of her as my softening cock bobbed at her backside.

Without being able to resist, I reached down to feel the evidence of our love-making dripping out of her. My dick jerked against her ass at the feeling of her slick slit dripping with proof of our love.

Love? Was this love?

I rubbed our release around her entrance before shoving it back up inside of her. Where it belonged. She whimpered and clamped down on my two fingers.

"God, you're so fucking sexy filled with my cum," I said in a husky tone, raspy from all the heated grunting.

She smirked at me as she took in my expression in the barely lit closet. As her lips gently placed a kiss on mine, the bell rang out, signaling the beginning of another day.

We really needed to be fucking careful.

CHAPTER 27

-HALEN-

The days flew, as they tended to during the winter season with the back to back holidays and events. I was almost a week into my break from school. I spent most of the time reading or on video calls with Sawyer.

I was beginning to have some concerns about Nicky. That day that I had come home from school expecting him to be waiting in my room, I was shocked to find it empty. I reached out to him multiple times over the last few days but he would always give me a vague response.

Something wasn't right, and I didn't know how to handle it. Sawyer told me to give him space as he might have been coping with the loss of Evan in his own way. But whatever *his way* was, wasn't safe, if The Overlook was a prime example.

I did have two indecipherable messages from him that were both sent just before sunrise. In my gut, I knew that he was likely plastered to unreasonable levels.

My phone chimed in my bag as I looked through the shelves of the local bookstore for the book that I drew from the popsicle stick jar. I had a feeling it had some naughty things inside because it wasn't available to borrow from the school library.

After finishing my mission, snagging the book off of the shelf and checking out, I grabbed my phone and checked the message that I had missed.

Gregory: Hey wifey, I'm bored. Our parents are busy partying it up and I need some quality troublemaking to keep my blood flowing. It's practically sludge at the moment from

lack of movement.

Groaning, I stopped walking in the middle of the sidewalk and looked at my surroundings as if to find an answer there. Unlucky for me, the answer was not found in the awkward five second eye contact with Earl the local homeless drunk.

I continued walking to my car as I shot back a response.

Me: Not your wife, G. You're lucky I'm not in mixed company. That comment might have caused you and I both some issues. What did you have in mind?

His answer was immediate.

Gregory: Ouch, wifey. I'm hurt. What do you say to a little snowboarding?

My eyebrows shot up and I could actually feel some real interest piqueing at his suggestion. I hadn't been snowboarding before. My parents sure as hell weren't going to take me unless it was in Switzerland, and when they did, they usually just left me behind with a nanny.

Feeling the sting of hurt from rejection all of those years, I stomped the remaining distance to my car and slammed the door closed behind me as I sat in the driver's seat. I inhaled a calming breath.

Putting myself first needed to be more of a priority. I was always picking up pieces from Evan and Nicky's messes. Or taking care of things that my parents definitely should have been responsible for.

I may have been eighteen years old, but the truth was, that I grew up in my pre-teens. Now it was time to enjoy myself. Make my own decisions. Not let others dictate my life. Halen decided for Halen.

Me: I'm in. Pick me up at my place in an hour?

Gregory: Fuck. Yes. <fire emoji>

He showed up at my door half an hour later. Eager little shit. After grabbing my snow bib, jacket, snow boots, mittens, and beanie, I was ready to go!

"You look great!" He said, letting his eyes track down my

body.

I curtsied and lost my balance in the heavy layers. Falling to my side on the ground, I felt my cheeks flame red with embarrassment. I occasionally had some dizziness that stemmed from my loss of hearing. The eustachian tubes would give me vertigo sensations.

"Yep. This is gonna be interesting." Gregory said through his laugh as he helped me back up to a standing position.

We darted to the car and I got all settled in. My phone began ringing with a call. Gregory pulled out of the driveway and began heading towards whatever resort we were going to snowboard at. I dug through my pockets and pulled out my phone.

Teach.

Panic prickled my system as I realized I didn't tell him I was heading out with Gregory. My fiance. My panic shot through the roof when I saw that Gregory saw my face and the caller ID.

"You can answer it, Halen. I know that you aren't interested in me like that. It's okay."

No it wasn't okay. Sawyer wasn't just a guy I was dating. He was over twenty years older than me, and my teacher. He was absolutely off limits.

"You don't understand," I whispered.

The ringing of my phone stopped and my stomach rolled with unease. I had to make a decision. Tell Sawyer and Gregory. Or omit the truth from both.

Guilt immediately began eating away at me at the thought of hiding anything or lying to Sawyer. I knew what my decision needed to be. I'd never do something to hurt him. Ever.

I cleared my throat. "He's older than me."

Gregory glanced my way, assessing me before watching the road again, a smirk on his face.

"I'm older than you too. So what?"

"Actually. He's much older. Twenty-One years to be specific." He didn't need to know that Sawyer's birthday was soon.

His smile dropped as he looked back at me. "Holy fuck. You're dating an old man? Over me?"

I winced. "He's also my teacher."

His mouth dropped open in shock. "Now I'm really hurt. I lost my wife to a man twice our age and with a peasant salary."

I could hear the humor lacing his tone and I exhaled my relief. I didn't realize how nice it was to tell someone. I was so happy to finally say it. Make it real.

"It's obviously not public knowledge, so if you could," I gestured zipping my lips and his responding grin was truly beautiful.

"Of course. I won't say a word." He squeezed my hand and focused back on the road. I clicked Sawyer's name on my phone and video called him back. After a few rings, his masculine voice filled the car.

"Are you calling while driving? Pull over, Squid." I didn't miss the questioning look from Gregory at my nickname. That was a later discussion. Deciding to just get it over with, I pointed the camera toward Gregory to show Sawyer I was actually not the driver.

Rumbling sounds flowed through the phone so loud that I could have sworn I felt the vibration in my fingers. I rushed to explain.

"We are just friends, remember? He is taking me snowboarding. He's also the only one I can openly talk to about us."

"He knows?" Sawyer growled again.

"He does," I responded. "So please trust that I would never hurt you. Okay? I just wanted to call before I get a face full of snow."

I saw his features softened slightly. "Fine. But don't think about pulling any shit with my girl or I'll break you like a twig." He raised his voice at the last part, directing it to my fiancé.

Gregory saluted, and mumbled his agreement.

After a brief chat, I hung up with Sawyer and we pulled into a parking lot of the local sketchy grocery store. The lot was nearly empty though. My nerves were spiking, and it didn't help that Tension by Conley was blaring from his car speakers.

"Uh. Why are we here?" I asked.

"We are meeting up with a few of my friends. Don't worry, you'll like them."

Nerves ran through me as we pulled up next to another car parked along the outer edge of the lot. Three boys stood outside smoking cigarettes and laughing. When they saw us pull up, they waved at us.

Okay, friendly so far. That's good.

Gregory and I got out and walked over to the boys. He gestured to the one on the left with dark black hair that fell slightly over his eyes, making him look broody and kinda scary. He had tattoos peeking out from his t-shirt that ran up his neck. "This is Vesper." He nodded, saying nothing.

Gregory gestured to the next boy in the middle. "Kyle." His honey blonde hair reminded me so much of Evan's. It was short on the sides and long on top. He fit the pretty boy aesthetic perfectly.

"Last but not least, Zafar." He pointed to the tanned boy on the right. His eyes were golden, but his darker middle eastern skin tone made them almost glow.

"Like from Aladdin?" I asked, cocking my head at him.

His brows pinched together as the guys looked at each other questioningly. It was Kyle who broke into a loud laugh.

"Oh my god! That's Jafar." He pretended to wipe his eyes of tears from his giggles. "Holy shit, alright Greg, keep this girl around. I like her."

Jafar, um, I mean Zafar looked less than amused as he sent me a dirty glare. I shrugged my shoulders and let his annoyance roll off of me.

Greg was chuckling as he pulled me into his side and kissed the top of my head. "This is Halen, guys. And she is definitely not escaping me. Till death do us part, baby."

After a few more rounds of laughs, the boys pulled out a rope from the trunk and all of the snowboarding gear. Confusion clouded me as I watched Gregory get all snapped in. Vesper tied the rope to the hitch of the vehicle and the scene started to make more sense.

"You want to... street snowboard? Are you fucking crazy?" I snapped.

"Like a bat. Kinda like you," Gregory quipped.

"Bats are blind, not deaf, you idiot," I deadpanned.

Kyle chuckled, mumbling under his breath. "Burn."

Gregory held his hand out to me.

"No way."

"Come on, Halen. Live a little."

I huffed and looked around at the boys. They were both indifferent to my argument with Gregory and eager to get things rolling.

Remembering the promise I made to myself, I placed my hand in his and he stepped me up onto his snowboard so that we were sharing the same one.

"They better drive crazy slow, G. I mean it."

"At least we will go together if we die."

It ended up being the perfect day. I laughed. I smiled. I forgot about my troubles and the troubles of those around me, for just a moment. We switched turns with the others and before we knew it, hours had passed. The only downside was that I missed Sawyer. But I needed this.

As we sped through the parking lot in circles, sliding everywhere on the board, my eyes caught on a few men in hoods near the side alley of the store.

My troubles came slamming back into me as I watched Nicky grab a prescription bottle from some stranger's hand and slap money in the same palm.

He was buying fucking pills.

Gergory grabbed my waist more firmly as we made our last drag across the parking lot. A little yelp unleashed from my throat and I felt Gregory's chuckle, but couldn't hear it due to the adrenaline.

By the time the car came to a stop, and I jumped off of the board, Nicky was already swinging his arm back and launching into Gregory's face. This time, I really did scream in shock.

"Nicky! No! What are you doing? Stop!"

"Why are you groping my fucking girl?!"

The boys went crashing down to the ground, in a brawl as they both threw punch after punch. My stomach bottomed out, and panic filled my veins as Vesper, Kyle and Zafar jumped out of the car and threw themselves on Nicky and dragged him off.

Kyle and Zafar each had one of his arms, while Vesper inhaled the tobacco from his cigarette and held it like a weapon. I looked over right as Gregory spat a glob of blood on the ground, staining the layer of snow on the pavement crimson. He was livid.

His eyes found mine and then looked over to Nicky. "You fucking asshole. What is your problem?"

"He's a junkie, clearly," Kyle scoffed. "Look at his eyes, man. Definitely on something."

I was worried that was the case. He had been slipping in ways that even I couldn't help him from. But that didn't mean I would give up trying. Vesper made a step forward holding the glowing side of his cigarette just inches from Nicky's arm.

"Vesper, no!"

He inched even closer.

"I mean it. Don't make me hurt you," I said firmly.

Every head snapped my way, revealing shock at my demand. Except for Nicky. He was too fucking high and exhausted. My eyes met Vesper's, and I gave him my most pleading puppy dog eyes.

He flashed his teeth in anger but pulled the cigarette back to his lips for another drag.

"Fine. But you now owe me a debt." His eyes narrowed

further, clearly pissed that I was standing up to him.

"Deal."

This time he smiled. But there was absolutely nothing nice about it. It was cruel, and eager, and more dangerous than anything I had ever seen written on a face before.

I looked over to Nicky, assessing his current state. The anger had quickly faded as whatever he was on was really starting to work its way through his system.

Walking to Gregory, I gave him a quick hug. "Im sorry," I whispered. "I'm gonna get him home and sobered up. Text me, okay?"

He nodded and softened his tense frame.

With the help of Kyle, I managed to get Nicky into a ride-share and back to my house, where he would sleep off his mistakes. Again.

CHAPTER 28

-SAWYER-

Squid: Merry Christmas!

The notification chimed against my countertop where the phone was sitting while I made an omelet for myself. Snow was pouring from the sky beyond the large windows surrounding the room.

I wasn't a fan of the cooler weather, but having a white Christmas was always magical. It always reminded me of easier times when my biggest worry in life was if Santa was going to forget to stop at our house.

I grinned as I typed out a response. I thought about her every waking minute, and while it consumed every part of my day, I tried not to be too needy for her time. She still had people that she needed to interact with.

Last I had heard, Nicky was staying with her while she nursed him back to health. I was initially jealous as fuck, I suppose I still am, but she explained that he has no one and is struggling with Evan's passing still.

I wasn't going to tell her no. I just didn't like it one fucking bit. But I trusted her above anything else. She told me that he would no longer sleep in her room, and got him set up in the guest room. I nearly cracked my phone when she told me she slept next to him.

It's okay, she isn't Victoria. You trust her.

Me: Merry Christmas, baby. Your present should be delivered later today.

Squid: Aw, thank you, Teach! Yours is in the guest room closet, underneath the spare blankets.

My brows pulled together in confusion. When had she been here? I hadn't brought her here since Connor was in town. She wouldn't have bought a present back then.

Fully believing that she was messing with me, I raced to the closet and pulled up the blankets. Sure enough, there was a nicely wrapped box with a sparkling bow on top. It even smelled slightly of waterlily. Like *her*.

Me: How?

Squid: I slipped the doorman a Franklin.

My laugh escaped my lips, echoing through the room as I sat down on the couch with the box. Opening it eagerly, I saw a whole sketching kit. It was clearly expensive. High end pencils. A thick and sturdy sketchpad. Erasers. Pulling it out, I saw the note that was tucked underneath it.

To replace that piece of crap you have suddenly started using. Draw the world around you.

She was perfect.

Halen and I spent every single free moment that we could together. She started coming over to my place when Ressner would disappear randomly. Likely to get high. My anger was still palpable from when Halen finally revealed that he had gotten into a fight with her fiance.

Ew, that's a statement I never want to think about again.

Nicky had called Halen his girl. *His girl*. Oh, how very wrong he was. He needed to get his head out of his ass before he lost Halen completely. I could tell she was wearing herself thin. She was so consumed with helping him cope that I didn't think she really fully coped herself. Though, she was much better than she was. She was sleeping. Tiny blessings.

She mentioned that her and Astrid had even gone to grab a cup of coffee together. That was shocking news to me to say the least. Though it turned out that Astrid was just trying to find her way and needed a clean break from the people who got off on hurting people.

She turned to Halen for friendship first. The girl that she bullied. That took fucking balls. And it took the heart of an angel to accept her so openly after everything.

New Years came and went, which we spent kissing each other under the fireworks that displayed over Niagara Falls. She made me feel like life wasn't too late for me to live to the fullest. I was considering switching over to teaching art. We danced in our underwear to 90s classics. We fucked constantly. I wasn't able to get enough of her.

As I packed my work bag for the first Monday after break, a notification on my phone. My eyebrows pinched together in confusion as I read the work related email.

Meeting request with Principal Derek Howard, Sawyer Bennett, and Victoria Trexler.

Worry sent chills skittering across my skin. I wasn't afraid of losing my job if Victoria was spouting her mouth about harassment or some shit. But I did need to uphold my reputation if I planned on teaching art in the future.

Zipping my bag with a little too much force caused little threads to come undone at the seam. Growling my frustration, I charged out of the condo and headed to work.

What did she need to say that concerned our boss?

Thankfully and unthankfully Derek had to reschedule our meeting later that morning due to being stuck in Wisconsin for an extra few days from a winter storm. I was glad to have more time but at the same time, the unknowing was eating at me.

I spotted Ellen and Brent standing shoulder to shoulder in the cafeteria, watching the students eat and chatter amongst themselves. I grabbed a snack from the lunch line and began making my way to the Library to check on Halen when I came to a dead stop.

She was sitting at a table with Astrid, laughing and signing while she spoke. I could see her cochlear was in, but she was still signing. It was beautiful. Astrid watched her movements as she laughed with her and nodded.

Hearing about her making friends outside of Ressner was one thing, but seeing it in action was something that made my heart skip a beat. She deserved this. People were shitty to her. Kids were even shittier. She was finally thriving.

With that thought in my mind, my attention was dragged over to Ressner as he stepped out from the lunch line and caught sight of my girl.

That's right, my girl.

His distaste was palpable and he sneered in their direction before dumping his tray in the trash and leaving the cafeteria. I knew he wasn't mad at Halen, but more likely jealous that she was swimming while he was sinking. She was constantly trying to help him, but it seemed like every time she did, he walked away.

I passed by a few fellow teachers as I left Halen to enjoy her lunch period with her friend. Turning the corner, I smacked right into none other than my ex. She smiled at me, though the movement didn't meet her eyes.

"Just the man I was looking for. Can we have a quick chat? I wanted to wait until our meeting, but I think I'd rather air this out quickly given the unforeseen delay." Blood fell from my face as I nodded and walked to my classroom with her quietly following. I knew that look she gave me. It said she was sitting on a gold mine. And that was never something you wanted Victoria to have access to.

As she closed the door behind her, I walked to my desk and sat down. She parked her ass right on the edge of it so she appeared taller than me, more in control. But I didn't show her my concern.

"Spit it out. I don't have time to fuck around," I snapped.

Her grin was feline. "Oh, but you do, don't you? Have plenty of time to fuck around, that is?"

Oh, I definitely did not like where this was going.

With her eyes still on me, she watched every muscle as she placed photo copy images of my sketches from my old sketchbook down on my desk. One by one. I wanted to gag as her acrylic nails scraped against the crisp paper.

It was a mixture of real things I had seen and decided to put on paper and things regarding Halen that were purely sinful fantasies on my part. Some were explicit. Very explicit.

I gritted my teeth and felt a muscle pop in my jaw. That was exactly what she wanted because she chuckled.

"Ah, *there* he is."

"Why do you have my sketches? Did you steal my fucking book?"

"Hmm. Yes."

I was contemplating strangling her to death right there on my desk. I almost felt my body budge the slightest inch in anticipation. These were always meant to be private. Halen had seen most of them already, but by letting them into the wrong hands, she was at risk of public humiliation.

My skin heated as my blood pressure rose. My fists clenched to keep from reaching out to her pretty neck. I didn't often get pushed to this point, but she was pushing me there without a worry of the repercussions.

"What do you want, Victoria?" I asked through clenched teeth.

Her mask dropped for a fraction of a second, fear starting to sink in a little. The vicious smile that she was wearing began to droop in pain, but she quickly snapped back into the manipulative bitch she had always been.

"Right to business, huh? Alright, suit yourself." She looked right into my eyes, unlinking. Studying me. You know how some people would say that eyes are windows to the soul, or some shit like that? Well, behind her windows was hell.

After another uncomfortable few seconds of her looking at me like a snack she wanted to rip apart with her teeth, she spoke. Gently and quietly.

"You *will* stop seeing that girl. She *will* be dropped from your class. Then we *will* go back to trying to be in the loving relationship that we had."

I was already shaking my head in disbelief. "You need to be medicated. You know that, right?"

"Because I am feeling generous and not in the mood to let you bait me. I'll agree to your negotiation. Everything I had mentioned before, plus a little pick-me-up from a psychiatrist per your request. No biggie."

She outstretched her hand, waiting for me to place my palm in hers. I stared at it like she was going to give me leprosy. Holy shit, this chick was a nutcase. She didn't seem nearly this bad while we were in a relationship.

Thoughts of my sketches becoming available for public view at Halen's expense was pushed to the front of my racing thoughts. A feral need to protect her rushed over me. I gripped Victoria's hand. Hard.

Her wince gave me the exact victorious feeling I was looking for. She wasn't trying to destroy me, break me, hurt me. But she was willing to do all those things, and likely more, to my Squid.

Standing up I walked out of reach of her as her arms tried to grab at my shirt in a needy and pathetic way. I kept walking but turned my head just enough so she could hear my parting words as I left the classroom.

"I'll play by your rules for now. But you *will* regret this." With that, I continued through the atrium and out the side doors of the school to get some fresh air. The snowflakes whisked around my face as painful cold air raked over my skin.

I inhaled deeply, savoring the burn in my lungs. Without a second thought, I pulled out my phone and shot off a text to the only person that I knew could help me out of this shit show.

Me: I need to cash in a favor. It's urgent.

CHAPTER 29

-HALEN-

The end of the week came quickly, and time felt like it was rushing past me these days. I could have pretended that Sawyer had no play in that, but I wasn't going to lie to myself. I was happy. Genuinely fucking happy and in lo–.

Stop. Too soon.

I walked through the doors of the house as I basically skipped down the hall, eager to get to my room. The sharp smack of something pelted against the side of my face. I yelped and grabbed my face as I moved my furious gaze to find the culprit.

My mother was standing in the living room, her hands firmly planted on her hip and sporting a scowl that was surely going to cost her a pretty penny in botox to remove. My eyes turned to slits as I looked from her, then down to my feet where an expensive metal black pen rested.

A pen? She threw a fucking pen at me?

My gaze snapped back to her, and I slowly made my way closer. It was when I moved deeper into the room that I realized she was not alone. Three women and a man sat around the seating area holding different binders and papers.

I looked back to my mother with a hardened expression. *"What is so important, Jennifer?"*

She immediately straightened her spine and looked over to the others with a sympathetic smile. I watched her mouth mumble something that I couldn't make out from this angle but I think she was apologizing on my behalf for speaking with my hands in a way that they couldn't understand.

Her eyes met mine again as she spoke slowly and likely dripping with venom if the crunch of her nose was any indication. "Why are you unplugged, dear? Go put yourself together and come back down. We need to discuss some important things."

I rolled my eyes and turned around, only one finger as I marched off in the direction of my room. The others in the room didn't appear to know sign language, but sure as fuck understood what I had just said.

After grabbing what I needed and unpacking my books onto my bed, I made my way back downstairs to see what it was that involved a committee of some sort and myself.

I could hear the clinking of fine china and chatter as I got closer. The sounds of porcelain rubbing together made me wince slightly, but I finally joined the others as I sat down in a seat and grabbed a pre-poured cup of black tea.

"Thank you for finally properly joining us, sweetheart," my mother said with a little bite to her tone at the end. "If I may introduce, Vena Terrura, wedding dress designer to everyone who is anyone. I'm sure you have heard of her."

I hadn't. I nodded and smiled at Vena.

She continued. "Davis Sheppler, music coordinator for local musical talent. Loretta Kane, wedding planner and personal friend to the Jaffly family. Then of course Sandra Hurst, wedding cake designer. The last wedding cake was for the Spectra family. Can you believe it?"

She clapped her hands together with excitement as I nodded in greeting to the others. It wasn't their fault that they worked for rich assholes, like Jennifer here.

"Halen, we have so much down as a reference already from your mother regarding the wedding, but if there is anything that you have dreamed of having or want to mention to any of us, now is the perfect time so we can work as a team to make it happen." Loretta beamed as she slid a binder my way labeled 'G + H Jaffly'. The initials were harsh block lettering while underneath the Jaffly name was written in a beautiful script.

I reached for it and offered her a gentle smile. Flipping through the pages, I quickly realized this was not even close to my dream wedding. This was my mother's dream wedding, if she had the opportunity to throw another one for herself. Everything looked obnoxiously over the top.

Spotting the wedding dresses, I tilted my head to the side and studied the styles. I found one that I actually really loved. It was lacey material from top to waist and transformed to tulle from the waist to the floor. The ballbown cut worked surprisingly well with the long lacey sleeves and neckline.

I turned the binder to face everyone. "I want this one." Vena's eyebrows rose and a smile broke out across her face. "In all black." The smile dropped as quickly as it appeared.

"No," my mother snapped.

"Black. That's what I want."

Vena tilted her head and studied the image for a second before she regained her excitement at my decision. "I think I can make a beautiful black gown like this. Especially if the theme is more black-tie."

Loretta looked to my mother for input, but shrugged her shoulders as she took a sip of tea. "It could work, Jennifer."

My phone chimed and I pulled it out as the rest of the group continued their wedding conversation. Let's be real, I was here as a formality more than anything else.

Teach: I need to see you. I miss you.

I smiled as butterflies danced in my stomach. This man was quickly becoming the only thing I wanted to think about. If I was planning my wedding with him, instead of Gregory, this would have been an entirely different experience.

Me: I miss you too. In a meeting about wedding planning. Gag.

Teach: I'm a level headed man, Squid... but the thought of you planning your wedding to that boy is making me want to kidnap you and and just leaving this mess behind.

"Halen! What could you be possibly doing?" My mother's tone was short and I could tell she was ready to lose it.

"Just looking at wedding inspo on Pinterest."

Her eyebrows shot up and her angry stance calmed a fraction as she took in my response that clearly stunned her. "Um. Oh. Okay, well make sure to keep doing that and pass any important details you find over to Loretta. The last major details to iron out are what type of cake you would like and the type of music."

"What's your favorite flavor of cake, Halen?" Sandra chimed in. She was an older woman with lots of aging to her. I had no doubt that she could make a damn good cake with all of the years of experience under her belt.

"Red velvet with matte black fondant."

"Oh, heaven help me." My mother pinched the bridge of her nose. "Fine. But only because I can't argue this with this migraine forming."

I smirked and placed the wedding book back on the coffee table in front of us. "As for music, I think I would like anything deep and heartfelt. The cello. No harp bullsh–"

"Halen!" My mother snapped.

Raising my palms in surrender, I looked over to Davis to make sure he understood my meaning. He was nodding while holding my eye contact. "I can definitely work with that."

Smiling, I hopped up from the seat and gave the most horrendous and clearly fake curtsy before saluting my mother.

"Well, it appears that is all. Let me know if there are any updates. Thanks, everyone." I basically ran to my room where I curled up underneath my covers before grabbing my book jar from my nightstand.

I looked at the dwindling amount of popsicle sticks that were left and felt the frown tugging down on my lips. What happened when I had no books left? Shaking the jar aggressively as I watched the sticks fly around the inside, I thought of Sawyer and the hard work he put into designing this for me.

I opened the lid and picked a stick out, reading the title. A dark romance, interesting. I placed the jar back where it belonged and pulled out my phone to snap a picture of the stick.

Me: My next read. Any tropes or details I should know about before diving in?

I inserted the image with the text and shot it off. I got comfortable as I waited for a response. It didn't even take a minute for my phone to buzz.

Teach: It's a forbidden romance with a touch of mafia edge to it. There are also some mentions of pegging.

My eyebrows pulled together, but after a quick Google search, my questions were quickly answered. Pegging. Hmm. Kinda hot.

Me: Would you ever be interested in that?

Teach: Absolutely not. The only thing getting pegged, is you, baby.

Me: Boo... how boring. Anyway, I'll chat with you soon. I'm eager to learn more about this pegging experience. I'll keep you updated on all of the male ass play.

I chuckled at myself, knowing that he was likely red in the face from uncomfortability or lust, or both. His response was once again immediate.

Teach: You're killing me, Squid.

Teach: Don't forget to unplug.

Me: Yes sir.

Teach: Great, now my cock is hard. I'll be thinking of you while I take care of some needed business.

Well done. Now it was my turn for my cheeks to burn red. The thought of him stroking his hand up and down his shaft as he muttered and moaned my name created a dampness between my legs that I was slightly annoyed I couldn't do anything about.

Was he leaning against the shower wall while he used the water to add slickness between his velvet skin and his hand? Maybe he was laying down in his bed , thrusting his hips upward to meet the pumping strokes.

I shook my head to clear my clearly slutty thoughts. I could not be thinking about Sawyer like that right now when I couldn't do anything to remedy the need throbbing between my thighs. We had visitors here and I didn't want to risk them hearing me screaming for my teacher.

I huffed a frustrated breath as I turned on my kindle and downloaded the book that I needed. Remembering Sawyer's annoying reminder, I unplugged and was immediately immersed in silence.

Okay, he was onto something with that one.

But I would never admit it to him.

"Open the hell up, Nicky!"

My fists pounded on the wood door, threatening to splinter it right there. He had been radio silent more than usual and I was absolutely done with it. He was slipping so quickly. It was like sand falling between my fingers. I could feel him falling from my grasp, but there wasn't a damn thing I could do about it besides try to catch as many pieces as possible.

"Damn it, I will break down this motherfucking door if you don't answer in the next fi–"

My words cut off as the door swung open and I was greeted with a very disheveled version of Dominic Ressner. Not my Nicky. His eyes were red rimmed and his cheeks were so gaunt that he looked like his body was literally eating away at itself for nutrition.

I eyed him from top to bottom. "What the fuck is going on with you? Where have you been?" I snapped. Tough love was all that I could give him at this point.

He narrowed his eyes at me and his upper lip curled. "Where have *I* been? Halen, where have you been, huh?"

"I've been trying to pick up your pieces at every turn, that's where! You're pulling away, Nicky. I don't know what to do, but I can see you slipping and I am trying so hard to stop it from happening. What should I do?"

The tears began slipping down my cheeks as I poured my heart out to him. I couldn't stand the look of him before me. He was so fucking, broken.

Pain flashed in his eyes but only for the smallest of seconds. His muscle mass was clearly taking a hit, and his hair was greasier than I had ever seen it in my entire time of knowing him. That was saying something considering we occasionally had week-long camping trips together with Evan. When he was alive.

An ache formed in my chest at the reminder that without him, this is what we had become. He would have been so disappointed in us. I knew that. It only strengthened my desire to pull Nicky away from whatever fucking demons he was facing off with.

"Maybe you should ask Astrid or your fiance what you should do," he huffed. "Considering they are the ones that you have been involving yourself with now."

The hit struck, but I doubled down. I knew Evan was watching, and I needed to show him I could pull Nicky out of this bullshit haze he was in.

"What the fuck is wrong with you? Evan would be so fucking disappointed with how you're acting right now. He soaked up all the beauty of life more than the both of us combined. He would *not* want you to be self-destructing like this!"

"Don't you dare bring him into this! This is about *us*. You and me, Twerp!"

The nickname didn't warm my heart like it normally did. Instead it was filled with anguish and pain that was clearly being mirrored from the heartbreak coming from Nicky.

I couldn't get in a word before he continued. "You have been coping just fine, but some of us are struggling. You left me to drown. You decided that without Evan, you could be the person that you were meant to be. The selfish rich cunt who becomes besties with Black Grove's mega bitch. The cute but deaf arm candy to the one and only Gregory Jaffly. How fucking sad. You left me. You fucking left me. Tell me what Evan would think of *that*! All to whore out your pussy for some trust fund frat boy!"

I snapped. Rage had nowhere to go. It was heating my skin, my heart, my soul. "You think *he* is the one I chose over you?"

The rage that I felt just moments ago seemed as if it was doused with water. I knew I had made a mistake in so many ways. I not only hurt Nicky with that gut punch, but I also had just put Sawyer at risk. I knew it the moment his features went from defensive anger to murderous.

"Who?" His words were quiet, but not gentle. The warning was definitely there.

"Maybe you would know if you even bothered to answer a number of my calls or texts. Or maybe if you didn't flee to get high every time I put you back together. Maybe if you cared about me in the slightest."

"What the hell? I fucking love you, Halen! I told you that! I care about you more than I care about my own goddamn life. I'm *in love* with you. Always have been. I've been tearing myself apart with sadness every single minute that I don't have you."

At that moment clacking could be heard behind him from inside the house. We stared at each other, the space between us growing larger and larger as the unmistakable sound filled it.

At first his face showed the perfect balance of pain and frustration, but I could see clearly what it was morphing into by the second.

Worry.

Arms slid from behind view, across the front of Nicky's chest. Red manicured nails gripped the front of his chest, rubbing seductively.

A head finally poked from the side of his arm, and peeked to take a look at me. My heart slammed to a complete stop. A deadline.

Katherine.

My eyes met his, and for a moment, his dark orbs looked like the ones that I knew so well. But I couldn't hold back any more. "Right… you're *really* broken up about it." I didn't let him get a word in before I walked in the opposite direction. Maybe he was too far beyond saving.

I didn't care that he had been sleeping with other women. I loved him, but strictly as my best friend. What hurt was that he was sleeping with someone who bullied me to the point of considering unspeakable things, and was using Evan's death for clout.

She was a terrible person. He knew that. I *thought* he knew that.

"Halen, baby! Wait!I can exp–"

I slammed my car door shut and simply drove off back to Sawyers without a glance in my rearview. I hit the gas pedal and let the car take me where I felt safe. Where I belonged.

CHAPTER 30

-SAWYER-

The sounds of Halen's steady breathing, as she slept naked beside me kept me feeling sane and grounded. I had nearly driven over to Ressner's house when I saw her fall into my arms in a heap of tears a few days ago.

Thankfully, he hadn't shown up to class so I let the whole thing go, at her request. I wanted her to move on so it was probably for the best that I didn't unnecessarily involve him with myself or her.

It would have also been a dead giveaway if I had shown up at his doorstep, ready to throw punches, over a girl that was supposed to only be my student. I had enough blackmail bullshit from Victoria without adding Ressner into the mix.

I heard a whimper from next to me, and pulled her tighter into my bare chest where she wrapped herself more around my body and nuzzled her face into my neck. I felt the hairs on my arms rise. It wasn't lust exactly. It was so much deeper than that. Something that I hadn't realized I had never felt in this capacity before.

"I love you," I whispered into her hair.

She didn't hear me, obviously. She was fully unplugged, as she should have been. But the deep parts of me wished she had heard it. Because it was real. It was a leap of faith that I wanted her to see I was willing to take.

I picked up her hand and placed it over mine, my fingers were held in an awkward form, but I held them as long as possible. Kissing her temple, down to her neck, she finally stirred and instinctively grasped the hand back.

It took her a second, but once she pulled herself away enough from her dream state, she ran her fingertips around the shape of my hand. I knew the moment that she realized what sign I was holding up. Her breathing picked up. And she drew even closer to me, if that was possible.

"I love you, too." Those words whispered in the dark were everything and more. I seized her lips with mine as our tongues battled for dominance. The heat was burning both of us, but it was a welcome sensation. She was everything that I realized was missing from my life. What a sad life that would have been, without her.

I moved my body on top of her as I spread her legs with mine. Her moan into my mouth was the only thing I needed to proceed. The kisses grew hungrier and I could feel my erection drilling into her stomach as she dry humped me.

She wasted no time lining her already soaking entrance up with my hard as granite dick, and sliding up onto it. The arch of her hips and back had me meeting her half way with a guttural moan that I couldn't contain even if I wanted to.

"Fucking hell, baby. You feel so damn good." Realizing she couldn't hear me saying all the things that I was begging for her to hear, I reached over to my nightstand and turned on the lamp, bypassing her cochlear.

After the very dim glow illuminated the room, I lifted my hand between us and signed.

"That's better. How else are you going to hear all the ways I am going to destroy this pussy?"

Her eyes fluttered shut as she grasped what I was saying. Her hips rocking up into my pelvis to meet me thrust for thrust was better than porn. It was absolutely going to be in my spank bank for life. He eyes snapped open again.

"God, yes. Harder, please, harder. Harder. Yes!"

Her signing was becoming sloppy and frantic as she grew closer and closer to her orgasm. I flipped us over so that she was now riding me, because I knew that if I sacrificed a hand to strum her clit, I wouldn't have a hand to sign to her as the other one was holding me up, hovering over her.

She took charge the moment I flipped her on top. Her rocking was pornstar worthy. I knew she couldn't hear it, but the sounds that were being pulled from us had me almost bursting inside of her right then and there.

"Yes, baby, like that! Fucking hell, you are perfect. Take it, Squid. Good fucking girl." I pressed my thumb to her clit and watched her shatter on top of me while her pussy rippled around my shaft, sending me right into oblivion with her.

"Fuck!" I growled out, while she called out my name in response without realizing it. It only made my cock throb harder and longer. We were the perfect puzzle pieces. Words weren't always needed to communicate. We operated fine without them, actually. I was convinced now more than ever that this woman was my soulmate.

I gathered the remaining papers that needed grading when my phone began ringing from my pocket. Everyone that would call my phone was either in class teaching or learning. Or...

I reached into my pocket quickly and scanned the caller ID. Sure enough, the only other person that would not know my daily schedule was pasted on the screen.

"About fucking time." I growled into the phone.

"Don't be greedy. These kinds of things take time, you know, but don't worry, it's been handled."

"Handled? What do you mean handled? Con, I don't want her killed!" Truth be told, if it had come down to it, I would have allowed it, but she was only making threats at the moment, so I couldn't justify it. *Yet.*

"Fuck bro, what do you take me for, an assassin?"

"Aren't you?"

Silence. "Eh, not exactly. Mercenary. There *is* a difference, you know."

My brows pulled together trying to understand his point. "Yeah yeah, I don't care. What do you mean it's handled? I need specifics."

His chuckle sounded almost demonic as it met my ear. "Don't worry. You should be finding out in approximately," a pause, "ten minutes."

My eyes found the nearest clock which was hanging above my classroom door. I studied the second hand that was moving at a pace that was sure to send me into an early grave.

"Okay. Are you coming back anytime soon?"

"Unlikely." His answer was short and to the point. Very in-character for him. I knew he couldn't always go into detail over the phone when things were sketchy on his end.

"Is what you are doing or about to do, worth it?"

More silence. This time it stretched for nearly a whole minute. The only thing that kept me reassured that the line hadn't been disconnected was his breathing on the other side.

"Have you heard of the Crimson Elite?" He asked.

"No, why?"

"Look them up. You won't find news articles but you will find blogs and random claims on the internet. Once you do, then you tell me. Is it worth it?"

I pinched my lips together and tried not to let my pain for my brother bleed through the phone. I had wished that he had become something more, dull. Something safer. But truth be told, he was out there saving lives that wouldn't have been saved otherwise, and taking lives of those that had deserved to be sent to hell long ago.

He was the grim reaper, and he loved every second of it. He was the kind of person that we needed to rescue our mother. I'm sure the thought crossed his mind when he chose this path.

"I love you, Con. Let me know if there is anything I can do to help. Thank you, by the way, for the Victoria stuff," I still didn't know what was happening, but I knew that whenever I asked him for help, he was going to put his neck on the line to do it.

After we hung up, I sat down at my desk once more, and this time pulled up the web browser on my computer.

Crimson Elite. Sex Trafficking. Cult. Corruption. Secret society that controls the local government. Cannibalism.

The words from all the blogs and statements ran together as I took in the horrendous claims that people were making.

"Is it worth it?" His words echoed in my head.

The truth was, yes. I understood why he saw it was worth it. He was a hero. My little brother was my goddamn hero.

The bell rang for lunch and I followed my usual routine of tracking down Halen. I didn't find her in the cafeteria sitting with Astrid like I was expecting. Instead I saw Astrid sitting quietly at a table, talking with a boy. She still hadn't acknowledged any of the popular kids recently, so I had a feeling that her intention to cut them out of her life was authentic.

Walking through the halls again, I went to the one other place that I had a feeling she was. She never liked being in the noise-ridden cafeteria but I had a feeling Astrid was helping her get out of her comfort zone, while Halen was doing the same for Astrid in return.

The library was empty aside from the assistant librarian sawing wood at her desk. Her mouth was hanging open as she sucked in each loud as hell breath. I glanced over the large shelves and finally found exactly what I had come for.

She was sitting with her back leaned up against a shelf as her eyes tracked from left to right across the pages of her book. I smiled but slightly jumped when I heard the sound of an aircraft taking flight.

Nope, nevermind, just the old broad snoring again.

Studying Halen's face, I wondered how the sounds weren't bothering her every few seconds, but quickly pushed down a smile as I remembered her reality. She was unplugged, just like I had asked her to be.

I walked over in her direction, and as my feet must have gone into her field of vision, her head snapped up. The smile that stretched her face had my heart beating so much faster.

"Come here often?"

Her giggle was everything I needed for today. A simple speck of her happiness to pour into my life. I squatted down in front of her while I maintained a foot of distance just in case we were interrupted. I noticed the breathing pick up in her moving chest. My eyes were drawn instantly to the small bit of cleavage peeking from her black satin blouse.

She licked her bottom lip and my cock began stirring in my pants. I was just about to throw our rules right out of the window when I heard the distant sirens. Lots of them.

I looked over to the large windows and could see Halen's confusion at my reaction as she followed my line of sight. We were both stiff when we saw the red and blue lights of over six police vehicles pull into the school lot.

Did we break a law? A technicality? Did Victoria manage to release those explicit drawings? My nerves were shot but I was thankfully side by side with Halen and it instantly calmed me.

After a few minutes of agonizing patience, my eyes were wide as I saw them marching Victoria out in handcuffs. She was squirming in the grip of two officers. Her hair was a damn mess, with loose strands falling out of the bun haphazardly.

I looked over to Halen and saw her shocked face taking in the same scene. She looked over at me and pinched her lips together. I could tell there was nothing unhappy about it. She was absolutely trying to keep her smile at bay.

That in itself had a lighthearted smile stretching across my face. Once she saw that I was more than okay with what was happening, she finally let the grin break loose.

"Don't look too broken up about it," she signed with a giggle.

"It apepars she stepped on the wrong toes on her way up the

scheming ladder."

Her head cocked to the side as she studied my face.

"What did you do, Sawyer Bennett?"

I shrugged and raised my hands in mock surrender. *"Wasn't me, Squid. Ask Connor."*

She didn't believe a single bit of it. *"Right... and did you ask Connor to do something about her? And did it happen to do with scheming?"*

Damn, she really was a smart little cookie. I wasn't interested in hiding the truth. It was best if she knew the kind of shit Victoria was trying to pull.

"She was blackmailing me with my sketches of you. Even the ones I drew from my fantasies. I will risk myself every single day if it means protecting you, but I will never risk you. I couldn't let your chances at Gallaudet be squashed by a scandal like that due to her holding on to something that was no longer there."

Her eyes softened as she looked at me with such love and affection before turning a fierce glare out of the large windows in Victoria's direction.

"What a twat."

This time I barked a laugh and heard the choking inhale across the library as I realized that I had woken the assistant librarian. She was glancing around quickly, trying to assess her surroundings.

When her eyes found mine and Halen's, she offered a sweet smile and went about whatever business she had on the computer in front of her.

I turned back to Halen, but stepped slightly further away from her after realizing how close we had drifted together. We were like magnets, always being drawn into each other's natural pull.

"I have to go before I do something I absolutely shouldn't. Tell me I will see you after school, though." I was surprised to see her eyes drifting away, almost looking guilty. I grabbed her chin gently and turned it back to face me.

"Tell me," I signed while holding her chin.

Her lip quivered, but she maintained her composure, not letting any tears fall.

She pulled away and reached into her bag to grab her implants before wincing at the loud world surrounding her.

"I can't. I have to meet up with my family this evening. They want to have dinner again with the Jaffly family."

I held her gaze. "You could just tell them to fuck off and come live with me. I don't have tons of money stashed at the moment, but I will always make sure you are taken care of."

She bit her lip and looked away. I could tell she was lost in her own thoughts. I didn't know what she was holding out for or why, but I figured she would tell me when she was ready.

I cut her a break by breaking the silence growing between us. "Tell me you're still mine. Always mine. *Only* mine."

Her shoulders relaxed as she looked at me with a soft smile touching her lips. "Always."

That was good enough for now.

CHAPTER 31

-HALEN-

I smoothed the creases from my dress as I scanned over my body. It was sophisticated and pink. I fucking loathed it. I didn't mind a sophisticated number, but strutting around in fuschia when my hair was red was a clashing nightmare.

I looked ridiculous. I winced as I spun lightly to soak in the entire view in the full length mirror. With a sigh, I threw on my heels and grabbed my clutch for the evening.

With one last look in the mirror, I felt my phone vibrate with a call inside the clutch. I quickly dug into it, hoping to talk to Sawyer before I left. As I looked at the screen, my hope died in my chest.

Nicky.

He had been calling once every half hour since I left him looking like the asshole on his porch days ago. I was willing to help him, for so long, but the moment he started hurting me, I knew I had to protect myself first.

I wasn't ready to cut him off completely and go 'no contact', but for now it was what needed to be done. His dad wasn't going to notice or care about his bullshit, so eventually, Nicky was going to have to admit defeat and ask for help in getting better. I would obviously be there for him when the time came. However it seemed like it was going to take some time.

I clicked ignore and sucked in a breath before joining my family in the car. It was dead silent except for the obnoxious humming of the car. There was a slight whistle coming from somewhere but neither of my parents said anything about it, so I tried my best to push down my annoyance.

The city passed by as my gaze tracked the different visuals and beauty even in the not so great areas. Sawyer had really begun to teach me how to view life like that.

A valet opened my door and I startled at the embarrassing realization that I had zoned out. Grabbing my clutch, I stepped out of the car and followed my family inside. My father glanced back every minute or so to make sure I was keeping up. My mother didn't give two shits whether I kept up or not.

My dad wasn't the best out there. I knew that. He rarely hugged me, and mainly only listened to me if I had something to say that involved a negotiation. He was, and would always be, a business man at heart. He didn't make the big bucks any other way.

Where my father was cold but could be swayed with propositions, my mother was a cold hearted bitch with too high of a limit on her credit card. My father also needed me. It was a bargaining chip I was getting desperately close to playing.

He needed an heir to his empire. He couldn't really afford to lose his only child. Everything in his name would default back to my mother, and I knew that the possibility of that happening was going to eat away at him.

"Ah, Jennifer," a female voice cut in as we were guided to our table. "You look stunning! Wow, Halen, you look so radiant in that dress. What a vibrant color choice." Her eyebrows twitched with amusement. I think.

Fucking Botox.

I rolled my lips inward to stifle a laugh. Clearly she was in agreement about the god awful color. I felt an arm slip through mine as a strong presence of Burberry cologne wafted up on my right side. Glancing at the dashing young man, I caught his smirk just before he turned his attention back on his mother.

"Now that everyone is here, shall we take a seat? I'm sure my wife-to-be is starving."

He gave my arm a light squeeze and I rolled my eyes

at his nickname for me. His chuckle told me he caught it. I couldn't help the small smile that touched my lips.

Gregory wasn't someone I was romantically interested in, but he was quickly becoming a good friend to me. Not many people shocked me, but his personality was not at all what I was expecting, in the best possible way.

As I sat down in my seat next to Gregory, I looked over the menu trying to locate the chicken nuggets. I didn't know what Foie Gras was, but it didn't sound appetizing in the slightest.

"What are you getting? I was hoping for something a little more, normal," I whispered to Gregory.

He leaned closer to me and looked over the menu before pointing his finger at one.

Coq au Vin.

"Easy. When in doubt go with this one, or the classic Lobster Bique."

My nose scrunched as I read over the basic ingredients for the first one. "So, no weird organs or snails?"

I felt the attention of our parents snap to us when his chuckle rolled out a little too loudly. They were watching us. I could feel it. It soured my mood almost immediately. It wasn't Gregory's fault. We were on the same page. It just sucked that I couldn't even be genuine friends with him at the risk of our family getting the wrong idea.

Time passed slowly as we ate and talked about the wedding and how the merger would look once it's all finalized. I was drowning in boredom. The only thing keeping me from escaping through the bathroom window was the large amounts of delicious wine and occasional rounds of thumb war under the table with Gregory.

"I think we will all feel a lot better once Halen gives birth. It will be the final binding to this arrangement that will surely give us all the security we need."

I stiffened at hearing the words leave Edward Jaffly's mouth. Give birth? Were they shitting me? First our families were controlling our marriage, and now they were dictating the potential birth of our children.

Gregory's hand moved to rest on my knee. I hadn't realized that I began to stand in my haze of anger. My eyes locked with his and all I got back was pleading in his. Why? Okay, maybe we weren't on the same page.

"I agree! A grandchild would perfectly tie this beautiful future together. I can start Halen on supplements now, so that she is in prime condition when the wedding rolls around." My mother beamed.

Oh, hell no.

I stood up quickly, causing my chair to scrape loudly across the wood floor. A few tables looked over but only for a glance. I looked over Edward and Eleanor, before meeting the pissed off stare that was my mother's. My father was mostly just curious.

"Gregory and I would like to get some fresh air, while everyone talks... *specifics*," I said flatly.

"What a wonderful idea. You lovebirds scoot along," Eleanor said with so much hope in her voice that I almost felt bad. She wasn't a bad person from what I could tell. She was into preserving as much of her youth as possible, but that didn't make her bad.

I grabbed Gregory's hand and pulled him from his seat so that we could make our escape.

"Richard, maybe when the reception concludes, you can accompany me to the island I mentioned to you," Edward says in a lower voice. I only caught a brief snip of the conversation as we left the table.

How nice that they were able to just live it up on the beach, making decisions for everyone, while nobody made decisions for them. How fitting.

I also didn't miss Eleanor shifting uncomfortably in her seat as she resumed her independent conversation with my mother. I didn't have the time to dissect everyone's personal problems though, I had a mountain of my own.

Busting through the doors, the cold air shocked my system, bringing me down from the near panic attack I was likely sprinting towards. Gregory didn't hesitate to pull me in for a hug.

"We aren't actually going to get married and have kids, right? We both know that this is temporary?"

He pulled back to search my eyes before responding. "Of course. You never hid your intentions, wifey. I understand. I just," he paused as he looked out at the cars passing by on the street. "I don't know, I just think we should wait until the absolute last minute to break that news to my family. Specifically my father. I don't want to give him time to manipulate the situation in his favor."

"Maniupulate the situation, or manipulate you?"

His eyes pulling away from the cars and back to mine was like the crack of a whip. There was pain behind his. Genuine pain and frustration. I had hit a nerve, clearly. But was he going to push me away, or trust me with what troubled him?

After a minute of silence, him opening and closing his mouth like a fish out of water, I gave him a reassuring hug and pulled back with determination flowing through me now.

"Do you want to blow this bullshit dinner and go have some real food? I know a pretty good chef."

He rocked his head back and forth in thought. "You know a chef? I'm shocked. But, yeah, let's do it."

I smiled and ordered a rideshare. As the car pulled up and called off the address to the driver, Gregory's brows pinched together.

"What did you say the chef's name was again?"

"Sawyer Bennett. My boyfriend."

"Holy shit, bro. This is fire!" Gregory moaned around a mouthful of cranberry grilled cheese.

"It shouldn't be spicy, I used my regular ingredients.

Do you have any allergies to food?" Sawyer lifted a brow and watched Gregory carefully, obviously looking for any signs of respiratory distress.

I chuckled and bit into my grilled cheese before drawing the sandwich back creating the perfect cheese-pull. Gregory swallowed his bite and shook his head with laughter.

"Sawyer, man, if you are gonna date my wifey, you are going to need to stay on top of the lingo for her generation."

A growl rumbled through Sawyer's chest, and his fierce eyes locked on hard to Gregory. I quickly shoved the stretched cheese strings into my mouth before dropping my sandwich and jumping up to step in front of Sawyer.

"She is *not* your wifey. She will *never* be your wifey, you lit–"

"Teach, stop! It's okay. It's just a nickname. Gregory and I are crystal clear on expectations between us. Our friendship is just that, a friendship."

I looked behind me to see Gregory watching in amusement as he took another hefty bite. "It's true. I'm growing to love her, but mostly in a way that I would see a sister or a friend. You have nothing to worry about from me."

I felt Sawyer relax a little at Gregory's admission. "Thank you for the compliment on the sandwich. You're welcome to join Halen and I for one anytime." His words were genuine but you could tell that they had irritation laced in them. Gregory and him were going to butt heads in the future. I couldn't quite decide whether it was going to be funny to watch or annoying to play referee.

"That Dominic kid on the other hand," another bite. This time he let the words hang in the air while he chewed, shaking his head. He chewed and chewed. Slowly. That little butthead was absolutely trying to get under Sawyer's skin. "Now he is someone you should keep an eye on. I don't believe for a second he will be as accommodating as me. Something is off about him."

Sawyer grunted his agreement and started digging into

his own food. I sat back down and tried to move the conversation in a different direction. It hurt my heart to be in this situation with Nicky. I felt like a piece of my soul was cracking off, ready to join the other lost piece that went with Evan.

After another hour of chatting, Sawyer and I walked Gregory to the elevator where I gave him a tight hug and Sawyer shook his hand firmly. Too firmly based on the fact that his knuckles were draining to a white hue.

"See you later, Wifey."

"Get out."

My lips rolled inward as I tried my absolute best to hold in my laugh. It ended up coming out as a heinous snort, which absolutely did not go unnoticed by Sawyer. Gregory smirked and pulled out his phone to text someone as the elevator doors closed him off from view.

Sawyer and I spent the rest of the night cuddled up, embracing one another as the minutes ticked by. His hand massaged my scalp as he threaded his fingers between the auburn curls. My eyelids didn't stand a chance. As they grew heavy, the last thought I had was about how he was quickly becoming my life. My joy.

I only slightly roused from sleep when I felt warm firm hands pulling the implants off of my ears, sinking everything into silence.

Then, I really drifted into dreams of *him*.

CHAPTER 32

-SAWYER-

The elevator dinged signaling the arrival of someone entering. I looked at the clock on the wall, seeing that it was way too early for it to be Halen as she had an obligatory meeting with her wedding planner. Unless something went wrong.

The whole wedding situation made me nauseous. I wished she would just tell them all to 'fuck off' and move in with me. Letting my uneasy thoughts take root in my head, I got up and started walking towards the elevator area.

Right as I rounded the corner from the living room, I saw a young man, maybe a couple years older than Halen, about to light up. Inside.

"Um, first of all, can you not smoke inside? This technically isn't my place. Second, who the hell are you?"

He stood there frozen, with a cigarette perched between his lips as the bright flame of his Zippo lighter lingered a mere inch away. His eyes looked up at me slowly through the gap in his hair strands.

He had something terrifying lingering underneath those eyes. I didn't have the time nor the energy to try to decipher it at the moment. I had too many other things up in the air that needed my focus. Halen's engagement, my future living situation, and the piles of papers that needed grading were just a few.

He flicked the lid of the lighter to smother the flame and stood straighter. It was then that I noticed the large manilla envelope tucked under his arm. He slowly tucked the lighter in his pocket and wedged the cigarette behind his ear.

Classy.

"I'm Vesper. Your brother sent me. Thought you might want to have this. I would have dropped it off sooner, but I had better things to do." He extended the package out to me and I eyed it suspiciously but grabbed it from him. He said it was from Con, and that was all I needed to trust it.

I ripped the seal open and reached inside, dragging out the perfectly leather bound book. My sketchbook. The one that Victoria had stolen from me. I quickly opened it, shielding it from the view from the creepy motorcycle president wannabe. Everything appeared to be in place, the sketches of life here, my Squid, and the beauty that I found around me.

"The one on the desk is my favorite," Vesper said in a dry tone. No emotion in his words at all.

I registered his words and took a threatening step forward. "You looked?"

This time he smiled, but there was nothing kind about it. It felt dark and clouded, possibly evil. Fuck if I knew. My blood was boiling at the idea that he got a look at the sketch I drew of her.

He shrugged. "I had to. I did a full sweep on that crazy broad's place. So I had to make sure that I inspected everything I came across. Connor filled me in on the main thing I needed to find."

I snapped the book closed and held it to my chest protectively. "Fine. But if you mutter a single word, I will end your life."

He scoffed. "Whatever, old timer. You're welcome by the way." He walked towards the elevator and stepped inside. I called his name right before his finger could hit the lobby button.

"What are the cops holding Victoria on? Is there any chance she is getting out soon?"

He stared at me, unblinking. Why wasn't he blinking? Weird ass motherfucker.

"It's unlikely. Not impossible, but not likely. I planted

enough drugs in her apartment to pin her as a distributor for Black Grove. We needed a fall-guy for that anyway. I also paid a few students to sign an affidavit claiming that she sold to them on campus."

My eyes widened, but I couldn't help the small upwards tug of my lips. She deserved it. She was a shitty teacher and an even worse human being. I had no sympathy for her the moment she jeopardized Halen.

"Well, thanks for that, kid. Well done."

He clicked the button for the lobby and the doors began to slide closed. "No problem. Tell Halen I said I'm looking forward to seeing her again." I had no time to process his words, let alone respond before the doors clanked together. I stood there for an extra moment, speechless as the whirring of the elevator lowering to the lobby filled the area.

What the hell?

I marked error after error on essays while Halen was sprawled out on a few of the student desks that she pushed together. She had a book perched in his hands while she laid on her stomach and read silently.

I couldn't contain my gentle smile every time I heard a light gasp, or the rustle of her body shifting to get comfortable. A few of those times I could tell her cheeks were flushed crimson, so she was likely reading something naughty.

Knowing that I needed to get through my papers, I suppressed the hard-on I was sporting in my slacks. Being around her was like being dosed with Viagra constantly. She wasn't just a balm for everything wrong in my life, but she was also everything that I didn't know I wanted in a woman.

Fierce. Independent. Driven. Full of love. Full of hope.

I heard her phone vibrate, but kept myself focused on the really shitty explanation of Wuthering Heights. I could definitely tell which kids read the book and which ones watched the movie.

Halen groaned but it almost sounded sultry to my ears. God, I was fucking turned on. Everything about her flipped this switch in my head, demanding me to claim her, to breed her. I looked up to finally plant my eyes on her. It had been about a few minutes since I last had. Sue me.

Her head began shaking angrily as she typed out a rather aggressive text. My heart began to race slightly as all the possible scenarios raced through my mind. She was finally opening herself up to so many different people after being brutally bullied for her differences.

Her eyes met mine.

"*What is it,*" I finally signed.

"*Nicky.*"

I waited for her to continue and expand on what it was that was bothering her. She just huffed and crossed her arms while she stared out the window.

"*He said he is coming to school early today to talk to me. I don't have anything to say to him until he agrees to get help. I offered to pay for it all and I even have a connection to a rehab in Oregon, but he is dodging the demand. I'll need to meet him in an hour to tell him, again, to clean up or he'll end up dead.*"

My eyebrows rose and I watched her face battle between crumpling and hardening into the brave woman that she was. She was tired of crying. I understood. I felt similarly when I lost my mother. It was with that thought that I realized what was happening.

Grief.

She was grieving her friend. Not the one that died, though I knew she still had her moments of grief over that. This was grief over the friend that *didn't*. The friend that kept choosing to live a worthless and meaningless life, even though his was spared while Evan's was not. She was grieving the loss of her one true remaining friendship.

I stood and walked over to where she was sitting on the student desks. Her eyes were filled with tears but not a single one dropped. I grabbed her chin to keep her still and steadily looking at me.

In that moment, the only thing I could do was gift her my most reassuring and loving smile. Her face slowly softened out as her tears dried within her eyes.

God, she really was breathtaking.

I leaned down to capture her lips with mine. It wasn't urgent or fierce. It was patient love and eagerness to drown in each other. While we didn't hold back when it came to fucking, this was so much more. Everything.

Even with the kisses being gentle and romantic, I felt her slide her hand down to my crotch where she gave my raging erection a light squeeze. I could feel the precum drip from the pressure from her grip. I felt her smile against my lips when I groaned into her mouth.

She lightly bit my bottom lip, and let it snap back into place before sliding off of the desk, leaving me panting for her. It wasn't a long wait though. She sank down to her knees in front of me, and I swear to God, I nearly busted right there. She was a walking fantasy for me, but here in this moment she was recreating an actual scene I fantasized about. So much that I memorialized it in my sketchbook.

Fuck, the real life version is a shit ton better.

She reached to unbutton my dress pants, and I let her. I caressed her soft auburn curls, running my fingers through the strands. She flicked her eyes up to me as she pulled my cock from my pants.

Holy shit, I was going to hell for sure.

Her mouth stopped right at the crown and she opened her mouth to flick her tongue against the slit, collecting a bead of precum that was eagerly sitting there for her. My breaths quickened and this time she slipped her whole mouth over my cock.

The warmth of her mouth surrounded me, causing my head to tip back and eyes to roll. I gathered some of her hair in my fist and helped her move her hot mouth up and down. The slide of her tongue against my shaft caused my hips to lift to her warm silky mouth.

"Jesus ever-loving Christ, you're doing so good, baby," I panted out, knowing she couldn't hear me since she was still unplugged. She must have read my lips though because her responding moan around my shaft send vibrations surging through me.

"Oh, fuck, yes," I moaned out as I began to quickly move her head up and down faster. My cock nudged the back of her throat where she gagged slightly before correcting her methods. I personally liked her gagging on me like this but I wasn't going to push her too far. She was still exploring new things, with me as her first.

Just the thought of her being only touched by me had me rocking my hips into her eager mouth. My hand that wasn't holding Halen's hair caressed her cheek where I could feel the slight outline of my cock while she tried to swallow it while.

This time I knew I was game over. *"Halen, baby, I'm gonna come. Are you going to take it down your throat like my perfect good girl?"*

Her nod was eager and excited and it threw me right over the edge and into the abyss of pure pleasure. Everything that flashed behind my eyelids as I shot ropes of cum down her throat as she quickly swallowed it down, was her.

Light. Joy. Excitement. Growth. Pleasure. Kindness. Desire. Halen. All Halen.

After I was done emptying myself, she gave me one final lick and pulled away. My breathy chuckle had her giving me a sinful smirk before wiping her lips.

A thud against the door had me sobering from our desire immediately as I snapped my attention to the entrance of the classroom. Halen caught on quick because she immediately grabbed her implants from the desk and poked her ear out to listen for whatever I had heard.

There was nothing and no one in the door's window, so my shoulders relaxed slightly. It was unlikely that the teachers were strolling in yet. It was barely 6:45 AM.

"It was probably the air pressure from the heaters kicking on for the start of school or something."

She didn't look convinced but she still gave me a small smile before going back to her desk and sitting in it correctly like the ideal student.

This girl was going to be the death of me.

CHAPTER 33

-HALEN-

"God, I can't believe she did that. I'm sorry," Astrid said with genuine sympathy lacing her words.

I shook my head in disbelief at the situation I was in. My eyes tracked down the paper in my hands once more, studying every word. I was so full of rage that I could feel myself considering whether the jail time might actually be worth it.

That little calculating little bitch.

"I mean, she could have given you something more serious like HIV," she said, giving a placating shrug and a small wince.

"She gave me herpes!" I snapped out. My eyes widened for a moment, before looking to my right and seeing two students staring at me with their mouths gaping open. When they finally registered my hard glare, they quickly scurried off.

"Astrid, she is going after my reputation. This can't happen so close to being accepted into Gallaudet. It's the only reason I haven't broken the engagement off with Gregory yet. If I move out, my mother will absolutely tamper with my future acceptance to keep me under her thumb. I'm waiting for the official offer before I pull the plug. But if Katherine keeps doing this shit, it's not going to matter!" I scrunched the paper in a ball and chucked it into the nearest trash can.

"Come on, we have to make it to physics. Let's just get your mind off of it." We turned the corner of the hallway to find about twenty more copies taped to the walls and rows of lockers.

"Ah, shit," Astrid muttered under her breath. She didn't

waste another second before running up to the nearest set of lockers and snatching down the fake health assessment which had my name at the top. In bold.

Giggles could be heard at the end of the hallway, echoing loudly for all to hear. I grabbed another paper from the wall as a loud male voice, dripping with venom, cut through the laughter.

"What the fuck are you guys laughing at? I'll be the one laughing when your blood is dripping from my skin. Leave!"

With a few yelps and gasps, the girls scurried off like their lives depended on it. In a way I suppose it did. The old Nicky would have absolutely killed for me. This Nicky seemed to be just begging for forgiveness that I wasn't willing to give unless he agreed to get better.

With another crumpled paper in my fist, I shoved it into my backpack, not seeing a close enough trash can. I didn't want to spend more time than necessary disposing of this shit. I still had class that I was sure I was going to be late to, and I could feel my annoyance hitting an all time high.

"You too, Astrid. Beat it." I felt his body heat prickling my skin but I kept my gaze firmly planted on my backpack. Maybe if I didn't look, he would go away.

Astrid leaned down next to me, completely ignoring the angry growl coming from Nicky's direction.

"Are you going to be okay? If not, just say so and I'll tell him to fuck right off."

I couldn't contain my small smile at her words. She was quickly getting her backbone back and this time she was playing for the good team. Not her ex-friends that made her life hell and encouraged her to drag everyone down with her.

I nodded. "I'll be okay. See you in a few minutes." She gave me one last look over and squeezed my hand before signing to me. "*Give him hell.*"

Nicky scoffed, clearly understanding what Astrid signed as she began to stand and walk by him. He didn't hold back from spewing one last stab at her as she passed.

"Bitch."

"Demon," she quickly retorted.

When she was fully out of ear shot, I faced Nicky head on. I wasn't going to cower, and I sure as fuck wasn't going to let him talk shit to me or Astrid just because he was fucking up his life.

His appearance sent a jolt of sadness through me. He seemed to be getting worse by the day. It was like the healthy muscle was just falling off of his bones and his already sunken eyes were so painfully dark and full of suffering.

The leather jacket and jeans that he would have normally rocked were nowhere to be seen. Instead he was wearing a pair of jeans with stains on them and a shirt that I couldn't even confirm was his own. I had never seen him wear it before. It didn't look like it fit at all but that could have been due to the weight loss.

"Halen..."

I hardened myself, knowing that all he saw was my sadness for him and how close I was to breaking. But, I had to remain strong. For *him*. He was going to kill himself slowly otherwise. I refused to watch that.

"Halen," he repeated, reaching for my arm. I stepped back. The pain across his face was palpable and I could physically feel my heart cracking from so much anger and hurt. "I'm sorry, okay? I shouldn't have said the things I did. You know I didn't mean a word of it. It's not what you think, regarding Katherine. I didn't fuck her."

"You're allowed to fuck who you want, Dominic. I just thought you had better taste. You criticized me for being friends with Astrid while you were busy with Katherine doing what? Hmm?" I didn't let him speak. The question was rhetorical. "Right, like I said. I have to get to class. The offer still stands on rehab. Say the word and I'll be by your side the whole time."

I moved to walk around him but he grabbed my wrist and snapped his words out, causing me to jump a little.

"She's my dealer!"

I went still and looked back to him with pinched brows. "Your dealer? As in your *drug* dealer? I want you to be crystal clear right now." His lips pinched together, battling between snitching and shutting the hell up.

Thankfully he chose the former. "Yes. I get some of the harder stuff from guys in town, but for lighter highs, I have been utilizing Katherine."

That cunt! She needed to be swiftly dragged to hell.

I swallowed the anger as best as I could. "Thank you for telling me. However, it changes nothing. You need to get clean, Dominic. This isn't right. Please, just accept the help."

"Stop calling me that. I know what you're doing. You can push me away all you want, but we are fated, Halen. You're my best friend. My beginning and end. I don't need help. Sure, I might be going a little overboard lately with my fixes, but I can cut do—"

"No! You don't need to cut down. You need to detox completely and safely. You're an addict, Domi— Nicky. An addict. Let me help you." This time I reached my hand up to rest against his jaw that had overgrown in the past few weeks. His eyes fluttered shut momentarily as he leaned into my touch. I couldn't see it but I could have sworn I felt the slightest quiver of his chin against my hand.

When his eyes opened again, they were stern yet pleading. "I don't need help."

My hand dropped and I let a breath come out that was anguish and acceptance of my own. This was it. This was the moment that I had to protect my own peace. The moment I realized that he was never going to let himself get clean without the right motivation. Motivation that wasn't *me*.

"Let me know if you change your mind, Dominic."

This time he didn't stop me as I hurried off to the class I was now extremely late for. Thankfully Astrid had saved me a seat and I was able to quietly slip in and catch up on the notes being displayed.

"Are you alright?" Astrid leaned over and whispered as Mr. Teller continued his lecture.

I didn't look at her. I knew that if I did, the tears that I was barely keeping in check would finally fall. She didn't need to see though. She knew.

I felt her hand slip into mine on my desk and give a firm squeeze. I held it back with a grip that I was sure was not comfortable. But I needed it. I sucked in a lung full of air and released it.

Newton's Laws... right. Focus.

My fingers gripped the envelope, so tight that my knuckles were turning a shade of white. Anxiety rushed over me as I stared at the piece of mail that was addressed to me. The sender, Gallaudet University Admissions Office.

Blood roared in my ears as my fingers trembled on the perfectly sealed edges. My heart rate picked up, causing the pounding in my chest to thump so powerfully that I had to take a step back from the mailbox.

Snapping back to reality, I grabbed the rest of the mail pile from the mailbox and dashed back into the warmth of my home. I didn't waste a spare second throwing every piece of mail, except for my own, on the entryway table and running as fast as possible to the privacy of my room.

"Miss Halen, is everything alright?" Enzo paused in the hallway with my mother's suitcase in hand. She was likely going on another vacation. Lucky her.

Not wanting Enzo to relay any information regarding my college status to my mother, I kept my pace down the hall until I finally worked my way past him. "All good, Enzo! It's just, uh, my period starting. It's about to be a scene out of The Shining in a minute."

As I made it to my door, I snuck a peek behind me to see Enzo straightening his back and continuing quickly down the hall, clearly uncomfortable.

I sat on my bed and stared at the envelope again, eyes wide as reality began to smack me in the face. The tan and blue colors were vibrant with foil accents. They wouldn't waste such an elegant envelope just to reject me, right?

I squeezed the top and bottom, trying to gauge the thickness. My heart began racing faster as I felt the stack of more than one slip of paper inside.

Stop being a little bitch and open it!

Lightly tearing at the flap to preserve it as much as possible, I finally freed the edges from the glue and slid the papers out. I didn't want to accidentally tear anything. If I got accepted, I was definitely going to be scrapbooking it.

Taking a deep breath, I flipped the papers and stared at the letter directed to me from the admissions office.

Dear Halen Knox,
We wish to congratulate you on being accepted to our program at Gallaudet University. We are enthusiastic ab—

I didn't even finish reading the sentences before jumping up and down on my bed with tears of excitement pouring down my cheeks. I had done it. I had actually fucking done it.

I scanned the letter and found the necessary steps to accept my admission and enroll for classes in their program. I wasn't going to spare a minute. I was finally able to make moves about my life that were my choice, and I was not going to let a second of that slip by.

After an hour of getting all of my documents gathered and online enrollment done, I leaned back in my chair and stared at the ceiling, still in a state of shock. This was going to be the moment I took charge of my life.

I pulled out my phone and found the contact that I was looking for. Deciding between a text and a call, I opted for a text message in case he was pre-occupied.

Me: I've officially accepted my spot at Gallaudet. Care

for a roomie?

His response was nearly immediate.

Teach: Congratulations, baby! I knew you would. As for moving in… it's about fucking time.

My smile grew and the tears of joy just kept coming and coming.

Me: I just have a few things to wrap up and I'll be on my way to your place. Will you be there?

Teach: It's our place now. At least until we find something that is truly ours and not Con's. But for now, it's our home.

I hugged my phone and envelope to my chest and let myself feel all of the emotions releasing from my body. My mind couldn't help drifting to Evan. I knew he was looking down on me, so proud of the woman I was becoming. I just wished he was there with me to celebrate such an amazing moment.

I set my things down and went to my closet where I began to pack my suitcases full of my belongings. I knew there were some hard conversations to be had. It was time for me to pull the trigger.

CHAPTER 34

-SAWYER-

I paced around the kitchen, grabbing random things to organize just to place them back down in the original spot again. Halen had texted me that she was on her way home.

To *our* home.

Well, temporary home until we could find something that was fully ours. Washington D.C. was likely going to be the final landing spot until she finished her program.

I was in the middle of wiping down the countertops, again, when the ding of the elevator signaled her arrival. My heart was pounding in my chest and nerves were taking over. I was a grown ass man who had lived with, and was planning to be engaged to, another woman. However, the feeling of 'love' between Victoria and I fell painfully short to what I was feeling with Halen.

I hadn't felt this kind of belonging in a very long time. Likely not since my mother was still alive. Con and I always looked after each other and loved each other so much, but we had separate paths that always kept us at a distance.

This was someone I could share my feelings, pain, joy, ideas, sketches, and life with. My other half. Our gap in age didn't even come to mind anymore, and I honestly didn't give a single shit whether it made others uncomfortable.

As I walked next to the counter to head in her direction, I grabbed the bouquet of Strelitzia. I had rushed to the florist down the road when I had learned she was packing her things. I wanted tonight to be as memorable for her as I knew it would be for me.

God, you have turned into such a pussy.

Rounding the corner, I came face to face with an out of breath Halen as she dropped her rolling suitcases and duffel bags on the floor. Our eyes were locked as we walked straight into the most comforting embrace.

It wasn't rushed. It was a sensation of releasing a breath you were holding for slightly too long. My eyes shut as I pressed my lips to the top of her head in a gentle kiss. Her hands that were wound around my waist immediately tightened.

"Thank you."

I pulled back slightly to look into her eyes again. "What for?"

"For knowing exactly what I needed just now. For waiting. For loving me. For taking this step with me. For everything. I love you, Sawyer."

Her eyes began to mist over and I caressed her cheek gently with my thumb as I brought my other hand, holding the bouquet, in front of her face.

"One of many. Welcome to the new normal. I love you too, Halen."

Her smile lit up the room and I couldn't help smiling back. She inspected the flowers with wide eyes, looking at every single petal.

"Oh my god," she whispered. "These are absolutely stunning! I've never seen anything like these before!"

I chuckled as I rubbed her arm. "They are Strelitzia, but you may have heard referred to as Bird of Paradise. They represent freedom and taking on a new adventure. I figured we should start it on the right foot."

She looked at me with all the love in the world reflecting back in her eyes. "They are stunning. Thank you."

I lowered my mouth to hers, pressing a soft kiss on her lips. She wound her arms around my neck and the scent of the flowers surrounded us as she continued to hold tight to the bouquet.

After a few minutes of passionate kissing and and a fucking boner that was sure to take a bit to go down, I walked her to the bedroom to unpack her things.

"Let's get you unpacked. I have a whole night ahead of us to celebrate and I don't want you worrying about organizing your things or whether you left something at your parents."

"That works for me." She winked. "I have lunch scheduled with Astrid tomorrow, and then I plan to stop by Gregory's place so I can fill him in on where we stand."

I didn't like it, but she was trying to put an end between the fake relationship so I was going to grit my teeth and suck it the fuck up so we could be done with it all.

"Sounds good, baby. I should probably spend some time with a few assignments anyway. I might take some time to read as well. It's been a minute since I have had a moment to read a good book."

She began to place her clothes in the drawers I had emptied for her. She smiled and gave me poke on my chest.

"Speaking of, I am running low on popsicle sticks. So maybe you *should* read, so that you can start adding more to my jar."

I smirked and gave her a gentle kiss on the cheek. "Before you know it, we are going to be buddy-reading these."

"Now that would be the ultimate goal. I can see it now," she said as she closed her eyes, mentally building our future. "Hot tea, cuddles, the only sound of pages flipping and rain hitting the window." Her happy sigh made that rock solid organ in my chest feel a little less stone-like.

We spent the rest of the night cramming chinese food in our mouths, followed by popcorn and crappy candy as we watched romantic comedies and laid in bed. It was the perfect start to our first big step.

The next morning I woke up spooning her in our bed. Her warmth was everything. Her breathing was steady, indicating she was still asleep. I cracked my eyes open a tad more and surveyed the room, taking in the small little things scattered in places throughout, staking her claim on the area.

A hair clip on the dresser. Her cochlear on the nightstand. A book on the chair in the corner. I pulled her closer to me as I buried my nose in her neck, inhaling the familiar scent of waterlilies.

Pressure on my dick had my eyes widening for a moment before looking down between us. Her hips pushed back again, rubbing her pajama clad ass against my pulsing cock. The ache in my balls told me everything I needed to know. I needed her. Now.

Groaning as she continued to grind against me, I trailed the hand that was wrapped around her front, up underneath her tank. I tweaked her nipple lightly before soothing the area with gentle strokes. Her whimper pushed all blood flow in my body down south.

With her audible encouragement, I rocked my hips slightly against her ass as I slid my tongue up her neck, hovering over her pulse point, then finishing with a nip at her jaw. Her panting began to grow heavier, matching my own. I let my hand drop from her perky nipple down the front of her sleep shorts.

Her moan was music to my ears when my fingers brushed across her clit. I gently rubbed it in tight circles, groaning as my balls began to ache even more than I thought possible.

Her whimpering settled as I pulled my fingers away from her pussy. She looked curiously over her shoulder with a furrow to her eyebrows, and a jut to her lip.

My smile was wicked as I began to pull her sleep shorts completely off. Her understanding gave her the reassurance she needed to lay on her back and lift her hips.

God, the arch of those hips granting me permission was one of the sexiest movements. And here she was, giving me the permission to absolutely destroy her.

Fuck, I was going to enjoy every second of it.

"*Please,*" she signed.

I threw the sleep shorts aside and spread her thighs wide, exposing every inch of her. Without a second thought, I held her eyes as I bent down and slid my tongue along her slit. She pushed further against my tongue, begging for friction. I smiled as I latched onto her bundle of nerves.

"You like that, baby?" My fingers struggled to get my meaning across while I was holding her slightly shaking thighs open for me.

Her head nodded quickly as legs began to quake more and more. Using some of her dripping arousal, I ran my fingers along her pussy before I shoved two fingers deep inside of her, scissoring them. If only she could have heard the mewling sounds she was making.

Pre-cum dripped from my cock as I lapped at her, soaking in every breathy moan that I pulled from her. She ran her hand through my hair before gripping tight and grinding against my face. I curled my fingers rubbed against the perfect spot that I knew would send her over.

She detonated, and ran her fingers lovingly through the strands that she nearly pulled from my scalp. I leaned into her touch and then pulled my body up over hers, planting a fierce kiss on her lips. She opened, letting my tongue slide against hers, moaning at the taste of herself. I couldn't help the rumble that came from my own chest.

After a few minutes of claiming each other's mouths with lust and love pouring from us, I pulled back and lined my cock up with her entrance.

"I love you." Her hand said between our bodies. I pecked her hand with a kiss.

"You have no idea how long I have waited for you. Years, Halen. I love you more than fucking life itself, because if there was ever a life without you. It wouldn't be a life worth living at all."

Her smile took my breath away. It was only made even more intense as I pushed myself inside of her. My eyes rolled slightly back as her pussy squeezed me.

"Fuck, baby," I said aloud, losing all sense to sign to her.

Her hand slid up my neck and her fingers rested on my mouth. She knew how to read lips so I knew she understood what I had said.

I kissed her fingertips before she dropped them and grabbed onto the sheets next to her. I reached down and began strumming her clit with my fingers as I pounded into her pussy relentlessly.

"Sawyer," she moaned out.

My eyes stayed trained on hers as her grip on the sheets clutched tighter. My balls slapped against her ass and I started to feel the tingling sensation overcome me. I was seconds away from blowing.

Slamming my lips against hers, I gave her a bruising kiss as I continued to thrust in and out so hard that the headboard was knocking against the wall. Our tongues battled for dominance and I swallowed her moans as we reached our climax.

I felt a gush flood my dick as it was throbbing and spurting ropes of cum. My final thrusts were deep and punishing. When we both were left with heavy breaths, cuddling into one another, I pulled out, watching with interest as my cun began to leak out of her swollen pussy.

Knowing she was on birth control didn't stop me from pushing some of it back in with my fingers. Her soft exhales had my eyes meeting hers again. She was smiling with such admiration. I crawled back up to her and gently brushed my lips against hers.

"Want to take a shower?"

"Yes, please. Maybe you can give me round two up against the shower walls." She winked.

"You're absolutely fucking perfect."

CHAPTER 35

-HALEN-

"So what do you plan to tell Gregory's parents exactly? Aren't you worried that they are going to tell your parents that you are pulling out?"Astrid asked, peering at me above her iced tea as she took a sip.

"Yeah, well, they are all vacationing together on some island that Gregory's father recommended." I rolled my eyes. "We are all stuck here suffering through the last few cold months while they are likely getting tans while drinking margaritas. Gregory and I are talking with them over video chat at his place. United front and all."

She moaned, leaning back in her chair as her eyes closed. "What I wouldn't do for a killer margarita right about now."

I stuffed my mouth full of the pasta in front of me, my lip tugging up at her completely bypassing the other things I had said. "I know, right. I should get some to keep at my new place. I guess I'll have to ask Saw–" my words slammed to a halt as I caught myself before finishing the sentence.

"Yeah. You're likely going to need Mr. Bennett's ID if you are planning to stock a whole wetbar's worth."

My eyes snapped to hers, wide in alarm. I stuttered around my fettuccine. "Uh, wait, wha–"

She smirked and took another bite of her salad. "No need to play dumb, Halen. I know you. Not to mention he absolutely eye-fucks you whenever he is even slightly in your vicinity."

My eyebrows shot up. "You... you know? I mean, I guess

we should probably be more discreet. You seriously can't tell a soul. There are a lot of things hanging in the balance right now."

She gave me knowing eyes. "Of course I won't say a word. I wouldn't do that. I know we have a less than pleasant past, but I've learned the importance of choosing the right people to have in my life. I'm not the same cunt that you thought you knew through the years."

"Twat, actually."

"What?" She cocked her head trying to understand.

"I thought you were a twat. In fact," I said, twirling a fork in the hair in her direction. "I called you three the twat trio."

She choked on a mouthful of lettuce and buried her face in her hands, hiding a laugh. I was glad she wasn't offended. I mean, I wasn't going to sugar coat it. Those girls were a nightmare. But admittedly, Astrid rarely actually said or did things herself. She just supported the girls who really did the dirty work.

"Speaking of, I haven't seen much of Raya. What's up with that?"

She rolled her eyes and groaned. "She's back with Chad again."

I gave her a tight smile, studying her reaction. "And how are you doing with *that*?"

She shrugged, and while I saw some lingering sadness there, it wasn't anything like how I had seen her talk about Chad before.

"He told me that he made a mistake with Raya, and he thought the grass was greener because she was willing to put out. He wanted me back."

I waited for her to continue.

"I told him to fuck off, and left him sobbing in the school parking lot. I'm nobody's second choice."

My eyes widened at her admission and I dropped my fork to my plate, sitting back to soak in her words.

"You're my fucking hero."

She gave me a wink and took another bite. I never found myself to be a person with girlfriends, but Astrid was quickly becoming a comfort in my life. Someone to lean on and talk to when life was becoming too heavy. I think we helped each other grow stronger. I needed that in my life.

After another half hour of girl talk, I checked my phone for the time and realized I needed to jet out of there.

8 Missed Texts

4 Missed Calls

Nicky: What the fuck is wrong with you?!

Nicky: We need to talk. Right fucking now.

Nicky: I mean it, Halen.

Nicky: Pick. Up. Your. Phone.

Nicky: Come over before I lose my shit.

Nicky: I really need to look you in the eyes when we have this conversation.

What the hell was he so pressed about? Likely drunk.

Teach: Hey Squid, I hope you are enjoying lunch with Astrid. I love you.

Nicky: I just spoke with Katherine, Halen. This is important. I need to know if she is speaking out of her ass.

Katherine? Oh, he could kiss my ass. I punched out a quick response, pissed at his audcaity.

Me: Interesting. You and Katherine are gossip buddies now? Cute. You can pretty much count on it being a lie. Don't text me about her again, Dominic. I mean it.

His response was immediate.

Nicky: Twerp, please... I told you it's not like that. I don't trust her either, which is why I need to hear from you that it's false.

Me: Unless you are ready to get the help that I have offered you time and time again, please leave me alone. I won't stand by and watch you self destruct. Whatever it is that she said doesn't concern you anymore.

I huffed a frustrated breath before throwing my phone in my purse. I headed to Gregory's house and knocked on his door using the obnoxiously large lion door knocker. It was weird how some people found ways to display their wealth. My parents were no exception. We had shrubs throughout the property that were in ridiculous shapes that the groundskeepers maintained weekly.

Nothing says wealth quite like triangle hedges.

The door swung open and with it a gust of something swept over my face. Loud music was blaring from inside with a song I had recognized as Tension by Conley It took me a minute to register the smell, but when I did, I just lifted my brow in question.

"Hey, Wifey."

He was sporting a pair of grey sweats and a hoodie. It was by far the most casual I had ever seen him before. The more I got to know him, the more I actually liked him. He was caught up in a world he didn't ask to be in while deep down he was just a normal human being told what to do from someone with more power. I could relate.

But not for much longer.

"You're going to be high for this? Are you really that nervous?"

He shrugged and stood aside to let me through. I gave him a fake glare and walked inside. The living room already had the laptop set up on the coffee table and aimed at the couch.

I took a seat in front of it, leaving room for Gregory.

He plopped down next to me and leaned back to stare up at the ceiling for a minute. I gave him a minute before speaking.

"I'm sorry. I'm sorry that I put you in this situation. Just know that whatever happens, you will always have a friend in me."

He dropped his head back down to look at me. I could see the emotions written on his face. Anxiety, pain, insecurity, but there were traces of admiration and love there too.

"No, Halen. Please don't be sorry. You're just doing what every trust fund kid dreams of doing. You're brave. Never lose that about yourself. Honestly, I'm not concerned about telling them as much as I am concerned with what comes next."

"What do you mean?"

"I was arranged to be with you, but what happens if I am arranged with someone terrible next? What if she is ugly? Oh god, what if she is like our mothers?" He groaned and scrubbed his hands down his face.

I barked a laugh at that thought, but covered it quickly with my hand. "Sorry, I don't mean to laugh, but that would actually be quite tragic." I grabbed his hand in both of mine. "If that happens, I promise I'll get you out of it, somehow. I know she will have big shoes to fill, but give her a chance like you gave me a chance." I winked.

Shaking his head, he huffed but squeezed my hand back. "Alright, let's do this."

The call connected, plastering both Edward and Eleanor's faces on the screen. I pinched my lips together, trying not to laugh, when I saw that they were indeed holding glasses of what looked to be frozen margaritas.

Nailed it.

"Darlings!" Eleanor nudged Edward with her arm lightly. "Don't they look like us when we were young and in love? You both make an exquisite coup–"

"Mom, that's actually why we are calling. We would like to inform you and dad of a few changes to our relationship."

I saw her smile begin to immediately slip while a different emotion swept over her face. Fear maybe. She looked cautiously over to Edward before focusing back on the screen in front of her.

"What is this about, Gregory?" Edward's tone was firm. He knew. We both knew that he knew what we were going to say.

"Right, so, we have agreed to discontinue this engagement. Halen is currently building a future with someone else." My heart began to thump loudly in my chest but Gregory continued. "I support her completely."

I grabbed his hand and gave a thankful squeeze, but didn't let go. His presence was the only thing keeping me grounded for this conversation. Especially as silence, minus the sound of waves in the background, filtered through the speakers.

"What the fuck do you mean?! Miss Knox, what has your father had to say about this? I haven't spoken with him yet today as he and your mother are out on the catamaran. But believe me, I intend to."

I cleared my throat, trying to muster as much courage as possible. "Well, they don't exactly know. We wanted to give you the respect of informing you first. This is my choice, not Gregory's. He would have fully gone through with the arrangement. It's me who is breaking it. When you relay that information to my parents, you can also tell them that I am no longer living under their roof."

Edward's face began to flush red, and I could tell he was about to lose his shit. I decided to be the bad guy as much as possible to spare Gregory from his father's wrath as best as I could.

"Thanks for hearing me out Mr. and Mrs. Jaffly. I appreciate it. I wish you and your family the best."

"Young lady, you can't ju–"

I clicked the end call button on the laptop and heard Gregory's long release of breath.

"You okay?" I asked.

"I will be. I have plans to meet up with the guys and get shit faced. I'll need an alibi for the missed calls from my father so I figure blaming it on his friends' sons is the best possible way."

"You mean Vesper, Kyle and Jafar?"

He laughed and shook his head at me. "Zafar."

"Nah," I waved a hand dismissively. "I've decided to stick

with Jafar. He looks like a villain already, so it fits better. So does Vesper, but his name already has villain vibes so he can keep his."

That earned me another laugh.

"I'll make sure to pass that little nugget of information along to him tonight." There was a pause as he considered his next words carefully. "Don't lose touch, okay? Keep me in the loop with how you and Sawyer are doing."

I gave him the biggest hug I could manage and kissed his cheek. "I promise."

CHAPTER 36

-SAWYER-

I poured the coffee in my travel mug and Halen's coffee mug. I planned to drink mine on the go since I wanted to knock some grading out in the classroom. Today was the day that I was going to officially submit my resignation. Halen had taken a huge leap of faith by moving out of her house and cutting off her engagement with Gregory. It was time for me to do my part in giving us a real shot.

"Halen, your coffee is ready!"

I finished gathering my things, as I remembered that she said she was going to sneak in some reading this morning before school. If she followed the rules we agreed on, then she wasn't wearing her cochlear.

I walked in the bedroom to find her snuggled up amongst a ton of pillows, clutching onto her book as her eyes swept across the page.

I waved a hand, snagging her attention.

"I'm heading out. Are you sure you don't want to ride with me?"

She shook her head at me. *"It's not a good idea. Someone might see. Also, I'm just getting to the good part in this book. I'll just meet you there, Mr. Bennett."*

My cock jumped in my pants at the casual use of my professional name. Though we knew it was nothing casual for her. The red tint of her cheeks told me she knew exactly what she was doing.

"Don't be late, Miss Knox. I would hate to give you detention and smack your little ass with a paddle."

Her eyes widened before she smiled at me, biting her lip.

"I love you," I signed.

"I love you, too."

The drive to school was easy enough with little to no traffic. The gloominess of the winter was finally starting to disappear as the sun made its appearance. It was the start to a beautiful day.

Don't Go by Letterday was blaring through my car speakers as I pulled into one of the spaces of the faculty lot. A few teachers were making their way inside, likely here early for the same reason as I was.

I made my way through the empty halls until I reached my door and slipped inside, closing it behind me. Going through my same routine as I did every morning, except for the days when Halen didn't show, I prepped my classroom for the first class period and did some grading.

I suffered through an essay about The Scarlet Letter which consistently referenced how *Hester was done so dirty and totes shouldn't have been cancelled like that* and that she was truthfully a *total icon*. I rubbed my brows, trying to decide on the best way to grade this essay. At least the student put in the effort to read and understand the book.

The sun was still shining through the glass, putting me in a good mood for the warmer weather ahead in the coming months when the ball rang, and students started piling into the classroom.

I reached for my phone to sneak a text off to Halen, making sure she made it to school safely. I stood in the hallway, greeting students as they entered.

"Hey there, stud. It's been a minute. Haven't seen you at happy hour lately."

Ellen gave me a smile and greeted a kid walking by us that must have been one of her current students.

"Yeah, I've been meaning to," *Lie*. "Life has been kind of busy. Though I see Brent when I can. Speaking of, I heard that you both have been hitting it off. Congratulations. He is a great guy."

She straightened her spine and faced me full on with a broad smile. "He's talked about me?" Her eyes lit up like all she wanted was to be wanted. Poor thing. "Nothing exclusive has been discussed yet, but I have been enjoying his company lately."

"Maybe consider asking him to the botanical garden downtown one of these weekends. It's one of his favorite places to visit, and it's actually perfect for a unique date."

She nodded and gave me a nudge. "He's lucky to have you. You get an A plus for your wingman duties."

I gave her a smirk and held up my hands in fake surrender. " I have no idea what you are talking about Ms. Ferrier."

A few other boys grabbed Ellen's attention, asking about an assignment, but it was clear that they were using it as an opportunity to sneak a peek at her rack.

I shook my head and pulled out my phone from my pocket as the last of the students in the hallway made their way to class.

Halen hadn't responded for a few minutes and I started to get antsy, until I saw her walking with Astrid through the hallway, deep in conversation.

She glanced back at my classroom door to find me watching her with a heated gaze and gave me a wink before carrying on with her conversation.

God, I loved this girl.

I sat at my desk as I ate some leftover steak and potatoes from the night before and typed out a meeting request for today with Derek. Given that he was the principal, I knew he would be busy, but I made sure to emphasize that it was a pressing matter and would only take a few minutes of his time.

I printed the resignation letter and placed it in an envelope so I was ready to go at any minute. Right as I took my last bite, the door opened and none other than Katherine James walked in.

Her pink heels clacked on the floor as she made her way to my desk, a cheshire smile stretching across her face. I didn't like what was about to happen. Not even a little bit. I held my neutral gaze on hers before finally asking the question that I knew was going to bite me in the ass.

"How can I help you Miss James?"

She stopped in front of my desk while I tucked away my empty lunch bag into the desk drawer. She bit her lip, clearly contemplating something but straightened her spine and met my gaze head on.

"I just thought that maybe I would be a good girl, and give you a heads up about something that is currently in the hands of Dominic Ressner. You are innocent in this after all." She looked at me from under her lashes and gave me a smirk.

There was nothing good in this girl's body. From everything that Halen had shared with me, it was clear that she made bullying a blood sport. She couldn't stand not being the center of attention for any given moment, so she created madness around her to maintain power.

"Okay? I assume you aren't wanting me to spend my afternoon guessing. Care to elaborate on what it is that Mr. Ressner currently has?"

She twisted a lock of her hair between her fingers, putting on the absolute worst innocent act I have ever seen. After a few moments of silence, she finally opened her mouth.

"Dominic has been pulling away from me lately. He goes through waves of throwing a pity party, claiming he wants to be better. For himself, Evan, and Halen." She scoffed at the mention of Halen's name. "Then the next moment, he is floating through his own ecstasy, seeking comfort from me, as he should."

I continued to stay silent, trying to figure out where this was going.

"Well, yesterday he decided it was the final straw and he wanted to put down the drugs, the alcohol, and worst of all, *me*. That simply wasn't going to do. I've been waiting for this moment, you see. Halen didn't deserve Evan, and she doesn't deserve Dominic all the same."

I most definitely didn't like where this was going, but I clenched my fists trying to calm myself as I listened to her delusional speech about being second best to Halen ever since she had moved here.

"Anyway, I'm not letting him go. He is *mine*. Mine! He just needed a little push to see what a stupid little whore Halen is so he could finally let her trashy ass go. He will never forgive her now. I'm just so sorry that you also got swept up in it. I tried to hide your face as much as possible, but it was hard trying to get a good visual behind the door without being spotted."

"Miss James, I am going to need you to clarify. Now."

"I may have sent a video to Dominic, showcasing exactly the kind of skank he has been spiraling over. I'll tell you what, the choking sounds alone while she sucked you off is absolutely going to break him. And guess who he will run to. *Me*."

I shook my head in disbelief. A sweat had broken out over my skin as I contemplated the consequences. This was the second time that Halen and I's relationship was at risk and just like with Victoria, I couldn't let it implicate Halen.

The only difference now was that the evidence was literally in the hands of someone else. Not only that, but I hadn't had a chance to put in my resignation yet. I wasn't going to let this childish girl try to intimidate me. She had no idea who she was messing with.

"I think that will be all, Miss James. Please remove yourself from my classroom."

Her scrunched eyebrows told me I had definitely surprised her with my calm reaction. I wasn't going to give her my worries or any ammunition to use against Halen. She could fuck right off.

She dropped the innocent act altogether and turned her back to me, walking towards the door before stopping and looking back at me over her shoulder. "Tell your girlfriend that as of today, I have everything that she ever wanted. Maybe after graduation, I'll come for *you* next. Toodles, Mr. Bennett."

I waited a few minutes, digesting the information completely before jumping up and pacing the classroom. If I could change my official resignation, effective at the end of the day today, it would be fine. No harm, no foul. Well, maybe a little bit of foul, but nothing that could hurt Halen's admission into Gallaudet.

I just needed Derek to confirm that meeting. Snatching the phone out of my pocket, I checked my email. Relief flooded over me as I read the confirmation that he had an hour of empty time towards the end of the day.

It would be okay. I would just blame my resignation on a family emergency and use up my PTO, with the coverage of a substitute teacher, until they were able to secure another permanent teacher for the remainder of the year.

I pocketed my phone and exhaled a breath as I walked over to the windows and looked out at the beautiful day beyond the glass. I was itching to grab my sketchbook, but I knew I only had half an hour left of my free period. Not enough time to fully invest in what I wanted to capture.

I was so focused on what my future was going to look like, that it took me a few moments to register what I had heard.

Pop. Pop. Pop.

CHAPTER 37

-HALEN-

"Can you shelve these last few stacks, dear? After that, our return pile is empty, so you are more than welcome to make yourself comfortable somewhere with your book.

I gave Mrs. Lowell a smile and nodded before grabbing the cart with the remaining stacks. "Sure thing! Also, I meant to tell you, I placed the list of the damaged and missing books on your desk. I can place an order for replacements at the end of the week if you would like. Just let me know."

She crossed her arms over her chest and smiled brightly at me. "You're doing so much of my own job for me that I don't even know what to do with myself most days. It's going to be hard to replace you when you graduate. Do you have an order form for *that*?"

I chuckled. "Actually, I just might." She lifted her eyebrows in surprise. "Do you know who Astrid Baker is?"

She thought about it for a second before nodding. "Ah yes, I have seen her here and there through the years. Not much of a reader though."

I shook my head. "No, she isn't. But her little sister, Kayla is quite the nerd. I think she would love a position like this. She will be attending as a freshman next year. If you aren't against it, I can mention it to Astrid to gauge Kayla's interest."

"That sounds wonderful. Here you go again, taking tasks off of my plate." She gave me a faux glare before smirking and walking to her desk. I continued pushing the cart around the library as I restocked all of the returns.

Finishing within only a couple minutes, as I knew the library like the back of my hand, I grabbed my current book. I unplugged from the sound around me, and sat by the window like I always did.

The sun was warm on my face through the glass as I immersed myself into the story where I had left off. There was captivating romance and mystery, which kept me on my toes as I flipped from one page to the next.

I had held my bladder off long enough by the time I had finished a handful of chapters. Standing up, I set my book down, plugged my cochlear back in, and walked by Mrs. Lowell as I signed, *restroom.* She didn't know sign language but she knew a few basic ones that I had taught her just to make things easier.

She gave me a nod and went back to her business at her desk. The hallways were quiet as I walked along the white tiled floor. It wasn't quiet in the sense of sound as even the lightbulbs in the ceiling had a mechanical hum at all times, but in the way that there wasn't a soul in sight. It was still lunch period for some students and others were still in the middle of their classes.

I walked into the restroom and relieved myself, taking extra time at the sink to wash my hands and fix my appearance. My curls were actually looking decent. They dried out severely during the winter months, but as the temperature outside began to creep up, the dry and frizzy look thankfully began to calm down.

I walked back out into the hallway and got lost in thought as I ran my index finger along the lockers as I passed them. I traced the cool metal as I walked, imagining what Sawyer was doing at that moment.

He must have read my mind, because in that exact moment, I could feel my phone vibrate in the back pocket of my black skinny jeans. I paused my steps and pulled out my phone to see a missed call from Sawyer. Assuming it would be more discreet, I opted to text him back instead of returning his call.

Me: I was just thinking of you. Sorry I missed your call. I was in the restroom.

Teach: Where the hell are you?!

Scrunching my brows, I looked up and around me, trying to decide if I should just head to his classroom. Not wanting to bother him if he was in a teacher meeting or grading, I decided against it and responded.

Me: I'm in the hallway of the *elective wing*. Why?

Teach: Halen, listen to me, I need you to find a hiding space.

Teach: NOW!

Teach: I'll come find you.

Teach: HIDE!

The text came in seconds after one another, setting me more on edge with each one. I looked up and around me again, lost in confusion. Hide? Where the hell did he want me to hide, and for what reason?

Right as I was trying to figure it out, a yellow flashing light began illuminating the wall, rotating and flashing. An alarm rang out that had me wincing in pain from the sharp sounds.

I froze, trying to remember if that was the color for the fire alarm. It would have been stupid to hunker down in a building that is literally on fire. I stood rooted to my spot, weighing my options. Trusting his judgement, I saw a utility closet to my right and rushed inside.

Me: Sawyer, what's happening? There is a yellow light flashing in the hallway, but I don't know what it's for. It's not a fire, right? I don't want to burn to death.

Teach: Where are you hiding? I'm coming for you, baby. Active shooter.

Me: Cleaning closet. Across from the senior lockers. The one next to Mr. Young's class.

My phone buzzed again, and I was fully expecting it to be Sawyer, but felt a pang of pain as I saw who it actually was.

Dominic: Where are you?

Bile crept up my throat as I fully absorbed what Sawyer was telling me. A fucking shooter was in the school, and he was just wandering around out there trying to find me! What the hell was he thinking?

I shot off a quick reply to Nicky, telling him where I was and that I was safe before quickly opening up the text thread to Sawyer.

Me: Don't you dare leave your classroom to come find me. It's too dangerous!

He didn't respond for several minutes and my heart began thudding in my chest. I didn't want to risk getting shot by stepping in the hallway, but I wasn't going to sit around letting my thoughts go wild as Sawyer was in danger.

Not a fucking chance.

A moment later, I heard the click of a handle turning and bright light lit up the utility closet as the door to the closet was opened. My skin broke out in goosebumps as my panic skyrocketed.

It wasn't until I met the ocean blue eyes that belonged only to the man I was in love with, that I dropped my shoulders in relief. He quickly shut the door behind him and kneeled down in front of me, embracing me in a tight hug. His breathing ragged.

"Thank Christ," he murmured.

Pop. Pop. Pop. Pop. Pop.

This was the first time I was actually able to hear the gunshots. Whoever it was that was shooting was clearly making their way through the school quickly. Sawyer and I sat knee to knee, listening to the occasional series of gunshots followed by thundering footsteps of students running.

Screaming from the hallway outside of the door had me nearly hyperventilating as I clutched Sawyer's hands in mine, squeezing hard. The screech of a young girl just outside of the door pierced my ear. It was deafening, even with a slab of wood between us.

Sawyer's jaw was clenched tight, battling a war within

himself on what he needed to do. It wasn't until his jaw tightened impossibly harder that I saw he had come to a conclusion. His face was a void as if he tucked away his emotions into a box and shut it tight.

I could tell with every twitch of his fingers that he wanted to jump outside of the door and help the girl. I knew what he was thinking. We didn't have a weapon. Going out there would only put us right in the line of fire with no defense.

The sounds of a wailing cry pushed me over the edge as I let sobs rip from my body. I threw a hand over my mouth, trying to stifle the sounds I was making, desperate not to give away our position.

"Please, please, please! No! Help me, I don't want to die," a feminine voice pleaded.

Pop. Pop.

More cries and begging from boys and girls alike hit my ears. I started to hyperventilate just as I saw Sawyer's hands reach up, running his fingers through my hair, and tug the cochlear implants from my ears.

All the sounds of the suffering students around me ceased as I was plunged into silence. My eyes locked onto Sawyers as he was fully focused on me, showing as little fear as possible in his expression. I didn't really know if he was naturally brave or if he was just being brave for me.

I envied him either way.

I saw the light flinch of his shoulders at the same time that his fingers twitched in mine. It was subtle, but not enough for me to miss. I slid one of my hands out from his, and reached behind me to press my hand against the wall of the closet, in search of vibrations. Before my hand could make contact, Sawyer snatched it away, causing my eyes to snap back to his.

The sad shake of his head and single tear running down his face told me everything I needed to know. He was trying to protect me from the trauma of truly knowing what was happening on the other side of the door. He didn't have that capability. He was hearing it all.

CHAPTER 38

-SAWYER-

"Someone, please help me!" The voice of a male student pierced my heart at the same time that a tear escaped my eye. I was trying so hard to put on a front for Halen, to keep her calm. Little did she know I was just as horrified as her. Itching to run out that door to help the students that were likely bleeding out on the floor.

I couldn't do it. I couldn't risk her. If it was just me in this room, I would have marched out there, gun in hand or not, and tried my best to neutralize the threat. But putting her in danger was out of the question, especially when we didn't know who all was out there and if there was even more than one shooter.

"Wait, wait, wait! I can give you mone–," the voice said before it was silenced with the echoing sounds of gunshots. The weapon sounded like a pistol, loud enough that I could tell it wasn't a .22 caliber. I hadn't heard any signs of a shotgun so at least there was some chance that these kids would survive.

Halen's whimpers brought me back to the girl sitting in front of me. She couldn't hear after I removed her implants. It was an attempt at trying to spare her from the memories of hearing her fellow students beg to be spared.

I couldn't stop my flinching at each shot that rang out, which caused her to react based on my reaction. I was doing a terrible job at keeping her mind blank.

"Halen!"

My head snapped to the door as my eyebrows furrowed in confusion. I must have been hearing things, clearly starting to lose my shit with all the violence around us, maybe tinnitus that was playing tricks on me.

"Halen, where are you?!" The familiar voice echoed through the hall and into the supply closet where we were tucked away.

My eyes met Halen's tentatively where I found her already staring at me, studying my face. She lingered for a moment, doing what she does best, by peering into my very thoughts.

Before I could stop her, she reached over and snatched one of her cochlears off of the ground beside us. I gripped her wrist as quietly as possible in a plea to get her to stop, but she was adamant.

She plugged back in, cocking her head to the side, trying to hear what it was that had obviously caught my attention. I begged her with my eyes, but she knew whatever I didn't want her to hear was something big.

I had a hunch. A really bad fucking hunch as to what I would find beyond the door. Even if I was wrong in my assumption, and the person was just trying to get to the same safety she was in, it was still a risk to expose her hiding spot.

This was a lose-lose situation, regardless of how this played out. Her heart was going to break either way unless the shooter had moved on to a different area within the last twenty seconds.

Doubtful.

"Halen, please, come out! It's safe!"

Halen's eyes widened and met mine. Tears were freely running down her face as she registered who was calling out for her. I began to shake my head at her, gripping her hands hard. Begging.

I knew the moment that she had made up her mind. I saw the pain that flashed in her expression along with the urgency to get out there.

"No. Please, baby!" I whisper shouted at her.

"He could get hurt! I can't let him die, Sawyer! I can't

lose him too. I won't do it!"

She jumped up from the ground as I tried to grab at her. She was so quick, so eager to help her friend. I could feel the potential possibilities that would come if she were to open the door. None of them were good.

"Wait!" I jumped up behind her as she swung the door open and walked out into the hallway without a second thought.

Her loud gasp met my ears as she took in the scattered bloody bodies littering the hallway floors. Blood spatter stood out against the lockers and walls like a super fucked up version of a Jackson Pollock painting.

She gagged, trying to wrangle her disgust and pain. She finally ripped her gaze from the bodies of different students to meet the eyes of her best friend who happened to be wielding a pistol.

Dominic Ressner.

Extra clips to his gun were peeking out from the multiple pockets of his cargo pants. He came prepared for this, and it's clear he also came prepared to take far more than one life.

I stepped fully out from the closet, trying to reach Halen so I could push her behind me. Ressner's arm that was holding the gun flew up and pointed in my direction the moment he recognized who I was.

"Wait, Nicky! What the hell are you doing?"

I raised my hands in the air slowly, as a show of surrender at the same time that Halen did. Thankfully, I could clearly tell that the gun wasn't pointed at her. Instead it was pointed slightly to her right. At *me*.

"You piece of shit motherfucker," he snarled.

It took everything in me not to flinch as he gripped the pistol harder, jerking it towards me in aggression. "You fucking pedophile. She was *not* yours to touch."

I couldn't help the glance to my left, right into the face of the woman I fully intended on marrying, having children with, and dying old with. Her brows furrowed as she looked in my direction, question in her eyes.

"Katherine sent him a video of us, um," I cleared my throat, drawing all the confidence I could while having a gun fully directed at me. "We were in my classroom. You were blowing me." I whispered the last part, trying not to enrage the already fucking crazy person in front of me.

Halen sucked in a sharp breath and stood straighter, thoughts clearly battling for space in her head. After a few moments, her eyes finally landed on Ressner. Narrowed in anger. "He is not a pedophile, Nicky. We love each other."

He snapped his attention to her, eyebrows raised for just a moment before a fierce expression took over. "What the hell, Halen? What the fuck do you mean you *love him*?" He said the last part in a mocking tone.

"I mean that we love each other. We live together. He didn't take advantage of me. But that is not the point, Nicky. Why the fuck are you hurting innocent people?" She choked on the words, but powered through. "Please don't tell me it was some ridiculous war path you set yourself on because you thought my teacher was sexually assaulting me."

Her hands shook, still suspended in the air just as mine was.

She continued. "You–You've *killed* people." Her voice broke and I saw that his hand holding the weapon wavered slightly, but he regained his determination.

"I originally came here with the intention of killing this stupid dick, and Katherine. But when I got here, people got in my way, people that were horrible humans. Half of our school is filled with assholes that are probably better off meeting the slap of my bullet. The world is a better place without them."

My eyes narrowed to slits. Feeling braver than I actually was, I spoke. "What does that make you then? God? Or someone who needs to meet the slap of your own bullet?"

He took a menacing step forward, pulling at his hair with his other hand. "No, you fuck. God gave me an opportunity to not just confront you, but to also confront all of the other idiots gracing these halls."

"Nicky, no. This is so wrong," she cried. "Please just put the gun down. I will never forgive you if you hurt Sawyer. Please."

"You are mine, Halen. Always have been. I know I upset you by involving myself with Katherine. I know you were jealous. I'm sorry for that. I am cutting all the toxic people out of my life, and I'll cut them out of your life too while I am at it."

His eyes met mine, cold and empty.

"Nicky, I wasn't jealous. I was disappointed. Katherine has been bullying me since moving here. I was hurt that associating yourself with her was so easy for you when you knew the toll it took on me over the years."

"Well, you should be happy to know that she won't be tormenting you anymore," he said plainly.

She cocked her head to the side, her eyes dancing over his face. "What do you mean?"

He shifted on his feet nervously before jerking his head in the direction behind him. Halen leaned her body to the side slightly to peer around him. I did the same, enough to see what he wanted her to, but not enough to startle him into pulling the trigger.

Halen's hand slapped over her mouth on a sharp inhale. "Oh my god."

My eyes finally found the particular body he wanted her to see, slumped against the wall. Her eyes were open, staring at nothing. Blood lightly dripped from the ends of her hair. I followed the trail upwards to the hole right in her temple.

Katherine James.

Police vehicles could be heard in the distance, growing louder. They must have had their feet all the way on the accelerator because the escalating volume of their sirens grew by the second.

"Alright, well, as much fun as this has been, I'm done dragging this out. Any last words, you pedo prick?"

Knowing this was my last moment, I looked at Halen,

wanting her face to be the last one I saw. "I love you so much, Squid. Don't beat yourself up about this. It wasn't your fault. I'll see you again when you are old and grey."

A pained whimper escaped her, and as quick as lightning she jumped towards me, throwing her arms around my neck, laying a kiss on my lips that was full of heartbreak and pain.

Our teeth clacked together as her body jolted towards mine. I didn't even register the sounds at first. I was so focused on her touch that I didn't care about my inevitable demise at the hands of her best friend.

Everything finally came together in my mind. Her position, the pops, the jolting of her body against mine. When I released her lips from mine and looked deep into her eyes, the emotion in hers only displayed one thing.

Pain.

CHAPTER 39

-HALEN-

Searing pain forced its way through my back. Two spots of pure hellfire. I leaned back, arms still wrapped around Sawyer's neck. A pained whimper left my mouth before I could stop it.

"Oh, fuck! Oh shit. Halen, baby. No. It was an accident. No! Shit!" Nicky's manic voice sounded almost as if he were underwater but I didn't dare tear my eyes from Sawyer's.

My ears were still slightly ringing from the sound of the gun releasing the two bullets. I held on tight, in shock, and searched Sawyer's eyes which were wide with horror. His mouth hung open in pure anguish.

"I– I need t–to sit," I said through the pain.

Sawyer nodded frantically and sank slowly down to his knees before adjusting to sitting on the floor, taking me with him. He never let his eyes leave mine as he cradled me in his arms. The warmth of his body was more comforting than ever.

I could hear the repetitive muttering of Nicky in the background but I tried to ignore it as I processed all that was happening. I knew I had been shot. I knew I was experiencing pain. However, it hadn't quite set in that I was in a life or death situation.

When reality finally hit, I realized with brutal certainty what my future would be. I would take my last breath in this hallway. My face would be splashed on the news with fuck knows how many others, in memoriam. Candles would be lit outside of the school for the victims who were injured and lost their lives. When searching my name on the internet, the only thing that would populate would be the tragic events that took place today.

I felt shivers radiate throughout my body as my spine began to seize. I could feel my fists slowly clenching beyond my control. I focused my attention fully on trying to release the tension in my hands, but no amount of concentration helped.

Sawyer's eyes trailed down to my hands, catching on to where my attention was focused. I was dying. My body was on the defense, trying to save itself. He lifted his hand that was cradled on my back and brought it forward to inspect. Deep red covered his entire palm.

Warm thick blood trailed down his forearm as he looked at it as if it was a nuke. A pained cough pushed past my lips which had his attention snapping back to me. He placed his hand firmly back on the wound, smarting my back.

"Ah, fuck," I cried.

"I'm sorry, baby. I'm so fucking sorry. I'm here, okay? Help is coming. I can hear the sirens."

I sobbed as I started to feel a numbness take over my legs. To pass the seconds until an ambulance could reach me, I counted every freckle and stubbled beard hair that I could on Sawyer's face. He was beautiful.

I felt a hand cradle my cheek. Through blurry vision, I saw Nicky's face come into view. Torment was written over every feature. I thought he was broken before. I was so very wrong. *This* version of him was undoubtedly broken. Any part of me that felt he could be healed was officially squashed. Killing me would eat him alive.

"Halen, fuck... please forgive me. It wasn't meant for y–"

His words cut off as I felt my body jostle and Nicky's hand torn from my face as his grunt met my ears.

"Get the fuck off of her! You will never touch her again. You can snort and ingest all the drugs you want, but you will never forget the fact that you *murdered* the only person in this world that loved you unconditionally."

So much venom dripped from Sawyer's words, but my

brain only latched onto one thing. *Murdered.* Past tense. He fully believed I was going to die. He didn't say 'hurt' or 'nearly killed'. No, he had already accepted my fate. That was almost as brutal of a blow as the bullet itself.

"I'm dying, aren't I?" I asked in a whisper, my breaths choppy.

I saw his throat bob through a thick swallow as I felt his fingers slightly tighten around me. "Yeah baby, I think you're dying." The crack of his voice heartwrenching.

I saw the mental toll it took on him to admit that. I kept my eyes on his, tracing his furrowing brows and wobbling chin.

I nodded.

My attention from Sawyer was ripped away when Nicky's voice echoed through the hallway. It could have just been an echo in my own ears given that everything sounded distorted, but I couldn't quite tell.

"I am going to make this right, Twerp. I'm going to be there first, welcoming you with a hug alongside Evan so you won't be so scared. I have always been there for you, and won't stop now. So that's what I intend to do."

It took more energy than I was willing to admit as I turned my head to face Nicky, his nearly black eyes trained on mine, full of sorrow.

"I'm so sorry, baby. Don't be scared. I love you so much."

He raised the pistol in his hand up to his temple, holding for a moment as his eyes moved quickly back and forth, studying my face, like he was committing every detail to memory.

My brows pinched together in confusion, trying to register what he was saying. Seeing the pistol resting against his temple snapped me out of my haze, as I silently prayed that he would listen to reason.

"No! Nic–"

Pop.

Red exploded from the side of Nicky's temple as the

bullet traveled through one side of his skull and out the other. Blood spatter painted the lockers to his right. His body immediately collapsed to the ground. A howling cry unleashed from my body, using up all the energy I had left to give to this world.

No.

"No," I cried. "No, Nicky!"

I grasped onto Sawyer's arm as he pulled me close, hugging me tightly to him. His whispers in my ear felt hazy and I couldn't tell if the blood loss was causing auditory hallucinations.

"Squid, I need you to listen. You *cannot* die on me. Please. I won't survive it. I need you to really fight, okay? How else are we going to get married, you graduate from Gallaudet, and have babies? You need to start fucking fighting." His voice cracked, shattering my heart alongside it.

Tears fell down my cheeks as his words pricked my heart. I was trying. I didn't want to die, but the pull to sleep was so powerful. Definitely more powerful than an eighteen year old girl fighting massive blood loss.

"I'm trying. I w–want babies with you. I want it a–all." I said through the pain. "Even if I don't m–make it, please know that I l–l–love you. Don't beat yourself up about this. It wasn't your–r fault. I'll see you again when you are old and grey." The last few words came out gurgled as the taste of pennies filled my mouth.

I choked, my lungs starting to burn, as I heaved a cough. Through the blurriness of my vision, I watched in sadness as blood sprayed across Sawyer's face with the action. Though he didn't move a muscle to wipe it away.

His wailing cry pierced my ears, but the absolute devastation of him understanding my words had me tearing out my implants, submerging myself in complete silence to avoid the heartbreak of his screams. The last sounds I had heard was a mixture of wailing of the one I loved, and sirens that wouldn't find me in time.

I continued to watch his face, understanding what

Nicky was trying to achieve in his last moments. He was looking for peace and courage. I coughed again, as blood trailed down the sides of my mouth.

It dawned on me that he was going to lose me very similarly to how he lost the only other woman that he truly loved. His mother. I sent a prayer up that he would seek therapy and that Connor would step up for him.

I silently took in Sawyer's face as his crying turned to rage and screaming. His eyes bounced between mine and the hallway, his words clear as day even in the quiet.

"Somebody fucking help," he screamed out to the hallway of bodies.

Eyes on me.

"Electives hallway!"

Frantically searching.

"Fuck, please!"

Eyes on me.

This time his eyes never left mine.

The song I Found by Amber Run played through my mind, likely a coping mechanism for the loss of control that was overwhelming me. I had heard the song earlier in the day and couldn't get it out of my head. I didn't realize then what comfort it would bring. My eyes rolled back slightly, trailing the bright fluorescent lighting in the ceiling.

A light shake of my body jerked my focus back to Sawyer's. His hand cradling my cheek, as he spoke words I lost the capability to understand without my implant.

My eyeballs shuttered, trying hard to focus on a single point, but failing. Seeing the ruin of his expression, I brought my painfully clenched hand up to my cheek over his. Knowing speaking would only paint him in more blood, I hummed the song that was dancing inside of my head, trying to calm him.

"I love you. I love you. I love you," he mouthed as he planted kisses on my lips, his coming back bloody. As pain began to fully fade away from my body. I managed to give him a smile. Blood likely coated my teeth, but I needed him to know

I wasn't scared anymore.

With every ounce I had left, I pressed the remaining energy into shifting my fingers on his that covered my cheek.

"I love you," I weakly signed.

My lids pulled down against my will as darkness seeped into my vision from all sides, pushing me into the death that I knew would haunt him forever.

CHAPTER 40

-SAWYER-

A scream tore from my throat, uncaring of who saw. Bile burned my esophagus as I tried not to vomit from the agony overtaking me. Taking a moment, I looked at the path of destruction that surrounded me.

Bodies.

So many bodies laid lifeless, riddled with bullet holes. No different than the best person in the entire world currently cradled in my arms.

Looking back down at her eerily still body, I let the tears keep falling. Noises that sounded so unfamiliar continued to tear from my chest.

I read somewhere that sometimes when you lose a loved one, your body creates a distinct horrifying wailing sound that's called keening. I understood now.

It wasn't until I saw movement out of my peripheral vision. My eyes snapped over to see a handful of officers clearing the area and two paramedics carrying a stretcher, looking over the horrific sight in front of them. Their mouths hung open as they studied the carnage. The officers continued their sweep, doing their best to ignore the trail of bodies.

"SAVE HER! FUCKING SAVE HER!"

The middle aged woman jumped at my harsh demand, her eyes quickly training on Halen in my arms. She quickly switched into rescue mode and ran my way, but halted again as the police called out.

"Hold! We have to clear the area before any life saving measures can be made," a rookie looking cop shouted to the paramedic.

I felt the growling begin to vibrate through me as I considered ripping out his throat. Biting back my ire, I tried to use reason instead, hoping it would get Halen help quicker.

“The shooter is fucking down! Right over here, holding the gun,” I quickly snapped at the officer.

Looking back at the woman, and her male co-worker who looked no more than a few years older than Halen, I yelled again, my voice cracking. “PLEASE HELP HER!”

The younger man looked at the woman, his lips tightening into a thin line. “Fuck it.” He rushed over to us just as the woman made up her mind as well and hurried our way.

The man started barking out things I didn’t quite understand as he began assessing and working on her, communicating with his partner. “Starting intubation, keep bagging her as I prep,” he said quickly as he shoved everything on a sterile pad.

I was surprised at his confidence and concentration at his young age. He seemed to know what he was doing more than the woman who had likely been doing this for longer.

The woman squeezed the bag rhythmically, then stopped as the man performed his intubation. The sight of the tube shoved down Halen’s throat made my heart crack, but it also gave me hope that they could bring her back.

“Roll her with me! One, two, roll.” Halen's body was turned to her side as they used a pair of scissors to cut away the shirt covering her back. After a moment of bandaging her wounds, they placed her on the stretcher and walked with urgency, dodging the bodies on the ground that were beyond saving.

Jumping into the ambulance, I watched as they continued working on her. The man pried her eyelids open and flashed a light in them to gause pupil response. "Hey, sweet girl, my name is Remi. I need you to fight like hell for me. Can you do that?"

No response.

"She's deaf," I said in a voice that sounded like gravel.

The young man, Remi, continued talking to her in a soothing tone as the ambulence sped through traffic.

"I have healed soldiers way closer to death's door than you. So don't lose hope. Keep fighting."

I was frozen, glancing between my hands covered in her blood and her chest that was rising and falling with the breaths only maintained by the paramedics.

We made it to the hospital in record time. They rushed her back to surgery immediately as I stood, watching the doors she disappeared through. A nurse shortly came my way with Halen's bloodied belongings in a bioazard bag.

"Are you the immediate family of Halen Knox?"

Knowing I wasn't going to be able to see her or be told anything by her doctors, I felt no shame in lying. If anything, it was a delayed truth.

"She's my wife."

Her brows furrowed but didn't question me further, seeing the heartbreak written all over my face.

"She is in the OR being worked on right now. Here are her personal belongings for safe keeping. Do you need any medical attention?"

I shook my head, and grabbed the bloodied items.

"Thank you," I whispered and turned away, finding a seat in the waiting area. The sounds of families crying, shuffling papers, and the squeek of sneakers on vinyl floors echoed through the space. I tuned it out, though. All I heard was the was the gurgling sound of Halen choking on her own blood as I held her.

Repeat.

I wasn't sure how long my eyes watched the doors, unblinking, but my attention faltered as I felt her phone buzz from inside the bag.

Pulling it out, I immediately scanned through the large number of texts and missed calls, skipping to the most recent one.

Gregory: Please answer me. I'm outside of the school

but there are too many people here to find you. It's chaos. Where are you?

Not feeling an ounce of jealousy at this moment, I sent a text back from her phone with her location, before scrolling through the other messages.

Astrid: Are you okay? People are saying they saw you get into an ambulance! Were you shot?! Please call me back.

Flashbacks forced my eyes closed as I tried to hold back my tears. Not knowing how to respond, I clicked out of the messages and tried to calm my rapid breaths.

"Fuck," I whisperd, pinching the bridge of my nose.

An hour later, I heard a panicked snarling voice echo through the waiting area. Familiarity had my eyes looking around, trying to locate the source.

"She's my fucking fiance! What the fuck do you mean you can't share any information with me? Do you know who I am?! I will have your job before you can say wh–," his eyes caught mine mid sentence but didn't bother to finish his screaming match with the nurse.

He rushed over to me, worry etched over his features as he took in my appearance, covered in blood. "Is she okay? What the hell happened?" He rushed out.

I shook my head, and buried my face in my hands, sobbing. I felt his hand rest on my shoulder as I worked my way through this wave of sadness. After composing myself again, I looked at him. "She's in surgery. She was shot twice by Dominic Ressner. I tried to save her. I tried."

His face drained of color as he stumbled back a step.

"I tried," I repeated. "It's bad, Gregory. She wasn't fucking breathing. I tried. I tried. I tried. I tried." My resolve broke as my cries echoed around me, mixed with the sounds of other people crying for their hurt or dead loved ones.

Gregory fell into the seat beside me and squeezed my shoulder again as my body shook. Minutes passed and I sat straight again and looked over at him to see him staring into space, tears falling down his face. He didn't say a word.

We sat there in silence for hours. Neither of us said a thing as we waited, and waited some more.

When a doctor entered the lobby, we eyed him to see what name he would call.

"Family of Halen Knox?" The doctor called out to the masses of people.

Gregory and I both jumped out of our seats and rushed to the doctor wearing a neutral expression. "Here! We are the family of Halen!"

He looked exhausted as he drew in a breath, shaking his head. My stomach bottomed out at his body language.

"There was significant damage." My heart thumped wildly in my chest, constricting as I hung on to every wood. "We were able to insert a chest tube successfully and repair the damaged part of her lung that was penetrated by one of the bullets. The second bullet was thankfully easier to remove, missing anything major. She is currently in the ICU on a ventilator. She has lost a lot of blood and is currently receiving a transfusion. You can see her in a few minutes."

"When will she wake up?" I croaked out.

He gave me a sympathetic look, shifting on his feet. "We won't know until we see how she handles the next day or so. She is in critical condition, and while I am optimistic after her surgery, it's going to be a fight to survive. You need to prepare yourself for the possibility that her body just can't handle the strain of coming off of life support."

"Motherfucker," Gregory said to no one in particular, rubbing a hand over his face.

My eyes welled with tears, but I nodded. "Thank you, doctor."

As promised, a nurse escorted us back to the ICU. Entering the room, my breathing picked up as I took in all of the tubes, cords, and sounds surrounding Halen. She looked almost peaceful, like a sleeping angel. Her red curls framed her face perfectly and her arms laid gently by her sides.

I saw Gregory's hand cover his mouth, shocked by all

the machinery keeping her alive and the paleness of her already fair complexion. We didn't say anything, each of us taking a side and holding her hands so she knew she wasn't alone.

We were here.

Waiting for her.

CHAPTER 41

-SAWYER-

One Week Later

I watched as the doctor looked over her vitals, a small smile playing on her lips. "She's looking great. I think today is the day."

I sat straighter, looking between Halen and the doctor. "Really? Today? Can she handle it?"

Dr. Ullman smiled as she held her clipboard to her chest. "I think so. We will monitor her closely as we see what her lungs can handle, but I'm confident. She has been making huge strides. Hang on to this one. She's a fighter." She gave me a wink and left the room quietly.

Right as the door closed, it busted open again as a very out of breath Gregory came barging in. "Did I miss it?! Fuck! What did she say?"

"They are going to take her off of the ventilator today. She's showing signs that her lungs are working around it."

"Fuck yeah! I knew you had it in you, wifey!" He shouted at the still unconscious angel next to me.

I rolled my eyes and huffed an annoyed breath. "Not your wife."

"Not yours either, bro," he said, eyeing me. "Yeah I saw the paperwork you filled out for her. Apparently I missed the memo that you were her husband."

Ignoring his comment, I focused back on Halen, rubbing circles on her hand.

"I haven't been able to get ahold of her parents. I tried contacting mine to relay the message but they are pissed at me at the moment, so they aren't taking my calls or messages. I'll keep trying though."

I nodded without looking away. The days had begun to bleed together into a blur of tears, rage and complete helplessness. Gregory a I had made sure that one of us was always by her side. That way if she even slightly twitched, we would know. I had only left for an hour or so every couple of days to pack fresh clothes to take back to the hospital.

Gregory had personal things to attend to which required him to leave more often than me. I was okay with it. I hated leaving her side and nearly had panic attacks for every minute I was away.

Later that day, Gregory and I were asked to leave the room while they worked on Halen. I sat in a seat, holding a very shitty cup of hospital coffee while he slammed back his third energy drink.

"Oh, I meant to ask you," Gregory said as he tossed his can into the trash bin and sat beside me. "Can you send me the number for Halen's parents? I figured my time is better spent trying to contact them directly. Either my parents don't have a signal or I am currently blocked."

I nodded grimly, dreading the idea of them coming here to see her. It seemed like they weren't the type that deserved her. I also wasn't ready to confront them about our relationship. I wanted to officially resign before shooting myself in the foot.

I inwardly cringed at the choice of phrase in my head.

I pulled out Halen's phone from my pocket and powered it on. It took me a minute to navigate the new age tech bullshit, but I managed to find two contacts in her phone listed under *Devil* and *She-Devil*.

"I'm not sure if these are correct, but I have a pretty good hunch, " I said as I forwarded the contacts to Gregory's phone from Halen's phone.

After a few seconds, a chime sounded out loudly followed by an audio clip of Borat saying '*My Wife*'. My body stilled before I looked over at Gregory, deadly calm.

"So help me God... I will throw you out of that hospital window if you don't fucking change that."

He tucked his lips inward, biting down on a smile and a snort. When he saw my expression shift to violence he held his hands up in a placating gesture.

"Alright, alright!" I heard him muttering something about being an old wrinkly sour puss under his breath. I let it slide. Only because I couldn't risk being thrown out of the hospital right when Halen was making an attempt to wake up.

We waited for hours before being allowed back in the room with her. Days slowly passed but she still hadn't woken up.

Dr. Ullman assured us that she likely just needed more time. She managed to successfully breathe on her own without the ventilator, giving me just a little more hope that my baby was a warrior to her core and soon would open her eyes.

I was in the middle of reading a book out loud to her while holding her hand when Gregory came in the room with bags of food.

Thank fuck.

I had placed her cochlear in her ear every so often so she could hear my voice telling her stories, begging her not to leave me here alone, and giving her any good news when I could.

The smell of Mexican food permeated the room, making my stomach growl deep from hunger. Hospital food was the absolute worst. Did the cafeteria have something against seasonings? I had tasted better lunches from the cafeteria at Black Grove Academy.

"I was able to get in touch with Richard and Jennifer. They will likely be in tomorrow afternoon," he said as he placed the food down and unwrapped everything.

I nodded as I closed the book and ran a hand over my face in exhaustion. I wasn't going to complain in the slightest though. How could I when she was laying there, fighting through her own exhaustion and pain to make it back to me.

With no words between us, Gregory and I ate the food,

occasionally looking over to the broken girl on the hospital bed.

GREGORY

I sent out a text to Kyle with Halen's current status which hadn't changed from the others I had sent over the last few days. He had stopped by to drop off flowers a few days prior when he learned that she was here recovering.

Kyle was a good guy with a heart of gold, but it wasn't like him to display it so easily to others. Deep down it didn't surprise me that he immediately found friendship with Halen. They had hit it off really well while snowboarding.

I glanced at the sunflowers standing tall in a vase by her bedside, then over to her opposite beside where the bouquet of yellow roses Sawyer and I bought her sat. A stuffed bear sat next to the sunflowers, compliments of Astrid. She had stopped by a couple of times, but was struggling herself when she had learned that her ex was one of the thirty-two deceased. She didn't want to pollute the room with her negative energy. Her words, not mine.

Glancing at Sawyer, I took in his current state. His eyes were darkened around the edges and puffy from lack of sleep and crying, which he swore he wasn't doing. He looked more like his age than I had seen him before.

His grip was tight on the pencil, making aggressive swipes across a sketchpad. The sound of each swipe was loud and strained. He had been drawing a lot to pass the time.

Being the nosey guy that I was, I couldn't help leaning over a tad, sneaking a look at what he was creating so intently. He was likely drawing something stupid like a bowl of fruit or a vase of flowers.

My eyes moved across the page, taking in the perfect stroke placements. He was really talented. His hand kept swiping aggressively across the same spot, making it darker and darker. My brows pulled together as I finally understood what I was looking at.

A girl's head was propped in the lap of someone. You couldn't see the person holding her as the image made it as if you were looking down at her through their point of view. My eyes trailed over the girl's curly hair, and gentle eyes. Eyes that I had come to be very familiar with.

Halen.

The man's hand was placed over her cheek while one of her hands covered his. Smears of darker shades stretched across her face.

Blood?

A soft smile graced her face. It was clearly forced and painful, but still there. Liquid appeared to be leaking from the corner of her mouth, trailing down her neck.

More blood.

I followed the dark shadows of blood across the page, tracking it everywhere. The man, who I now understood to be Sawyer, had his legs slightly shown as they cradled her body. One of his pant legs were a completely different shade than the other.

Darker.

More blood.

I wanted to vomit. I had understood what happened from the news and what Sawyer had shared with me. But this... I was getting a full look inside his memories to see what he actually saw.

Hearing it was hard enough, but seeing her like that broke my heart. I clutched my stomach and heaved a deep breath, trying to steady the emotions that were slamming into me.

Sawyer's head whipped up and looked over to Halen. After seeing her still in the same condition, he met my eyes.

"What's wrong? Did you eat something bad?"

I shook my head, my eyes not leaving his. "Why would you draw that? Was that how she actually looked?" Another wave of nausea consumed me.

Sawyer's eyes hardened beofre he snapped his book shut

and tucked it into his bag. I pressed harder, needing to understand why he would do that to himself. Why would he want to look at that just to relive it over again? "Why would you put that shit on paper?"

His lips pinched into a thin line. I raised my eyebrows in response as if to say 'well, speak up' which only caused his fists to clench.

"These images are swirling through my fucking head all day, every fucking day. Putting it down on paper is the only way I can get the images to stop swirling. They still appear occasionally, but not every living second," he spat. "It's fucking haunting me."

His face slightly broke before he hardened his features once more. "I fully intend on burning them when I get a chance. I just needed to get them the fuck out of my thoughts. I can't live another second watching the blood bubble over her teeth as she tries to speak and breathe."

I leaned back in my seat, still clutching my stomach as I thought over his words. "Images? Plural?" I eyed him carefully.

Sawyer looked away, his eyes tight. "Yes."

I cocked my head to the side and opened my mouth to speak but was abruptly cut off.

"No," he said through clenched teeth.

"You don't even know what I was going to say."

"You were going to ask to see them. The answer is no. It is haunting enough to have witnessed everything firsthand. I won't be responsible for putting those images in your head. She would never forgive me for hurting you like that."

Looking over to Halen, my shoulders dropped as the potential fight died right there. He was right. I looked back to him and nodded sadly. "You're right. I'm sorry."

He looked surprised that I had given up that easily but just nodded and leaned forward on the bed to rub Halen's hand between his.

She needed to wake up. Soon. Before this guy followed her into whatever void she was currently inhabiting. With that sad thought, I leaned back in my seat further and closed my eyes.

CHAPTER 42

-HALEN-

Silence was the first thing I noticed. There was a complete lack of sound that indicated I was unplugged or floating in some pergatory. It was also dark as hell but I figured my eyes were likely closed.

The second thing I noticed was the screaming pain in my back. Flashes of memory danced across the inside of my eyelids.

Hiding in a utility closet.

Bullets burrowing into my back during a passionate kiss.

Nicky shooting himself in the head.

Sawyer's face above mine, screaming for help.

Darkness.

My breaths quickened as my heart shattered, and the pain in my back tripled but I managed to not release a sound, not fully convinced I could even use my voice anymore.

Cracking an eyelid, I allowed myself to take in the room. After adjusting the light I was able to open my eyes more and really focus on my surroundings. A heaviness was pressed over my right arm. Black hair, messy as if it was constantly being tousled, tickled my forearm. Tight hands gripped my palm as though I was going to float away at any moment.

Sawyer. My Sawyer.

Looking over at the other person in the room, I was shocked to see a sprawled out Gregory, who was also very unconscious. His entire body stretched over the hospital recliner, spread eagle. I couldn't hear it, but based on the movement of his mouth, I could tell he was snoring like crazy.

One side of my mouth lightly tugged up before pulling

down again as I looked back to Sawyer. His stubble has grown longer than I had ever seen it.

How long had I been out?

An ache formed in my chest at how disheveled he looked. I looked at the nightstand to my left and saw my implants sitting there. Grabbing them with my free hand, I gently put them in, trying not to wake either of the boys.

A harsh mixture of snoring, loud mechanical beeps, and footsteps outside of the door met my ears at once. I winced a tad as I adjusted to it all. Not being able to help myself any further, I reached over to Sawyer with my free hand and ran my palm against his light messy beard.

I felt him instinctively lean into the touch, making a small smile break across my face. His eyes snapped open and he shot up in his seat to find my eyes already on his.

"Hey, Teach," I rasped out painfully.

He searched my eyes for a moment and then completely broke. Tears poured down his face as he jumped up and leaned across me carefully to plant kisses on my lips as if it was his only lifeline.

I threaded my hand through his hair as his soft lips brushed against mine for a final time before pulling back and resting his forehead against mine.

"I thought I had lost you," he whispered. "You were slipping through my fingers and I couldn't do anything to stop it. Never do that to me again. If anyone is going first, it's going to be me. Understood?"

I gave the nod, knowing that it wasn't exactly something I could predict or prevent. He released a breath and relaxed a little at my agreement.

"Marry me," he said, his blue eyes piercing mine with so much love.

"Are–Are you serious?" I asked, my hands beginning to shake.

He nodded. "As a heart attack. The moment you are out of here, I want us to go somewhere beautiful and elope. You were always meant to be my wife, and I won't waste any more of my years not being able to refer to you as such. You're mine, baby. What do you say? Will you be Mrs. Halen Bennett?"

Tears pooled in my eyes, and I let them fall without question. These weren't tears of pain. These were tears that needed to be celebrated. Tears of pure joy.

"Yes. Yes! YES!" I repeated the words between kisses as he claimed my mouth once again.

The jolt of a chair had us breaking apart as we snapped our attention over to the sound. Gregory was standing, wide eyed, as he watched me carefully.

"Wifey?" His chin wobbled.

I gave him a watery smile, opening my arms out wide. He didn't hesitate rushing over to me to embrace in a hug while making sure to be careful of the tubes and wires attached to my body.

He sobbed in the crook of my neck but after a few minutes he was able to retreat and pull himself together. I watched as he wiped the straggling tears from his eyes, my heart breaking for him and everyone that had worried for me during this time.

Right at that moment, the door to the room opened as I saw my father walk in with a pinched expression. The door closed behind him, indicating that either my mother was further behind or decided to not come.

Sawyer and Gregory stepped back as my father came to my left side, dropping into the seat. His eyes never left mine as he looked over my body and the two other men in the room.

He gave Gregory a nod, before his eyes settled on Sawyer. Understanding flashed across his face, though he didn't say anything. Thank God for tiny miracles.

His eyes came back to me again as he tentatively reached out to offer his hand. I placed mine in his as I wrangled my emotions. "I'm sorry it took so long to get here. There were storms that delayed our flight."

I nodded slowly. "I understand. Thank you for caring

enough to come."

He flinched at my words before pursing his lips. "I'm sorry, Halen. I haven't been the best father to you, or fair in the slightest. I think... I think I have had my priorities mixed up for a while. I'm embarrassed that it took my little girl being hospitalized for me to realize it."

More tears fell from my eyes but I couldn't find the courage to respond with the emotions battling for dominance.

"*Please forgive me,*" he signed.

It was at that moment that my walls came crumbling down. Years of resentment and pain were wiped, replaced with the regret and love he was showing me.

I cried out a tad as I sat up more and leaned over to hold him in my arms. He hugged me tightly but I gritted my teeth through the pain. This was something I had wished for since I was a young girl. I had always known that he loved me, but I never got the loving hugs, kisses, and daddy-daughter days. Just memories of him working and not being present.

"Where is mom?" I pulled back to get a read of his face.

He cringed and then pursed his lips, deep in thought. "Your mother and I are getting a divorce. As I said, priorities."

That meant that she had decided not to come. She had such an aversion to concern for others, specifically me, that she couldn't have been bothered to show up for her potentially dying daughter.

Well the joke was going to be on her. She was officially dead to me. Not the other way around. I regained my composure quickly, accepting everything he had said with a nod of understanding.

Moving on from the irritating topic, I looked back to Sawyer who was watching the encounter carefully. He clearly was trying to give us personal space but didn't want to leave my side for even a second.

"Dad," I said looking back over at him. "I would like you to meet my fiance." I didn't miss the way his eyes flicked over to Gregory, thinking we may have decided to reconcile.

I grabbed Sawyer's hand in mine and squeezed. "This is Sawyer."

His eyes narrowed on Sawyer's for a moment before meeting my eyes, trying to search my face for something.

"Does he make you happy?"

I smiled brightly and nodded. "He does."

My father released a deep sigh but reached his hand out. Sawyer's eyebrows shot up in shock as he reached up to shake his offered hand.

Gregory's smirk had my smile turning into a full on beam. He winked at me as we watched the two men stare off mid-handshake, making peace with each other. For *me*.

Healing was harder than I thought it would be. I spent weeks in the hospital recovering from the damage done on my body. I had started my remote learning to ensure that I graduated on time. Sawyer had sent an email with his resignation the day after I was admitted into the hospital. A handful of other teachers resigned that day too, but after the shooting, nobody questioned them as to why they were leaving.

It was assumed that they couldn't handle working in that school anymore after those horrors took place. While that was also true for Sawyer now, it thankfully helped his already structured plan to quit.

I spent most of my time reading books that Sawyer brought to the hospital as I drew the titles from the book jar. We spent hours talking about characters and plots.

The elevator door chimed open. Sawyer's hand lightly landed on the small of my back in support as I slowly walked inside. The evening sun was just setting, the light illuminating a pink and orange glow behind the clouds. Colors splashed against the white interior, altering the space from beautiful to breathtaking.

Sawyer's hand dropped from my back as I turned into

the living room. A sharp gasp left my lips. My feet froze in place as my eyes bounced across the room, taking in the black roses everywhere. Tea candle flames were dancing throughout the massive floral display.

The thumping in my chest felt like it would punch through at any given minute. I turned quickly to find Sawyer down on one knee, an adoring smile on his face.

"I wanted you to have the real deal. Not just some panicked proposal in a hospital room. You deserve everything, Halen. You have been a force of nature since you entered my life. I never thought I would trust another woman again after Victoria. Then, I met the most interesting , beautiful, intelligent, and strong woman that I have ever met. It was as if the universe had you planned for me all along, and I just needed to be patient," he said as tears ran down my face. "And thank fuck I was, because life without you would have been a fucking tragedy. Will you marry me tomorrow, Halen?"

Pulling a red leather box from his pocket, he held it out between us, opening it to display the stunning pear shaped black diamond surrounded by intricate swirls on the band. My breath hitched as I met his eyes again and nodded eagerly, sticking out my left hand. "Yes!"

He jumped to his feet like a giddy teenager and placed the ring on my finger before slamming his mouth to mine. He swallowed my sounds of joy, lightly tracing his tongue on my lower lip, asking for entry.

I deepened the kiss, our tongues caressing as we panted through the desire. His hand wound into my hair, lightly tugging back to break the kiss. His lips kicked up in a smile as he peppered small kisses on my lips.

"Now you just need to pick a place, Squid. Anywhere in the world, because we leave tomorrow morning. Your bags are already packed," He said, not releasing me from his grip.

"Hmm. I think I know just the place. I just have to do one thing before we go."

His eyes searched mine, seeing the sadness creeping in.

He knew. He didn't need to ask. He could read me like a book and with that, he just nodded and gave me a kiss that made my belly swoop.

The next morning, the dew on the grass wet my shoes as I walked through the open green area. Looking around the large grounds, I finally found what I was looking for. A grey marble stone stood before me, new and unworn by the weather. I had picked it specifically for its durability, but this was the first time I was able to see it in person.

Dominic Ressner
May he rest in peace

The wind kicked up, blowing strands of my hair across my face as I felt the sting behind my eyes. I willed them back, promising myself that I had shed enough tears since the shooting. The scent of the carnations in my hands swept through the air, giving the sad place a hint of beauty.

I looked over my shoulder to see Sawyer standing at his car, leaning against the door, eyes trained on me like a hawk unwilling to let me out of his sight. He was hesitant to let me do this alone, but I compromised by allowing him to be nearby.

I turned back to the stone and kneeled down, placing one of the flower bouquets against the stone. I didn't immediately stand from my position, grief holding me rooted in place.

"I'm so sorry that your life turned out this way, Nicky," I whispered. "I'm sorry for whatever part I played in your pain. I was trying to save you, and also save myself. Instead I pushed you to a place where only demons dwell. I can only imagine what evil things they whispered to you that gave you the urge to do such a terrible thing to innocent people. Some of them were even kids. I will never forgive myself for not taking a different route in getting through to you. I know you left this world thinking I would be immediately behind you. I can't say that I am sad that I've been given more time here. Sawyer and I are leaving to get married. Maybe down the line, kids will be in our future. I hope you are looking over me right now, happy for my happiness."

I looked up and over across the graveyard, staring at a spot that I was all too familiar with. Looking back at Nicky's stone, I gathered all the remaining strength I had.

"I love you, Nicky. What you did was vile, but I know your heart, and I know that you weren't nearly in your right mind. I've heard mentions that you were having a psychotic break. I for–" my breaths quickened. "I forgive you, Nicky. I'll see you when it's my time. Rest peacefully until then."

With that I pressed a kiss to my palm before pressing it to the center of the stone. I slowly rose to my feet and walked over to the other stone in the distance, squatting down to place the second bouquet down.

"Watch over him, Evan," I said through a broken sob. "I promise to visit you both whenever I can. I love you."

Placing a kiss on his grave the same way I did Nicky's, I stood and walked towards the man of my dreams.

It was time to move forward.

I was going to be Halen Bennett, after all.

EPILOGUE

-HALEN-

Six Years Later

"Holy fucking hell," I grunted out, doubling over. Clutching onto my swollen belly, I took a steadying breath and counted to twenty.

Sawyer was at the studio instructing a class, so I was all on my own for the time being. We had bought the studio two years ago and turned it into a space where people could take classes or some to create their own masterpieces.

I winced through another jolt. This baby kicked like a fucking donkey. After a moment to calm the ache in my side, I continued to unfold and refold the baby clothes in the drawers.

Sawyer told me that the book he had read called it *nesting*. Whatever it was, it seemed like everything was constantly out of order and needing to be done. The smell of the baby detergent I washed everything in even brought me to my knees in tears one day. The powdery baby smell hit me in my hormonal heart.

Right as I placed a pile of folded overalls in their spot, another swift kick from within had me gasping and clutching my stomach again through a groan. A gush of liquid splashed from between my legs, pooling into a puddle on the tile floor.

"Ah, shit," I muttered.

Grabbing my phone I quickly sent out a text to Sawyer with a bunch of alarm emojis. Not even fifteen minutes later, he came barging through the door, muscles flexing through his shirt, eyes wild as they searched the house for me.

"Grab the bags. It's baby time," I groaned through a

contraction.

"Oh my God. Okay! Oh shit, alright, let's go baby."

He supported my arm as he walked me to the car and set me inside before rushing back in to grab the hospital bags that we had pre-packed. I used the few moments between contractions to send off a mass group text to our friends and family.

Me: Baby is about to enter the group chat.

Astrid's response came immediately.

Ass-trid: Hell yeah!! Praying for you guys. Send pics when you pop that sucker out.

Dad: Congratulations honey. I'll stop by in a few weeks to check in on you and the baby.

A moment passed before another text from him came in.

Dad: ...And Sawyer.

Sawyer and Dad had been warming up to each other over the years. They actually both had an interest in art which sparked a lot of conversations. Dad obviously leaned more towards the expensive pieces while Sawyer enjoyed finding up and coming artists to collaborate with and support.

Sawyer threw the bags into the back seat and sped off like a speed racer, making my stomach drop momentarily. I placed my hand on his, reassuring him that it was okay and we would make it in time.

My phone buzzed in my hand and I opened it to see that Gregory had responded.

Gregory: I'm gonna be an uncle! I can't wait to tell the guys!

I rolled my eyes and closed out of the text, unable to deal with his ridiculousness at this moment.

"Have you heard from Connor? Will there be any way to get word to him?"

Sawyer's sigh was deep and loaded. "No, unfortunately not. Him and his team are working with some people to take down a big fish. The last I had heard from him was a few weeks ago but Elise reassured me that there are contingencies in place to inform me if he is injured or..."

The rest didn't need to be said. I squeezed his hand and nodded, looking out the front windshield absently. "He will be okay. He's like a cockroach, not easy to kill," I said trying to lighten the mood.

Sawyer's light chuckle had my body relaxing, thankful that the joke landed where it needed to in order to cheer him up. Connor would reach out when he could. I knew that.

The hospital appeared fairly empty thankfully. Nurses were able to get us into a room within a few minutes. I took a moment to kiss my husband, searching his eyes for any indications on how he was feeling.

"Are you ready to grow our family, daddy?"

His eyes darkened at the nickname but a smile tugged his lips upward as he dropped his head to place a soft kiss on my lips. "More than anything. You're going to be an amazing mother, Halen. I love you."

"I love you more." I pressed another kiss to his lips before it was abruptly broken by a wave of cramping and my whimpering.

Five hours later our sweet baby girl entered the world.

"Wow, she's beautiful. Just like her Mama," Sawyer whispered as he rocked her swaddled form in his arms. "Have you decided on the name?"

We had discussed names that we liked but hadn't really agreed on anything as we didn't even know the gender until she was born. I had a few names floating in my head but there was only one that really felt *right* at this moment.

"Yes, actually," I said as I eyed him cautiously. "I'd like to name her Alva."

Sawyer's rocking stopped abruptly as his eyes snapped up to mine, wide and full of emotion. The slight shake of his chin before looking back down at our beautiful girl told me everything I needed to know.

Her name was Alva.

He slowly walked over to the hospital bed, placing Alva

in my arms, then immediately cradled my face in his hands. Tears fell freely from his eyes, but they sparkled with adoration.

"Thank you," he whispered.

I nodded, smiling, as I leaned my face into one of his hands. Just as things were getting too emotional, Alva tested her lung strength by letting out a cry, rooting for my breast.

Life was perfect.

◆ ◆ ◆

Six Months Later

"Is it supposed to be this chubby?" Connor eyed Alva suspiciously, cocking his head to one side as he studied each little roll on her thunder thighs.

His arms were extended, holding her out at arms length as if she would barf or shit on him at any moment. I gave him a scowl.

"Yes! That means she is healthy and getting plenty of nutrition. She has checkups with the pediatrician often."

"Hmm, whatever you say, Short Bus. All I'm saying is that she looks like she may struggle crawling with all of this extra fluff."

I snatched Alva from his hands and placed her on my hip. "She's fine and stop calling me that!" I exclaimed, my voice clearly carrying which drew Sawyer into the living room with us. Connor threw his hands up in surrender.

"Alright, chill." He walked over to sit his ass on the couch with a smirk playing on his lips. I waited, knowing him better now that he wasn't just going to let this go without another word. "She's cute. You both did good."

Not falling for it, I continued waiting.

His eyes met mine as he continued. "Thank you for honoring our mother by giving her a legacy. Knowing that her name will carry on brings me a sense of peace that I didn't realize I needed."

My eyes widened at his vulnerability. He was always a closed book. This was the most sharing I had heard him do in the years that I had known him.

I was just about to smile at him when he had to open his fucking mouth again.

"I didn't think you had it in you, Humping Halen."

"Con," Sawyer growled out.

Connor just smiled, trying to hold back a laugh. I flipped him off and tore out my implants, needing a bit of silence from that chode.

That evening Sawyer and I sat down on the couch with a bowl of popcorn and a shit load of candy. He was wearing a pair of sweats with no shirt on, looking like a snack himself. I was sporting a simple oversized tee and undies as it was perfect for middle of the night breastfeeding sessions.

We agreed on a classic rom-com as I snuggled into him. The sound machine in Alva's room sounded through the baby monitor on the coffee table but we were professionals at tuning it out now unless she was actively stirring or crying.

The movie was just about to start as I stuffed my face full of sour candy followed by a handful of extra buttery popcorn. Sawyer gripped my chin between his fingers, tilting my head up towards him to peer down into my eyes.

"You're so fucking beautiful. Even with sour gummy worms hanging out of your mouth."

Swallowing the last bit of the chewy sweets, I caught my lower lip between my teeth as I watched the hunger, desire and love pour through every expression on his face. His thumb moved up to pull the lip out from its trapped spot.

I didn't bother waiting. Leaning up, I crushed my mouth to his in a bruising kiss. My tongue swept across his lower lip and he parted them immediately. His hand wound into my hair as I lifted myself up from my spot and straddled him.

With a deep rock of my hips, a groan rumbled through his chest and into my mouth. I devoured every little bit of it.

His teeth nipped at my bottom lip before soothing it with his tongue. This time it was my turn to moan.

"Do you want me to fuck you right here, Mr. Bennett?" I asked between kisses.

He lifted his hips in response as he pulled my body down, grinding my core against his rock hard length. A whimper tore from my lips as he continued moving his hips back and forth.

I reached down in between us and tugged his sweats down. His hard cock sprang out, slapping him in the abdomen. I pulled back to break the kiss as I looked at how swollen and ready he was. He was thick and veiny, with a bead of pre-cum right at the tip.

Swiping over the tip with my thumb, I spread it around his cock as I gripped him tightly and gave him long and slow strokes. He leaned back into the couch, watching my hand move up and down, paying extra attention to the head.

I slid my free hand down the front of my panties as I continued to stroke him. Sawyer's eyes whipped to the movement and his hand snapped out at an unnatural speed, yanking my hand out.

"Hell no, Squid. You're going to sink that pretty pussy right down on top of me while I worship your clit like you deserve. Now be a good girl and bounce on my cock."

I drew in a sharp breath as he lifted me slightly, pulled my panties to the side and pulled my hips down over him so I stretched around every delicious inch of him.

"Oh, fuck," I said as I began to ride him like a fucking stallion.

"That's it, baby. Fuck, you look so good. Your pussy was made for me."

He reached down and began to rub circles on my clit as I continued riding him. The bundle of nerves was sensitive and felt like it was only going to be minutes before he would have me detonating.

I leaned down and captured his mouth with mine, savoring the whiskey on his breath. His free arm worked its way back into my hair like he knew I loved and gave it a firm tug. My head tilted upward but not enough to lose eye contact with him.

"Keep going. Shit. Yeah, like that," he said through panting breaths. His hips began to rise to meet my thrusts causing my eyes to roll back.

The tingling throughout my body surged into a full wave of euphoria as my orgasm slammed into me causing white flicking to take over my vision. I heard a feral roar rip from Sawyer as warm ropes of cum shot inside of me. My body fell forward to his chest as I no longer had the strength to sit upright.

We stayed like that for a minute, trying to reach a baseline again after coming down from such a large high. His hands were rubbing circles on my back at a soothing pace making me want to snuggle even harder into him.

"What are the chances we just made another baby?" I asked without moving.

I heard a gravely chuckle. "Honestly, kind of high."

I nodded against his chest, thinking it over. "Would that be good or bad," I asked quietly.

His response melted my heart and made it beat faster all at the same time. His lips pressed against my hair as he murmured, "I couldn't think of anything better."

THE END

THE END

ABOUT THE AUTHOR

Bree Rathbone

I decided to start my writing journey as a bucket list item that I could check off. Turns out, I love doing it. That doesn't surprise me based on the amount of books I read each year, but I didn't realize how therapeutic it would be to put thoughts on paper for myself.

I'm a mom and a wife first, so publishing may be sporadic but I hope that when I do release different titles, you'll be able to enjoy it anyway.

I write spicy, and usually dark, novels and novellas. With that being said, always check trigger warnings.

If you are family, turn around, and pretend you never saw this.

BOOKS BY THIS AUTHOR

Cracked Steele

This why-choose romance novel will take you down a road filled with sex trafficking, murder, and so much more. You may also see a someone you recognize!

On Kindle Unlimited now!

BOOKS IN PROGRESS

Want to see more of Connor?
No worries. You can catch him in Cracked Steele.
While this story isn't about him, you catch a glimpse
of where he was during Ruled by Silence.
He may have his own book coming. Maybe. Possibly. Likely.

What ever happened to Gregory, Zafar, Kyle, and Vesper?
Wouldn't you like to know, babygirl.
Maybe you will in 2027.

www.ingramcontent.com/pod-product-compliance
Lightning Source LLC
LaVergne TN
LVHW010638110826
845149LV00014B/2879

* 9 7 9 8 9 9 4 2 5 2 0 0 0 *